SUMMONING

It only took Gift a few moments to reach the ledge.

It wasn't made of a continuous piece of stone at all. It was rock mortared together long enough ago that the rocks themselves had cracked. It was slightly uneven and rough beneath his feet.

This was a man-made structure, built to look like part of the mountain. Except for the swords outside.

Stone swords, carved out of rock. They were taller than Gift. Two of them were embedded in the rock, points down. Another two were sticking out of the sides of the cave's mouth. A fifth sword stood balanced above its center.

"That's their religious symbol," the Cap said. His voice shook. "We need to leave."

"No." Gift grabbed the Cap's arm. He couldn't explain it, but he didn't feel any threat here. Just the compelling need to go inside.

"You can't," the Cap said. "You can't. If you die in there—"

"At least let me go first," Leen said. She stopped between the two swords and touched the closest with her fingers. Her hand was trembling.

Gift held his breath—

Also by Kristine Kathryn Rusch

FANTASY

The Fey: The Rival
The Fey: The Changeling
The Fey: The Sacrifice
Traitors
Heart Readers
The White Mists of Power

SCIENCE FICTION

Alien Influences
Star Wars: The New Rebellion
Aliens: Rogue (written as Sandy Schofield)
Quantum Leap: Loch Ness Leap (written as Sandy Schofield)

HORROR

The Devil's Churn
Sins of the Blood
Facade
Afterimage (with Kevin J. Anderson)

MYSTERY

Hitler's Angel (written as Kris Rusch)

STAR TREK NOVELS

Treaty's Law (with Dean Wesley Smith)
Soldiers of Fear (with Dean Wesley Smith)
Rings of Tautee (with Dean Wesley Smith)
Klingon! (with Dean Wesley Smith)
The Long Night (with Dean Wesley Smith)
The Escape (with Dean Wesley Smith)
The Big Game (written as Sandy Schofield)

ANTHOLOGIES

The Best from Fantasy and Science Fiction (with Edward L. Ferman)
The Best of Pulphouse

THE RESISTANCE

THE FOURTH BOOK OF THE FEY

Kristine Kathryn Rusch

SPECTRA™

BANTAM BOOKS
NEW YORK TORONTO LONDON
SYDNEY AUCKLAND

THE FEY: THE RESISTANCE

A Bantam Spectra Book/June 1998

ISBN 0-553-57713-1

Published simultaneously in the United States and Canada

Bantam Books are published by Bantam Books, a division of Bantam Doubleday Dell Publishing Group, Inc. Its trademark, consisting of the words "Bantam Books" and the portrayal of a rooster, is Registered in U.S. Patent and Trademark Office and in other countries. Marca Registrada. Bantam Books, 1540 Broadway, New York, New York 10036.

PRINTED IN THE UNITED STATES OF AMERICA

WCD 0 9 8 7 6 5 4 3 2 1

For Phil and Flossie Barnhart
with thanks for everything

ACKNOWLEDGMENTS

Thanks on this one go to Anne Lesley Groell for taking on such a large project; to Carolyn Oakley for her belief in the Fey; to Tom Dupree for loving the series; to Merrilee Heifetz for all the help; to Matt Schwartz for designing such a lovely web page (please visit @ www.horrornet.com/rusch.htm); to Nina Kiriki Hoffman for her trusty red pen; to Paul Higginbotham for sharing his expectations; to Dean Wesley Smith for nagging, brainstorming, and supporting; and to all the readers who let me know how much they're enjoying the series.

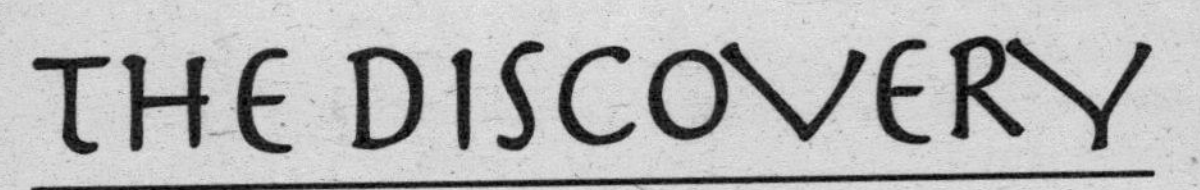
THE DISCOVERY

ONE

THE day dawned clear and cold on the Eyes of Roca. The Shaman wrapped a blanket around herself and watched the sun turn the mountains the color of blood.

She had not slept in two days, not since the Islander King, Nicholas, had arrived with his half-Fey daughter, Arianna. Arianna was unnaturally thin, her eyes sunken into her head. She had used her shape-shifting skills too often in her battle against her great-grandfather, Rugad.

The Black King.

The Shaman shuddered and drew her blanket tighter. She sat on a rock outcropping, her feet dangling above the snow. Behind her, Nicholas and Arianna slept in the cave the Shaman had found when the Black King invaded less than two weeks before. If she had not fled, she would have died with the rest of her people, the Fey who had come into the first invasion.

Failures, Rugad had called them, and according to Fey law he was right. He had no choice but to kill them. He could not trust them. He certainly could not trust her.

There was no wind. The air was so cold it chilled her lungs. Despite her lack of sleep, she was not tired. Her mind was too busy. She had Seen a dozen futures, and young Arianna, in her first Vision, had Seen a dozen others. The future was in flux.

The Black King had brought danger to the world when he had come to Blue Isle. For one of the Shaman's Visions had shown the insanity brought on by Black Blood warring against Black Blood.

She raised her head and looked toward the valley south of her. It spread below her, green and gold and crisscrossed with roads and buildings. In the distance, smoke still colored the sky, making it hazy. The Black King was there, in the city built by Nicholas's people, the city he burned according to Fey tradition.

The Black King had ignored the wishes of his granddaughter, Nicholas's wife, Jewel. She had sacrificed herself so that Blue Isle could become part of the Fey Empire. Peacefully. She felt that her children would link the Islanders with the Fey, and the Fey would leave the Isle alone.

They had not. Jewel's death and the strange magick that flowed through this Isle had created a rift so powerful not even the Shaman felt it could be mended. The events would play themselves out now. All she could do was counsel Nicholas, counsel his wild children, and hope the insanity would not come.

She wiped a strand of her coarse white hair from her face. Her hands were cold. She had seen a dozen dawns on this mountainside, and none of them had been this red. Something was in the air, a change of huge proportions. She could feel it.

Then she felt slightly dizzy. She let out a sigh and turned toward the cave. A Vision was coming. She wanted to get inside before it hit. The last time, she had wandered off and nearly died in the snow.

A Vision—

And then it struck, tilting her world, making her spin for a moment before she found herself in a cave.

Not her cave. A different cave. It was dark, and yet it glowed with an inner light. All around her, Powers flew, whispering things she couldn't quite hear. She was half in and half out of the cave.

She had been here before. On her pilgrimage as a young Shaman.

In the Eccrasian Mountains, the birthplace of the Fey.

It was the Place of Power.

But Visions never went backward. This was the future. In the Eccrasian Mountains? How did they get to Galinas? How did they go all the way back to the place where the Fey began?

Then she looked up. Nicholas was stroking her face, his eyes glinting with tears. He had Arianna over his shoulder.

She looked dead.

"What can I do?" he asked. His voice, usually so strong, was filled with panic.

What can I do?

Behind him, she saw Fey faces, peering out of the cave. Magick flowed beside them, like water.

The Place of Power.

She reached up toward him—

And the world shifted again. Rugad, the Black King, was lying among shards of stones, his body crushing an ornate chair. He had a healing wound on his neck, and bruises on his face—

—And the Black Blood boiled and spilled over everything. They were drowning, drowning, drowning in madness—

She came to herself facedown in the snow, her entire body chilled. She stood slowly, trying to get her balance, then she brushed the snow off herself. The cave that she had found, the one Nicholas and Arianna slept in, was still behind her. They hadn't awakened yet.

She gazed at it a very long time, remembering the shaky feeling she had had in her Vision as she lay within the entrance to the Place of Power. That feeling was familiar, yet unfamiliar, and mixed with it was a love she hadn't acknowledged.

Her reasons for fighting against her own people might not have been as altruistic as she thought.

Nicholas.

The Place of Power.

And the blood. All that blood.

They still hadn't prevented the worst crisis of all.

TWO

THE town at the base of the Cliffs of Blood was named Constant because, some said, King Constantine the First had been born there. Others said the town's name predated Constantine. The name Constant came because it was the oldest inhabited place on Blue Isle, older even than the capital town of Jahn, whose recorded history went back to the first Rocaan.

Matthias loved it here. He always had, even though the town had never loved him. He had been born here, in Constant, to a mother he never knew. Because he had been a long baby—nearly twice the size of the average Islander—he had been taken into the Cliffs of Blood and abandoned. Sometimes he almost thought he could remember his first days there, cold and starving and crying. But he supposed he had heard enough about them to create the memory.

And he had seen it enough. The people who lived near the Cliffs of Blood were hearty folk with superstition buried deep. They believed tall babies equaled tall adults, and tall adults were demon-spawn. Some people still clenched a fist when they saw him to ward off his hidden magick.

Still, he loved it here. The air was fresh and cool, the sunlight was brilliant, and the killing mountains had a beauty all their own, a beauty that he had never found in Jahn. After he had left Jahn in disgrace some fifteen years before, after he had abandoned his post as the Rocaan—something no one had ever done—he had come here, to Constant, and here he had found peace.

He had returned to Jahn only a few months before to test his scholarship, to try again to make a varin sword, as was described in the Secrets. The Secrets, which only the Rocaan knew, were considered a sign of power in the Tabernacle. But their purpose had been forgotten, or lost, and they had become a wealth of useless information. But Matthias had been the one to discover that holy water was more than a tradition; it was a weapon that killed Fey. And it made him wonder if the other Secrets had that same power.

He had yet to test the theory.

He sat on the doorstep outside his house and stared at the Cliffs of Blood. They were tall, the tallest mountains he had ever seen. They were part of the Eyes of Roca mountain range that ran from the Stone Guardians in the west to the Cliffs of Blood in the east. But the Cliffs were unique. They were taller than any other mountains in the range, and their edges were jagged, impossible, after a certain height, to climb. They were also an unusual color. The Eyes of Roca were brown, for the most part, except for their caps, which were covered in snow. But the Cliffs were red, and even the snow on the peaks was a pale pink. In the sunlight, the red deepened to the color of glowing coal, and it seemed as if the Cliffs burned from within.

Sometimes he felt that burning. At night, he would awaken with an urge to climb the mountain, as if it beckoned him, as if it wanted him. As a boy he'd feel that urge, and his adopted mother would have to physically restrain him to keep him from the Cliffs. He had left Constant, in part, to bury the urge, to stay off the mountain, which, he believed, might some day kill him.

Yet he loved the Cliffs. He loved their mystery, he loved their danger, and he loved the secrets they had stored within. The caves that riddled the Cliffs were filled with treasures, like the varin he was using to make the sword. The plants that grew on the lower mountainside were native to the region. Only a few grew elsewhere as well, like the seze that was in holy water. It also grew in the Kenniland Marshes to the south, and it had proved the ingredient that had nearly destroyed the Fey.

The early morning was chill. The sun still hid behind the highest peaks, but the sky was light. Days were short here.

Mornings started later than they did anywhere else on the Isle. But they were spectacular. Every sunrise was different, every storm that blew across the mountains unsurpassed in both strength and majesty.

He had forgotten how much he had missed this place. He had only been away two months, and he had felt incomplete.

Inside the house, he could hear stirrings. It was probably Denl. Denl was the only member of the strange band that had brought Matthias up here who had any religious sentiment at all. He called Matthias Holy Sir, even though Matthias had asked him not to, and he could not quite get over the fact that he traveled with the Fifty-first Rocaan.

It was Denl who said, when they learned of the death of the Fifty-second Rocaan, that Matthias was Rocaan once again. Actually, Denl had said that it was God's way of showing Matthias that he had never stopped being Rocaan at all.

A man canna stop bein Beloved a God, Denl had said, and in his heart of hearts, Matthias feared Denl was right.

Denl wouldn't come outside for a while. He still had his prayers to say and his breakfast to eat. In the week or so that they had traveled together, Matthias had learned a lot about the habits of this group. And Denl's were the most predictable.

Matthias's were the least.

Pain had awakened him only a short time ago. He had been stabbed in the face and shoulders by a Fey nine days before, and he had nearly died. The wounds had destroyed his face. He saw the handiwork for the first time in the Cardidas River after the group had escaped Jahn. Long jagged cuts ran from his forehead to his jaw. Marly, the only woman in the group, was something of a healer, and she had stitched the wounds together. She had warned him that on either side of the scars would be tiny dots. He would be disfigured for the rest of his life, bearing the mark of the Fey outside as well as in.

They were the true demon-spawn, although Nicholas had never listened to him on that. Nicholas, who had married one, bred with one, and corrupted the Roca's line with demons that had no soul. Matthias had proven that when he touched the head of Nicholas's wife, Jewel, with a small bit of holy water, and she had melted, as all the other soulless Fey had done. God hated them, and visited his wrath upon them every chance He got.

Matthias would make sure he would have more chances.

Now that he was back here, in Constant, and safe, he would explore the rest of the Secrets, and he would be ready when the Fey finally came this far north and east.

The Cliffs were the northeastern point on the Isle. They were difficult to reach, and most Islanders never traveled there. They had to go along the ridgeline of the Eyes of Roca, or take the road built beside the Cardidas River. The trip was long and difficult, and because the Blooders were so unfriendly, often unrewarding.

He shivered once and ran his hands along his sleeves. He no longer wore the robes of his office, hadn't since he had abandoned it after Jewel's death. Sometimes he still missed it, the heaviness and the comfort of it, especially here, in the Cliffs of Blood, where the air was never completely warm.

His house was, though. It was, like the other buildings in Constant, made of the gray stone that littered the base of the mountains. He had always thought it odd that the stone that had fallen off the mountain was gray while the stone it was made of was red. He had once asked his adoptive mother—the kind woman who had taken him and nine others abandoned on the mountain in—why this was so.

Mountains are living creatures, Matty, she had said, cradling his head with her hand as she spoke. *The rocks that fall away lose their life force and die.*

He had thought her answer fanciful, but he always thought of it whenever he saw the gray stone littering Constant. He always thought of her, and how much he missed her. How much he appreciated her kindness, and how her kindness hadn't mattered in the face of her husband, who had been determined to get rid of the children as soon as he could.

The door opened behind him, and he braced himself. Denl's religiosity disturbed Matthias, reminded him of his own failures, just as that young Aud had, the one who had passed through the tunnels on a Charge from the Fifty-second Rocaan, the one Matthias had lied to. Matthias still could see the boy's dirty, beautiful face, and Matthias had felt that urge, the one to hide what he had become.

Even so, he had spoken a partial truth: *I'm just an old Aud gone bad,* and that much had terrified the boy to his underdeveloped toes.

An old Aud gone bad.

A Rocaan without a following.

A man with a mission, a mission no one else could complete.

"What're ye doin in the cold?" The voice belonged, not to Denl, but to Marly, the woman who had tended Matthias's wounds and had, more than once, saved his life.

"Saying hello to the mountains," he said. He had developed a manner of speaking that kept him from moving his face too much. To his own ears, it sounded laconic and slow.

"Ye saw em yestiday, n the day afore that, n the day afore that." She stood behind him. He could feel her warmth against his back.

"But not from here," he said. "Don't you think they're beautiful?"

"N terrible," she said. "Too many ha died there. In the Soul Stealers."

He'd heard that name for the mountains before, but it was a local name. Marly, too, had been born here, but her family spirited her away to the Kenniland Marshes, where the height prejudice wasn't as severe. She spoke like a marshlander, but she had the talents of the tall folk from the Cliffs of Blood.

Her healing proved that.

"The Soul Stealers," he said, musing. He wondered if she knew where the name came from. He did. It referred to the babies left on the mountain, the babies who survived. They were said to be demons without souls.

"Aye," she said. "N they have an evil magick. Can ye na feel it?"

He did feel something different about the Cliffs of Blood, something beside his urge to go to them. He had worked near the Snow Mountains in the south and he had never felt the energy, the life, that he felt here. It felt as if the mountains watched the valley, as if they stood guard, as if they would move if they did not like what they saw.

Perhaps they would, when the Fey arrived.

"It doesn't feel evil to me," he said. What would she think if she knew he had been one of the mountain's survivors? Would she still tend him? Worry about him?

Touch him?

"Ye are the Holy Sir," she said.

He hated the reference. Especially coming from her. He stood. "No," he said. "I'm not. And I wish you'd stop referring to me that way."

He swayed a bit from the suddenness of the movement. He still hadn't recovered. Marly said it would take a long time for his wounds to heal. He had overheard her once, telling one of the others that she was shocked by Matthias's strength. A normal man, she had said, would have died from those wounds.

He nearly had. The Fey had attacked him in the river, in the Cardidas, and as he sank, blood pooling around him, he had heard a voice.

A voice of one of the Fey he had killed.

You have a great magick, holy man.

A great magick. Those words had echoed in his head for fifteen years, terrifying him. Yet he could not forget them. They often came to him, unbidden, as if the Fey he had killed had somehow put those words inside his head.

Matthias had once spoken to his predecessor, the Fiftieth Rocaan, about the beliefs of the Wise Ones, here in Constant—The ones who believed Matthias to be demon-spawn, who said that tall people from Constant had to die because of their special powers. The Fiftieth Rocaan, the man Matthias succeeded, said such powers came from God. Matthias wanted to believe that, just as he wanted to believe in God. But if God existed, He existed in distant form.

The more Matthias studied, the more he realized that God had given man the tools and then backed away. The secret was finding the tools and using them properly.

"Ye seem far away," Marly said.

"Just thinking," Matthias said. He put a hand on her for balance. She let him. She was a tall woman, and her reddish hair showed her Cliffs of Blood origin as clearly as her height. Her features were small and delicate, her eyes a sharp green that saw too much.

She had become dear to him in the short time he had known her. He tried to tell himself that was because she had healed him, tended him, touched him. No one had treated him with such kindness in a long, long time.

He told himself that, but he didn't completely believe it.

He would have smiled at her, but the memory of pain from the last time he had smiled stopped him. Instead he caressed her cheek with his free hand.

"Shall we go in?" he asked.

She leaned into his touch. "Aye," she said. "Tis na much we can do out here."

"Yet," he said, then glanced at the mountains. He had come

home for a reason, a reason deeper than the simple one of owning a house here.

The mountains had brought him back. He had answered their call, and he would learn why soon.

He could feel it.

THREE

GIFT stood beside Leen in the center of Constant, clutching several gold coins in his hand. The city, if it could be called that, was tucked against the mountains. From a distance, it looked as if it were part of those mountains. The buildings were small and rounded, built from the same gray rock that littered the mountain's base. It was the roads that gave the city away. They were brown and straight, and they looked man-made.

The buildings were dwellings mostly, although there was a large town gathering place near the base of the mountains. There were a few businesses, a smithy, several mining companies—most closed now—and the ubiquitous kirk. This one seemed small and unused, but it still filled Gift with dread.

The entire place made him nervous. He hadn't felt like himself since he had seen the tall peaks of the Cliffs of Blood. Something shimmered in the center of one of the mountains, and when it did, he could feel it, as if the shimmer happened inside him.

No one else seemed to feel it. He had asked Leen on the way to the city if she thought the mountains were odd, and she had looked at him as if he were.

Still, he had welcomed the chance to come into the city, to get out of the mountains, to see if the feeling he had made it all the way to the valley floor. It lessened a bit, but he didn't know if that was because his nervousness had risen.

The coins bit into his palm. He hadn't come into the city before. The others had: Coulter, Adrian, and even Scavenger. But Coulter and Adrian were Islanders. They were short and blond and looked like they belonged. Scavenger too was accepted here. His Fey features seemed to mean nothing. And his magickless, unclean status, the fact that he was a Red Cap, clearly meant nothing at all.

These people had never seen Fey before. None of the first Fey invasion force had traveled this far on the Isle. Rugad's second invasion force hadn't made it this far either.

But it was only a matter of time.

Gift shuddered, an involuntary movement he made each time he thought of his great-grandfather. His great-grandfather had invaded Gift's head less than a week before. He had traveled along the Link Gift had with Shadowlands, and he had arrived inside Gift, shoving Gift aside and looking out his eyes.

Each person was Linked through invisible threads to each person he loved, to each thing he created. Visionaries and Enchanters could see the Links, and their consciousness could travel across those Links.

Gift understood the procedure. He had traveled the Link between himself and Sebastian, shoving Sebastian aside countless times before he realizing that within that stone changeling body was a personality, one that felt and loved and thought just as clearly as Gift had. After that, Gift traveled the Link to talk with Sebastian. They hid in a corner of that stone body and shared information, shared lives. It was the only way Gift had ever seen his father, the first way that Gift had seen his sister, Arianna. And whenever he thought of them, he felt an echo of Sebastian's feelings, an echo of Sebastian's love.

Sebastian. Gift closed his eyes. Sebastian was dead. Gift felt as if a part of his own self had died with him.

Leen stirred beside him. She still acted as his bodyguard, even though their positions were equal now. Their families were dead—his adopted parents and her real ones—along with the rest of the Fey in Shadowlands. The Black King, Gift's great-grandfather, had killed them.

His great-grandfather had a lot to pay for.

But Gift couldn't be the one to exact the vengeance.

That would be Black Blood against Black Blood.

Stout people walked past them, their reddish blond hair reflecting the color of the sky above the mountains. It was just dawn, even though the sun hadn't come over the cliffs, and the city was bathed in a red-gold light.

He had never seen mornings like this before. But he hadn't been outside much until now. As a Fey from Shadowlands, his only sojourns outside were through the Links, to Sebastian.

His heart spasmed. The deaths of his parents and all the others he had known since childhood on had, after the initial shock, numbed him. But the death of Sebastian was a raw wound, as if someone had taken a part of himself and shattered it.

"I don't see any market," Leen said. She stood as close to him as she dared, her long black braid trailing down her back, her clothes travel-stained but brushed clean of dirt. She wore an Infantry uniform, even though it no longer applied. She was no more part of the Fey army than he was. The only difference between them now was that he had come into his magick—indeed, he had had it since he was young—and she hadn't.

"Adrian said it was in the center of town," Gift said.

"Whereever that is," she said. She looked around, and Gift did too. People flowed around them as if they weren't there. Every once in a while, someone would glance at them and then look away, as if they were seeing something forbidden.

No one spoke to them. No one even tried.

But then, Gift hadn't tried either.

"We could ask," he said.

She sighed. "I doubt most of these people would help us."

She was right. The people who passed them went out of their way to avoid being on the same side of the street. Ever since Gift and Leen had stopped, the people going by had given them sideways glances and had whispered with something like fear.

Adrian had warned Gift about this. Islanders, particularly Islanders from the north, didn't like tall people. That was why Adrian, Coulter, and Scavenger had done most of their dealings with townsfolk. At first, Coulter had spelled everyone so that even the Fey looked like Islanders, but that hadn't worked long. The spells didn't affect things like height, and they had taxed Coulter's waning strength. All the magick he had used in the last ten days had left him pale and thin, his eyes empty and his features gaunt.

If Gift weren't so angry at him, he would have felt some

compassion. But Coulter hadn't understood the troubles he'd caused. Or if he had, he hadn't cared.

"Adrian and Coulter should have come down," Leen said, echoing Gift's thoughts.

"They couldn't," he said. "By the time they're done in the quarry, the market will be closed."

Adrian, Coulter, and Scavenger had gotten pickup work in a nearby rock quarry. The work went to whomever showed up each day. They had worked there for the last two, and had received the coins that Gift now held in his hand. Gift and Leen had tried to apply as well, but were turned away at the gate.

They needed the money and the legitimate work because they planned to stay in this area until Coulter got his strength back. Adrian thought they might have to stay longer. He felt that this was the best place to hide Gift until they had a real plan. Gift didn't want to wait too long. The mountain made him nervous, but it was more than that. Each day that went by was a day that his great-grandfather solidified his position on the Isle. The Isle was Gift's home; and he didn't want that murderer in charge.

Still, they all seemed to assume that Scavenger's plan was best. Scavenger wanted to hide Gift until they could make Gift the equal of the Black King—the equal of a man who had ruled the Fey for generations and who killed without a qualm. Gift wasn't sure he could ever be like that.

Leen had moved down the street and peered between two of the buildings. The sun had risen higher, cresting the edge of the mountains and increasing the light.

"Hey," she said, "I think I've found it."

Gift took a deep breath. He had felt nervous standing still like that. Adrian and Scavenger had determined that the Blooders, as the people from this area called themselves, had no prejudices against Fey, didn't really care if the Fey were among them or not. They wouldn't try, as other Islanders might, to kill Fey in their midst. At worst, they ignored the differences.

Except height.

Gift would see how far that prejudice extended on this day.

He crossed the road and stopped at her side. The alley between the buildings here was paved with the same stone the buildings were made of. On the other side of the buildings, the stone continued, forming a flat plaza. On the plaza, several booths were built in. More stone. Behind those booths were people, laying out wares and talking with each other. Women, carrying baskets, were already making their way through the stalls, picking up fruits and vegetables and then setting them down again, or purchasing them with the same sort of coin that Gift held.

"Let's go," he said to Leen.

They made their way through the alley, and into the market itself. The conversations halted as they approached. Gift felt a flush warm his skin.

"We just came to buy food," he said.

Three women clenched fists at him. Another merchant did the same.

"Away with ye, demon-spawn," said a man near the front.

Gift held up a coin. "We can pay," he said.

"We dasn't take the money of demons," another man said.

"*And they came down from the mountaintops,*" said an elderly woman, obviously quoting something, "*with their gold and their beauty and their winning ways. 'We only want to buy,' they said, and came forward. When a merchant took the coin, his soul left through his eyes, hovering between them, before vanishing into the strangers' mouths.*"

She clenched her fists at him. "Begone, demon-spawn."

Gift was confused. He'd never heard anything like that before. "I'm not from here," he said. "Please. My friend and I would like to buy food."

The Blooders crowded forward, raising their fists one by one. Their eyes glittered with fear. Leen took his arm.

"It's no use, Gift," she said. "Let's go."

"I don't understand," he said. "It's money, same as what you pay. I'm no demon-spawn."

"The tall ones have returned," the elderly woman said, "just as the legends said they would."

"Begone," the crowd chanted together. "Begone."

"Gift," Leen said, tugging on him.

The hair had risen on the back of his neck. These people had no weapons and no obvious magick, and yet they had a collective energy that felt like magick. But he wouldn't show fear. He couldn't. Not now. It would give them too much power.

"I'm sorry," he said, wondering at the vehemence, at the strength behind their fear. "I am not from your mountains. I do not mean you harm."

"*Begone,*" they said again, moving closer.

He let Leen pull him into the alley. They walked backwards until they reached the dirt street, and then they turned and ran.

It wasn't until they reached the outskirts of town that they stopped. Gift was breathing hard. The fear that they had aroused in him had made little goosebumps on his arms. Leen had gone gray.

"That was a Chant," she said. "We were Compelled. Me more than you. But we were still Compelled."

Gift frowned at her. They had stopped over a small rise. The city lay below them, the stone houses glistening in the early morning sunshine.

"Impossible," he said. "They're Islanders."

"So is Coulter," Leen said. She shivered, visibly. "Maybe he isn't as unusual as we thought."

Gift looked down at the city. His people would have known. The Fey would have known if there was other magick on Blue Isle, more magick than the wild magick that had created him, his sister, and Coulter. They would have known.

They would have known and they would have told him.

Wouldn't they?

But no Fey had ever been here before. In this place, where the mountains shimmered and were the color of blood.

What had kept his grandfather away?

What had kept his great-grandfather away?

Distance?

Or something else, something less visible?

Like a barrier.

Like a Chant.

FOUR

A moan woke Nicholas. He turned on his side and looked at his daughter. Her hair was tangled around her face, one arm flung above her head. She was too thin, and she had deep shadows under her eyes, despite the four days of rest.

The cave was surprisingly warm. Sometime during the night he had kicked off his blankets. The fire that the Shaman tended still burned at the mouth of the cave, but she was gone. Outside, a thin golden light let him know that it was nearly dawn.

He thought he heard the moan again, but Arianna hadn't moved. He was worried about her. The Shaman said her exhaustion came from Shifting too many times in such a short period, but Nicholas wondered if it weren't more.

If it weren't the loss of her home, her city, and her beloved Sebastian.

Sebastian wasn't really her brother—something Nicholas had learned only two weeks before. He was a changeling, left by Jewel's father when he stole Nicholas's real son, Gift. Gift had been raised by the Fey, and Nicholas had raised what he thought was a child—a slow, sweet-tempered boy—who in fact turned out to be made of stone.

That stone had shattered a week ago, when Sebastian had

protected Nicholas from the swords of the Black King's guards. Sebastian had exploded in a blaze of light. His loss had hurt Nicholas, but it had devastated Arianna.

She had loved him above all else.

But if the moan hadn't come from Arianna, then it had come from outside.

From the Shaman.

Nicholas stood, and wiped the sleep from his eyes. The Shaman had continually surprised him, taking his side against the Fey not once but a number of times. She had saved Arianna's life when Jewel died in childbirth, and she had given him advice when no one else would. Sometimes, it seemed, she was the only one who still believed in the vision that he and Jewel had shared: that in combining their people, the Islanders and the Fey, they would be able to defeat the Black King and to leave Blue Isle intact.

But Blue Isle was no longer intact. Its king lived in a cave. Its major city had burned, and many of its people were dead. The Black King lived in the palace now, but he was not well. Nicholas had nearly killed him during their one and only meeting.

And lost Sebastian in the process.

When he reached the outside of the cave, he saw that the Shaman was sitting on her favorite rock. If she had had trouble a moment before, he couldn't see evidence of it now.

Except.

Except the snow was churned up near her feet.

Had she had another Vision? If so, she would tell him when the time came.

He had come to trust that too.

He pulled on his boots, and set Arianna's near her when she awoke. She had a Shape-Shifter's abhorrence of all things binding: shoes, clothing, rules. He often found that exasperating, especially these last few days, when he had been so worried about her health.

She still didn't stir, but her chest rose up and down as she breathed heavily in sleep. He didn't want to disturb her. Not yet. Besides, he had made some decisions, and he wanted to discuss them with the Shaman before Arianna awoke.

For three days after his arrival here, he hadn't been able to sleep. He knew he had to find a way to get the Black King off Blue Isle. He thought of raising armies, of fighting the Fey in their own way.

That wouldn't work. His people had some experience defending their homeland from the first invasion, but they were not a military people.

He could come up with only one solution, and he didn't like it.

He hoped the Shaman would have another.

He put the cape Arianna had stolen for him over the pants and shirt that she had also found, then went outside the cave and scrubbed his face in the snow. He had felt unclean for days, and he longed, more than he wanted to admit, for the comforts of the palace in Jahn.

"There is root tea and meal mush on the fire," the Shaman said without turning around. She had been cooking nourishing meals for them. He had worried about her food supplies, but she had merely smiled at him. When he queried some more, she said that all she had to do was go down the mountain, past the tree line, and she would find enough plants to keep her fed for months.

"Thanks," he said. He grabbed their only cup and spoon, filled the cup with mush, and then ate. When he finished, he melted snow in the second pan and cleaned the spoon, leaving it on its rock, where Arianna could find it. He rinsed out the cup, poured some root tea, and drank.

Over the last few days, he had gotten used to the tea's bitterness. He was beginning to like it.

Then he rinsed out the cup, set it near the spoon, and walked over to the Shaman. She was watching him as he did. He knew what she saw. The past two weeks had aged him. He too had lost weight, making the bones of his face prominent. A webbing of fine lines near his blue eyes gave him a look of perpetual worry. And his blond hair, once the color of the summer sun, seemed to have grown lighter. It was starting to go silver.

She had commented on it the night before. She had said, "A man could not endure the things you have endured without them showing in his face."

He wondered if that was why her face had so many wrinkles. She hadn't changed at all since he first met her, around the time he married Jewel. Her hair was white, and it circled her head like an explosion of light. Her mouth was a small oval amidst all the wrinkles. Only her eyes looked Fey. They were dark and bright and powerful, making her seem ageless somehow, even though Nicholas knew her to be of an age with the Black King.

Young, she said, for a Shaman.

"Morning," Nicholas said.

The Shaman patted a smooth spot on the rock beside her. "The sun has blood in it this morning," she said.

"It's from the fires," he said as he sat beside her.

The Black King had burned most of the city of Jahn. The Shaman had told him that it was the Fey manner of war. Destroy the cities, where much of the useless wealth accumulated. Leave the fields and the farms untouched. The policy destroyed the power bases and left the riches of the country intact.

"Perhaps," she said, but she clearly did not agree.

He felt a twist in his stomach that had nothing to do with the meager meal he had just eaten. "What else could it be?"

She shook her head, her eyes downcast. Something *had* happened this morning. He was certain of it.

"Did you See something?"

"Nothing I understand," she said.

"So you did."

She nodded. "But things are no different, not yet."

"And you think they will be?"

She raised her eyes. In them, he saw a sadness he did not completely understand. "I hope so," she said softly.

He was silent for a moment. He needed to talk to her, but her mood was odd. He sighed. "Sometimes I envy your Feyness," he said.

His statement clearly startled her. Color flooded her cheeks. "Because of the Vision?" she asked.

He shook his head. "Because your path is set by who you are. You will always be a Visionary, my friend, just as my daughter will always be a Shifter."

But in the last two weeks, he had gone from King of Blue Isle to a man whose country had been taken from him. From King to soldier at best.

Assassin at worst.

"You will always be King," she said.

"King of a conquered country." He folded his hands over his knees. "I have been thinking for the last two days. My options are few. I can surrender, give Arianna to him, and see what he does to her, how he molds her in his image. And he will. I have never met a man with a will like his."

"And the subtle magicks of an aged Visionary," the Shaman

said. "Links, Controls, Constructs. She wouldn't even know what changed her."

His heart pounded. The Shaman had just confirmed what he had feared most. If he gave up, he would lose Arianna completely.

"I could fight him," Nicholas said. "But my armies are decimated, and my people no longer trust me. They haven't since I married Jewel. They believe I will help the Fey. It would take more time than we have to convince them otherwise."

She waited. She was an excellent listener. The best he had ever encountered.

"I could stay here," he said, "and hide my daughter. You could search for Gift, and when you found him, you could bring him to me. The Isle would have to fight for itself, if it could. The Black King needs to find his great-grandchildren in order to move on to Leut. We would stall him until we became careless. And then we would lose."

"What of going to Leut yourself?" she said. "You could rule in exile, gather an army there, and bring it back."

He had thought of that. He had spent most of the last two days thinking about that option. But he knew nothing of the continent beyond Blue Isle. His people had only traded with Nye on the Galinas continent, and that had been before he became King.

"Abandoning Blue Isle to the Black King? Risking death at sea?" Nicholas smiled. "This is my home. And that path carries too much risk, even for me."

The sun had risen higher, but it brought no warmth. The reddish color remained in the light, almost as if the rays were filtered through a bloody cloth. The Shaman pulled her blanket tight. Nicholas felt the chill as well.

"You have found a course," she said. It was not a question.

"I think so," he said. "I can't seem to think of anything else. Perhaps your Vision—"

"Your course first," the Shaman said.

He took a deep breath. It wasn't real until he spoke of it. He bowed his head, ran a hand through his hair. His fingers were cold against his scalp.

"I am going to leave here," he said. "I want you to keep Arianna safe."

"You're not taking her with you?" the Shaman asked.

"I can't," Nicholas said. "She's too impulsive."

The Shaman's eyes widened. She knew what he was going to

say. It was all over her face, her fear, her disapproval. But he had already tried this before, and nothing had happened.

Except losing Sebastian.

But that had nothing to do with the Black Throne and its curses. Did it?

"Nicholas, you can't," the Shaman said.

"Someone has to," Nicholas said. He held out his hands, trying to warm them in the growing sunlight.

"You have no magick," the Shaman said.

"I don't need magick. The Black King is as mortal as the rest of us." Nicholas tilted his head. The sunlight streaked his skin, coating it in blood. "But only I can kill him."

FIVE

RUGAD, the Black King, stood on a balcony overlooking the garden. Plants he did not recognize bloomed below. Before the Fey came, Jahn must have been beautiful.

But now the air had an acrid scent. Some of the fires still burned. The city around the palace was a blackened husk of its former self—most of the buildings that could be burned had been. Only the palace remained completely intact. The palace and its outbuildings. The rest of the city had been leveled.

Or would be. He had yet to give the order, but he would. He would leave buildings between the palace and river, and rebuild the warehouses. The rest of Jahn—most of Jahn—would be completely destroyed. The foolish Islanders had built Jahn on prime farm land. The fires would replenish the earth, as they had done in so many other cities, after so many other campaigns, and then the Islanders, grateful for his generosity, would farm it.

The additional food supplies would benefit the Fey. Blue Isle itself would furnish supplies for the next campaign—the one that took him to the Leut continent.

Conquering Blue Isle had been easy, as he had expected. His son Rugar, who had brought the first invasion force here, had merely been incompetent. And his incompetence had led to Rugad's other problem.

His great-grandchildren. They were still missing.

Rugad touched the bandage around his neck. Jewel's husband, the Islander King, had nearly killed him a week ago. Only the quick thinking of Rugad's guards and the talents of the Domestic Healers had saved him. He had been without a voice for days, but he would remedy that this afternoon. He had been studying the old magicks, and he knew there was a healing spell that would give him the power of speech despite the damage.

The Healers hadn't told him because they knew the risks.

So did he.

Now.

And the decision was his to make.

Just as the decisions for this Isle were his to make. He leaned on the railing. He was still weak. The injury had been a serious one. He wouldn't be able to stand for long. But he had been injured seriously several times in his past, and he had learned that staying in bed only made the weakness last. Forcing the body to use its strength kept it alive.

Beyond the garden, he could see the towers of the palace's sister building, the Tabernacle. It stood on the other side of the Cardidas River, a river that Rugad planned to use as a major transportation route sometime soon. He had destroyed the Tabernacle and its Black Robes first, slaughtering the ancient religion before it could even rise from its slumber. The religion had caused the first invasion force much grief. The magick poison, which the Islanders called holy water, killed the Fey quickly and horribly. He had learned of the holy poison's power in a Vision. He had had his guards round up the remaining members of the Rocaanist sect on Nye—decades before, Rocaanists had tried to expand their religion to the Galinas continent, but it hadn't taken. Only a few had followed it, and they had been dying out by the time he learned of them.

He asked for and got a sample of their holy water. Then he gave it to his Spell Warders. They had used some of the blood and bone matter taken from the Fey dead to determine its effects, then to determine how best to combat those effects. Their solution had been a simple antidote, absorbed into the body before the troops entered Blue Isle. Apparently, the holy water had an ingredient, a magick ingredient, that destroyed his people, and the Warders found a way around it.

Rugad wouldn't get caught unawares, unlike his son.

His policy had been simple. Neutralize the magick and destroy its source.

He had won the Isle, and he could, logically, begin to plan his campaign to conquer Leut. But he hadn't come to Blue Isle just for its strategic position.

He had come because he was ninety-two years old. He still had, in the course of a normal Fey lifespan, another fifty years. But in those years, he hoped to train his great-grandson—or his great-granddaughter—in the ways of the Fey.

One of them, not his grandchildren still on Nye, would inherit the Black Throne.

And from what he had seen of his great-grandchildren's powers, his decision was correct. They had the brains, they had the Vision, and they had the power. They would rule as well and as ruthlessly as he.

If he could train them.

The girl was lost to him as long as she remained with her father. She was magnificent. She had the look of her mother, his granddaughter Jewel, and she had courage. She had faced him with fire in her eyes, hatred on her lips, and a plan in her heart. She had the cunning the Black Throne needed.

Rugad had yet to meet his great-grandson. He had touched the boy once, through a Link, and then the boy's protector, a powerful Enchanter, had blocked the Link. It had not been enough to gain a sense of the young man, but from what Rugad had heard, the boy—Gift—was exceptionally talented. Rugad had seen the results of the boy's early Vision during the short campaign. The boy had repaired a Shadowlands, something even an adult Visionary couldn't always do.

The great-grandchildren were his, but in order to get them, he had to find them, woo them to his side, and, in the case of the girl, destroy her loyalty to her father. Those were goals that would take time. And it was more important for him to take that time than it was to move on to Leut. The Leut continent would wait. They probably knew the Fey were coming, but few societies had defenses against the Fey. Leut would be no different.

It had been a surprise that the Blue Isle was.

A knock on the door made him turn. He could not invite the person in—people had been entering without his permission since his injury—but that would soon stop.

The door opened, and Wisdom entered. Wisdom's long hair was braided on two sides, the braids running down his back. His arms bore heavy scarification, a ritual he had learned from the L'Nacin people after the Fey had conquered them. Since Rugad's injury, Wisdom had been his voice, a situation Rugad did not like.

"I have sent for Seger as you requested," Wisdom said, his tone faintly disapproving. Rugad had requested the Healer in writing, using one of his precious pieces of handmade paper. He was getting tired of writing. He wanted to speak, to give orders as he was meant to instead of filtering them through his power-hungry advisor. "She says that I am to tell you that the spell will not repair your voice, but will instead use other muscles in your throat to create a raspy whisper."

Rugad waved a hand dismissively. He knew that.

"She also said to tell you that if you use the muscles too long, there is a chance that you will never recover your real voice."

Rugad nodded once. He knew that too.

"She will remind you of that before she performs the spell, in case you wish to change your mind."

Rugad crossed his arms despite his precarious balance. He wanted Wisdom to leave this topic alone. Rugad had made his decision. Better half a voice than no voice at all. Especially now, when he had to find and recover his great-grandchildren.

When he had to find and execute their father.

Wisdom stared at him for a moment, then nodded, as if he understood. "I will tell her to come, then," Wisdom said, and the reluctance was back. So he didn't like giving up the power that being Rugad's voice had given him.

Rugad made note of it. Time to find Wisdom a new position, one that seemed to have a lot of authority and in reality had none. Rugad had a bit of time. He would find the right position.

Wisdom did not yet realize that he had outlived his usefulness.

"There is one final thing," he said. "The Domestics have found, in the course of their cleansing of this place, a series of secret passages that run throughout. They lead through the dungeons and beyond. I suppose you would like them explored?"

Rugad held up a finger, indicated that Wisdom should wait before assuming Rugad's answer. Wisdom grabbed paper and handed it to Rugad along with a Domestic-spelled pen, one that did not need to be dipped in ink each time it was used. He and Rugad had gone through this ritual a lot in the past week. It was this, more than anything else, that made Rugad realize that the duties of command could not be fulfilled without a voice. Writing and hand signals left too much unsaid, too much room for interpretation.

He sank into one of the iron chairs at the edge of the balcony, and spread the paper on his knee. Holding the paper in place with one hand, he scrawled quickly:

Do not kill any Islanders found in the tunnels. Have our people remain unseen. Place guards on the Islanders and report to me.

He thrust the paper at Wisdom. Wisdom took it, read it, and frowned. "But sir," he said as he too often had recently, "don't you think it would be best to let them know of the Fey presence?"

Rugad slapped the paper with his hand. Then he clenched a fist, narrowed his eyes, and pointed to the door.

Wisdom nodded. "You're right, as always," he said. "I will give the order immediately, and make sure you are kept informed."

Rugad bowed his head once in acknowledgment, then stood, and turned his back on Wisdom. A moment later, he heard the door click shut.

Fool. For all his fancy L'Nacin name, Wisdom had none. He did not realize that only a handful of Islanders had to know about those secret passages. Good King Nicholas and Rugad's great-granddaughter were among them. Even if Nicholas and Arianna were not in those tunnels, the Islanders who were might know where the two were hiding. With luck, they might lead the Fey to the King and his daughter.

With luck.

As long as the Fey remained invisible.

As long as Wisdom gave the correct order.

Rugad clenched his fist and rested it on the balcony railing. Seger had better hurry. Rugad needed a voice before the day was out.

SIX

CON leaned against the cases of holy water. The large open tunnel, where he had first encountered the old Aud "gone bad" and his troop of cutthroats, was filled now with real Auds, several Officiates, and a large number of Danites. They had all survived the Fey attack on the Tabernacle and the subsequent fire by going to the catacombs beneath the Tabernacle and then crawling under the bridge as Con had done hours before.

In this large man-made cavern that smelled faintly of smoke and the river was all that remained of Rocaanism, Blue Isle's religion. And tragically, the Rocaan, the leader of the religion, the Keeper of the Secrets, was not among them. He had died from a fall from one of the tower windows, and had been eaten by the beasts that were controlled by the Fey.

Or perhaps those beasts were part Fey. Con did not know nor did he understand. He was only thirteen, although he felt as if he had aged a decade in the last two weeks. He was an Aud himself, the lowliest of the low in Rocaanism, as demonstrated by his bare feet, his unadorned flesh-colored robe, and the small silver sword he wore around his neck. The Officiates, members of the highest order to have survived the attack, wore plush black robes, had sandals, and the swords they wore around their necks were filigree, handmade, and expensive.

Not that it mattered any more. Rocaanism without the Rocaan was probably doomed.

Now the survivors were scattered all over the cavern. Many slept. Others tended wounds received in the fighting. Some prayed. Five torches burned in select corners of the cavern, giving faint light. In the days Con had been down here, he felt as if he had lost a bit of himself to the darkness, as if it had sapped much of his strength.

Beside him, he heard a small groan and then an odd creak—the sound of stone grating against stone. Sebastian was awake.

Con shuddered. On the day the Tabernacle burned, he had received the Rocaan's last Charge: go to the palace through the tunnels and warn the King that the Fey had invaded. Con had made a long, tortuous trip through the passageways, nearly getting captured by the old Aud and his gang of cutthroats, and had arrived at the palace in time to see the troops the King had dispatched go up the tunnels to fight the Fey.

It had done little good. The Fey had been victorious anyway. But Con, on his Charge, had gone into the palace, and had arrived in the Great Hall, near the wall of swords. He had pushed the hidden door open to find Fey waiting for him, and he had grabbed a sword off the wall, only to discover that it killed Fey as easily as holy water had.

The sword was beside him now, as was the other thing he had rescued from the palace: Sebastian, the Fey-like creature made of stone, who was King Nicholas's son.

"We . . . must . . . leave." Sebastian spoke slowly, his voice deep and rich, as a stone's might be. Con turned. Sebastian sat up, his hands behind him, bracing him. In the week they had known each other, Sebastian had never made a suggestion, let alone given a command.

"Leave?" Con said.

Sebastian nodded in his curious fashion. His head went down once and then up again, as if the movement were difficult for him. All movement seemed difficult for him. Con did not know if that was unusual.

He had discovered Sebastian by accident. Con had hidden in a room in the palace, a room filled with rubble. He had set his unusual sword on that rubble. Then there was an explosive sound, like booming thunder, and all the air seemed to disappear from the room. Con was thrown back. When he came to himself, he saw that he was not alone.

Sebastian sat in the middle of the room, naked, lines and cracks running through his body as if he were a shattered goblet that had been poorly repaired. The rubble was gone. And Con recognized Sebastian for what he was: the King's half-witted son.

It startled Con that the result of a mixed marriage between a Fey and an Islander would result in a young man who seemed to be made of stone instead of flesh, whose mind, while intact, moved as slowly as a mountain, and whose soul seemed as fresh and innocent as that of a newborn babe.

"We . . . *must* . . . leave," Sebastian said again, and Con frowned. He had felt that way for days, but the Officiates refused to let anyone out of the cavern. They were afraid that people who explored the tunnels would find Fey and lead the Fey back here. The Officiates weren't protecting the cavern for its holy water supplies—holy water had been rendered useless in the battle against the Fey—but for all the other supplies: food, extra water, and even blankets. It was as if the gang that had hidden here had abandoned everything quickly and under duress.

"I know," Con said, hoping that would placate Sebastian. Sebastian had proven difficult in a whole manner of ways. Once he got an idea into his mind, it seemed to stay. He had wanted to look for his sister and father after Con had rescued him from the palace. Con had finally lied to him, telling him that they were going to search in the tunnels below.

A day later, Sebastian had said, rather sorrowfully, "We . . . aren't . . . look-ing . . . any-more."

And they weren't. The King had disappeared, leaving his son to fend for himself. It wasn't that the King was dead—Con had seen him ride out of the palace on a horse. The King had left without his son, a son and heir who was at a disadvantage at all times. It was an unusual cruelty, given Sebastian's capacity or lack thereof. Con found that he couldn't abandon Sebastian too. He felt that Sebastian was part of his Charge. The Rocaan hadn't known that Sebastian needed guarding, but the Holy One had. And He had sent Con.

"Now," Sebastian said. His grating voice held an urgency that Con had never heard before.

Con turned to him. Sometimes he found it hard to look at Sebastian, with all the lines and cracks running through his grayish skin. Now they seemed like sorrow lines, all pointing to the fear that made his chin jut forward, his mouth turn down.

"Why?" Con asked, in spite of himself.

"Magick . . . shifted," Sebastian said.

Con didn't know what that meant. But he did know that Sebastian was half-Fey and that he might know things that Islanders wouldn't. It had been what the Officiates feared when Con stumbled on their hiding place.

Take him away, they had said. *He's Fey. He does not belong here.*

He is the King's son, Con had said.

We cannot have him here, they had said.

He is my Charge, Con had said.

And that had silenced them. They had argued about Sebastian a bit later as well, but by then, Con had another answer for them. If they let Sebastian go, he might lead the Fey to them. They had extrapolated that answer to all the people hiding in the cavern and now no one could leave.

"Where would we go?" Con asked. He had been asking himself that for days. He hated the darkness here, the sense of waiting, the anticipation of doom. The Officiates seemed to have forgotten the Words Written and Unwritten:

A man's strength lies in his ability to rescue himself and others.

The Officiates may have forgotten that, but Con hadn't.

"I . . . do . . . not . . . know," Sebastian said. "But . . . we . . . must . . . go. Now."

"All of us?"

"No." Sebastian's sorrowful look seemed to grow deeper. "You . . . and . . . me."

Con rubbed a hand over his face. The fear that had been bottled up inside him flared. He had fled here because he hadn't known where else to go. He had planned to go back to the Tabernacle, but it only took moments for him to realize that the Tabernacle—and the entire city—were gone.

He supposed they could try to find his parents, to see if his family had survived. He had been a second son, sent young to Rocaanism, as was the tradition. His family gave him away, and he belonged to the Roca now. It had been such a wrenching parting, a loss that had ripped through him and left him speechless for months, that he did not want to face them ever again.

He wasn't even sure he wanted to know if they lived or died.

"We have nowhere to go," Con said. He could imagine them, scavenging through the countryside, trying to avoid the Fey. Sebastian could not move quickly. If a Fey spotted them, they were doomed.

Sebastian shuddered. Con could feel it, a deep rumbling from within, as if the earth actually moved.

"I . . . know . . . one . . . place," Sebastian said. "But . . . I . . . have . . . never . . . been . . . there."

"Great," Con said. "How are we supposed to find it?"

"I . . . have . . . mem-o-ries . . . not . . . mine. . . . I . . . will . . . ex-plore." And then he vanished from his eyes. Con had never seen anything like it. One moment, he was talking to a living, breathing person, the next he sat beside a statue. The fear he had been fighting grew. If this truly was his Charge, then it was a strange one. But he could not deny it. The King carried the Roca's blood. He was a direct descendent of the Roca's bloodline. And that meant his son was, too.

And with the death of the Rocaan, that meant the King's family, within their bodies, guarded one of the most precious pieces of Rocaanism.

Con had always wondered about the Roca. His advice, recorded in the Words Written and Unwritten, seemed so wise, and yet his final action, the one the religion celebrated, seemed on the face of it so foolish. The Roca, when asked to choose between leading his people into a battle they could not win or slaughtering the Soldiers of the Enemy, decided instead to offer himself as a sacrifice. He cleaned his sword with holy water before letting the Soldiers of the Enemy run him through. And then he was Absorbed into the Hand of God, where he now interceded for his people.

Although he hadn't done a lot of interceding lately.

Con clenched a fist. The thought was blasphemous and he knew it. But the Islanders were faced with the Soldiers of the Enemy for the second time in twenty years, and each time God had done nothing.

Perhaps He was displeased with the uses holy water had been put to. Or perhaps He expected more from his people, as the Words Written and Unwritten said.

Then, suddenly, Sebastian was back in his own eyes. The change was startling and subtle at the same time. Con couldn't explain the difference, but he felt it. It was like a breeze suddenly coming up on a warm summer's day.

"I . . . can . . . find . . . it," Sebastian said. He slowly reached across the distance between them and took Con's arm. Sebastian's grip was firm, almost painful. "We . . . must . . . go."

"All right," Con said. He knew that leaving, despite the Officiates' orders, would be easy. The darkness would give them cover, and no one paid attention anyway. They were all too involved in their own loss. "I'll get supplies, and then we can leave."

He wasn't sure about trusting this creature beside him, but he knew it was better than remaining here, beneath the ruined city, waiting for the Fey. He had fought the Fey once, and that was more than enough.

SEVEN

"YOU are not the only one who can kill the Black King," the Shaman said. She wrapped her blanket tighter around herself, as if her own words made her cold.

Nicholas felt unusually warm, despite the snow, despite the chill air. The sunlight was thin, and seemed to have no heat. But the warmth he felt came from within, from a decision soundly made.

He had no other choice.

"There are others—"

"Who won't even get close."

She tilted her head toward him. Her hair looked pale in the thin light. It formed a nimbus around her head. She was only one of two Fey he had ever met whose hair was not black.

"You won't get close either," she said. "He expects you now. He sees you as a worthy adversary, and he will expect you to try again. He will do everything he can to prevent that."

"I'll figure out something. I know passages in the palace—"

"And I'm sure he will soon if he doesn't already." The Shaman turned slightly on her rock. Her dark eyes were like holes in her face. "Nicholas, you have never met anyone like him. He has held continents under his hand. He is the smartest military leader the Fey have had in generations, and we are a military people. You were lucky the first time, and you nearly killed him. You will not be lucky again."

"Have you Seen something?" Nicholas asked.

She stared at him. Then closed her eyes. "I have Seen many things. Mostly, I See death."

Nicholas shook his head. There was death all around them. Arianna was his heir now. She could rule if something happened to him. If there was something left to rule. And the only way that would happen would be to eliminate the Black King.

"I can try to get close," Nicholas said. "I have been known to have amazing luck."

"You would need it," the Shaman said quietly. "The Black King probably has orders out for your execution."

The thought didn't shock him. He knew it. He might use it to his advantage if he had to, although he wasn't quite sure how.

Yet.

Something scraped behind him. Nicholas turned. His daughter stood at the mouth of the cave. She was wrapped in a blanket, but her thinness was still painfully apparent, her Fey features all the more severe because of it. She used to have some of his roundness. That was all gone now.

Only her bright blue eyes and her pale brown skin showed his paternity. He had never noticed how frail the light skin and dark hair made her look. Not even as a newborn that couldn't keep its shape had she struck him as this vulnerable.

"Dad can't get close, but I can," Arianna said. She sounded confident, but her eyes looked haunted.

"You cannot get close, child," the Shaman said without turning around. She continued to face the valley, as if she could see something in the villages below.

"I can," Arianna said. In the past, that sentence would have had fire behind it. Now it only had a quiet determination. "I can look like a hundred different Fey. I can get in so close he wouldn't even know I'm there. I could look like his most trusted advisor."

"With practice," Nicholas said. His heart had contracted in his chest. He didn't want to think of her there, with the Black King, so close to his power and his temptations.

And his soldiers.

"With practice," she agreed.

"And then what would you do, child? Would you try to reason with him? Would you make him leave? Would you offer yourself as a sacrifice, pretending to work with him, while saving Blue Isle?"

Arianna's eyes flashed. Blue and bright and deep. "I would kill him."

"You cannot," the Shaman said. "It will destroy the Blood Magick."

"I don't believe in that," Arianna said. "Dad stabbed the Black King and nothing happened."

"Your father did not kill him."

"I may not be considered part of the Blood," Nicholas said.

"But you might be," the Shaman said. "Do not underestimate the Mysteries and the Powers. They hold the secret to all."

"And they seem to be capricious," Arianna said. "I can try."

"You would risk a Blood war?" the Shaman said. "You would risk being wrong? The Black Throne is held together by Blood Magick. If that Blood—and you are part of it, child, through your mother—if that Blood turns on itself, insanity will reign. Millions will die. You can gamble with your own life, child, on a hunch, but you cannot gamble with the lives of millions. And neither," she said, looking at Nicholas, "can you."

"I already have," he said. "I tried to kill him."

"Did you?" she asked. She hunched forward, but she still did not turn. "You are a warrior, good Nicholas. Warriors do not fail."

Nicholas's heart was in his throat. Arianna frowned at him, as if she did not understand.

"Why wouldn't you try to kill him?" she asked.

"I did," Nicholas said.

"And something within you prevented it. Something stopped you from severing his head from his body," the Shaman said.

"Yes," Nicholas said. "The toughness of his throat."

Arianna crossed her arms. The blanket fell away. She was wearing britches and a linen shirt, and she looked cold.

The Shaman shook her head. "I think it was more," she said. "I think it was the knowledge of the consequences if you were wrong. You are a man used to making decisions for countless people. You do so instinctively. You did so that day."

"You sound so sure of yourself," Nicholas said.

The Shaman turned then. Her face was gray, her eyes dark. "I've Seen it," she whispered. "I've Seen the Blood turning on itself. The insanity."

"When?" The question was Arianna's, and it had a sharpness to it.

"The first time I Saw it was the day you and your father escaped the Black King," the Shaman said. "I had a series of Visions, and the last showed Blood against Blood, the Fey lunatics, killing all in their path. I have Seen that Vision over and over, child. It is a likely possibility."

"I didn't See it," Arianna said.

"We don't See all," the Shaman said. "We only See parts. And sometimes we See nothing at all. That is why Visionaries compare Visions. You Saw something that day. I did too. We should compare."

The warmth Nicholas felt had fled. Instead, a chill colder than ice filled him. He believed in Visions. He knew their limits and their strengths. Arianna was alive because the Shaman had had a Vision, a Vision that someone needed to assist at Arianna's birth. Otherwise, both Arianna and Jewel would be dead.

"You saw the result of Blood against Blood," he said, his voice wavering slightly.

The Shaman nodded. So that was the difference he had seen in her since they arrived. Not just the fact that she had denied her training and abandoned her post in the Shadowlands, unwilling to die with all the other Fey from the first invasion force. Not just the fact that she was worried for him and Arianna. But the fact that she was terrified for the whole world.

Everything rested on what they all decided.

Together.

He had already seen his world explode twice in his lifetime, but the Fey had an odd way of conquering. They didn't destroy indiscriminately. They kept fields and crops and people alive so that the land would earn for the Empire.

But if the Shaman's Vision were true, even that would disappear. The Fey would become lunatics, and the Fey-ruled world would turn upon itself, exploding in conflagrations not seen since the Fey began conquering other countries.

The very thought made his stomach turn.

"You believe her?" Arianna asked.

He nodded. "Don't trifle with Visions," he said. "Your mother tried, and walked right into hers."

Arianna took a step out into the snow. "But they can be wrong. You said they can be wrong. You said my grandfather followed a false Vision. That's why he failed here, why he didn't conquer Blue Isle."

Nicholas glanced at the Shaman, hoping she would explain. She, in turn, nodded her head toward him.

"He failed," Nicholas said, "because he didn't compare the Visions. If he had compared his Vision with your mother's he would have learned that she was going to die here. As it was, he had incomplete information, and it cost hundreds of lives."

"So your Vision could be incomplete," Arianna said to the Shaman.

The Shaman nodded. "It could be. I'm sure it is," she said. "But we do not know in what way, yet. It might be that if we compare Visions we will learn that you have Seen the path to the Blood against Blood and I have Seen the result. The result is worthless without the path."

"Not worthless," Nicholas said. "You'd never had that Vision before that day, have you?"

She shook her head.

"So something we did then might lead us to the insanity you're talking about. Something changed that day, and we might be on that path."

"That's right," the Shaman said.

"Would it be so bad?" Arianna asked.

Nicholas turned to her, the chill deepening. He must have looked shocked because she raised her hands in self-defense.

"I mean, I know that all the deaths are bad," she said. "I know that. But they would happen in the Fey Empire and nowhere else. If we don't stop the Black King, there will be more deaths on Leut and in the rest of the world. It seems to me that we're trading Fey lives for real lives. It might be worth it."

Nicholas was staring at her. She looked the same. The birthmark on her chin made her the Arianna he had always known. Tall, slender, with the look of Jewel. But he hadn't given her this ruthlessness, this utter disregard for life.

Had he?

"Your child is truly Fey, Nicholas," the Shaman said, and there was disappointment in her voice. "She could kill the Black King with no remorse."

"I'd feel the remorse," Nicholas said.

The Shaman slipped a hand out from under the blanket and put her fingers on his arm. Her skin was cool, as if nothing could keep her warm.

"That is why you cannot go to him," she said. "You're not a killer, Nicholas. You are a warrior. You cannot kill in cold blood. If you could do that, you would have killed that Black Robe, the one who murdered your wife."

Matthias. Nicholas clenched a fist. He had wanted to kill Matthias that day, but killing him would have made Nicholas no better than Matthias was.

"It's not an acceptable risk, Arianna," Nicholas said. He put a hand over the Shaman's. His fingers were warmer than hers were. "I can't believe you don't understand that. I can't believe you don't understand the value of life."

"She is a Shifter raised by a Shifter," the Shaman said, and sighed. "If I had known that Solanda would rise above herself and remain with the child for life, then I would have intervened somehow. I thought your attitudes would form her, not attitudes of a pure Fey."

"Nothing's wrong with Solanda," Arianna said. Her voice rose. "She's been good for me."

And she's probably dead, Nicholas thought. "If Jewel had lived, Arianna would have been raised by a Fey."

"If Jewel had lived," the Shaman said, "Arianna would not. I would not have come, and Jewel was not equipped to handle such a powerful Shifter's birth."

Arianna's eyes narrowed. "You can stop talking about me like I'm not here," she said.

Nicholas shook his head. He would have to deal with his daughter later. The enormity of her callousness was more than he could handle at the moment.

And he had anointed her to follow him because he did not know his son Gift. Because he was afraid of this very thing, this Feyness, from his Fey-raised son.

"The Black King won't stop until I'm out of the way," Nicholas said, "and he has Arianna and Gift. Then he'll move on to Leut and continue his rampage through the countries of the world."

"It is what the Fey do," the Shaman said.

"Then why are you helping us?" Arianna asked.

"Because it must stop someday. The Fey Empire needs no more land. The men in your family—your Fey family—see the world as a toy, and conquering it as a game. It is a measure of your great-grandfather's prowess that he has expanded the empire so. Once conquering was a matter of Fey survival. We were a small race with little land and even less ability to provide for ourselves. Somewhere, we ceased seeking to improve ourselves. Somewhere we became blind and power-hungry and greedy. And it must stop before it reaches Leut. It can stop here. Nicholas and Jewel made it so. They gave us children who lead two races. Symbols of peace."

The Shaman emphasized those last three words, as if she were trying to drill them into Arianna's head.

Arianna's face flushed. "If you believe that, why don't you kill him?" she asked.

"Because I will lose my powers, child. And I think my counsel and my Vision are more important to you and your father than my death."

"Even if it means the Black King lives?" Arianna asked.

The Shaman squeezed Nicholas's arm and withdrew her hand. "Even if it means he lives," she said. "You are not ready to rule. You are too young, too impulsive, and you have no understanding of life outside your small sphere. The Black King will not move on until he has you or your brother. That gives us time."

"Time for what?" Arianna asked.

"Time to work with you," the Shaman said. "And time for you, Nicholas, to find someone who will destroy the Black King, without all the repercussions."

"I thought you said he shouldn't try killing the Black King," Arianna said.

"Not directly," the Shaman said.

"As if indirectly would work," Arianna said.

Nicholas felt his heart roll over. A possibility, and one that he could do. He believed in political assassination to stop a war. He knew that at times it was better to take one life than thousands. He just hadn't been sure he was capable of taking that life.

And he didn't know if the Fey magicks would let him.

"Indirectly does work, child," the Shaman said gently. "It is the favored method of assassination for people of Black Blood."

"What does that mean?" Arianna asked. "The favored method?"

"Exactly what it sounds like, child." The Shaman spoke softly, gently, as if she were imparting wisdom instead of tales of death. "Your great-grandfather killed your grandfather in just that way."

"I thought Solanda killed my grandfather," Arianna said.

"She did," the Shaman said, "but your great-grandfather had had a Vision, a Vision that your grandfather would fail here. And failure meant death."

"Because my great-grandfather could kill him then?" Arianna asked.

"No," the Shaman said. "Because losing a war usually means the commander dies. It is to Rugar's credit that he lasted as long as he did. And his invasion here was not a complete failure. It resulted in you and your brother, two of the most powerful Fey ever."

"I don't know what good it does me," Arianna said, "being powerful. I couldn't save Sebastian."

"Sebastian died," Nicholas said, his voice breaking, "trying to save me. It was my fault."

And something he would have to live with. He had grown to love that boy, even if the child had been made of stone instead of flesh, even if he wasn't really Nicholas's blood kin. Sebastian was his child and he had shattered trying to prevent the Black King's soldiers from killing Nicholas.

Then a thought struck him, a thought he didn't like. "Did your Mysteries take Sebastian because I tried to kill the Black King?" he asked the Shaman.

She shrugged. "I do not understand the Mysteries," she said. "None of us do. They are capricious, more powerful than anything we are familiar with, and they lead us in odd ways."

"So you don't know," Nicholas said.

"It's possible," she said. "As possible as it is impossible."

He glanced at Arianna. A tear ran down her cheek. She had loved Sebastian beyond reason, and she had barely spoken of his death. Perhaps Nicholas had judged her too harshly. Perhaps he had failed to take into account what she was going through. She had lost everything—her home, her land, and her beloved brother. She had gone from being a princess to living in a cave. She had discovered great power while experiencing great loss.

He put out his hand to her, and she came to him. He hugged her close, feeling the bones of her shoulder blades against his palms. She was thinner and she was fragile, and the Shaman was right; Arianna was not ready to make decisions. Not for herself, or for her family or for her country.

Not yet.

He had a daughter to raise, and to keep safe. Right now, she was too easily corruptible. Part of that was his fault: he had kept her sheltered. He hadn't given her a chance to know anyone outside the palace. He hadn't allowed her to live, because he had been too afraid to lose her.

And now he was faced with losing her heart and soul.

He was right and the Shaman was right. The Black King had to die, but not by Nicholas's hand. The method had to be indirect and unexpected. And it would require some thought.

"What are we going to do?" Arianna said against him. She was probably speaking of Sebastian, but there was nothing they could do about that now. The boy was dead. They had to move on.

"We're going to find your brother," Nicholas said before he had a chance to consider the decision. "Your real brother."

Arianna pulled back. She held him at arm's length. The Shaman was staring at him, as if he had startled her.

Nicholas looked at both of them. "The Black King came here for his great-grandchild. Both of his great-grandchildren are Visionaries. He may not come for Arianna. He might search for young Gift. And it won't matter which one he finds. He'll mold that person to him. We have to find my son before the Black King does."

"And do what?" Arianna asked.

"Protect him," Nicholas said. "Just as we're protecting you."

EIGHT

PAUSHO was the first to reach the Meeting Hall. The large stone building was empty and dark despite the early morning light. She opened the doors, pulled the curtains away from the windows, and set her basket on the table. The other Wise Leaders from Constant would be here shortly. They would have to send for the rest.

Her heart was pounding. The sight of that tall thin creature in the market was almost too much for her aging heart. She had remembered the Incantation, though, had remembered more than the gesture, and that had united the people enough to drive it and its tall thin woman away.

This time.

Her mouth was dry. She was nearly seventy, a keeper of the ancient wisdom, who never believed she would do more with it than keep the Blooders pure. Even at that she had failed. Of all the babies condemned to the mountain, over two dozen had survived. Some due to the misguided kindness of childless women, others due to the young Auds who had come here from other places. Those religious children knew nothing of their heritage. They did not know that the compassionate drivel in the last chapters of the Words Written were added generations after the death of the Roca.

The original Words were kept in a stone box, in a stone vault, beneath this very hall. She had studied them, as had the other Wise Leaders, and they knew, unlike the Tabernacle, what had been added over the generations and what had been taken away.

She took a deep breath and put a hand over her heart. The scratchy wool of her sweater tugged at her palms. She was dressed for early morning: sweaters, heavy skirt with leggings beneath, and boots. She would be too hot by the time the meeting ended. But it was too late to run home now. Too late to change clothes. Too late to warn her husband of the meeting. Too late to bring food.

The emergency was upon them, and she needed to act quickly.

They all did.

"Tall ones."

She whirled. Zak was behind her. He was older than she was, his red hair gone yellow with age. The lines on his face were deep; sorrow lines. He had once said to her that a man could not condemn babies, however evil, without the torment showing up on his face.

"I saw them," she said. "In the market."

"I heard." His voice was deep, warm, compassionate. He leaned on his cane as he hobbled to the table. "I heard you drove them away."

She nodded. "We Incanted."

"It was good you were there." He spoke softly. His words hung between them. The entire city could have been lost if someone had so much as taken a coin from the tall one. It had been bad enough to allow Matthias back, all those years ago. As if the Wise Leaders could have kept him away. He had a place in Constant the day Elda had misguidedly rescued him from the mountain.

The traditions were quite specific on that: anyone the mountain spat back deserved to live.

But strangers, tall strangers who came from outside, were pure evil. They had to be driven away, and if they could not be, they had to die.

"The tall ones were seen two days ago," Zak said, "trying to find work in the quarry, but no one reported it until now."

She sighed. So many were raised without proper respect for the traditions now. She blamed the Auds for that. The Auds and the encroaching Tabernacle, who believed its version of the past was the only one.

At least there were no Auds in the kirk at the moment. She had managed to keep the last Aud's death hidden from the Tabernacle.

A stair creaked. Tri stood outside, his long red hair flowing about his face like a cloud. At forty, he was the youngest of the Wise Leaders, brought into the traditions when his father died, only one year before.

"They say the legends are coming true," he said. His voice quavered, and Pausho heard his disbelief. She had thought it a mistake to bring him into the leadership. He had been raised in Rocaanism, named Dimitri for a King of Blue Isle, and listened more to his religious mother than his wise father. Still, tradition demanded approval from only three Wise Leaders, and all had supported him. All except her.

"There were tall ones in the market today," she said. "I saw them."

"Strangers?" The disbelief still hadn't left his voice.

She nodded.

He came in, but he did not meet her gaze. Instead he went to Zak, pulled out a chair, and helped Zak down. She watched Tri, but he gave no more indication that he was upset, no indication that this meeting was anything more than an inconvenience, a way to take away the business at his forge.

"Have the others been sent for?" Tri asked.

"Yes," she said, wondering if he thought her a fool. She knew how to call a meeting, even though it was never done. The Leaders met only on the day of the full moon, and only for a very short time.

But she knew the procedures. She knew that the sighting of a tall one required a meeting, just as a demon birth did.

At that moment, Fyr entered. She was out of breath. She carried a basket on her thick arm, and she too wore her early-morning clothes. She was fifteen years older than Tri, and she had just become a Wise Leader a year before he had.

Pausho longed for her old group, the ones she had served with most of her career. The ones who approved a removal to the mountain without all the debate, who believed in the traditions and the legends without the corruption of outside stories, who knew the necessity of acting quickly and without thought.

"I saw Rin," Fyr said. "She's coming now."

Rin was the fifth and last of the Wise Leaders of Constant. She had been brought in just after Pausho, and they were so close it sometimes felt as if they were sisters.

Rin came through the door. She was out of breath, her round face flushed. She looked as if she had come a long way.

"Tall ones," she said, and in her voice, Pausho heard a terror matching her own. They were the old leaders of the Wise Ones now. It seemed like only weeks before they had been the youngest, looking to people decades older than they were for guidance.

Decades older, and now dead.

"Tall ones," Pausho said. "Please close the door."

Rin did. She was short and round and her curly brownish gray hair hadn't even been combed. Her clothing was mismatched and barely fastened. Someone had awakened her, and she had clearly dressed quickly and come.

"We need to send for the other Wise Leaders," Zak said.

He meant the leaders of the other villages, the leaders who represented the small enclaves throughout the mountains, and the leaders who represented only their families, living in isolation near the Slides of Death.

"We will," Pausho said. She had become, in the last year, the head of this group, a position she still was not comfortable with. Zak was the oldest, but he had no desire, indeed no ability, to lead. He merely suggested. She enforced. "But first we must warn our people. We must prevent the tall ones from doing commerce in this place, from touching our children, and from seducing our young people."

Tri sighed. "I think we're overreacting. We have no idea who these people are or what they want. And now they probably think we're a superstitious backwater."

"Does that matter?" Fyr asked quietly. "Do we care what others think?"

Tri shrugged. "I do. If they rode in, their horses may need shoeing. Perhaps they have weapons that need repair. I can always use new business in my forge. By Pausho's own statement, they had come to the market. They were going to spend coin. That's good for us—"

"Good?" Rin sat down in one of the chairs. Her twisted fingers were working the buttons on her sweater, attempting to fasten it better. "You are a Wise One and you do not know the stories?"

"Tall," Tri said. Then he stood. He was Pausho's height, Rin's height. Zak's height. Most of the people in the Cliffs of Blood grew no taller. They had purged the tall ones from their lines years ago. Only a handful got through.

A handful that survived the mountain.

"Tall," Tri said. "I am tall to our children. Does that make me evil? And what is tall? Perhaps the old stories don't mean men of Matthias's height. Perhaps they mean giants. The legends speak of 'creatures who scale the mountains.' Does that mean creatures who can climb the mountains? Or creatures who in some way compare in height to the mountains? We don't know. We're dealing with stories passed down from generation to generation. Just because Pausho believes these people were tall does not mean that they were the tall ones of legend."

Pausho crossed her arms. "You have no place here," she said.

Tri raised an eyebrow. "Because I question you? Because I'm not comfortable with the tasks of the Wise Ones? Because I refuse to condemn people to death without asking a few questions first?"

"Because you don't understand," she said quietly.

"Then make me," he said. "Make me understand. Tell me what would happen to all of us if these 'tall ones' spent their coin in our town. Matthias spends his coin here. You put him on the mountain, and when he survived, you reversed yourselves, saying that survivors belong like the rest of us."

"Matthias is no longer in Constant," Fyr said.

"Matthias returned last night, along with several other people," Tri said.

"Perhaps it was these tall ones you saw," Zak said.

"It was Matthias," Tri said. "His house is next to mine. I watched them all enter. Strangers, every last one of them."

"Were the tall ones with him?" Pausho asked. Her heart was beating hard. She had not known, all those years ago when she became a Wise One, what it meant to hold the life and death of others in her hands. She had not realized that she would never get used to it, never completely shake the feelings that Tri argued with now, the feeling that she had no right to make these decisions, that she was as confused as the rest of them.

"There was a woman who was of his height," Tri said. "Redhaired also. But I had never seen her before."

"The tall woman I saw was dark," Pausho said. "Dark hair,

dark skin, dark eyes. She had a look that made her not of here. The man did too."

Zak put a hand on her arm. "Was it night when he returned?"

Tri nodded.

"Then you cannot know if these tall ones were with him."

"I know these tall ones were in the quarry two days ago. They were searching for work," Zak said.

"And there is a strange man in the quarry now," Fyr said. "He is not tall, but he is dark, just as you described. He is not from here."

"Could Matthias have returned a few days ago, but not gone home?" Rin asked.

"Why?" Tri said. "Why would he stay away from his own shelter?"

Pausho's mouth was dry. "You have become friends with Matthias?" she said to Tri, voicing a question she had held for almost a year now.

"We have spoken," Tri said. "We're neighbors."

"And does he stop at your forge?"

Tri shrugged, but his gaze moved away from hers. "Everyone uses my forge."

"Does Matthias?"

Tri didn't answer. Fyr stood and touched his arm. He didn't look at her. His gaze was down.

"Tri," she said. "It's important."

"Important so you can persecute a man for how he is built rather than for who he is? He became Beloved of God," Tri said. "Surely that must count for something with you."

"He renounced it," Rin said.

"And you, who believe the Tabernacle is misguided, should relish that even more," Tri said.

Pausho didn't move. She stared at him, her heart pounding. A Wise One cavorting with an outcast? Had they made such a mistake bringing in Tri? Had they hurt themselves that badly?

"What did you do for him?" she asked.

Tri raised his chin slightly. "I found him some varin."

Varin. An ore native to the Cliffs of Blood. Touched only by a handful, mined by a specifically chosen few, and hoarded by the Wise Ones in the vaults below.

"Varin," Pausho whispered.

Fyr took a step back from him as if he were somehow contaminated. "Why? Why would you do that?"

"Because he asked?" Zak said.

"Because he paid." Rin spit out the phrase. "I cannot believe you would cavort with an outcast."

"You said he wasn't an outcast," Tri said. "Not since the mountain gave him back."

"We said he could live here. We did not say he wasn't—" Pausho stopped. She couldn't explain it any better. "Don't you understand your vows? Your duty to your people?"

Tri crossed his hands over his chest in the position he held when he took his vow. " 'I promise to support, defend, and lead the people of Constant in all ways,' " he said solemnly, " 'no matter the cost to me, my family or my peace of mind.' Seems pretty vague to me."

"Vague?" Zak shook his head. "It is not vague."

But Pausho was beginning to understand. "It is vague, if you haven't read the Words, learned the history, or studied the legends."

"Have you done that?" Rin's voice was soft, but it held steel.

"We asked him to," Fyr said.

"It's required," Zak said.

"Have you done it?" Rin asked again.

Tri let his arms fall. "Some of it." His response sounded reluctant.

"What part?" Rin asked. Her voice was rising with each question.

"I have looked at the Words."

"But not read them," Pausho said. "What about the history? What about the legends?"

"They have nothing to do with now," Tri said.

"They have everything to do with now," Zak snapped. "A tall one was in the market this morning. If you don't have the history, you don't have the understanding. If you don't have the understanding—"

"I won't feel the need to murder innocent children," Tri said.

"Is that what you think this is about?" Rin asked.

Pausho's heart was beating hard. She had sensed this. She had sensed it from the beginning with Tri. And now she finally understood why he had joined them. Not to help, but to dismantle.

"Of course that's what it's about," he said. "That and leadership so old it cannot provide for Constant in any meaningful way. Of course I gave varin to Matthias. I saw no need to hide a valuable ore from someone who wanted to use it. And I would vote against killing a child, especially a newborn, simply because we do not like its looks. That's barbaric."

"And you joined us to change us." Zak sounded terrified. He looked at Pausho, his eyes red-rimmed, his skin paler than it had been a moment before. " 'When the tall ones return, the betrayals will be revealed and the mountains will crumble.' "

"That prophecy is part of the legends," Pausho said to Tri. "If you had studied—"

"If I had studied, I'd be as brainwashed as all of you. Can't you see what you've become? Murderers in the name of tradition. Don't you know what that does to all of us, how that affects this entire community? Pregnant women sneak away in the middle of the night, more willing to face the dangers of travel than to have their babies judged by you. Entire secret societies have sprung up in order to hide children from you. People watch the mountain so that the babies placed in the snow are rescued."

Pausho felt as if she had been stabbed in the heart. She grabbed for a chair, sank in it, and stared at Tri.

He seemed larger than he had before, more powerful. "And that's not all," he said. "You deny our community the coin it needs by keeping our most valuable and unique riches for ourselves. You hoard varin, give seze to the Tabernacle, and forbid the picking of blue naries. You keep us poor and isolated. You didn't even attend the ceremony for the new Prince, despite your invitation. You act as if we aren't a part of Blue Isle at all."

"We keep our people safe," Zak said.

"At great price," Tri said.

"You don't understand the price," Rin said. "We've kept our people pure. We are the only ones—"

"It doesn't matter." The sentence came out of Pausho before she could stop it. Her words silenced the room. Everyone looked at her.

Looked down at her. It felt odd to be the only one sitting, the only one who seemed defeated by Tri's words instead of challenging them.

"You can stop arguing with him," she said to her friends, to the other Wise Leaders, the ones who had voted him in. "You cannot convince him. He joined us to change us, to be silent until he was established or until he faced his first difficult choice, and then he would reveal himself for what he is, just as he has done."

"He gave varin to Matthias."

"And I'm sure he warned more than one family to sneak away into the night." Pausho clenched a fist. She knew of at least two pregnant women from families with a history of long babies who had disappeared shortly after the Wise Ones decided to monitor their pregnancies. "But it stops here. You can leave us, Tri."

"But the Wise One takes his oath for life," Tri said.

She nodded. The exhaustion she felt grew. "He takes his oath for life," she said, "and he remains a Wise Leader as long as he keeps the oath. You have never kept an oath. Not from the moment you made it. Your intent was always to break it." She ran a hand over her face. The skin was soft, the eyes so hardened by life, she had no tears in them. "You have no idea what you've done."

"I've tried to protect my people," Tri said. She could hear a ragged edge to his voice that hadn't been there before. "I think your leadership is outdated. It's based on things that don't matter any more."

"We had tall ones in the market this morning," Zak said.

Pausho removed the hand from her face and sighed. She stood slowly, feeling each one of her seventy years. "Do you know what varin is?"

"It's an ore. It has properties that make it particularly difficult to forge, but once forged, it provides a wicked blade that does not shatter with use."

"That's only a small part of it," she said. "Varin can kill with a single touch. If forged into a blade, it can slice anything with no effort at all. But it likes the slicing. It likes the blood. It will continue, unless contained by someone who knows its use, its powers, and its controls. Do you?"

He frowned at her.

"Of course not," she said. "You who hate tradition. Does Matthias know this? No. He only knows that varin is part of a recipe he learned in his position as Beloved of God."

She couldn't keep the sarcasm from the last words.

"Matthias is no more Beloved of God than I am. The position he held was not his to hold. It belongs to the descendants of the Roca's second son. It is a hereditary position, just like the position of King belongs to the descendants of the Roca's oldest son. These recipes were not meant to be known by men such as Matthias. They were meant for men who could use them, for men who had the blood of the Roca running through their veins."

Her entire body was shaking.

"You have failed, Tri. You have no place here. The betrayal is done. You have destroyed your vow."

Zak swallowed hard. He glanced at her, then said to Tri, "You have no place here."

Rin and Fyr echoed the statement.

"If you are found here again, if you come into this place, if you touch anything within this hall, you will receive our punishment," Pausho said.

"Death, right?" Tri shook his head. "You people are sad and predictable. The bad part of this is that so many innocents rely on you. They believe in you. They let you come into their homes and steal their children. They listen to you when you deem something demon-spawn or evil or wicked. And they live in fear of you. Well, I won't live in fear of you. I'm sorry you're sending me away from here. I think I would have done a lot for our community. I would have wrenched it from the past and made it part of the present. I would have—"

"Embraced the tall ones and sealed our doom," Rin said. She crossed her arms. "Get out."

"Get out," Zak said.

"Get out," Fyr said. She moved closer to him as if to push him away.

He stared at all of them. "Don't you know that what you're doing is wrong?"

"Get out," Pausho said.

He shook his head once, then turned and left. Pausho followed him, pushed the door closed and kept her hand on it. It was ironic. Ironic and sad. In arguing with them, in admitting his betrayal, he confirmed that the tall ones had come back.

Demon-spawn.

She shuddered, then turned. The others were watching her.

"Now what?" Zak asked.

"Our numbers are diminished and so is our power," Rin said. "Right when we need it the most."

Pausho shook her head. "We are not diminished," she said. "We are strengthened. We would only have been diminished if we had allowed him to remain."

"That still doesn't tell us what to do," Zak said.

"We follow the legend," she said. "We listen to the prophecy."

"But we need a smith," Rin said.

"There are others." Pausho wasn't sure who she would hire now. She too had been counting on Tri.

"We have to find one quickly," Fyr said, "before the tall ones come back."

"If they've even left," Zak said.

"They won't leave," Pausho said. She closed her eyes against the truth of the prophecy. "They won't leave until they own us."

NINE

ADRIAN leaned on his pickax and took a deep breath. The sun was barely up, and he was already covered in sweat. His back and arms ached from effort, and the blisters he had gotten on his hands the day before had burst.

He had thought farming was hard work, but it didn't compare with this.

The rock quarry extended as far as he could see, and throughout it were muscular men, their shirts off despite the morning cold, breaking large ore-filled rock into smaller pieces. Other men used wheelbarrows to carry the smaller rocks into the foundry, where the experienced workers extracted the ore. The remaining rock was then broken up farther, into gravel, and used on the more important roads.

He would never get that far in the quarry hierarchy. He was a day worker—he and Scavenger and Coulter. He had flirted briefly with settling near here while they worked with Gift. They didn't have a lot of time; they had to refine Gift's powers and teach him how to lead.

Adrian wasn't sure how they would accomplish that. He wasn't sure if they could accomplish that. But they had to try.

And all the while, they had to keep Gift away from his great-grandfather, the Black King.

Adrian liked it here. He had been skeptical when Scavenger first proposed it. No one came this far east or this far north. They had reached the edge of the Eyes of Roca mountain range, the easternmost edge, where the Eyes of Roca, which covered all of the northern side of the Isle, rose into the Cliffs of Blood. They had traveled to the Cliffs by the river route, coming up from the center of the country, heading east and slightly north until they reached the Cardidas. They had had difficult times crossing it, but they had made it.

And now they were in territory most Islanders never came to. Most of the Isle knew they were unwelcome here. So Adrian had thought Scavenger a bit mad for proposing this as a hiding place. But then, he had thought Scavenger hadn't known about the unusual nature of this part of Blue Isle.

Adrian had underestimated Scavenger once again.

Scavenger was Fey, but he was an unusual Fey. He had been a Red Cap, a short, squat magickless Fey. Red Caps were forced to work with the dead, carving the bodies for useful magickal parts and cleaning up after battles. The Fey thought of them as less than Fey, filthy, foul creatures who did a thankless job. Scavenger had escaped the Fey, escaped the work, and had become more Islander than anyone Adrian had ever met.

An Islander with a deep understanding of magick, for Scavenger had made a lifelong study of it. He figured that since he didn't have it, he should at least understand it.

Scavenger was the only one of the three of them who could work consistently. Since they had arrived at the quarry before the sun was up, he had broken red rock after red rock, the muscles on his broad back rippling.

Coulter seemed to be having a tougher time. He had worked hard the first day, slower the second, and his face was white with pain on this one. He wasn't used to this much physical labor.

Coulter was as tall as Adrian, which meant that he only came up to Gift's shoulders. His face was round, his eyes blue, and his hair a straw blond. He had been born six months before the first Fey invasion—and he had magickal powers that made Adrian tremble. Coulter had saved their lives twice since the Black King had come to Blue Isle, each time using magick and the power of his mind.

He was still shaky from that, not because of the magick depletion, although Scavenger said that was part of it, but because of the loss of life. Coulter was one of the most gentle people Adrian knew. The fact that he had had to kill, more than once, to save the life of a friend who didn't completely understand it, tore him apart.

Scavenger had argued that Coulter could change pebbles into gold coins, and the spell would remain until the group was long gone. But Adrian knew that Islanders would remember such an occurrence, and that would provide the Black King a trail directly to them. He worried that Gift and Leen were showing their faces in the villages, but Coulter simply didn't have enough reserves to continue making them look like Islanders. Gift was the one who finally called a halt; there were enough Fey on the Isle that sooner or later some would come here, the most hidden part of the Isle.

The Black King might not guess that the first ones were the ones he was looking for.

It was a gamble the entire group decided to take.

Adrian wiped his sore hands on his filthy pants legs, then grabbed the pick and slammed it onto the rock before him. The metal edge rang as it hit, echoing with all the other clangs around him. The work was almost musical: the ring of picks against stone, the grunts of the men around him, the squeak of the barrow wheels as they moved past.

His blow cracked the stone, but did not break it. He had noted before that when the rock finally shattered, and the pieces fell to the ground, the rock's color changed from red to a dull gray. Scavenger had looked at their first broken rock with something like horror.

"I don't like the feel of this," he had said.

But Adrian hadn't pursued Scavenger's feelings any farther—they would be kicked out of the quarry if they talked too much—and by the time he returned to camp for the night, he had forgotten Scavenger's comment.

He didn't forget it now. Each time he hit the rock, a deep red line would form, and then disappear, until he hit it again.

He was glad they had agreed to only a few days of this. It was backbreaking, mind-numbing work. A few days would give them enough coins to eat for a week. By then they'd be in another town, another place. They'd find the permanent hideout Scavenger was certain they'd need, and they would be left alone.

He hoped.

A hand brushed his sweat-covered arm. It was Scavenger's.

"Keep working," he said softly, "but look."

He had moved close enough to be heard only by Adrian. Then he scuttled back to his own rock. His pick had made a dent in the center, but had yet to find that perfect place in the middle, the place where the pick actually split the rock.

Adrian kept working, but he moved a bit slower as he did so. He scanned the area until he saw what Scavenger meant.

A man he had never seen before stood at the mouth of the quarry, talking to the owner. The man was wearing a sweater, warm breeches, and boots: the clothes of a mountain dweller who did not have to work hard in the cool air. He was gesturing as he spoke, his hands rising as if indicating something large.

Or tall.

"I don't like that," Coulter said. He had moved closer as well.

"I don't either," Adrian said.

"Do you think it has something to do with us?" Coulter asked.

"I think we should assume so," Scavenger said.

"But you're paranoid," Coulter said, and he wasn't joking. He had stopped joking in the last two weeks.

"I am," Scavenger said, "and I'm still alive."

"I think we need to find out what they want," Adrian said.

"I think we need to leave," Scavenger said.

"We haven't received the day's pay," Coulter said.

"We haven't worked a day," Scavenger said.

Adrian felt the tug between their arguments. The hair was rising on the back of his neck. This didn't feel good, but he didn't want to leave without knowing what was happening, what was going on.

"You two go," he said softly. "Get Gift and Leen, and wait at our camp. If I'm not there by tomorrow's dawn, go on without me."

"We can't leave you," Coulter said, his voice rising.

"You can leave me," Adrian said, "and you will. Gift is the important one right now, and you know it."

Coulter shook his head. "I'll stay with you. I can defend you."

Adrian smiled. Coulter was more his son than his own son at times. Adrian had shown that by leaving Luke behind, letting him tend the farm, while traveling with Coulter. He and Coulter were bound by the Fey imprisonment and all those years they had spent helping each other.

Saving each other's lives.

"You need to be with Gift," Adrian said. "The Visions show you with Gift. I'll come. I just want to know what's going on before I do."

Coulter swallowed so hard that his Adam's apple visibly bobbed. Scavenger slammed his pick into the rock, then grabbed Coulter's arm.

"Come on," he whispered.

"I'll be all right," Adrian said again.

Coulter nodded. He understood. He obviously didn't like it, but he understood.

Adrian knew he would. Coulter loved Adrian like a father, but he was Bound to Gift. If Gift died, so would Coulter, and vice versa. It almost made them two parts to the same whole.

Scavenger tapped Coulter's arm. They carried their picks, as they had agreed, away from the spot, dropped them in separate places, and threaded their way through the pile of rock. Adrian had been with them when they planned the escape route. It would take them some time to get out of the quarry.

The escape route had been planned with the Fey in mind. Adrian had thought it would only take the Black King a few days, maybe a week, to get to the northeast corner of the Isle. But so far, he had not sent any of his people here. Maybe the wound that Gift had Seen him get was fatal; maybe the news hadn't yet come to this isolated place.

But even as he had the thought, he knew it was wrong. The Black King wouldn't die. Not yet. Not without the person he came for.

Not without Gift.

Adrian brought the pick down again, determined to keep working until he was sure that Coulter and Scavenger were gone from the quarry. The muscles on his back ached, and his arms were sore. Each thud into the rock shuddered through him as if the ax had pounded into him. His mouth was dry, and he was scared.

He knew that the man talking with the owner had come because of Gift and Leen.

He knew it. He should never have asked them to go to the market. He had known that after they were turned away from the quarry when they all came looking for work. But the group was running out of food, and he didn't want Scavenger to steal any more. They were also running out of Isle, and they didn't want Islanders after them as well as Fey.

But there were no Fey here. None. Scavenger, Gift, and Leen stood out. And if it hadn't been for the strange reaction to Gift's and Leen's height, they would have been working the quarry too.

What was it that Scavenger used to say? Height went with magick.

Until Coulter. Coulter wasn't very tall.

"All right," a voice said behind him. "Knock off."

Adrian stopped slamming the ax into the stone. He kept a grip on the ax, turned, and tried not to look nervous. The owner was behind him. The owner and the man who had been talking with him.

The owner was an older man, face as smooth as the stone that Adrian worked. His eyes were a deep gray, and his mouth a thin line. In the few days that Adrian had worked for him, he had never seen the man smile.

The other man had an entirely different look. He was slender and bowed, as if the weight of the world were on his shoulders. His face was deeply lined, sorrow-lined, as Adrian's wife used to say. Only his eyes held no sorrow. They were as cold and as hard as the mountains.

"Where are your companions?" the owner asked.

Adrian shook his head. "They didn't show this morning."

The owner crossed his arms. "The foreman said they left their markers."

The owner had a simple pay system. Leave a marker in the morning, and pick it up at night. When the worker retrieved his marker, he received a few coins for his daily work. Only a certain number of markers were taken each day. When the quarry had the right amount of workers, everyone else was turned away.

Adrian had forgotten about the markers. "I haven't seen them this morning," he said.

"I thought you three were together," the owner said, his eyes narrowing.

"We arrived together. We made acquaintance." They had agreed on that too. It was better. It prevented too many questions.

"But you're not friends," the owner said, clearly unconvinced.

"No," Adrian said.

"Three strangers, who arrive together, who are not friends."

Adrian shrugged.

"Five strangers," the other man said. His voice was deep, with such subtleties of inflection that Adrian thought the man could hum and be understood. The man had spoken these two words with so much disbelief, it was all Adrian could do to keep from flinching.

"There's only been three of us the last few days," Adrian said. He had been a captive of the Fey for a long time. He knew how to control the inflections in his own voice. He could lie so smoothly no one would ever know what the truth was.

"You arrived with two tall ones," the man said.

"No," Adrian said. "This morning I arrived alone."

"Not this morning," the man said. "Yesterday."

"Yes," Adrian said, "there were some tall ones in the group. But they weren't with me."

"You spoke to them," the owner said. "You made a pact to rendezvous with them."

"Of course," Adrian said. "They gave us breakfast that morning. We agreed to pay them for it when we finished work."

"You took a gift from tall ones?" the man's voice held a shuddery horror.

Adrian shrugged, wondering what local custom he had just stumbled into. "We shared breakfast," he said. "It wasn't a gift. We paid them for it."

"You had commerce with tall ones," the man said.

"Of course," Adrian said. "Tall ones. Fey. You've heard of them, I presume. They've been on Blue Isle for twenty years."

"Rumors," the man said.

"You've seen them," Adrian said to the owner. "That's all they are. They're as much a part of the Isle now as we are."

He didn't want to say more. If the news of the Black King's invasion hadn't yet reached here, he didn't want to bring it.

"Why do you travel with these outsiders?" the man asked.

"I don't," Adrian lied. "I came up here looking for work."

"No one comes here looking for work," the man said. "You sound like you're from Jahn. Men from the city do not need our help."

Adrian sighed. He would have to tell this part. If he didn't, they would remember him when the Black King did come searching.

"They need your help now," he said softly. "I'm probably one of the first. There'll be a lot of strangers up here soon."

The owner crossed his arms as if he didn't believe anything Adrian said. The other man narrowed his eyes, and Adrian could feel the evaluation.

"More?" he asked.

Adrian nodded. "There's been a second Fey invasion. This time, it's their Black King. He's brought thousands of troops with him, and he's determined to overthrow our king."

"Then why were you accepting food from these tall ones?"

"Because they're not part of the invasion force. The second invasion force," he corrected. "They're part of the first. The Black King will try to destroy them as well as Islanders. It's part of their custom."

"And these Fey, they are tall?" the man asked.

"Some," Adrian said, wishing he understood this obsession. "But that little guy who I worked with that first day, the one you hired"—and he nodded to the owner when he said it—"he's Fey. And he's not tall."

The owner frowned and turned away.

Now for the question Adrian had planned to ask. He had to do so in a way that wouldn't reveal his own interest. He leaned on the pick. "Why are you after these people anyway? Did they do something?"

"No," the man said, "except that they tried to have commerce with us."

Adrian swallowed. So Gift and Leen had gone to the marketplace, and their appearance had caused this confrontation. Not because they were Fey. But because they were tall.

"So you're saying that I can't use the money I'm making here to buy things in Constant?" he asked.

"You may," the man said. "They may not."

"Why?" Adrian couldn't keep the shock from his voice.

"Did they teach you nothing in Jahn?" the man responded, an equal amount of shock in his voice.

"Apparently," Adrian said.

The owner and the visitor glanced at each other as if Adrian had confessed that he didn't know how to eat. Then the man said, "I assume you are a Rocaanist."

Adrian nodded, even though that wasn't really true. He hadn't been to any kind of worship service in decades, but he had been raised in a kirk, and learned the teachings of the Tabernacle as a young boy.

"Then you know the story of the Roca."

Adrian frowned. "I do. But I don't know how it's relevant."

"He was from the Cliffs."

"I thought he was born in the Snow Mountains," Adrian said. "I had heard that years ago."

The man shook his head. "We have unbroken knowledge of his history here. The people of the Snow Mountains took our stories and perverted them centuries ago, in an attempt to seize religious power. We have the original copy of the Words."

Adrian leaned harder on his pick. He felt as if he were suddenly in an intellectual thicket, one that was beyond him.

"There are many writings, and many legends passed down from the Roca's day," the man continued. "Most of those writings and legends were not recorded by the Tabernacle. Most of them were lost—deliberately, we believe—as the Tabernacle solidified its powers."

Adrian blinked. He had expected some strange story, but nothing like this.

The man pushed back the sleeves of his sweater. It was beginning to grow warm. The sun had finally cleared the mountains.

"Many of these stories are about the tall ones. They are evil and they must be destroyed."

Adrian shook his head. He had never heard anything like that. "But I thought people from the Cliffs are tall."

The owner swore softly. The man shut his eyes for a moment, and then opened them, as if he had heard something difficult to bear. "I told Pausho that," he said to the owner. "She would not hear it."

"What?" Adrian asked.

"There is a tall strain in our family lines. We destroy it. Many women—pregnant women—leave before allowing us to take care of it."

The hair rose on the back of Adrian's neck. This man had just calmly spoken of infanticide. "So the tall Islanders that come from the Cliffs are—evil?" He nearly choked on the last word.

"And must be destroyed," the man said in that same calm voice.

Adrian's breath had left his body and he didn't quite know how. He felt as if he had received a blow to the chest. His own culture. These were his people. They looked like him, but they were nothing like him.

They couldn't be.

Could they?

"You—kill?—tall people here," he said, not even trying to hide his disbelief. Gift. Leen. Had they made it out of the market? Had he unknowingly sent them to their deaths?

"We must. It is law," the man said.

"Because the Roca said so?" Adrian asked, still not believing what he was hearing.

"It is not in the Words used by the Tabernacle."

Adrian felt a slight relief at that.

"It is in the Words excised by the Tabernacle."

"They cut the Words Written and Unwritten?"

"The Words were altered by the Tabernacle," the man said as if he were speaking to a child. As if it were the most fundamental thing in the world. "They cut much that they did not want to believe. It is in our Words, in the original."

Adrian's palms had grown moist. He could feel the rising heat of the day inflaming his face.

"He does not want to hear it, to hear anything about his tall friends," the owner said.

Adrian shook his head quickly. "No, no," he said. "I want to hear. I do." But he had to explain his physical reaction. "I'm just shocked that the Tabernacle would change something sacred."

"So are we. But it happened generations ago. The Tabernacle became too involved in itself, and not in the souls of the living. It forgot its roots. Even the Rocaan had no relation to the Roca. That too is a violation of tradition."

Adrian didn't want to hear about that. He wanted to hear about the tall ones.

"So these tall strangers you saw this morning," he said, unable to hide the fear in his voice. And here he had prided himself on his composure. But the Fey had never shocked him like this. "Those people I shared breakfast with. You killed them, and now you're coming for me because I associated with them?"

He had initially meant the question to explain his fear, to let them believe that was what he was afraid of. But it wasn't until the words were out of his mouth that he realized he had asked something that truly terrified him.

Gift and Leen were dead, killed in the place they had come for safety.

And he was next. He wouldn't be able to warn Scavenger and Coulter.

"No, they are not dead," the man said. "We do not kill tall strangers, unless they remain. We ask them to leave. If they do, they will be safe."

Adrian swallowed. He couldn't hide his nervousness now. "Then why did you come to me?"

"If you are associated with them," the man said, "you must leave as well. If you are not associated, but if you are acquainted, you might want to warn them to stay away from Constant."

"But my only contact was the one I told you about," Adrian said.

The man shrugged. "Then you may remain. But realize that if you are caught lying about tall ones, you will receive the same punishment they do."

"Punishment," Adrian repeated. "For doing nothing."

The man raised his chin slightly. "Tall ones can corrupt simply by breathing," he said. "There are many who believe we are too lenient by allowing them to leave. Many believe we should kill tall ones on sight."

"But you don't," Adrian said, hoping he was right.

The man's gaze softened slightly. His face seemed less severe, his eyes warmed. "The Roca was a harsh man who lived in a harsh time," he said. "He always said those times will come again, and we must prepare. We have prepared for generations. But because we have prepared for so long, we must also remember that the Roca urged us to exercise compassion."

Then he smiled, and the look transformed his face again. This man rarely smiled. His face could not accommodate it. The smile looked painful somehow.

"We have exercised compassion with these tall strangers. The next time we see them, we will remember the Roca's words, and prepare for the harsh times." His smile faded. "This is your only warning."

Then he turned and walked away. The owner remained. Adrian felt a shiver run down his back.

"I've been watching you," the owner said. "You are a good worker. You may remain as long as you come to work alone."

"Thank you," Adrian said. The words were strangled in his

throat. His voice sounded strange, even to himself. But the owner didn't seem to notice. He nodded once, and followed the man.

Adrian watched them until they reached the mouth of the quarry. Then he picked up his ax. If he left now to warn Gift and Leen, then he might bring the wrath of the whole town on them.

He would stay until sundown. And then he would make sure they left this area as quickly as they could.

TEN

LUKE dipped a rag into the pail of water he had brought into the kitchen and wiped the sweat off his face and neck. The morning was hot already and it wasn't yet midday. He scooped some of the water out with a cup and took a long drink.

This lack of sleep was beginning to catch up with him.

He stared through the open doors at the fields beyond. The first corn crop was near harvesting, and he would have to do it alone. The Fey who were in charge of this area had offered to help him, but he didn't want them on his father's property.

On his property.

Luke shuddered despite the heat. He hadn't heard from his father Adrian since he had left with Coulter, Scavenger, and Jewel's son Gift two weeks before. He wasn't sure he would ever hear from his father again.

The Fey were here now, and they owned the Isle. The word had arrived quickly. King Nicholas was defeated. Some said he was dead, others said he was in exile and his oldest son had been slaughtered by the Fey.

Luke knew that the child who had died had not been Gift. It had to have been the golem, Sebastian, and that really had been no loss. The creature would have taken the throne from its rightful heir, and that had always made Luke uneasy.

But then, Gift had made Luke uneasy, with his Fey features pressed on pale skin. Gift looked like his mother Jewel, the woman who had imprisoned Luke and his father Adrian among the Fey and put a Charm spell on Luke so that he would believe he had fallen in love with her.

He still dreamed about her sometimes: her beautiful upswept eyes, her long black hair. She would speak to him in those dreams and he would long to touch her. Then he would realize it was a dream and force himself awake. The Fey had done other things to him in that short imprisonment. They had placed a spell on him that made him into an assassin. He had gone out of himself and nearly killed the Fifty-first Rocaan. If the Rocaan hadn't thrown holy water on him and broken the spell, Luke would have committed murder for the Fey.

Luke had stayed on the farm ever since.

He had never thought the Fey would come to him.

He sighed and took out the last of the bread. His father had baked before he left, and Luke had baked just after, hoping that his father would return. But he hadn't. He had gone with Coulter who was, in many ways, more a child of his heart than Luke was. Luke's father and Coulter had been damaged in similar ways by the Fey. During their imprisonment—Adrian's was long because he had traded his life for Luke's—they had bonded in such a tight fashion that they seemed like father and son. Adrian never excluded Luke, but he didn't have that closeness with him, either.

Luke always told himself it didn't matter.

But it did.

Especially now. Especially when Luke had been left behind, while Adrian went away to protect Coulter.

As if Luke didn't need protection too.

Maybe he didn't. He was a full adult, fifteen years older than Coulter, old enough to be the boy's father. He didn't need to be jealous of him. Adrian said that Luke needed a family of his own so that he wouldn't be quite so tied to this one.

Maybe his father was right.

But that didn't settle the matter of the crops. Nor did it resolve the nagging feeling in his stomach that something had changed, something had happened to his father. The last thing Adrian would suffer through was another Fey imprisonment. He had once told Luke that he would die first before going through that again.

Luke put some cheese on the bread and ate standing up. He had so many chores to do and no time to do them. He should have been in the field now, but he was waiting for one of the neighbors to come by.

The Fey frowned on meetings between neighbors, but Luke had found a way around it. He had said he needed help with the farm—which was quite true. The Fey military leader had offered the help of some of his soldiers, but Luke had declined. Years of experience among the Fey had taught him that soldiers were not Domestics. They might listen to instruction and they might even do well, but they wouldn't provide the help he needed.

At least, that was what he told the Fey who came by the farm. The leader, a man about his own age, had shrugged and told Luke that it was fine, he could do what he wanted. But if it looked as if the corn was going to die on the vine, the Fey would send soldiers anyway. The crops were the important thing. The Fey had taken Blue Isle, the leader said, for its abundant riches, and any attempt to sabotage those riches would be seen as treason against the Fey Empire, punishable by death.

Luke was planning treason, but not such a simple and fruitless kind.

The neighbor who was coming today was the last Luke was going to see. He wanted to start a resistance to the Fey, a resistance as subtle and divisive as he could conceive.

The idea came to him when he spoke with the Fey leader. If King Nicholas was alive and in exile, then the Islanders owed it to him to fight. They needed to prevent the Fey from gaining a stronghold on the Isle.

And Luke had a lot of ideas on how to do so.

He was starting by speaking to his neighbors, and telling them his ideas. If one of them turned him over to the Fey, so be it. Then he would at least have tried.

He couldn't have stomached letting the Fey overrun the Isle without trying to fight them.

He finished his lunch and washed it down with more water. He knew that midday was a bad time to see anyone, especially in farm country, but the Fey had forbidden night gatherings. He had to take this time from his own work to see what he could do.

Then he heard a rap on the side door. He turned. His neighbor stood there. Luke hadn't seen him coming, but then, Luke had been looking at the corn, not at the road.

His neighbor Jona was a slender man, a few years younger than Luke's father. He had several children, most of them grown now, and the wiry look of a man who had worked the land all his life.

Luke pulled the door open. "Thanks for coming," he said.

"Make it quick," Jona said. "I have crops to tend."

He came inside anyway. He was covered with dirt and had sweat runnels lining his face. He probably didn't look much different from Luke.

"Water?" Luke asked.

"Please," Jona said. "It's this hot already. The day will be unbearable."

Luke nodded. He dipped another cup in the water pail and handed the cup, dripping, to Jona.

"Have the Fey been to your farm?"

Jona took a long drink, then said, "They have. They want an accounting of all of our yield. They want to know time worked, and the land-use plan. We've never done these things before. I didn't even know what a land-use plan was until I spoke to one of them."

Luke leaned against the counter. His father had built this house with his bare hands. The counters, the cabinets, the woodwork were all additions he made after his Fey captivity, as if being held by them for five years gave him ideas that no Islander had ever had before.

Like a land-use plan.

"One of the Fey told me that King Nicholas might still be alive," Luke said, lowering his voice.

Jona brought his head up. "They told me he was dead."

"They want us to believe that," Luke said. "But my father taught me to speak Fey, and I asked one of them in his own language what happened to the King. He said no one knows exactly. There were rumors that he stabbed the Fey ruler and rode out of the city on a horse."

Jona set his cup down, then he pulled out a stool. "Mind?" he asked, and didn't wait for Luke's response. He sat anyway. "If the King is alive, we have hope," Jona said.

"Even if he isn't, we do," Luke said. "We outnumber them. The Isle was ours for generations."

Their voices had grown even lower. Even though the Fey

had been in control of the Isle a very short time, it quickly had become clear what disobeying them would be like. The second night after they had took control of the area, they called a meeting of all the farmers. They had had to watch as the Fey punished two prisoners, and were then told the same punishment would happen to them if they didn't listen to the Fey.

"We outnumber them, but we lack their power," Jona said.

Luke clenched and unclenched his right fist. "Power isn't everything," he said.

"But magick is."

Luke shook his head. He had learned a lot of lessons from the nonmagickal Scavenger. "The Fey believe they're all-powerful, that no one will oppose them. If we do small things to sap their confidence, small raids, small victories, we might be able to gain a foothold in their territory."

"Raids? You're proposing taking them on?"

Luke nodded. "Until we know what happened to King Nicholas or his children. We have an Isle to preserve. Already they're working us harder than we're used to. They talk about land use and high yields because we have to grow ten times the food we've grown before."

"Why?" Jona asked. "We've always had a surplus."

"*We* have," Luke said, "but the Fey Empire hasn't. You watch. After this year's season, they'll have us grow crops that can travel well. They'll store some and ship the others back to the countries on the Galinas continent. And, if we let the Fey advance from here to Leut, they'll ship our produce to Leut as well."

"We can't support all of that," Jona said.

"Not now, we can't. But the Fey have Domestics who use different farming techniques than we do. They'll change the way things are done here."

Jona frowned. "They said we could keep our land."

"As long as we produced the right amount of food. The amount determined by them."

Jona let out a bit of air. He seemed to grow smaller. "I hadn't thought of that. But they still won't confiscate."

"Scavenger"—Luke spoke the name with trepidation; the neighbors had always been afraid of Scavenger—"said they will confiscate and then force the former owner to work the land anyway. It takes years sometimes and it's done under the guise of a legal transfer. Very few nonmagickal beings can maintain the kind of crop yields the Fey need."

Jona's hand went for his cup. He played with the water beads on the side. "Where is Scavenger?"

"He's with my father and Coulter." Luke couldn't resist a look out the door. The corn swayed in a slight breeze. It stretched for rows and rows, all the work he could never, ever do alone. "They left to fight the Fey two weeks ago and haven't returned."

"Do you think the little bastard killed them?"

"Scavenger?" Luke asked. "He hated the Fey, maybe more than any Islander ever could. No. I don't think he killed them. I think they died fighting the Fey."

There. He had finally spoken the words aloud. And that belief, more than anything, made him want to fight here. He had to preserve something of his father's, even if it was his father's house and lands.

Jona was staring out the door, too. His slender face was almost expressionless. "Died fighting, eh?"

"I don't know. But I haven't heard, and that's what I think. There were so many troops, and my father was going right into them. He'd never allow himself to be captured again."

Jona leaned forward. "I let them come to my door. They knocked so politely, and they told me that Blue Isle was now part of the Fey Empire. They told me that I would answer to them now, and that someone would eventually talk to me about my land. They said I would still own the land unless I offended them in some way, according to Fey law. They said the Fey put a great stock in law, and any citizen of the Fey Empire had recourse under that law. Then they thanked me and left."

Luke's mouth was dry. He had heard the same speech. Only he had listened to part of it before he started asking questions. In Fey. They thought then that he was on their side and relaxed a bit with him. And that's when he realized what Scavenger said was true. The best way to conquer a Fey was to conquer his mind.

They weren't used to opposition.

They weren't used to losing. King Nicholas had learned that. Luke's father had learned that. The Fey were always startled by failure. They had no tolerance for it.

It was a way to turn the Fey against themselves.

"I just let them tell me that they were in charge, and I said to my wife, 'I guess it doesn't matter. We never heard from the King anyway,' as if he were supposed to talk to every private citizen. She had left the room. Angry at me, I suppose. Angry at me for not standing up."

Luke had heard variations of this speech all week. Each of his neighbors had been so stunned by the matter-of-fact way the Fey had taken over that they had done nothing.

And, truth be told, there was nothing to do. At least individually.

"You couldn't have stood up," he said. "Not by yourself. None of us can do this by ourselves."

Jona looked at him. The man's eyes were haunted. "What do you propose?"

"I propose that we become model citizens of the Fey Empire by day, and that we try to destroy it at night. They can be surprised, just like we can. They can die just like we can. And they can be demoralized. We did that to them once before. We can do it again."

"We didn't do it," Jona said. "We kept farming. King Alexander did it. And he's dead."

"Actually, it was King Nicholas and the holy water from the Tabernacle," Luke said. "And there's a good possibility he's not dead. The Fey just want us to believe he's dead. Because if he is, we have nothing to cling to. I think that's the first order of business. We need to make sure the entire Isle knows that the King lives."

"We can't do that and farm too."

"Sure we can," Luke said. "We find excuses to talk to each other, and we spread the word. I found an excuse to talk with you."

Jona's face split into a grin. It transformed him, made him look younger suddenly. "I guess you did," he said. "But your excuse is a real one. You need help farming this place. You can't do it alone."

"I know," Luke said. "I just don't want Fey help."

"What about female help?" Jona asked. "My sons are enough for me. I am able to do even the extra work with them. My daughters know how to work a harvest. They can also plant. I know it's not customary, but—"

"I don't mind working with women," Luke said. He wasn't like the older generation of Islanders. He had seen the Fey when he was young enough for it to make an impression.

Women didn't have to do household tasks. They were strong and powerful and could manage difficult tasks like a harvest as well as a man.

"I can't pay much," Luke said. "Mostly in crops."

"They don't need much," Jona said. "I am not doing this to help with your harvest. I'm doing this to keep the Fey off your land. If what you say is true, then we have to keep the Fey away as much as possible. The girls will help with that."

"Thank you," Luke said.

Jona stood. "You know that soon talk won't be enough. We will need to take action."

"I know," Luke said.

"Have you a plan?"

Luke smiled. "I have the beginnings of one."

Jona nodded. "That's more than I had this morning," he said. He grabbed the doorknob. "I will send the girls over as soon as I return."

"Thanks," Luke said again. He eased the door closed and watched as Jona crossed the fields. Then he let out a breath.

He had lied. He didn't have a plan yet. Only an idea. He knew that he had to attack and demoralize the Fey. He just wasn't sure how yet.

But he did know what kind of risk he was willing to take.

His father had been willing to give up everything to keep the Fey from holding Luke prisoner all those years ago. It was time for Luke to pay his father back. It was time to pay the Isle back.

Losing everything was a small sacrifice to get rid of the Fey.

Everything—including his life.

ELEVEN

"I don't want to find him," Arianna said. She pulled her arms tighter, as if she were holding herself. "You don't know this Gift. He's evil."

Nicholas put a hand on his daughter's back. She was shaking, not so much with cold but with some deep emotion. She was expressing it as petulance, but he suspected something else.

Fear.

Her first encounter with her real brother had terrified her. She had nearly made the largest mistake of her young life, and she had been unwilling to admit it ever since, going to the point of denying that Black Blood fighting Black Blood could cause a problem.

She had nearly killed her own brother, and she said she didn't regret it.

He believed she did.

"Gift is not evil." The Shaman finally turned around on her rock. She was hunched against the cold, her nose red. Her mood had been odd all morning, and Nicholas couldn't quite place the cause of that either. The Visions she'd had?

The ones she wouldn't talk about?

"He hurt Sebastian," Arianna said, her voice quavering.

"He helped Sebastian, child. He was part of Sebastian. There would be no Sebastian without Gift."

"That's not true." Arianna let go of herself and ran her right arm across her nose. She sniffed at the same time.

Nicholas stood very still, listening to the discussion. He had never seen his son as an adult. He remembered the newborn vividly, the baby's small hands, and active mobile mouth. And how, suddenly, the boy had lost interest in everything. He had gone from being a squirming bundle of curiosity to a leaden child, heavy and tired all the time.

Jewel had thought him ill.

Nicholas hadn't known the ways of babies. He hadn't realized what had changed.

What a fool he had been. His daughter and the Shaman had both seen his son, and he never had. He wanted to, and he was ashamed to admit it out loud. Afraid, somehow, that in wanting to see his flesh-and-blood child, he was turning his back on the boy he had raised, his stone-son, the one who had saved his life.

"It is true," the Shaman said softly, gently. She too knew how fragile Arianna was right now. "Your brother, like you, Arianna, is a Visionary. Visionaries can travel Links."

"I know," Arianna said.

"But you've never done it. You don't really know."

"I *know*," she said, in that tone that brooked no further discussion.

"Well," the Shaman said as if she hadn't heard it, "what you may or may not know is that Visionaries can leave parts of themselves in someone whose Link they have traveled across. But the parts can be autonomous."

"Solanda told me this," Arianna said.

"She did?" Nicholas asked. "Even the leaving of the self?"

"Yes," Arianna said. "You were there."

He was there. He remembered it clearly. He had thought, the way Solanda had described it, that Gift's leaving was accidental.

"Visionaries do this on purpose?" Nicholas asked, deciding to ignore his daughter. "You mean Gift created Sebastian intentionally?"

"No," the Shaman said. "I don't think he did. He was too young. He was using Visionary skills as a child, untutored. That has never happened before among our people. But usually Visionaries do such a thing on purpose. They create a construct in someone's mind. The construct must grow, of course, like your Sebastian did, but over the years, it becomes dominant."

She leaned her head back, sighed, and said, "Haven't you wondered how a Visionary, with no offensive or defensive magick skills, controls the entire Fey?"

"Through constructs?" Nicholas asked, horrified. He had visions of none of the Fey controlling their own actions, all being controlled by a Visionary. By the Black King.

"Only in a very few select cases. Usually Enchanters who become unwieldy. They are too valuable to destroy, you know." She sounded as if she were speaking of a horse. "And they all go mad. A wise Visionary will plant a construct in an Enchanter decades before the Enchanter's insanity strikes. For another decade, the construct controls the Enchanter, and keeps the insanity at bay."

"See?" Arianna said softly. "I told you this Gift was evil."

Nicholas didn't see the connection at all. "How do you come to that conclusion?" he asked.

"Because he created a construct in Sebastian."

"The construct is Sebastian," the Shaman said. "The boy you love as your brother is part of your real brother, and always has been. Gift is a warm, giving, and compassionate child."

"He's an adult."

"He's still a boy," Nicholas said, remembering what it was like to be eighteen. He thought he had known everything then. He hadn't been quite as impulsive as Arianna, but he had been close. "Even though he doesn't think so."

"You're determined to accept him, aren't you?" Arianna asked.

"He's my son," Nicholas said.

"He's Fey." She spit out the last word.

"No more than you are," the Shaman said.

"Oh, much more," Arianna said. "He was raised by you people. He has all your evil traits."

"Arianna," Nicholas said. "The Shaman has helped us."

"Helped us?" Arianna spread out her hands. "Look at where we are. While the Black King lives in our home, and rules our people."

"We're going to change that," Nicholas said.

"Not with her help, you're not," Arianna said. She narrowed her eyes as she looked at the Shaman. "You were in none of my Visions."

"I know," the Shaman whispered.

Nicholas raised his head. She had hers bowed. His heart started pounding, hard. "Not you too," he said. "I'm not going to lose you too."

She raised her head. "I'm fine, Nicholas."

But she didn't deny it. She didn't say she was going to survive.

She pushed a strand of hair off her face. "I know where young Gift is," she said.

"I know," Nicholas said. "You told me that when we first saw you."

"You can't believe her," Arianna said.

"I can," he said firmly, not sure how to deal with his wild daughter when she was this distraught. "I can, and I do."

"I will take you to him," the Shaman said. Her back was straight, her eyes meeting his. "I think it is for the best."

"Arianna and I can go alone if this is dangerous for you."

The Shaman shook her head. "Being on Blue Isle with the Black King is dangerous for me," she said. "It doesn't matter where I am."

"I don't want to find him," Arianna said.

Nicholas ran his hand along her back. He could feel the knobs of her spine. "I do," he said.

She turned toward him. "Aren't I enough, Daddy? Aren't we family enough?"

He nodded. "You are, and always will be, my closest child. Mine from the start." He had held her when she was only moments old, when she could barely hold her shape.

His wife, dead, before the fire.

He shook the memory away. "But the Black King has come for his great-grandchildren. And if we are to defeat him, we need him to come to us."

"The Shaman says we can't kill him."

"We can't," Nicholas said. "But we can stop him from getting you or Gift."

"I don't care about Gift!" Arianna said.

"I know," Nicholas said. "But your great-grandfather does. He doesn't need the power that Gift will bring him."

"And we do?"

Nicholas pulled her close. He couldn't explain his longing for his other child. He couldn't explain the sudden need he felt to protect the boy. But he could give Arianna a reason she understood.

"We need the Black King to come to us and us only," Nicholas said. "He'll come wherever you are. Wherever Gift is."

"And if we're together, he'll be there," she said.

"That's right."

She sighed, then leaned her head on Nicholas's shoulder. So fragile and vulnerable and impulsively difficult. How had he ever lived without this child?

"I'm not going to be nice to him," she said.

"Just don't hurt him," Nicholas said.

"You might want to remember," the Shaman said, "that the Sebastian you loved came entirely from your brother Gift."

Arianna pushed away from Nicholas, and faced the Shaman, face red. "I'll never believe that."

The Shaman shrugged. "Then you deny yourself another member of your family. One you could love."

"You're biased."

"And so," the Shaman said softly, "are you."

Nicholas took a deep breath. He'd had enough. They could argue as they walked. "We have to get ready," he said. "Can we reach Gift by nightfall?"

"No," the Shaman said. "But we can be there by dawn."

Dawn. His son. His children together with him for the first time. Another step toward rebuilding.

Toward defeating the Black King.

Toward hope.

TWELVE

TUFT flew in the center of the tunnels, the tiny spark of light created by his body the only illumination. His wings flapped above him, his arms were tucked against his chest, and his legs were pulled in tight. The lack of air in this place bothered him, and so did the hay, the dust, and the spiderwebs. He was afraid of many things as he flew, afraid that his small spark of light might ignite a fire in the dryness and the hay, afraid the dust would overwhelm him, afraid he would get trapped in a web and be unable to free himself.

Now that he was far away from the palace, it was clear that these tunnels hadn't been used in a long, long time.

The Black King had sent him on this mission personally. Tuft still wasn't used to being one of the most important Wisps in the invading force. Flurry, the Black King's favorite, had never returned from his mission to find the great-grandson. Neither had Cinder. Two other Wisps had been injured during battle, and many of the more senior Wisps were scattered along the Isle, doing scouting business and the things that Wisps were good for. Tuft was one of the few remaining in the Black King's entourage, and he was the most senior, even though his battle experience on Nye was slim.

Tuft had been sent into the tunnels to see what he could

find. The Black King believed that these tunnels had been used by the Islander King in his counterattack. The Black King also believed that many of the palace staff had escaped through here. Wisdom imparted all of this information to Tuft when he assigned Tuft the task of exploring the tunnels.

"The most important thing," Wisdom had said, "is to find out how far they go, where they end up, and what their real purpose is."

Tuft couldn't divine a purpose. He'd been following the tunnels all morning, and they were vast. An entire catacomb below the city was certainly more than a single Wisp could map out in a single day. He kept expecting the tunnels to end soon, to dead-end in a brick wall somewhere, but so far they hadn't. At some point, he thought, he would have to hit the river. The tunnels couldn't go through that.

He had noted many things worth reporting. The area around the dungeons was relatively clean, and got cleaner when he was under the barracks. This, he supposed, was where the counterattack was staged.

He took a side tunnel near the dungeons and found two sets of footprints in very old dust. They went to a hidden door. He squeezed his small frame through that door, and found himself back in the palace, in the Great Hall with all the weapons. A few of the Fey had said that a Black Robe had magickally appeared in this place, carrying a mighty sword.

The magick hadn't been magick at all. Simple, old-fashioned ingenuity.

As he flew now, he found himself in a tunnel still filled with cobwebs. They were the things that bothered him the most. He had visions of himself caught in the sticky strands, unable to grow large because of his panic. His thrashing would cause a spider to come down from her lair and entrap him farther. He had heard stories of Wisps dying this way in the ancient homes on L'Nacin, but he didn't know if the stories were true.

He didn't want to find out.

There were footprints in this tunnel as well, a single set moving toward the palace and a double set moving away from it. They appeared old, but he couldn't tell how old. He suspected they dated from the most recent attack on Jahn. Someone had come through here, and then two others had left the same way. He didn't know if these prints were related, but he did assume they would help him follow the main tunnels.

He kept flying. He felt as if he had been flying too much since he had arrived on Blue Isle barely a month before. First he did scouting, then he searched for the Black King's great-grandson, then he fought a bit in the attack on the city, and then he explored.

These tunnels were the worst of it, though. He hated darkness like this. Being the only illumination made him feel so exposed. Usually man-made places had torches burning or fires in the fireplaces, so he could pretend to be a spark. No one noticed him then. If he ran into anyone here, they would notice a single dot of light, flying alone, with purpose. They might assume he was Fey and crush him between two open palms.

His mother had died that way, slapped like a gnat between the palms of a Nyeian merchant during a scouting mission. Tuft had seen it all and narrowly missed being crushed himself. He still had nightmares about giant hands closing in on him, about the seconds before the pain began.

He shook himself and kept flying. His mission was to follow the tunnels to their end, and he would do so. He had brought no supplies with him, but he had seen lots of side tunnels, and a few other hidden doors. He assumed he could go to the surface anytime he needed refreshment. The Fey owned Jahn now. Finding a place to get food and water would be easy.

The tunnel made a banking turn up ahead, and he thought he smelled the rusty stench of the river. He heard echoes, too. At first he thought they were simply the sound of water against stone, but then he realized he was hearing voices.

Whispering.

The hackles rose on the back of his neck, and his wings stuttered. He dropped halfway to the floor before he could recover himself.

Why would anyone whisper down here? Why not speak aloud?

Unless they were afraid of being heard.

But by whom?

By what?

These tunnels appeared empty, and he hadn't noticed any sound carrying. If it did, he assumed he would have heard the sound of the Fey above, going about their day-to-day business.

He heard nothing.

Until now.

The whispering was getting closer. Despite his aversion to cobwebs, he flew toward the ceiling of the tunnel and slowed down. He didn't want to be noticed. He merely wanted to observe.

He went around the corner, and found himself in a large cavern. If he weren't so close to the ceiling, he probably wouldn't have noticed that the cavern was man-made. But it was. Each brick had been put in by hand. Many of them were moist. The river was nearby, and its wetness trickled in the side of the cavern.

But that wasn't what startled him the most. What startled him, and nearly made him flee back up the tunnel, were the preponderance of Black Robes. Even though Rugad's Spell Warders had neutralized the Black Robes' poison, Tuft had heard stories. He knew that it melted Fey with a single touch. He also knew that he had been given an antidote. But his fear was that these Black Robes had other tricks up their sleeves, tricks they had been unable to use in Rugad's quick and surprising attack on their stronghold.

They were hiding here now. A hundred of them, maybe more, with crates of vials stacked up against the wall, and the stench of the river around them.

The Black King would be happy to know of this enclave. He would destroy them as surely as he had destroyed their stronghold two weeks before.

This was enough. He could explore the rest of the tunnels later. The Black King would want to know this information immediately.

Tuft was about to turn back when he heard a whisper that caught his attention.

". . . gone," said the voice in Islander. Tuft's Islander had been mediocre when he came to the Isle. It had gotten better in the last month. "I woke up and Con had disappeared. The Auds say he left with the King's son."

The King's son. That was the phrase that caught Tuft.

Of course. If the boy had been hiding here, no Wisp would have seen him. Rugad hadn't even known about the tunnels until recently.

"Good riddance, I say," another voice whispered. Tuft didn't even look for the source. He clung to a crack in the bricks along the line between the wall and the ceiling, trying to be as invisible as possible. He had to work to make purchase in the grout. His tiny fingers could barely hold on, and he didn't want to flap his wings too much. These bricks were old and crumbling. He didn't want to send a spray of dust onto the Black Robes below. They might look up and find him.

"That boy isn't right in the head," the second voice continued. "And he looked so strange, as if he were coming apart from the inside out."

Tuft frowned. He didn't know what would cause that. Usually the Fey bred well with other races. It didn't create health problems. It usually made them stronger.

"You're sure they're gone?" the second voice asked.

"I haven't seen them, and I looked. Con was in my service before the Rocaan called him to that Charge. He's a good boy. I'm worried about him, especially with the King's son. He seems to think the King's son is part of his Charge, but I think he's wrong. And that sword, did you see it? It's all covered with dried blood."

Tuft shuddered. Probably Fey blood. This was very interesting, more interesting than he expected. Probably more interesting than the Black King had expected.

"I saw it," the second voice said. "He's not been acting like an Aud. That sword, and that attitude. Not wanting to stay here when his betters say he should."

"They'll punish him," the first voice said.

"If they find him," the second voice said.

"If we can get the religion back on its feet."

The sentiment seemed to depress both of them, and they were suddenly silent, staring at their hands. Tuft clung to the grout, watching them, and trying to put the information together in his head. The King's son had been here, but he was gone, traveling with a Black Robe. For what? Protection?

The important information, though, was that the boy had recently left. Tuft would be able to find him in the tunnels.

And then do what? Ask him to wait? Tuft was just a Wisp. Even if he grew to full size, he wouldn't be able to fight a Black Robe with a sword.

Better to go to the Black King. Better to let the Black King plan an invasion of the tunnels. With hundreds of Fey in here, the great-grandson wouldn't have a chance. He would belong to the Black King.

Tuft smiled. And he would be the hero. The one who brought the Black King's great-grandson home.

THIRTEEN

CON slid out of the narrow passage, clinging to his sword. The dust swarmed around him, and he tried not to cough. The air smelled of smoke—not fresh any more, but cloying just the same. He leaned the sword against his leg, then turned around and grabbed Sebastian's hands.

The feel of Sebastian's skin was always startling to Con. It was cool and smooth to the touch. If Con didn't know that Sebastian could breathe and talk, he would think him as dead as the stone around them.

Sebastian gripped hard. He was still in the passage. Getting him out would be interesting.

The entire morning had been interesting. After Sebastian's warning, Con had led them through the tunnels until they came to the passage that Con dreaded. It was built under the bridge that spanned the Cardidas River. The builders had placed a tunnel below the walking area, and time and lack of use had made the passage so narrow that Con had had to crawl through it two weeks before.

Two weeks.

It seemed like a lifetime.

The passage had gotten, if anything, more narrow. The smell of smoke hung in it, overpowering the scent of the river. Rocks had fallen from the roof of the passage, probably caused by the hundreds of Fey feet that had crossed the bridge in the last two weeks.

Or maybe nothing had fallen. Maybe Con had remembered it slightly wrong. But it didn't matter. The problem had been getting Sebastian through it.

Sebastian was tall and slender, but he had no agility at all. Con had to show him how to crawl through the narrow space, and more than once, Con had to back up to find Sebastian. Sebastian would be stuck and crying in a small area, head down, arms extended forward. Con never wanted to hear Sebastian cry again. The sound was like rock grating on rock, and it made his hair stand on end.

Sebastian had been crying a lot since Con found him. The loss of his family, particularly his sister, made him seem lost. He had almost no coping skills, and had never, Con discovered, been outside the palace grounds until Con led him away. The tunnels terrified him, and the narrow passage made things worse. But Con didn't have to explain to Sebastian the importance of leaving the cavern. Sebastian already knew it, and he wanted out more than Con did.

The warning had chilled Con. He knew they had to escape that place sooner or later—the Fey would find them eventually—but something in Sebastian's manner had really convinced him. Sebastian had Fey magick, and if he claimed he could feel other shifts around him, then Con was inclined to believe him.

Sebastian needed a protector, and Con would be it, until he found the King, or until Sebastian could be on his own.

"All right," Con said, holding Sebastian's hands tightly. "I've got you. Ease forward, and I'll brace you."

Sebastian inched forward. Con moved his hands down Sebastian's arms, until he held Sebastian's shoulders through his robe and guided him out. Sebastian was heavy. He seemed to weigh twice as much as Con expected, given Sebastian's slenderness and the fact that he never ate much. He never complained about being hungry or thirsty. On that level, Sebastian's needs seemed to be few.

"Where . . . is . . . the . . . ground?" Sebastian asked, his voice raspy from disuse and smoke.

It had taken a long time for Con's eyes to get used to the darkness, but Sebastian's didn't seem to be adjusting at all. Not only was he struggling through the passages, he was struggling through them blind.

"It's quite a ways down," Con said, wishing that Sebastian were agile enough to slide down, face first, like Con had. "I'm going to keep bracing you until you can get your legs out."

The passage's opening was wider on this side. Con hoped that by bracing Sebastian, Sebastian would be able to maneuver his legs forward, and then ease down. Con would have to carry him for part of it, but not for all of it.

Con kept one hand on Sebastian's shoulder and moved the other to Sebastian's chest. Sebastian's hips were nearly out.

"All right," Con said. "Can you get on your knees?"

"Yes," Sebastian said. He slowly moved up, crouching on his knees. Con couldn't reach him anymore, but Con kept his hands up anyway, to catch Sebastian if he fell.

Or to break Sebastian's fall.

Con shuddered. He wasn't certain if he was strong enough to survive Sebastian's weight on him if Sebastian did fall.

Sebastian braced his hands on the passage opening, as Con had instructed him. Then he put one foot out, followed by the other. He didn't get tangled, as Con had feared he would, in his own robe. He was sitting, his feet dangling off the ground.

"Great," Con said. He lowered his arms. His right arm tingled. It was going to sleep. And his shoulders ached. He wasn't sure how much longer he would have been able to support Sebastian. "Now put your hands on my shoulders and slide down."

Sebastian leaned forward. Con could almost hear the creaking of Sebastian's body. At times, he was furious at the King for abandoning this boy.

Sebastian's large hands fell on Con's shoulders, firm and solid and heavy. Sebastian put all his weight on them and slid his legs forward. It was everything Con could do to keep from staggering backwards.

Sebastian's slide seemed to take forever. But finally, he reached the bottom of the new tunnel, and stood like a child, proud to be on his feet. He kept his hands on Con's shoulders and smiled.

"We . . . did . . . it," Sebastian said.

"Well, we got across the river," Con said. "But I'm not sure how far these tunnels go. The Tabernacle isn't far from here. Where are your friends?"

"South," Sebastian said. He blinked a little, then added, "A . . . day's . . . walk . . . for . . . you."

"And what about for you?" Con asked, still wondering how

Sebastian knew all of this if he had never been off the palace grounds. This borrowed memory thing was disturbing. But then everything about Sebastian was disturbing. Especially his needy affection. Con wished Sebastian would remove his hands, but didn't know how to ask without hurting Sebastian's feelings.

Slowly Sebastian removed his hands, as if he had read Con's thoughts. But he couldn't do that, could he? Con shuddered again. Maybe he could. Sebastian could do a lot of things that made Con uneasy.

"I . . . do . . . not . . . know," Sebastian said. He loomed large in the semidarkness. They were lucky to be able to stand here. Con's back hurt from crouching for so long.

Con thought. It had been a long time since he had been outside Jahn. Sebastian had explained to him how to reach the farm. In what Con was beginning to recognize as Sebastian's thoughtful, cautious manner, Sebastian explained the entire route in case they were separated. Sebastian had thought of everything. He wasn't slow-witted like they said, but he was slow at everything else: movement, speech, and action.

"Well," Con said, "I don't think we can hurry. We'll have to see where these tunnels lead us, and go as far as that. I don't want to go above ground too soon. The Fey are everywhere, and they'll want you."

"And . . . you," Sebastian said softly.

Con frowned. He wasn't sure about that. But he did know that the Fey feared the Rocaanists. He had gathered that much from the survivors on the other side of the river. They said the Fey believed the Rocaanists had more "magick" like holy water, and would find a way to destroy the Fey.

Con did have extra magick. He had the sword leaning against his leg. But it had nothing to do with the Rocaanists. He had found it in the palace. It made him wonder what else was there, right under the Black King's nose.

He grabbed the sword. "Let's go on," he said.

Sebastian nodded. Con let Sebastian get ahead of him. He didn't want to lose Sebastian in the dark.

The air smelled foul the farther along they went. The stench of stale smoke grew, and Con's eyes burned. The smoke smell was mixed with something else, something older and more primitive. It made the hair rise on the back of Con's neck.

Death.

It smelled like death down here.

He made himself swallow. Of course it did. There would have been bodies above, and some of that smell would have had to seep below. But even as he thought it, he knew the explanation was wrong.

"Stinks," Sebastian said.

"I know," Con said. They turned the only corner, and then Sebastian stopped. Con came up beside him. A body stretched across the passage. It was barely recognizable. It had rotted for two weeks.

"We have to go around it," Con said.

Sebastian grabbed his arm. "There . . . are . . . more. . . . I . . . can . . . smell . . . them."

"So can I," Con said. "But we have to try."

He stepped around the body, careful not to touch it with his feet. Sebastian did the same thing, leaning heavily on Con for balance. Con wished he had something to cover his nose. The stench was growing. He made himself breathe through his mouth. Then he clenched a fist and kept going.

Of course there were bodies. Of course. There had been a full-scale attack on the Tabernacle. The Elders in the cavern on the other side of the river had done a small ceremony for the desperately wounded and ill left behind. Once they saw that passage under the river, they had known that only the healthy ones could get through it. The others were supposed to go back and see if they could find another way to escape.

Obviously some didn't make it.

Con wasn't sure the group on the other side of the river would make it either. They were assuming that the Fey would leave Jahn eventually, and they were hoping that they could wait out the Fey.

Con didn't think the Fey would ever leave. They had Blue Isle now. Unless someone took it from them.

The only hope Con had was that the King was still alive. But that was a slim hope. What could one man do against the magickal Fey? What could any of them do?

Con put one hand over his nose. With his other hand, he grabbed Sebastian's. He had a hunch the next few yards of passageway would be ugly and difficult to traverse.

"Come on," he said to the King's son and the heir to Blue Isle. "We can get through this."

And he hoped he was right.

FOURTEEN

BOTEEN stood in the palace garden. It smelled of flowers and grass mingled with the charred scent that had hung in the air for a week. There had been no real wind to speak of in all that time, and the smoke from the fires had lingered, like a poison, in the air.

Rugad had neglected many things since his injury. He needed to give direction to the Weather Sprites. They weren't bright enough to think of wind on their own. They needed guidance or they would experiment with esoteric things like the difference between the purity content of a raindrop and the purity content of a snowflake. They were lazy, ineffective magicians unless they had guidance, and they would take none from Boteen.

Even if he was their better.

He straightened to his full height. He was the tallest Fey on record, and probably the thinnest, although that detail concerned him much less. He ate his fill, but he consumed enough energy that food scarcely seemed to sustain him. He was constantly honing his skills.

It frustrated him that an Enchanter's magick was limited. He could perform all spells with great power initially, but his reserves would deplete. And some of the more complex magicks were almost beyond him. He could perform them, yes, but not with the degree of competence that, say, a Weather Sprite might use in creating a hurricane. Boteen might create a bad windstorm or a hurricane that lasted only a few moments. He couldn't create the devastation needed to destroy an entire coastline, like the Sprites had done during one of the battles in Nye, no matter how hard he tried.

He wondered if the others could.

The others. He took a deep breath and clenched his fists. Enchanters were rare things. He was the only one who traveled with Rugad, indeed, the only one known among the Fey from Nye to L'Nacin. He suspected an Enchanter had been born to the Fey remaining in the Eccrasian Mountains, but he had nothing more than a sense, on a particularly stormy night, of a child's birth and its flare of magick.

Since the flare had come from the Mountains, he had felt no concern. It did not jeopardize his position.

But the two Enchanters here, on Blue Isle, did. Rugad claimed to have encountered one. That Enchanter protected Gift, the great-grandson. He was, they say, an Islander, blond and round and short as the rest of them. But Boteen wasn't certain. Expert Enchanters could Shape-Shift. They could do so only for brief periods of time and at great personal risk, but they could do so. Perhaps this Enchanter had.

Although that did not explain the stories that had come from the Failures in Shadowlands. They claimed to have among them an Island-born blond boy whose Enchanting talents had gone unknown by all the but the Shifter Solanda. When he had finally been discovered, Gift—as a young boy—had saved him, and got him out of Shadowlands.

Now Gift was traveling with him, or so Boteen assumed. It would seem logical. Find the Enchanter and find the boy.

Although it would not be easy. Rugad had said the boy had closed off Gift's Links. The Enchanter would have closed his own as well, and perhaps disguised his trail.

If he were sophisticated enough.

But it did not answer the question of the other Enchanter. No one claimed to have seen him. Not the Failures, not the tortured Islanders, not anyone.

Yet Boteen could feel him.

He had felt him from the moment he had touched the cliffs to the south, a great reservoir of power, untapped and leaking.

This Enchanter did not know how to use his power, and that made him dangerous.

That made him invisible.

That made him deadly.

Boteen clenched his fists. He was here on Rugad's command. Rugad wanted the boy. He believed that Boteen could track the Enchanter. Boteen could, up to a point. It wasn't as easy as Rugad thought. Nothing was, really.

But Rugad didn't care. He wanted results, not complaints.

Boteen glanced at the sky. The sun had come up, but the smoke and ash in the air made the sky gray. His task would be easier if he could get the Sprites to make a wind. But he didn't want to usurp Rugad's authority. Rugad had no tolerance for it. He would kill a trusted advisor—he would destroy his only Enchanter—before he would tolerate any appearance of sharing power.

He had always made that clear.

It had become clearer when he sent his son Rugar here. When Rugar had died, Rugad had shown no grief, no remorse. Only relief.

Black Blood could not turn on itself—overtly. But the wise leaders, the ones who ascended to and kept the Black Throne, had found ways around that conundrum the Powers had sent centuries before.

Rugad was only maintaining an ancient tradition.

Boteen took a deep breath, hating the burning sensation that filled his lungs. He had no Link to the other Enchanter. So far as he knew, no one did. But there had to be trails. Trails etched in the ground, in the very air he breathed, in everything he touched.

Trails were different than feelings. Trails were simply paths that the Enchanter had once walked. All things left them. All things magick left obvious trails that faded with time.

Boteen could track anyone as long as there was a trail.

And there was an Enchanter's trail in this city. But only one. It was as if the second Enchanter had never been here. The question was, which one protected Black Blood?

He could only guess. And he would guess that the one that protected Black Blood had been once lived in this city for a long time and had been gone almost as long. The trail was very old and had almost faded. It was so old that it had lost much of its form. He couldn't see its color anymore, or its essence. He could barely feel that it had belonged to an Enchanter.

The trail dated from the days of Jewel, when the Failures had first lost Blue Isle. The Enchanter had not been in the garden, but he had been in the palace many times, and his trail went from here to the streets to the river.

His essence was strong in the river, almost as if he had lost part of himself there.

Boteen smiled. He would study the trail. He would learn its scent, its form, its basic nature.

And then he would follow it, silently tracking, until he found the Enchanter.

Until he found both Enchanters.

And until he found Rugad's great-grandson.

Gift.

FIFTEEN

RUGAD touched his neck. The still-vivid wound was ridged under his fingers. It would remain there, a blazing scar testifying to the strength of the King whose palace Rugad now inhabited.

He was standing near the balcony door. Seger, the Healer, was still on the balcony, collecting her things. She was gaunt, and had the leathery look of a Weather Sprite who had been too long in the sun. The last few weeks had taken their toll on all the healers. They had all lost weight. A few had begged him for a day's respite so that they could allow their powers a rest. Healers believed, some said rightly, that a Fey could diminish his powers to nothing.

Rugad had never seen it, but then his magick was never in such constant use. Healers could work for days, weeks, without getting sleep, without stopping to replenish themselves both physically and mentally.

That last series of Visions Rugad had had, the ones that had appeared to him in the rout that King Nicholas had engineered, had left Rugad exhausted. He just hadn't been able to show it.

Seger came in the balcony doors, carrying her herb pouches and the blanket she had placed around his neck. She clutched a small jar in her fingers. She claimed the jar, which looked empty, held his real voice.

She handed it to him. The glass was warm to the touch. "Where do you want this?" she asked. "I don't dare keep it. If it got out, then you would take my head."

He smiled. She knew him well. He set the jar on one of the occasional tables that dotted the room. He would put the jar away after she left, when he was alone. No one else would know where it was, nor how to use it.

"I'm going to tell you this one more time," she said. "If you want to have me restore your real voice when your throat is completely healed, then do not use this false one much. Otherwise, you will be stuck with this false voice for the rest of your days."

"A ruler without a voice has no power," Rugad said. His new voice was a mixture of breath and depth. Seger had spelled the muscles in his throat to allow them to reverberate, to create some sort of noise. It sounded nothing like him, and the pain that shot from his mouth to his chest was staggering.

"Your false voice will never have more power than it does right now," she said.

He took a deep breath. "What of the pain?"

"You either have pain or silence," she said. She stood in front of him, showing no fear. She did not seem in awe of him, and for once, he was grateful.

"Forever?" he asked.

"As long as you use that voice." She smiled. "That should be incentive enough to get your old voice back."

"I do not have the luxury of waiting," he said. "I have waited too long already."

"As you wish," she said, sounding doubtful. She nodded once, then carried her things out the door, leaving him alone.

He picked up the small jar and held it to the light streaming in from the balcony. He could see nothing inside nor did he entirely understand the reason for removing it.

A *man cannot have two voices*, Seger had told him. *He must speak with one, and use its authority only. The other voice would only confuse matters, and would, eventually, cause harm.*

He did know enough about healing magick to know that his old voice could be inserted into something—or someone—else. That was why she wouldn't let it fly on the winds. Someone might see it, capture it, and then speak with his voice.

Whoever had his voice had his authority.

He took the jar and carried it with him into the large bedroom he had been using. He took a pouch from his stack of clothes, and placed the jar inside. Then he tied the pouch to his waist. He too was going to be cautious with the voice. He would guard it as if it were still part of him.

No one would ever speak for him, especially not using the voice he had used so well for ninety-two years.

Rugad touched his neck again. Damn Nicholas. And damn Jewel for marrying him. This small Isle should have been an easy conquest, a mere boot stomp on the way to Leut.

Not a barrier. And certainly not the kind of barrier it had become.

He made his way back into the main room. He had warned himself when he arrived not to underestimate these Islanders, and then he had.

And nearly died.

He put his hands on the back of one of the ornate chairs, letting the curved wood cut into his palms. This place had been designed for comfort, not war. The hints of war were merely that: hints. When he had arrived, he mistook the easy conquest of the Islanders to the south as an inability to fight. He was more willing to believe in his son's incompetence than in the Islanders.

He should have trusted Jewel. Jewel had been extremely competent, and she had seen no way out. She had married Nicholas, given him children, and conquered the Isle the old-fashioned way. Comingling blood.

And then she had been murdered.

Rugad's great-grandson had been raised by Failures.

His great-granddaughter had been raised by Islanders.

Neither of them knew the Fey ways. And the only way he could teach them was to win them over first.

To have them at his side.

And for that, he needed to find them.

A knock at his door startled him. Then, without waiting for a response, the door opened.

"I can speak now," Rugad said, pain piercing his throat.

Wisdom slipped in the door and closed it behind him. "I'm sorry, sir," he said. "I hadn't realized that Seger had left."

"You will never enter again unbidden," Rugad said. He still hadn't decided how to deal with Wisdom. His inclination was to wait until Wisdom was particularly vulnerable and then to strike.

But reducing Wisdom's power bit by bit might be more onerous to the man. Rugad would have to decide which was the better course.

"Forgive me," Wisdom said, bowing a little. "I have news."

Rugad clasped his hands behind his back and waited.

Wisdom blinked once in surprise, and then continued. "One of the Wisps you had sent into the tunnels has returned, quite agitated. He claims to have found your great-grandson."

Rugad let out a breath. "Send him in," he said, moving toward the door.

Wisdom pulled the door open and beckoned someone to enter. A Wisp came through. He was slender—too slender, as many of Rugad's hardworking troops were these days—and his wings were pressed flat against his back. His dark hair was cut short in the Nye tradition, and plastered against his head by sweat. He was covered with cobwebs, dust, and dirt.

"Forgive my appearance," he said. "I came as quickly as I could."

Rugad held up a hand. "Leave us, Wisdom," he said.

"But, sir—"

"*Now.*" The pressure that Rugad put on his voice made it feel as if his throat were about to split open.

"Yes, sir," Wisdom shot a worried glance at him, then spun and let himself out the door.

"Come," Rugad said to the Wisp, and led him onto the balcony. The breeze fluttered the Wisp's wings, and toyed with Rugad's hair. Rugad closed the balcony doors. He didn't want Wisdom to be privy to this, and if he were listening at the hallway door, he would not be able to hear.

"Your name?" Rugad asked. He had once known the names of all his troops, but had stopped long ago wasting precious memory with such trivial details. Now the only names he remembered belonged to people who had made an impression on him, good or bad.

"Tuft, sir," the Wisp said.

"Sit, Tuft," Rugad said, indicating one of the lounge chairs. Tuft sat on its side so that his wings would have space. Rugad sat on the other lounge chair in the same way. "You have found my great-grandson?"

"No," Tuft said. He glanced at the door. "Is that what Wisdom said?"

"That is what Wisdom said." Rugad kept his voice calm. The pain in his throat was becoming an unbearable burning.

"No, I said I think I know where he might be." Tuft looked distressed. He knew that giving false information to the Black King was punishable by death. "I never said I knew where he was."

"Tell me what happened," Rugad said.

So Tuft told him of exploring the tunnels, of finding a cavern filled with Black Robes, and of the conversation he had heard.

"This is important," Rugad said. "You say they believe he was slow. He spoke slowly? He moved slowly?"

"Yes," Tuft said. He had clasped his long hands together and was twisting the fingers in a washing motion.

"And his features were marked by lines?"

"I don't know, sir. I never saw him."

"Is that what they said?"

"They said he looked strange, sir."

Rugad nodded and rested his elbows on his knees. Not his great-grandson, but his great-grandson's golem. Which, in some ways, was almost as good. "Do you believe he's still in the tunnels?"

"Yes, sir. That's why I came here instead of finishing my exploration as instructed. I thought if we got some Infantry down there in the passages we would be able to find him."

Rugad smiled. "Excellent thinking. Infantry will help. We will guard all the exits and entrances we find, too. And I will have the Wisps redouble their efforts in searching the tunnels. We will find the boy, thanks to you, Tuft."

"I would like to go back to the tunnels myself, sir, and see if I can find him."

"You do that," Rugad said. He stood, and that allowed the Wisp to stand as well. "You did well, coming to me. I appreciate a man who understands our priorities, and knows how to act on them."

"Thanks, sir," Tuft said, and then shrank to his small size. Within an instant, he became a spark which caught the breeze and disappeared.

Rugad watched him go. The golem. If he could turn it, it would be a wonderful tool. A physical representation of King

Nicholas's loss. The people of Blue Isle would think their Prince had made some sort of pact with the Fey.

And if he couldn't turn the golem, he could still use it. For it to have lasted so long, it had to be Linked. Rugad could travel those Links. And, he suspected, on the other end he would find his great-grandson, his great-granddaughter, or King Nicholas himself.

Then they would see the true extent of Fey magick.

Then they would really know what it was like to lose.

SIXTEEN

MATTHIAS sat at the table in the main room of his house, his head tilted back, eyes closed. Marly had her hand on the back of his skull, bracing him. With her other hand, she painted his still-healing wounds. The liquid she used stung. She had done this every day since she began treating him. When he asked her why, she had said it was because the wounds needed to remain clean. The stinging was almost unbearable, and when it ended, the itching began. She said the itching was a good sign, a sign of healing.

He hated it.

He also hated the look of his face in the silvered glass he had in the large bedroom. The wounds ran from his hairline to his jawline, cutting through his cheeks and narrowly missing his right eye. The thread Marly had sewn through them to hold them together was knotted on the outside, making him look as if he were a piece of cloth, poorly stitched. In repose, his mouth twisted slightly to the left, and his right eyelid drooped. He had not been a handsome man before, but he had had an interesting face.

It had just gotten more interesting.

The others had scattered for their day. He had dug some coins from his stash and had the men go to the market, with strict instructions to buy—not steal—several days' worth of food. He didn't know what he was going to do with all these people, this band of thieves who had inadvertently saved his life. They had been operating out of the tunnels in Jahn for the past several years and had stolen everything from food to coins to holy water from the Tabernacle itself. They had found Matthias, dying, on the river bank and had taken him to Marly for healing the night before the Fey invasion—apparently the group felt itself responsible for the life and limb of the common people. Sometimes, Marly had told him, they even shared their food with those who needed it.

From what Matthias had seen, these thieves were less kind-hearted than they imagined. They had warmed up to him quickly enough because Marly defended him and because she was Jakib's sister. Jakib was not the leader of the thieves, but he had put the band together.

The leader was Yasep, and even though he claimed to have accepted Matthias, he did not like him.

Still, Matthias had brought them here. They needed a place to escape the Fey, and he needed physical laborers. The Fey were entrenching themselves on Blue Isle. Titus, the Fifty-second Rocaan, was dead, and Matthias was the only one who knew the Secrets now.

One of the Secrets had killed Fey. He hoped to find out if any of the others did as well.

Marly's light touch on his face stopped. The pain shuddered through his skin.

"There," she said, bringing his head up. Her hand left his curls. He opened his eyes. The room was still dark, even though it wasn't quite midday. The windows he had built onto the mountain side of the house had yet to capture any light. He had spent many of his exile years here, studying and learning all he could about the origins of Rocaanism. The things he did learn had astounded him. The early history of the religion was a history of rivals, of bloody factions fighting each other to gain supremacy. It was one of the reasons the Secrets became secret. Once, it was rumored that the man who possessed them could not be killed.

A knock on the door startled him. He glanced at Marly, who shrugged. He got up, moved aside a chair, and made his way into the entrance area.

He had redesigned the house when he gained it. It had been

left to him by an old friend of his family, an elderly childless man who believed that Matthias's young years were an abomination, a sin committed against him by the Wise Ones. Matthias had received the house, which had then been a single room, and had expanded it, designing its interior as if it were a suite in the Tabernacle: a main room with a bedroom off to the side. Once he began to plumb the Secrets, he had added the entry area so that he wouldn't track dirt into his home. The second bedroom came even later than that when he realized that he needed a place for others to stay.

The knock sounded again. He squared his shoulders. He knew what this would be. One of the Wise Ones, wondering what he was doing in Constant again. Beneath the seemingly concerned question would be a desire for him to leave.

They hated seeing him. They hated having him anywhere near them. He was a reminder that sometimes their policies failed, that sometimes simple compassion won out over fear.

He gripped the knob and pulled the door open.

His neighbor, Tri, stood before him, cloak wrapped around his sturdy frame, red hair loose and flowing down his back.

"They sent you this time, huh?" Matthias asked. Tri had become one of the Wise Ones in the last year, and at first that had frightened Matthias—having a Wise One right next door. Then he realized that Tri was using the office differently, that Tri didn't believe the old teachings and was going to inject new life into the council. That too disturbed Matthias—he had learned that sometimes the old ways had relevance—but it also relieved him. Tri wasn't going to persecute Matthias, at least not in the way the others had done.

Tri was staring at him as if he had never seen him before. Matthias resisted the urge to put a hand up to his ruined face.

"What happened to you?" Tri asked.

Matthias shook his head. "Long story," he said. He didn't feel like going into it now. "Tell me what they want and get it over with."

"They didn't send me," Tri said, "but I do need to speak to you. May I come in?"

Tri had never made that request before. Matthias frowned and winced at the sudden pain going through his face, but stood back, holding the door open. Tri slipped in, glancing over his shoulder as he did. Matthias looked too. The sunlit street was empty. The houses across the way had a midday silence. If anyone was watching them, it wasn't obvious.

Matthias closed the door behind him. Marly appeared in the entry way. "Tis all right?" she asked.

Tri's eyes opened wide at the sight of her. He glanced at Matthias, as if asking who she was. Matthias ignored him.

"Yes," he said. "Tri is my neighbor. Can you give us a moment, Marly?"

She sighed, but disappeared from the doorway. She was protective of him, and he found he liked that.

No one had been protective of him before.

He led Tri to the table that he and Marly had been at moments before. Her poultices and healing creams were still scattered around the table's surface. The room smelled faintly of herbs and burned hair.

"She's a healing woman?" Tri asked.

"Among other things," Matthias said, not yet willing to answer questions about his companions.

"She looks like she was born here, but she doesn't talk that way."

"No, she doesn't," Matthias said. He slid out a stool with his foot, and indicated that Tri should sit in it.

Tri shook his head, and crossed his arms. His cape billowed slightly, revealing the traditional costume of Blooders; the sweaters, the heavy breeches, and boots. "I came to ask you a few questions and to warn you," he said.

Anger flared through Matthias. He leaned against the table in an effort to control himself and his voice. "I thought you said they didn't send you."

"They didn't," Tri said. "But I just came from the meeting. I got away as quickly as I could. I know you came into town last night. At dawn, just as the market opened, two tall strangers were seen in the area and forced out."

Things like this happened in Constant all the time. They were terrified of strangers. Matthias had been able to come here after leaving the Tabernacle only because he was known here. He had worried about bringing the crew here, then decided that of all the people he knew, this group could take care of themselves.

"You thought it was my people?"

"You didn't arrive alone," Tri said. "And your woman is tall."

"She was here." Then he put a hand to his face. The others had been asleep then. "You're sure this was at dawn?"

"Just past. The market opens before the sun comes over the mountains."

Matthias's stomach turned. "What did these tall ones look like?"

"I don't know," Tri said. "I didn't see them. But the woman who did said they were tall and thin and dark."

"Dark," Matthias whispered. He blinked and tried to think. His heart was beating rapidly. "How dark?"

"I don't know," Tri said. He sounded confused now. "What's happening here, Matthias?"

"Have you ever seen Fey?" Matthias asked.

Tri shook his head. "I've only heard you talk of them. In all these years they've been on the Isle they've never come this far."

"They've never been on the Isle in such large numbers before," Matthias said. He gripped the side of the table for support. "You are sure of this description? Tall and thin and dark?"

"As sure as I can be without seeing them," Tri said. "And I don't think you can talk to the woman who saw them. She's one of the Wise Ones."

"You thought it was my people. You came to warn me." Matthias's face was beginning to itch. He gripped the table harder. "What are your 'wise' ones going to do to these tall ones?"

"Throw them out of town if they can," Tri said.

"And if they can't?" Matthias asked.

"You know the Wise Ones' solution in those instances."

Matthias shuddered. He knew it all too well. "You came to warn me that my friends would be killed if they stayed."

"And to offer my help," Tri said. He bit his lower lip after he spoke, as he waited.

"Why would a Wise One help me?"

"I'm not a Wise One anymore," Tri said. "They threw me out."

"This morning?" Matthias stared at Tri. That wasn't possible. That had never happened, in all the years that Matthias had known of the Wise Ones. "Nice try, my friend, but the only one way to escape the Wise Ones is death."

"Or shunning," Tri said. "I was shunned."

"For what? Questioning their wisdom?"

"Sharing varin with you," Tri said.

Matthias felt the blood leave his face. The itching grew worse. "How did they know about that?"

"I told them."

"You *told* them?" Matthias raised his voice. He heard Marly stir in the other room. "You *told* them? Why?"

"Because they were wrong. They saw the tall ones and were instantly afraid. I joined them for just this sort of thing, Matthias. I'm there to make sure that no innocents are hurt."

"You don't know who these tall ones are," Matthias said. "If they're Fey, it's Constant that'll be hurt."

"And if they're not?" Tri said. "Then we condone the killing of innocent people because they look different than we do? That would mean you have to die, Matthias. You and that pretty woman in the other room. You don't want that."

"I don't want you to pay for helping me, either," Matthias said.

Tri shook his head. "I'm not paying. Leaving the Wise Ones is good for me. I hated being a part of the group. It's insidious, their paranoia. It was changing me, seducing me. I didn't want to be part of it anymore."

Matthias understood that feeling. It didn't quite describe his reaction to the Tabernacle—he had always respected the believers like the Fiftieth Rocaan—but it did describe his impatience with the nonbelievers, the political ones who were in the Tabernacle for personal gain. Sometimes he felt as if they tainted his experience, as if they had somehow corrupted him.

Tri apparently misunderstood Matthias's sudden silence. "I can still find varin for you, if you want it."

Matthias smiled, then winced. He still forgot how simple movements hurt his face. "I do want it," he said, "but that wasn't what I was thinking about."

He wasn't about to share his deepest thoughts about the Tabernacle. He rarely discussed his life there with anyone.

"I'm worried about these tall ones," he said. "If they are Fey, Constant is in trouble. The Fey rarely travel in pairs. They rarely travel anywhere without their armies. If this is a scouting mission, perhaps we can—"

"You want to kill them too," Tri said, shaking his head. "Is that the only response people here have to outsiders?"

Matthias felt a chill. Nicholas had called him a murderer after the death of Jewel. And he was, in his way. He had killed dozens of Fey, and thought little of it.

Was he no better than the people who put him on the mountain as a newborn?

"What do you suggest?" he asked.

"I suggest we find them, these outsiders," Tri said. "We find out what they want, find out why they're here, and find out if we can help them in any way."

"Why should we help them?" Matthias asked.

"Why shouldn't we?"

"If they're Fey—"

"If they're Fey, then we'll deal with that. If they're not, we can warn them away from the Wise Ones." Tri's eyes narrowed. "I thought you were a good man, Matthias."

"What do you mean?" Matthias asked, his mouth dry. He couldn't answer the question directly.

"A good man, a man of God, would try to help others. Isn't that what the Words teach?"

"They also teach protection," Matthias said. He took a deep breath and then released it. "You haven't seen the Fey. You haven't seen what they do. They burned the entire city of Jahn and killed most of its inhabitants. They're bloodthirsty and powerful, and they're destroying all that Blue Isle is. They even burned the Tabernacle."

Tri's eyes grew wide. Of course he hadn't heard. No one here had. This place was so far away from anything and so distrustful of outsiders.

"And the Rocaan?" Tri asked.

"Is dead."

Tri finally sat on the stool that Matthias had offered him. "Which makes you Rocaan."

"No," Matthias said. "I renounced the post."

"I don't think you can," Tri said. "The Secrets—"

"May not be of religious use," Matthias said.

"What does that mean?" Tri asked.

"I'm not sure yet," Matthias said. "That's why I wanted varin from you."

Tri scratched his head. "If Rocaanism is dead, then what happens next?"

"I didn't say it was dead," Matthias said. "I said the Tabernacle was burned and the Rocaan dead."

"But that was the religion."

Matthias almost smiled, remembered, and resisted the urge. "That from a Wise One? How interesting."

"Oh, you think the pockets will rise and become the religion."

"I think the Tabernacle tainted Rocaanism and remade it in its own image. I think that the religion may find its purity now."

"With you at the helm," Tri said.

Matthias shook his head. "No. I do not represent the Tabernacle or the religion. I merely hold its Secrets. Help me, Tri. Get me more varin, and we'll see if we can remake Rocaanism in our image."

Tri frowned. "Sounds dangerous," he said.

"It would have been if the Tabernacle still exists," Matthias said. "But it doesn't."

Tri ran a hand over his chin, then slapped his hands on his knees. "I will get you varin on one condition. Help me find those tall ones. Help me warn them away from Constant. It sounded like they didn't know the prejudices up here, and that may kill them."

"What if they're Fey?" Matthias asked.

"You can't spend your life afraid of the Fey," Tri said. "If they're here and there's only two of them as you said, let's find out why. It can't hurt."

"Oh, but it can," Matthias said. "It can."

SEVENTEEN

SCAVENGER climbed the steep path, then paused and levered himself on the rock. He used his hands and arms to pull his entire body up, then sat for a moment, panting.

Coulter was ahead of him, scurrying along the path, trying to reach Gift.

Scavenger needed a moment to himself. No one had followed them. He doubted anyone had seen them leave the quarry.

He scooted back on the rock and looked away from the mountains.

The valley spread beneath him, the gray stone houses tucked against the mountain, the dirt roads leading into the town. His heart was pounding. He and Coulter had run once they left the quarry, and hadn't stopped until they reached the mountainside path leading to their camp.

He hadn't liked the place they camped. It was still farther up the path, in a natural alcove created by the rocks. It wasn't too far from the rock quarry, but it was some distance from town. Gift and Coulter had liked that.

Scavenger hadn't. Gift and Coulter hadn't studied the geography of Blue Isle like Scavenger had. They weren't learners. They were intuitive leaders, something that disturbed him somewhat. Perhaps all magickal people relied on themselves like that, but he didn't. Even though he was Fey, he had never had magick. He was one of the unlucky ones. In the Fey Empire, the short, magickless Fey were forced to work as Red Caps, doing the jobs that none of the other Fey would touch.

He hadn't done that work for twenty years.

He hadn't been part of the Empire that long.

He had lived alone for years, and then he found Adrian and Coulter as they escaped the Fey Shadowlands. He had helped them elude the Fey, and they, in turn, had given him a home on Blue Isle.

He owed them for the companionship and acceptance, for the warmth they had always shown him even when they doubted his word.

They didn't have reason to doubt now. His knowledge had proven valuable all along on this trip. He had studied Blue Isle when he decided to make it his home, just as he had studied magick when he realized he had to survive without it in the Fey Empire.

And his study of Blue Isle had him worried.

They had reached the northeastern end of the Isle. The Eyes of Roca, the mountain range that began long before the valley that housed Constant, was on the northernmost tip of the Island. The range ended in these tall mountains called the Cliffs of Blood.

If the town of Constant was as unfriendly as he feared, their little band would have only two choices: It would have to go into the mountains themselves and hope it could survive there, or it would have to go back south.

If they went south, Scavenger would want to hug the mountains all the way. Once they passed the Cliffs, they would reach the eastern end of the Cardidas River. Crossing it had been difficult earlier. At this part of the Isle it might be impossible.

And then there were the Slides of Death on the other side.

The very name made him shudder. This mountain range was huge—the Cliffs were high and imposing—but he had heard that the Slides were even more dangerous, even more threatening than the Cliffs.

He didn't want to see that.

He didn't want to face it.

But he might have to. He was a Failure too, now that the Black King had arrived. If Gift was to be believed—and Scavenger had no real reason to doubt him—the entire troop of Fey who had brought him here all those years ago were dead. Killed by Rugad because he could not abide failure.

And because he did not want dissension in his ranks.

Sometimes Rugad outsmarted even himself.

Scavenger took a deep breath and stood. He wiped the dust off his pants and used a rock to brace himself as he climbed the rest of the way to the trail.

They had found this hiding spot after they had approached the rock quarry. Actually, Gift and Leen had found it when they learned they couldn't work. They had brought their meager food supplies here, and all his weapons. He had felt naked without them, but he knew he couldn't have them for work. He had hoped that Gift and Leen had brought weapons with them into town.

He also hoped they hadn't had to use them.

Coulter had initially wanted to find a place in the town to live, but Adrian wouldn't let them look. He was worried about precisely the problem that had appeared: fear of tall ones. Scavenger didn't entirely understand it—why would Islanders, who had never seen Fey, fear tall people? Because of magick? But that didn't make sense either, since Coulter had all the magick of an Enchanter without the height.

Scavenger believed, though, that they still needed to find a place to hide. He didn't like their current camp. They needed someplace better, somewhere that would give them time. He needed to train Gift how to think like a Fey.

Scavenger was afraid the task was hopeless.

And then there was Coulter. The Islander was clearly an Enchanter, but he knew little about Enchanter's magick. Scavenger knew what sort of spells an Enchanter could do, but he did not know how to conjure them. All he could do was tell Coulter that such spells existed.

Still, Coulter would try them.

But there were so many and there was so little time, especially while the group was on the run.

And Scavenger didn't know how long that would last. He never doubted the Black King's abilities. Rugad wanted Gift, and he would do everything he could to find him, including using tricks that Scavenger—as a magickless Fey—simply didn't know.

He sighed and made his way down the trail. His heart was still pounding, but his breathing was coming regularly now. He was worried that Gift and Leen had never made it back from their task this morning, but that was a fear he had whenever the group separated.

To lose the boy, though, after all of this, would be a great tragedy. Especially if they lost him through error or carelessness.

The trail was narrow, barely wide enough for his small feet, and Scavenger wondered, as he had when they first found it, if this was an actual trail used by Islanders or if some animal used it regularly instead.

He wasn't sure he wanted to see the animal that lived up here in the scraggly mountainside. It would take a tough and hardy creature to survive the winters here.

He didn't want to be one of them.

Then he rounded a corner, and saw the rock formation. The rocks jutted up from the ground like pillars, and above them was a flat ledge. It wasn't quite a roof, but it was close enough, if the five of them scuttled back against the rock wall. The space between the pillars was dirt and bits of rock. They had spent the first evening clearing out the large stuff and smoothing the dirt so that they could sleep easily. Scavenger's weapons were stored near that far wall.

Coulter was already inside the formation—Scavenger could see flashes of his yellow hair—and Leen was sitting on a boulder outside. She was at alert, her back straight, her knife near her hand. She looked tired.

"Where's Gift?" Scavenger asked.

"Inside," Leen said.

"Coulter say anything?"

"No," Leen said. "He needed water first. You two shouldn't have run like that in this dryness."

"Maybe not," Scavenger said. He wiped a hand over his mouth. He could use some water too, but he knew that Leen wouldn't offer it to him. She was still too Fey for that. She barely deigned to talk to him. "But something strange happened at the quarry."

"What happened?" Gift appeared between the pillars. He held a water skin. Coulter appeared behind him. Dirt ran along Coulter's face, and had streaked into his hair. He took the skin from Gift and handed it to Scavenger.

Scavenger drank. The water was gritty and warm but it tasted good. He hadn't realized how thirsty he was.

"What happened?" Gift repeated.

Coulter stared at Scavenger. Coulter and Gift still weren't speaking to each other except when necessary. Apparently Coulter didn't think this was one of those moments.

Scavenger removed the skin from his lips and let it dangle from his fingers. "A strange man showed up at the quarry. He seemed to be asking questions. Adrian stayed to find out what was going on."

"You didn't wait to see if this concerned us?" Leen asked, contempt in her voice.

Gift put a hand on her shoulder. "It did concern us. After this morning, it had to. They must be trying to find us."

Scavenger closed his eyes for just a second. It was as he feared. Something had happened when Gift and Leen went to the market.

"What happened this morning?" Coulter asked. Scavenger could hear the concern in his voice, even though he tried to hide it. He was standing slightly behind Gift, and his fair cheeks had reddened when Gift mentioned that something bad had happened.

"We went to the market, offered to spend coin there, and they reacted like we were—I don't know—evil, or something," Gift said.

Leen had turned slightly so that she faced Coulter not Scavenger. "It wasn't because we were Fey, either. I don't think they've seen Fey."

"It was because we were tall. I think Scavenger could go in there and no one would bother him."

Scavenger walked the rest of the way up the path, stopping beside Leen's rock, as much to annoy her as to get closer to the conversation.

"So what happened?" he asked.

"We left," Gift said.

"They made us leave," Leen said. "They held their hands up in fists and said *Begone*. We were Compelled."

"It was a Chant," Scavenger whispered, and for the first time, Leen really looked at him.

"Yes," she said. "It was."

"And these were Islanders?" Coulter asked. He leaned against one of the pillars and put a hand to his head.

"Yes," Gift said. "It was odd, too, because it felt as if we were pushed backwards. Leen reacted more strongly than I did, but we both felt it."

"Islanders," Coulter said again, as if in contemplation.

Scavenger was watching him. The boy was beginning to learn that he was not unique. Was it a revelation for him? Or was it relief?

Scavenger braced one hand on the rock and peered toward the valley. It looked no different than it had the day before, but his perception of it had shifted, suddenly, as if the world had moved slightly to the left.

The Fey had come out of the mountains too, centuries ago. The Eccrasian Mountains. The peoples nearby had no magick, but the Fey, the original mountain dwellers, had.

"You're sure it was because you were tall?" Scavenger asked again.

"They called us tall ones," Leen said.

Scavenger's gaze met Gift's. "Tall ones have magick," Scavenger said.

"Not on Blue Isle," Gift said. "Look at Coulter."

Yet, from what Scavenger had seen, Coulter was just a bit taller than the locals. Sometimes a bit was all it took.

"Maybe he's tall enough," Scavenger said.

"You can't put a Fey interpretation on Islander responses," Coulter snapped. He dropped his hands. His blue eyes were blazing, almost as if they were lit from within.

"No, I can't," Scavenger said. "But it was the first thing that came to mind." He took a deep breath. "It's only Domestics who use Chants among the Fey. They use it as a secondary defense system, and only when they're terrified."

"These people were terrified," Leen said.

"But they didn't kill you," Scavenger said more to himself than to anyone else.

"Obviously," she said.

"Interesting," he said. Among many of the Domestics, deliberate killing of any kind destroyed their magick abilities. Healing magicks did not tolerate deliberate violence to the body, unlike the dark magicks. But the Fey had cultivated the dark magicks. It served war so much better. The healing magicks were often forgotten.

But that was Fey. Fey. He had to remind himself of that. This was Islander magick, and it might be very different.

"Did they follow you?" Scavenger asked.

Gift shook his head. "We watched. No one followed us."

"But they're searching for you," Scavenger said, and he was not asking a question.

"We don't know that," Coulter said. "That man could have come to the quarry for any reason."

"He could have," Scavenger said. "Or he could have been coming to ask about tall ones. Remember the comments made when Gift and Leen were there yesterday?"

"We should wait for Adrian. He'll know," Coulter said.

"Yes, he will," Scavenger said. "If he finds us in time."

"Why wouldn't he?" Coulter asked.

"Because they fear tall ones. They know that Gift and Leen are nearby. They're *searching*." Scavenger felt a shiver run through him. He'd had enough war to last him a lifetime. He really didn't want to fight again.

"But how could they find us here?" Leen asked.

"This is their mountain," Scavenger said. "They have Chant. Maybe they have other magicks as well."

"But if they're afraid of tall ones, then wouldn't they be afraid of magick?" Coulter asked.

"You can't put a Fey response on Islanders," Scavenger snapped.

Coulter nodded once, as if in acknowledgment.

"But we might have to," Gift said softly. "We might have to put a Fey response on them. We don't know what they can do. We should expect the worst."

"The worst is they find us, capture us, and kill us," Scavenger said.

"So we need to find a better place to hide," Leen said.

"Do you have any suggestions?" Scavenger asked. "We are at the very end of this island."

Gift looked up at the side of the mountain, near the top. "I have an idea," he said.

Coulter put a hand on his arm. "I don't think it's a good one."

Gift shook him off. "Can you feel it?" he asked Scavenger and Leen. "Can you feel the power of the mountain itself?"

Scavenger peered at Gift. He didn't like how this was going. "A mountain is a mountain is a mountain," he said.

"If that were true," Gift said, "why is this one red? Why does it feel different?"

"And why do the stones lose their redness when they're broken from the mountain itself?" Coulter asked.

"I thought you didn't like his idea," Scavenger said.

"He hasn't heard it," Gift said.

"He doesn't have to," Coulter said. "I feel the mountain, and I don't like it. And I don't think you should either."

Scavenger sighed and closed his eyes. They were fighting again. He hated that. Hated that they couldn't settle this difference between them.

He slipped off the rock and walked to the edge, looking at the valley. So far he saw no one. He would wait for Adrian. Once Adrian came back, they would have a rational voice.

And then they could make a decision about their future.

He only hoped it wouldn't be too late.

EIGHTEEN

THEY came out of the snow faster than she expected. Arianna stopped on the narrow path and sat on a boulder. The mountainside continued down, disappearing into a layer of trees. Behind her, there was only snow, below her, trees, and beside her, the narrow rock crevice that provided the path she, her father, and the Shaman walked on.

Her father and the Shaman didn't see her sit. They continued, making a perilous way along the trail. Her father carried a makeshift bundle on his back. It was large and bulky and held the supplies the Shaman had hidden in the cave. Arianna had a similar bundle on her back, only hers was smaller. The Shaman wore pouches on her belt. They carried herbs essential to her magick.

Arianna brushed the snow off her boots. It had been wispy for the last way down. Now there were only traces of it on the path ahead. Maybe the three of them wouldn't have to be as cautious. The Shaman had been warning them about the dangers of disturbing this loosely packed snow; how, on steep mountainsides, it could slide, killing them all.

The rock was cold through her thin pants. Her soft boots were wet. That was partly because they didn't fit properly. She had stolen her clothes—and her father's as well—before the two of them had gone up the mountain with the Shaman, and nothing fit exactly. She could grow her feet to fit better in the boots, but it seemed like too much effort.

Everything seemed like too much effort these days.

Her father and the Shaman were already farther ahead of her on the path. She watched them go. Maybe she would Shift and catch up to them.

And maybe she wouldn't.

Shifting had gotten harder too. The Shaman had said it was because Arianna had exercised her magick so much in the last few weeks. Her body needed time to rest and replenish itself.

They had gone only another few feet when they realized she wasn't with them.

"Ari!" her father called.

"I need to rest!" she yelled back. Her voice was rusty with disuse. She hadn't said anything when they decided to leave the cave, even though it was one of the hardest things she had ever done. It had become a safe place in her mind, the only safe place she could find. It was home, in a strange way, home after all the turmoil.

After losing Sebastian.

She missed him. She missed him beside her. She missed his cool hands and his cracked smile and his soft, halting voice. She had never experienced life without him. One of her earliest memories was of him staring at her over the railing of her cradle, staring at her and smiling.

Her father made his way back to her. "The Shaman says there's a ledge just around those rocks over there," he said, pointing. "It would be a good place to rest and have a bit of food."

Arianna wasn't sure she could make it to the ledge. "She knows everything, doesn't she?" Arianna asked, letting her bitterness show. "She knows where this Gift is, she knows where the next stop is, she probably knows if we're going to succeed or not and is just unwilling to tell us."

"She's walked this way before," her father said, his voice soft, compassionate. He'd been looking at Arianna with a mixture of perplexity and concern ever since they'd left the palace.

Ever since everything had changed.

"Aren't you worried?" she blurted. "I mean, giving up everything for this Gift?"

He smiled. It was a tired smile, and it didn't quite reach his eyes. "What everything, darling? We woke up in a cave this morning."

"At least it was safe there," she said, and to her surprise, tears burned in her eyes. She blinked hard, holding them back.

Her father sat beside her on the boulder and took her in his arms. She hadn't realized how much she needed to be held. Her breath hitched. She promised herself she wouldn't cry. She didn't need to. She could make it through this. She knew it.

But there was no "through this." Every time she had told herself that in the past, the crisis had been small. She had made it through, and then life had returned to normal.

Now normal was gone. The Black King had taken her home, and he had burned the town she grew up in, and his people had killed the only brother she had ever known.

Her father put his hand on the back of her skull. He was warm and smelled of old wool. She rested her head on his shoulder. It felt strong and able to withstand anything. That's how he had felt to her from the moment she was born.

Able to do anything.

She took a deep breath. "Daddy," she said. "This Gift, I don't think it's right to find him."

"I know, baby, you said so before." Her father's voice rumbled against her hair.

"But you're not listening to me. Please. Listen to me."

Her father sighed. "All right," he said.

"I saw him. He's smart."

"How smart, Ari?"

"Smart as me," she said. "Maybe smarter. And he was raised by *them*."

"The Fey," her father said, his tone flat.

"Yes."

"Why do you fear them?" he asked. "They're your mother's people."

"They burned down my town."

"Not the Fey who raised your brother. They lived on Blue Isle in peace."

"In hiding," she said. "The Shaman called them Failures."

"They're the ones who raised your brother. The Shaman says he's like Sebastian."

"Why do you believe her?"

"Why should I doubt her?"

"Because she never told you that the Fey had this Gift."

Her father sighed again. "She tried," he said.

"But not hard enough."

"It's not up to us to understand the Shaman."

"But we should," Arianna said. "She's the one leading us to this Gift. She's the one who says it's safe. And I think she's *lying*."

Her father was silent for a moment. Maybe he thought so too. "I don't think she's telling us everything," he said. "I don't know if that's lying."

"Why do you trust her more than me, Daddy?"

"I don't," he said.

"Then why are we going?"

Her father pushed away from her so that he could see her face. His had grown thinner. It had more lines than it had before. Her father had grown older in the last week, and he looked tired. More tired than she had ever seen him.

"I loved your mother," he said. "Did I ever tell you that?"

Arianna shook her head. In the distance, she saw the Shaman. Waiting. Out of earshot.

"We made you out of that love. We made Gift. I remember him."

"How? Sebastian was there."

"Not for three days. For three days he was a different child."

She didn't like to hear this. She didn't want to know her father longed for his other child. "He wasn't a person. He was a baby."

Her father smiled. "He was a person. Just like you were. Right from the start."

"I'm sure the Fey changed him," she said.

"It doesn't matter," her father said. "He's in as much danger as you are. Maybe more, because all his friends are dead. We're all he has, Ari."

"*You're* all he has," she said.

"*We* are," her father said. "He's your brother too."

"Sebastian was my brother."

"And so is Gift."

A tear ran down her cheek. She swiped at it angrily. He brushed another one off her face.

"You're my girl," he said. "My baby. Nothing will change that."

Her lower lip trembled. He pulled her closer. She let him hold her as if she were a little girl, not caring what the Shaman thought. His warmth was refreshing. It kept her torso comfortable while the rock chilled her legs and buttocks.

He would always be her father. She knew that.

She wasn't being fair.

"Aren't you worried?" she asked.

"I'm very worried, Ari, but I don't think we have a choice."

"He could turn us in. He could send the Black King after us."

"No, Ari," her father said. "Gift may have been raised Fey, but he was raised by the Shaman's people. And they're all dead."

"So?" Arianna asked.

Her father's arm tightened around her. "You know how we feel without Sebastian, without our home. The Black King did the same thing to Gift. He has no home any more. Everyone he knows is dead. He's alone out there, and probably more confused than we are."

"He won't replace Sebastian," Arianna said.

Her father leaned his head on top of hers. "I don't want anyone to replace Sebastian," he said quietly. "I'll love and miss that boy until the day I die."

"Then I don't know why you need this Gift, Daddy," Arianna said. "You have me."

"Yes, I do." Her father's voice was soft. "And if the world were different, you and I would continue on the path we planned a few short weeks ago. You would have been the mind behind Sebastian. We would have let Gift go his own way. But we can't now. We can't let the Black King get to him. Gift is as powerful as you. Blue Isle needs both of you on our side. Not you against him. Imagine what a disaster that would be, Ari."

"I could beat him," she said, not sure if she believed it. She remembered seeing him that day, as he stood beside Sebastian. His face had been the template for Sebastian's, only Gift's had more angles and no cracks. And his eyes were so bright that they were nearly blinding. He had outrun her, had nearly outthought her, and provided one of the few challenges she had had until the Black King arrived.

"You don't dare, Ari."

"I know," she said. "This Black Blood thing. You really believe that."

"I've seen too much of Fey magick to disbelieve any of it,"

her father said. "We have to be cautious. If we're not, we could lose everything."

"I thought we already did," Arianna said.

"No, baby," her father said. "We still have each other."

"Do you think we'll lose that?" she asked.

"I lost your mother," he said. "I lost your brother."

Of course he thought it. Of course.

"You'll always have me, Daddy," she said.

His smile didn't reach his eyes. "I know that, honey," he said. But she could tell he didn't believe her.

NINETEEN

THE stench was almost unbearable.

Con walked slowly through the pile of rotted and decaying bodies, Sebastian at his side. Sebastian had to set the pace; he couldn't keep up with Con. Sebastian had tripped more than once trying to get past the bodies.

The tunnel had widened, and Con recognized it. They were in the catacombs under the Tabernacle. The bodies sprawled around him wore robes like his. Beige robes, black robes, canvas robes, and velvet robes. Death had spared no one.

The bodies were too far gone for him to recognize faces.

He didn't even try.

He was more concerned with how to breathe. The smell was so strong it turned his stomach, but he didn't want to breathe through his mouth. He didn't want to taste this horror anymore than he already was.

It was as if the odor had seeped into him. It was thick on his tongue, coating his throat, making a path all the way to his stomach. His eyes burned.

Sebastian also noticed the odor, but it didn't seem to be bothering him like it was bothering Con. Sebastian seemed more distressed by the bodies around him, glancing at each as if to see if he knew them.

Con knew them. Con had spent every day with them for the past two years. They had come into the catacombs when the Fey invaded, and they had come for safety.

Instead, something had killed them, and that something didn't look like the Fey.

These bodies were scattered as if they had fallen in an attempt to get to the tunnels that Con and Sebastian had just left. The acrid odor of smoke still filled the air here, and Con wondered if, somehow, the fires that had spread across Jahn had killed the Rocaanists below.

It seemed logical to him in this tight space, smoke instead of air, heat making the area tighter than it really was. So many of them were lucky to have made it to the other side of the river.

Funny that the group he had stayed with had not spoken of the carnage they left behind.

Maybe they didn't know.

Maybe they thought the Fey had killed their brethren.

The stone walls here were black, and so was the floor—what little of it Con could see. The light was better here. It filtered through in small patches, as if tiny parts of the ceiling had given way.

He tried not to touch anything as he walked, stepping cautiously to avoid bodies sprawled along the floor, wincing as his feet touched the slimy floor itself. When he got out of here, he wanted to throw away his robe, douse himself in the Cardidas, and clean off the stench.

It had nearly become a part of him.

Sebastian had reached a small turn in the corridor. Three bodies lay across it, blocking his way. He stopped and turned toward Con.

Slowly.

"Should . . . we . . . go . . . back?" Sebastian asked. Con almost thought he heard hope in Sebastian's voice.

"No," Con said. "We're almost to the end of the catacombs. My map of the tunnels doesn't show any other way to go. It looks like the tunnels end at the Tabernacle, but I'm hoping that there'll be a side passage so that we can continue heading south this way. I really don't want to dodge the Fey above ground."

"Me . . . ei-ther," Sebastian said. He turned back toward the bodies. "But . . . I . . . do . . . not . . . want . . . to . . . go . . . this . . . way."

"The faster we go, the sooner we'll get out of here," Con said. And the sooner they got out, the sooner he could breathe.

He finally reached Sebastian's side. The bodies were long and swollen, covered with soot and dust. They were packed into the small space. To go through the opening, Con and Sebastian would either have to move the bodies, or walk on them.

Con didn't like either option. As an Aud, he didn't wear shoes. The idea of walking on bodies was as grotesque to him as touching them with his hands.

Sebastian wasn't agile enough to jump.

Con wasn't sure he wanted to try.

"What . . . is . . . be-yond . . . this . . . room?" Sebastian asked.

"The last main chamber, if I remember right," Con said. The catacombs had looked different the last time he was here. The last time, the Fey had been outside the Tabernacle, and the catacombs had been empty. They had been full of dust and cobwebs, much like the parts of the tunnels near the palace. Only the catacombs also had the remnants of furniture, from the days of old when the Auds used to live in complete darkness, without light.

"Then . . . we . . . can . . . leave?"

"Or see if we can find another passage," Con said.

"Can't . . . we . . . do . . . that . . . here?" Sebastian asked.

Con frowned. He really didn't want to walk on those bodies any more than Sebastian did. His memory of the main catacomb cavern was imperfect—he had been in such a hurry that afternoon two weeks before (it seemed like another lifetime ago) that he hadn't stopped to explore any of the side rooms or to really notice anything about the catacombs themselves.

"I don't see any more passages here, do you?" Con asked, hoping that he had missed something.

"No . . . ," Sebastian said.

"Then I guess we go forward."

"How . . . ?"

Con closed his eyes for a moment. It would be easier to walk than it would to pull the bodies away, although it would be less respectful to the dead.

His feet were already filthy. His hands were somewhat cleaner.

"We walk," he said.

He opened his eyes, murmured a small request for forgiveness, and braced his hands on either side of the stone doorway. Then he put one foot on the back of a corpse, and felt it sink soggily into the slimy cloth. A shudder ran through him.

He put his other foot on the same cloth, then jumped to the far side of the doorway.

Goo had slithered between his toes. He wiped his feet on the stone, shivering and swallowing, trying to keep his stomach under control.

The corpse he had walked on had footprints in its robe.

Sebastian watched, slate gray eyes glittering. He looked even less alive than usual at that moment, almost as if his body were a statue in which someone had imprisoned a man.

"I . . . can-not . . . jump," Sebastian said.

"Then walk," Con said. He wanted Sebastian to hurry, wanted them both to be away from this place.

Sebastian put his hands—carefully—where Con had put his. Then he put his right foot on the footprint Con had left in the robe.

Bones snapped and popped. Sebastian sank to the floor with a cry of terror.

"Keep coming," Con said, knowing that if Sebastian stopped now, he would stop for good.

Sebastian put his left food on the spot where Con had walked. There was more snapping, more cracking as bones shattered beneath Sebastian's weight.

"Come on!" Con barked, making the words into a command.

The lines in Sebastian's face had deepened. He was whimpering. He took another step and nearly lost his balance, pinwheeling—if that's what the slow, round movement could be called—one arm so that he didn't fall.

Con extended a hand. "Here," he said. "Grab on to me."

And Sebastian did, with his free hand, in a grip so crushing that Con thought he might break some bones.

Sebastian took another step, slipping as more bones crunched. Then, when he took his final step, a wet squish made him whimper even harder.

Con finally understood what Sebastian was saying.

Under his breath he was moaning, "Sor-ry . . . sor-ry . . . sor-ry."

"They're dead," Con said, hoping he could calm Sebastian. "They can't feel you."

Sebastian finally stepped onto the stone beside Con. His grip remained tight on Con's hand. "Are . . . you . . . sure?" he asked.

"Yes," Con said. As sure as he could be. He didn't know what happened to the unblessed souls of unburied bodies.

He wasn't sure he wanted to know.

"Come on," he said, pulling Sebastian forward. "Let's get away from here."

The bodies in the main room were clustered near the doorway they had just come through, and the bottom of the entry on the other side of the room. A pile of bodies had gathered there, as if someone had dropped them from a great height.

The death smell had lessened here, or perhaps Con was growing used to it. The scent of smoke had faded too, and the air was cooler, as if a faint breeze were blowing into this part of the catacombs.

The main passage was wide here. The ceiling was arched and had murals on it. It looked like part of the Tabernacle. Doors opened all along the passageway. Con had looked inside them before and knew what he would find: the remnants of cots and tables from the days when the catacombs had been used as Aud quarters.

Sebastian still clung to him. The pain in Con's hand was immense.

"Sebastian," he said, looking down.

"Oh . . . ," Sebastian said, and released Con's hand. Instantly it flooded with warmth. A pins and needles feeling he hadn't realized he had grew momentarily unbearable, then ceased.

Con resisted the urge to cradle the hand against his chest.

"How . . . do . . . we . . . get . . . out?"

"There is only one way," Con said. He pointed at the end of the passageway, where the bodies were piled.

"I . . . do . . . not . . . like . . . how . . . it . . . looks."

"Neither do I," Con said. "But we need to see. Come on."

The floor of the passageway was relatively clear of bodies. Con's skin still crawled from touching that last. He made his way across the cold stone floor, peering in each side room as he passed. He didn't know what he was looking for—maybe even someone alive in all this mess—but he looked anyway.

And, midway through the passage, he stopped. Sebastian stopped with him.

In the room to Con's left were crates. Con recognized them. They were food storage crates from the Tabernacle's kitchen.

Apples, carrots, and other fruits and vegetables were stored in them. The faithful always donated to the Tabernacle, and always gave the Tabernacle more than it could use.

Con stepped over a body to enter the room. Sebastian waited outside.

"What . . . are . . . they?"

"Food," Con said. And he hoped it wasn't spoiled. He didn't know if the stench could spoil food like that.

"Holy . . . food?"

"No," Con said. But there were vials of holy water all along the ground. "You'd better stay out, though."

He didn't know if holy water was deadly to a creature like Sebastian, but he didn't want to take the chance.

The crates were covered with the black film that seemed to coat everything. He grabbed the corner of one of the crates, and pulled. Black stuff poofed off it, landing on his skin and in his already overtaxed nose. He sneezed, and wiped his face with his sleeve. It felt as if something had smeared across his skin. He winced, but continued.

Inside the crate were turnips. They were clean, though, and only the ones on the end were covered with the black stuff. The top layer was soft, as if it had been cooked.

His stomach growled. He hadn't realized how hungry he was.

"I was right, Sebastian," he said. "It is food."

"Holy . . . food," Sebastian said. Con recognized the tone. It was Sebastian's stubbornness. He wouldn't eat.

"I don't think so," Con said. He took a turnip from the middle of the pile. There they weren't soft or covered with black stuff. "I've never heard of the magickal properties of food. Except to make a person feel better."

He took a bite of the turnip. He'd always hated the things, and yet this one tasted delicious. Eating the tak and the meager portions in the cavern had never really satisfied him.

He went to the door and handed Sebastian a turnip.

"Try it," he said.

"I . . . do . . . not . . . need . . . food," Sebastian said.

"But you want something to eat, don't you?"

"Not . . . this," Sebastian said. "Too . . . dan-ger-ous."

"Come on," Con said, not really wanting to have this argument. "We all need to eat."

"I . . . do . . . not." Sebastian dropped the turnip as if it had burned him.

"You were eating at the cavern."

"Yes . . . ," Sebastian said.

"The supplies were meager there. Here we have an entire room full of food."

"I . . . ate . . . so . . . no . . . one . . . thought . . . me . . . strange."

That failed, Con thought, but said nothing. "You sure you'll be all right without food?"

"Yes . . . ," Sebastian said. "I . . . am . . . different . . . from . . . you."

That was true. Con still hadn't figured out the extent of Sebastian's abilities, but they seemed strange to him. Strange to him, even though he had been born after the first Fey invasion.

"Mind if I eat?"

"You . . . need . . . to," Sebastian said.

Con pulled open another crate, and then another. Turnips, potatoes, apples. There was enough food to feed him for the rest of his life.

If the food didn't spoil.

The turnip had tasted all right, as turnips go. But he took a potato and bit the end off it, letting it crunch beneath his teeth. He was so hungry he had to remind himself to eat slowly.

Sebastian stood at the door and watched. At first, it bothered Con, and then he didn't care. He filled his face until he was sated, and then he looked at one of the bottles of holy water.

He was so thirsty, and there didn't seem to be real water here.

Would the Holy One mind if Con used holy water to quench his thirst?

Con minded. If there was other water, he would drink that first.

"Sebastian," he said, "would you see if there are water stores in any of these rooms?"

"I . . . do . . . not . . . want . . . to . . . go . . . in," he said.

Con was beginning to understand Sebastian's hesitation. He had been warned about holy water his entire life; he had told Con that. In fact, as they hurried (as much as Sebastian could hurry) through the tunnels that first day, Sebastian had asked Con if he were carrying holy water.

He had been, but it had been lost in the fight.

"You don't have to go in," Con said. "Just see."

He wiped some juice from his chin and stared at the food

stores. He wasn't willing to stay down here indefinitely. Sebastian had told him that the walk to his friends' place was at least a day. That meant that Con would need food.

He couldn't carry much. The sword was awkward enough. He kept it threaded through his makeshift belt most of the time, but sometimes he had to hold it.

His robe had a few pockets. He would stuff them full. Then he would see if Sebastian would be willing to carry some food, too. As terrified as Sebastian was, Con suspected he wouldn't help.

He could hear Sebastian shuffling through the passageway. Con put a hand on his stomach. It felt heavy and bloated. Not as satisfied as it had been earlier. In his haste, he had overeaten. But at least he had some nourishment.

At least he would get through this day.

"There . . . are . . . more . . . bod-ies," Sebastian said, his voice echoing through the passageway.

"No water?"

"I . . . have . . . not . . . looked . . . in . . . all . . . rooms," Sebastian said. But he sounded doubtful.

Besides, water was not stored in crates, it was stored in animal bladders. With the stench and the soot on everything, the water would be tainted.

Con hadn't thought of that before.

The only water stored in vials was holy water.

He closed an eye, and murmured a small request for forgiveness to the Holy One. Water was only an issue down here, Con prayed. Once he reached the top, he wouldn't need to carry his own.

Only this once.

Only this once.

He crouched beside the vials and picked up one. It had the same black film that everything else had. Then he uncorked it.

His hand was trembling. He could hear Sebastian, walking along the passage. If Sebastian saw him doing this, then he would be even more frightened.

But Con couldn't spill. He didn't want any of this liquid near Sebastian. Con had heard that the touch of holy water on cloth had killed Sebastian's mother, Jewel. He didn't want to do the same thing to Sebastian.

But Con was so thirsty.

He held the vial gingerly by its neck. Then he drank.

At first the water tasted like potatoes and the stench outside. Then he could taste the water itself.

Bitter.

So bitter that it would have made tears come to his eyes, if he had any tears within his body.

He drank the entire vial, put the cork back on, and set the vial in the corner. Then he took a bite of a potato to clean the taste from his mouth.

How awful. No wonder no one drank it. He hoped it wouldn't harm him, like it harmed the Fey.

Holy water wasn't made for drinking, after all.

But it had quenched his thirst.

By the time Sebastian made it back to the door, Con was standing. "Would you help me carry some of this food?" he asked.

"I . . . have . . . poc-kets," Sebastian turned out the pockets of his robe.

"Good," Con said. "This will help me once we get out of here. Even if we can take a little bit, then we'll be all right."

"I . . . do . . . not . . . know . . . how . . . to . . . get . . . out," Sebastian said.

Con suppressed a sigh. "I told you. By that pile of bodies. There's a rope ladder."

"No . . . ," Sebastian said.

"I came down it," Con said.

"There . . . is . . . no . . . lad-der," Sebastian said. "And . . . no . . . more . . . tunnels."

"That you could see," Con said with authority, although his stomach was jumping.

"Right . . . ," Sebastian said.

Con stepped over the body, and pushed past Sebastian. He hurried down the passageway, not stopping to peer in rooms. No wonder it had taken Sebastian so long to look around. Sebastian had gone a considerable distance.

The bodies at the opening were piled as high as Con. It looked as if they had fallen in their attempt to escape the Fey.

Either that, or climbed over each other in an attempt to get out of here.

The stench was back, but it wasn't as bad as it was before. He peered at them, then above them. Way above, he should have seen the rotted stairs, but they were gone, too.

So was the door.

Light filtered into the shaft, illuminating the body on top.

Around the opening were burned timbers.

The Tabernacle fire had destroyed the stairs and the rope ladder. The bodies in front of Con hadn't come because they were trying to get out of the catacombs, but because they had fallen in.

He glanced around at the walls. Soot-covered, but smooth. The doors on this side opened to unfurnished rooms.

Nothing more.

There had to be another passage out.

There had to be.

He pulled the map out from his robe. The map, which the Rocaan had given him only two weeks before, was crumpled and coming apart. It was older than Con, older than the Rocaan had been, maybe even as old as the Tabernacle itself.

It showed passages, all right. The palace side of Jahn was honeycombed with them. But the Tabernacle side only showed this one.

Leading from the Tabernacle to the bridge. What few branches had existed were, as he learned on his first trip, dead ends.

Dead ends.

Like this one.

Unless they could figure out a way to escape this place, they were trapped.

They would have to go back to the other side.

Back to the place that made Sebastian frightened.

Back to the magick that awaited them.

Back to the ruined city now owned by the Black King.

Con turned and saw Sebastian making his slow way through the corridor.

"What . . . will . . . we . . . do?" Sebastian asked.

"I don't know," Con said. "I really don't know."

TWENTY

TUFT flew into the tunnels. Unlike the last time, only hours before, the tunnels were alive with sound. The Infantry marched.

Rugad was as good as his word.

The sound of hundreds of feet marching in unison on stone accompanied Tuft as he made his way through the tunnels. Occasionally voices echoed back and forth, but for the most part, the Infantry leaders did not speak, and the Infantry itself was too well trained.

Tuft didn't speak either. He was one of a dozen Wisps searching the passageways for the Black King's great-grandson. They would find him.

They had to.

The Black King did not tolerate failure.

Wisps were not the only searchers. The Infantry searched, in its own way, and Rugad had also sent a group of Spies, Beast Riders (Rat Riders, from what Tuft had seen), and Charmers. They would be able to deal with the Black King's great-grandson—hold him, and not kill him.

Tuft wended his way along the familiar passages. He had come from the palace. Apparently Rugad had gotten word quickly to all the Fey. Tuft had come across dozens of troops—

half Infantry and half Foot Soldiers—already. Some were searching the tunnels.

Others were heading the same direction he was.

Toward the cavern.

He wasn't far from it now. It amazed him how knowing the route made the journey quicker. The troops had gotten rid of the cobwebs. They had disturbed the dirt and dust; particles floated through the air all around him.

Because he was at his smallest size, some of the particles looked as big as boulders. He had to dodge them as he flew.

The tunnels were also hot. That many people were bound to have an effect on the small space, an effect that even Tuft could feel.

At least the tunnels were light this time. The Infantry had hung Fey lamps in their wake. The tiny Islander souls batted against the glass like moths, their small hands clenched into fists that pounded fruitlessly against the glass.

Sometimes, when he was in a taunting mood, he flew up against the glass and pounded back. Most souls didn't realize they were dead. Most of them didn't realize that the hands they used were composed entirely of their essence and their thoughts. If they thought themselves trees, they would be trees.

Trees made of light.

Of brilliant pure light.

The Fey lamps made from Islanders burned brighter than any Tuft had seen. It was as if someone had brought hundreds of rays of sun below.

The bright light illuminated the tunnel even more for him. The cracks in the stone, the layers of dirt and grime, even on the ceiling, told him that these tunnels were centuries old. They had been built for another reason, a reason he didn't know and didn't comprehend.

He doubted the Islanders did.

The Black Robes were using this place as a dwelling, hiding like rats.

And like rats, they would be flushed out.

He passed a group of Rat Riders flowing toward the cavern. They looked more menacing than other Beast Riders somehow, perhaps because he couldn't believe anyone would choose to be a rat. Beast Riders chose their creature when they came into their magick. They could look like a Fey, although eventually they would adopt parts of their creature—Bird Riders often had featherlike hair—or they could look like the creature with a Fey riding on its back. Only that Fey did not have legs. Its torso disappeared into the creature's back. The Fey on the back of the Rat Riders were small, and looked as mean as the rodents they rode.

Tuft shuddered. He was glad they weren't searching for him.

He was heading to the cavern, not to see the capture of the Black Robes, but to figure out the direction in which the great-grandson had traveled. Tuft had a hunch, a hunch he did not explain to anyone.

He believed the great-grandson would go south.

It seemed logical to Tuft. The palace was to the north. The great-grandson seemed to be, from everything Tuft had heard, of limited intelligence. Therefore the boy would figure that going south—the opposite direction from the Black King—might prevent the Black King from capturing him.

As Tuft got closer to the cavern, the sounds intensified. The marching feet were fading, going off in different directions—searching.

The sounds he heard were screams.

Male voices raised in terror, howling, shouting warnings. A few of the Infantry were uttering the undulating Fey victory cry.

They had been two weeks without battle, and the battle lust, apparently, had yet to die within them.

Tuft rounded the last corner before the end of the tunnel. The well-lit floor was black. Water ran along it as if the river had broken through the walls.

Water—

And blood.

Tuft wondered if Rugad had had enough foresight to send Red Caps. Someone had to stop all this magick material from going to waste.

Tuft flew the last of the way, hearing the cries grow, smelling the copper scent of blood. When he reached the cavern, he instinctively rose with an updraft, and narrowly avoided a strip of skin whipping through the air.

Careless. The Foot Soldiers were being careless.

Tuft looked down. Three Foot Soldiers flayed a Black Robe—or what was left of him—on the ground below. They were saving his head for last.

The scene repeated all through the cavern. Fey lamps were stacked on crates, set on the floor, hanging from torch hooks, but there weren't enough to illuminate the entire room. Shadows lurked everywhere, and in many of them, Black Robes were huddled, clutching vials of their holy poison.

A lot of vials had already been smashed against the ground. Shards of glass mingled with skinless bodies, and other dead still wearing their robes, skewered by the Infantry.

The Infantry was farther ahead, swords flashing in the uneven light. The clang of metal on metal echoed through the cave, mixing with the screams of the not-yet-dead.

The Rat Riders had found some Black Robes as well. The rat part of the Rider gnawed on the corpses while their Fey halves urged them on. Tuft shuddered as he watched them gorge. Sometimes even his own people disgusted him.

Up ahead, some Black Robes were running into the tunnels, only to be turned around by Infantry there. The sound of shattering glass resounded, followed by laughter, and cries of pain.

This was the last stand of the Black Robes. There would be no other. Their hiding place discovered, their future gone. They would pay for murdering an entire troop of Fey.

All of them would pay.

Tuft had no qualms about turning in their hiding place. He had seen what their holy poison could do. A Fey body had been removed from the bridge the night one of the Wisps had come to Jahn to announce the Black King's invasion. The body was melted into a round ball. Only an ear and a protruding hand identified it as Fey.

He flew across the cavern, hoping for a sign, for anything that would lead him to the Black King's great-grandson. The boy clearly wasn't here. If he were, the Black King would never have allowed this attack.

He had thought the Black King wanted no one killed.

That order must have changed. He knew how it would. The Black King had them searching for a Fey. There clearly were no Fey here.

Tuft hoped the Black King wasn't relying solely on Tuft's word. That would be a bad idea, since Tuft had never seen the boy himself.

Tuft shoved the thought from his mind. He let the air current carry him across the carnage, toward a darkened area of the cavern. Lights marked where the Fey had already been.

Darkness pointed the way to uncharted territory.

Besides, this dark spot was, if he was not mistaken, on the cavern's south side.

He slid around a corner, and went up a steep incline. No one had come here. Not even terrified Black Robes. But his own small light illuminated a recent trail.

His heart started to pound hard and his mouth went dry.

A recent rail.

He was tracking something.

He only hoped it was his quarry.

The tunnel narrowed and he paused. Was it too narrow to fit an Islander-sized person?

Probably not, for the trail continued.

The trail.

Finding the Black King's great-grandson would be the pinnacle of Tuft's career. Forever after he would be known as the Fey who saved the Empire.

He tried to contain his excitement.

It was too soon to count a victory where there was none.

But it was close.

He knew it was close.

He could sense it.

TWENTY-ONE

THE Cardidas River smelled faintly of blood.

Boteen crouched beside the bridge and dipped his hand in the water. It was murky and brown, and looked as it had since he arrived on the Isle.

Pure enough.

But the scent of blood was nearly overpowering.

Boteen closed his eyes and kept his hands in the water. The river held much blood. Ancient blood. Blood that had been shed over centuries. In its murky bottom were secrets as yet unopened, secrets that could lead him—

He opened his eyes and pulled his hands from the water. Therein lay madness. Enchanters could not follow every trail, could not search for every scrap of history, no matter how intriguing.

He was following the trail of the Islander Enchanter. It was fresh here. Fresher, anyway. Only a few weeks old.

How strange, since most of it was over a decade old.

This new part of the trail was clear: It had a gold center with imprints upon it, imprints he couldn't read. Around the edges, the gold faded to silver, and now as he reached the fresher trail, the silver had turned red.

The sight of it made shivers run through him. This Enchanter should have died twice.

Twice his magick saved him.

He was a powerful man.

The ground near Boteen had a large imprint, the size of a body. Boteen had run his hand along the grass. He dug his fingers into the dirt, but could get nothing. The near-death was the only story here, and it had nothing more to tell him.

But the river.

The river fairly screamed at him.

The river smelled of blood.

Of the Enchanter's blood.

Boteen wiped his wet hand on the grass and decided to try again. This time he took a deep breath. He would control the path this time. He would deal with the other magick in this water later.

He plunged his hands into the coldness, letting his mind search and search the murky depths until he felt the brush of a rope. His fingers caught it, squeezed it, and it squished against his skin, as if he were trying to hold mud.

He opened his hand, and tried again. The rope reformed. This time, Boteen stuck a finger in it. A flash caught him. A flash—an image—an impression—

As he sank, the blood leaked out of the wounds on his face. The blood floated upward, darkening the moonlight waters.

He was drowning—

Boteen caught himself, made himself breathe. *He* was not drowning. He had air. He was touching an old memory. A memory floating in the river—

But he wanted to live. He needed to live.

He kicked, feebly at first, but then with more strength. His legs were uninjured. His lungs ached but they didn't burn. How long could a man hold his breath underwater?

He didn't know—

Boteen could feel it. Circling magick. This was an important moment. The Islander Enchanter gained his red here—

He kicked again, harder, the power of his legs forcing him toward the surface. The blood swirled around him, then it congealed and formed a ropy string that he could tug on.

He was delirious.

He was dying.

The string broke—

The rope Boteen felt slipped from his finger.

"No!" he cried, and reached for it, nearly falling into the river.

Then he realized the panic he was feeling was not his. It was residual panic from the Islander Enchanter.

Boteen sat back on the bank, keeping his fingers in the water.

"Come back to me," he whispered. "Come back."

The rope reformed. He could feel its presence in the water, thick and slimy and warm.

Almost hot.

Like blood.

The smell of blood was even stronger than it had been.

He waited until the rope brushed his hand, then he shoved his finger inside again—

The blood came together, and braided itself, like a rope. He continued to pull, and kick, and pull. He still didn't need any air. Maybe he was already dead.

If so, he would claw his way to the Face of God. He wouldn't remain in the dark and the cold and the wet forever.

He kicked again, pulled on the string, and then his head broke the surface. He was still in the Cardidas. The moon shone silver on the water, except where his blood flowed. There the river appeared black.

The river appeared black.

The images faded. Boteen took his hands from the water and leaned back on his haunches.

A few weeks ago, just before the invasion. This blood trail was fresh.

The Islander Enchanter had used his powers to save his own life.

He had done that before. Once. Near the palace. Boteen had gotten faint impressions there, but they were covered with a patina, a gloss that made it seem as if someone else's magick had done the trick.

Someone Fey.

Fey.

A revulsion rose within him, a revulsion so strong it almost turned his stomach.

There were Fey about. Fey on the bridge. Fey—

He stopped. Those were not his feelings, not his emotions. He wiped his hands on the grass and sat.

The Islander Enchanter was strong. He was just coming into his full powers, so he was young. And he hated Fey.

This was the man protecting the heir to the Black Throne?

It did not fit, unless the Enchanter could get past the Fey part of the heir and see only his Islander heritage.

But that made no sense either. This heir, the young Gift, had been raised by the Failures. He was, most certainly, as purely Fey as a half-breed could be.

Boteen sat down, his calves aching.

Perhaps he had the other Enchanter, the sloppy one, the one whose magick could not be contained within him. The confusion fit, but the rope of blood did not. Could an untrained Enchanter save himself in such a way?

Boteen did not know.

He did not know which trail he followed.

If this were the other Enchanter, the one who leaked, then what happened to the one with Gift? Had he ever been in the city?

Had Gift?

He closed his eyes and touched the huge imprint, trying to find the continuation of the trail, trying to see where it would lead him.

TWENTY-TWO

GIFT pressed himself against the rock pillar. Coulter was standing a bit too close. Gift still hadn't gotten over the anger he felt at his old friend. It flared at unusual moments, then faded into a dull ache.

He blamed Coulter for Sebastian's death.

If Sebastian and Gift had remained Linked, Sebastian would still be alive. Gift knew it.

Leen was still sitting on her rock, staring at the Cap. The Cap looked odd. The news of the Chant had frightened him somehow, made him seem uncomfortable.

This whole area had Gift uneasy. He longed to make his own Shadowlands and hide them all in it, but the Cap still warned him away from that.

The Fey would be looking for a Shadowlands, he'd said. *It's the first thing they'd find.*

That sounded logical to Gift, but that didn't change his desire to build one. He had lived most of his life in a Shadowlands. He wanted to go back to something familiar, if only for a moment.

The real world had too many pitfalls, too many differences for him to entirely comprehend. He still wasn't sure why the townspeople had reacted so poorly to him. Perhaps if they had called him Fey it would be clear.

But they hadn't.

They had called him tall.

Beside him Coulter stiffened. He looked at the sky, then at the ground. The Cap stood and looked too, but not in the same places. He did it as if he were trying to see what Coulter saw.

Leen glanced at Gift. His heart was pounding. Something had changed.

He could sense it.

"What is it?" Gift asked.

"A strange magick," Coulter said. "Those presences that I've been feeling—one has been getting closer."

"Presences?" the Cap asked.

"The ones like me. I told you of them," Coulter said. He hadn't torn his gaze from the sky. Gift would have thought he was looking at clouds if he hadn't known better.

"No," the Cap said. "You didn't."

Gift was standing stiffly. He felt an ache in his back from the oddness of his position. *The ones like me.*

"There are two others just like me on the Isle," Coulter said. "There used to be only one."

He snapped the words as if the Cap should have understood them on his own.

"Like you," Gift said. "Enchanters?"

"That's what the Fey call it," Coulter said. "I *told* you."

"You might have," Leen said soothingly, "but so much has happened. Perhaps we didn't remember this."

It didn't seem to matter what she said. Coulter stepped away from the pillars. He was scanning the sky. Then his gaze moved down, down toward the village.

"Looking for trails?" the Cap said.

"Yes," Coulter said. "No one's been here. Except Gift, of course. No one else."

He stepped onto the footpath, then moved slightly beyond it.

"But someone's coming," he whispered.

The hair rose on the back of Gift's neck. "How soon?" he asked.

"Today. Tomorrow. Next week. I don't know."

"What do they want?" the Cap asked.

"That's not clear either," Coulter said. His voice was

strange, as if he were answering questions without really thinking about them, as if the answers were coming from some part of him not attached to his brain.

"What does it mean, the magick has changed?" Leen asked.

"Just that," Coulter said. Then he whispered, "Just that."

"We don't understand," Gift said.

"You're not supposed to," Coulter snapped. He stepped farther away, then crouched and reached out his hands. He sat like that for a long time.

The Cap approached his back, hovering there. Leen got off her boulder.

Gift didn't move.

He felt odd himself.

He had felt that way all day, though. It had to be the morning, the strange start they had had. And the lack of food. Their supplies were dwindling. Someone would have to go into the town for food in the morning.

Someone short.

And the mountain itself. The feeling he got, the strange compulsion it gave him, was growing.

Then Coulter shook himself and stood. He turned. His face was pale, but the color was returning. His eyes looked like his own again.

"We have to get Gift out of here," he said.

"We will," Leen said. "When Adrian arrives."

"We can't wait," Coulter said.

"I thought you said you didn't know what the magick changes were," the Cap said.

Coulter licked his lips. He looked frightened. "The others—they've done something. I can feel their changes. And they are focusing here. The changes are coming here."

"You're sure?" the Cap asked.

"I can feel it." Coulter walked back toward them. His face was turning red. It was a startling change from the paleness of a moment before. "We have to get Gift out of here."

"We can't leave Adrian behind on the strength of a feeling," Leen said.

"It's Coulter's feeling," the Cap said. "Adrian can fend for himself."

Gift glanced up the mountain. The strangeness inside his belly had grown. "We can wait for Adrian," he said.

"We can't," Coulter said. "It's not just your life, Gift. You have more importance than that."

Gift stared at him. There was real fear in Coulter's blue eyes. "What will waiting for Adrian hurt?"

"I don't think we have time," Coulter said. "I can't explain it better than that."

"Where would we go?" the Cap asked. "We're already at the edge of the island."

"I guess we'll have to go south," Leen said. "It would be better anyway. That Chant this morning was terrifying."

"No," Gift said.

They all looked at him. He must have spoken with more strength than he had planned.

"We're going up the mountain," Gift said.

"We're already too close to the snowline," the Cap said. "We can't go much higher. Air gets thin up there. Besides, there's nothing for us."

"That's not true," Gift said. "There is something for us. I can feel it."

"More feelings," Leen said and sat.

"A Vision?" Coulter asked.

Gift shook his head. "It's as if it were almost a Vision, as if something were shimmering just beyond my range of sight."

Coulter looked up the mountain. "Where?" he asked.

Gift came away from his rock pillars. He walked to Coulter's side and pointed up.

Above them the footpath faded into the jagged peaks. Huge boulders marked the way, and stone ledges marred sheer cliff faces. Trees grew on some of the ledges, until, farther up, the trees disappeared and the snow began. The redness of the rock grew the farther up the eye went, too. It almost looked as if the stone were bleeding.

The place Gift pointed to was just beyond the footpath. It looked, to him, like a dark spot on the mountainside, an obvious opening in the stone.

"That shimmer?" Coulter asked.

"I don't see a shimmer," Gift said. "I see darkness."

"I don't see anything," the Cap said.

"Me, either," Leen said. "Dark spot or shimmering. It's red up there. Red and sheer and terrifying."

"Terrifying, yes," Coulter said. "But there's magick above us. And it fairly shines off that mountain."

"Why didn't you see it before?" the Cap asked.

"I did," Coulter said. He looked at Gift. Gift bowed his head. He had tried to get them up there earlier, and Coulter had said no. The Cap had been confused by that small interaction, but Gift hadn't.

"Then why didn't you mention it?" the Cap said.

"If I mentioned every stray bit of magick I see, I'd be talking all the time," Coulter said.

He was understating it. Gift knew it. Coulter did too. He didn't look at the Cap as he spoke.

"You saw it too and didn't mention it?" the Cap said to Gift.

"What do you think it is?" Leen asked the Cap.

"It could be a hundred things," the Cap said, but his expression had grown dark, as if he didn't like what the possibilities were.

"It could be nothing," Coulter said.

"It's something," Gift said. He didn't want to understate the power he felt above them. He wanted the others to know what they were getting into. What he knew, anyway. "That darkness has been there from the start."

Everyone looked at him again. He shrugged. He couldn't explain it better. The darkness was like looking at a Shadowlands that he could hold in his hands, a Shadowlands before he made it large enough to hold people.

Perhaps it was a manifestation of magick, like Coulter said.

Perhaps it was.

"What if it's nothing?" Leen said. "We'll go up there for no reason. We'll be trapped."

"No more trapped than we are now," the Cap said. "And we can stop on those ledges. We might be able to see a different path away from that town below us."

"It's going to be hard to climb in the dark," Leen said.

"Coulter can make us some light," Gift said.

"And the entire valley will see our progress." The Cap shook his head as if Gift hadn't a brain in his. "That's not a solution."

Gift glanced up. He didn't want to go there in full darkness either. This mountain scared him enough, with its blood red color and its chill.

And the people below.

"We don't have to go at night," Coulter said.

"Oh, and what do you suggest?" the Cap said. "Waiting until tomorrow? You're the one who's in a hurry."

"He doesn't want to wait for Adrian," Leen said.

"Adrian is my friend," Coulter said. His temper had been close to the surface ever since they had returned from the quarry. Gift suspected the problems he'd had in town hadn't made Coulter any calmer. Sometimes, with Coulter, temper hid fear.

"He's my friend," Coulter repeated. "You people may not understand that."

He crossed his arms and turned his back on them.

"So what does that mean?" the Cap said. "That we should appreciate how hard it is for you to choose between Adrian and Gift?"

"I don't want there to be a choice," Gift said. "It's me we're talking about. I want to wait for Adrian."

"It's you we're protecting," the Cap said. "You don't get an opinion here."

"You're not letting me finish!" Coulter had turned to them, fists clenched, eyes bright. "I'm going to stay here. I'm going to wait for him."

"You can't," Gift said.

"Why not?" Coulter asked.

"You'll never be able to find us."

"I can see it as well as you can, maybe better," Coulter said.

"And what if nothing's there?" Leen asked.

"Then I can follow your trails. All three of you leave trails."

"That's a problem," the Cap said and sat down. "If we're being followed by another Enchanter, all he has to do is follow the trail."

Coulter nodded. "I thought of that. But we don't know exactly where they are. If we stay ahead of them, we have a better chance of staying away from them."

"But what if—" Gift swallowed. The question was hard to ask. "What if they find you after we've left?"

Coulter looked at him, as if he had heard the concern in Gift's voice. "They're not looking for me."

"We don't know that."

"Oh, we do," Coulter said. "You're the prize, Gift, and you will be as long as the Black King is alive. The rest of us are secondary."

Gift shook his head. He hated this. He hated it all. "How long do we have to run?" he asked. "How long until they stop looking for me?"

"They'll stop when they find you," Coulter said.
"Then maybe I should just give myself up."
"You're not ready," the Cap said from his spot on the ground.
Gift felt a chill. "You think I'll want to give myself up?"
"Oh, absolutely," the Cap said. "When you're strong enough to take over the Fey Empire, you'll allow yourself to be captured."
"I can't kill my great-grandfather," Gift said, his chill growing.
"You won't have to," the Cap said. "By then, you'll be able to out-magick him—and out-think him."
"He's the greatest warrior of the Fey."
"Yes, he is," the Cap said. "And he's an old man who's afraid of dying without a worthy heir. Someday you'll be his worthy heir."
"I don't want to lead an Empire."
"But you want to stop running," the Cap said.
Gift crossed his arms. His heart hurt. "Those are my only choices?"
"At the moment," the Cap said. "I'm sure, given time, we can think of a few others."
"Time is what we need," Coulter said, "and I'm going to buy some by waiting here for Adrian. You go up that mountain. We'll find you."
Gift wrapped his arms tighter around himself. He didn't like this. He didn't like any of it.
"What happens if you never come?" Leen said.
"You wait as long as you think fit," Coulter said. "And then you get Gift to safety."
"There is no safety on this Isle," the Cap said. "The Black King is too close."
"We've kept Gift away from him this long," Coulter said. "With each passing day, we gain a greater and greater victory."
"Maybe," Gift said. "Or maybe we just exhaust ourselves. I'm not learning anything new."
"Not yet," the Cap said. "We haven't had time."
"That's my point," Gift said. "How do we get the time? Or do we just run until they find us?"
Coulter came to him, and put his hand on Gift's shoulder. It took all of Gift's strength not to flinch. "You're going to have to trust me sometime," Coulter said.
"No, I don't," Gift said. "You killed Sebastian."
"You couldn't have done anything, Gift. If anything, you might have died with him."

"We'll never know, will we?" Gift backed away. He brushed off his shoulder, even though he knew it was childish. "Maybe I could have saved him."

"Maybe," Coulter said. "We'll never know. It's done now."

"It's not done," Gift said. The anger was flaring again, and he couldn't stop it. He didn't want to stop it. "It'll never be done. Not between us."

The Cap got between them. He grabbed Gift by the waist. The small Fey was surprisingly strong. "Stop. Stop now," he said.

"Why?" Gift asked. He was shaking. The Cap had tried to kill him once. He wasn't convinced the Cap wouldn't try again. "Because it bothers you?"

"We'll have time for this kind of fighting when the Black King is vanquished. Not before." The Cap shoved Gift back. Gift stumbled, then caught himself. "Now, the three of us will go up the mountain. Coulter will remain here. Got that?"

Gift brushed himself off. He hated being pushed around, especially by a Red Cap. "I don't see why we have to listen to him."

"He has more magick than the rest of us," the Cap said.

"Except maybe you," Leen said to Gift. She peered at him hopefully. "Have you had a Vision about this?"

He stared up at the black spot on the mountainside. It seemed to pulse. "I don't think so."

"You don't think so?" the Cap asked. "Either you've had one or you haven't."

Gift clenched his fists. He was beginning to really dislike that little Red Cap. "I don't *think* so," he said. "I won't know until I get there. Sometimes I only get fragments of things. I may recognize a fragment when I get closer."

He almost added, *I don't expect you to understand*, but he didn't. No sense in antagonizing the Cap farther.

"Well, then," the Cap said as if Gift hadn't spoken. "If you haven't had a Vision about it, we do as Coulter says."

Coulter was watching all of this, his blue eyes hooded. He had his arms crossed. He looked calm, but Gift got a sense that Coulter was as scared as the rest of them. He just wasn't admitting it.

For a moment, Gift got the feeling he'd had when they were friends. A brush of concern, a slight worry, then he suppressed it. Coulter didn't need Gift's concern. Coulter could take care of himself.

"I don't want to go up the mountain without Adrian," Gift said.

"I don't care what you want," the Cap said. "You're going. And Adrian would be the first to admit this is the right path."

Gift ducked back into the pillars. The small camp had seemed like home for a brief time. He would gather his things. He would go. But he wouldn't like it.

At least he'd be free of Coulter for a while.

He sighed, sat down, and put his head in his hands. Up until a few weeks ago, he'd had a life. He'd known what was going to happen from day to day. He had his friends, his adopted family, and his escape—Sebastian. He'd known how to be and who he was, within that context.

Now, the Cap wanted to train him to be the Black King's equal, as if a magickless Red Cap would know how to do that. Now Gift didn't know where he'd sleep from night to night. He had no place to run, and he had no say in where he was.

He didn't want to be the Black King's equal. He didn't ask to have these Visions or to be of Black Blood. He had liked his quiet life. He wanted to go back to it.

Only there was no life to return to.

And that made him deeply sad. He knew, in some, such loss brought a killing rage, but not in him. In him it brought rage, yes, but not of the kind that allowed him to become like his great-grandfather. Gift didn't want to be a man who slaughtered innocents because their parents made a mistake.

Gift didn't know how the Cap's training could change something that fundamental.

He wasn't sure they should even try.

Leen poked her head in between the pillars. "Scavenger wants to go right away."

"We have a few things to pack up," Gift said.

"Leave some for Coulter and Adrian."

Gift nodded.

"How far do you think that place is?" she asked. "That place only you two can see?"

"Not far," Gift said. He could feel its pulsing now, even inside the pillars. It was as if acknowledging its presence made it even stronger.

He glanced up, again, involuntarily, even though he knew he couldn't see it.

Something was waiting for him up there. Something he

wanted to see. He had learned to follow these hunches over the years.

But that didn't stop him from feeling nervous.

"Is it going to be all right?" Leen asked.

He wasn't sure if she meant the trip, leaving Adrian and Coulter behind, or the future itself.

"I don't know," he said, and wished, for the first time in his life, that he could conjure Visions at will.

At least he would have answers then.

Even if they were answers that he didn't like.

TWENTY-THREE

MARLY stood near the table, her arms crossed. She was watching Matthias pull tak from the containers, and put it into a small pack. Tri was holding a vial of holy water.

Matthias could feel her disapproval from across the room.

"Ye canna go searchin," she said. "I'll get Denl n Jakib ta go."

"They don't know what they're looking for," Matthias said.

"They know Fey jus as well as ye do," Marly said.

"Not nearly as well," Matthias said. "I've fought them for years. I've won."

"And ye nearly lost that night near the river," Marly said.

He raised his head. "Are you saying you're worried about me?"

"Aye, Holy Sir," she said, putting an emphasis on the last two words.

He flushed. It felt painful beneath his battered skin. He had thought, perhaps, that she was worried about him, not about what he knew.

"She has a point," Tri said. "If there are Fey, I may not be able to protect you."

"Tis na jus' protection I mean," she said. "He was serious wounded."

"And I managed to walk here," he said.

"Aye, with help."

Matthias shrugged. He didn't want the lecture.

"If what you say about the Rocaan is true," Tri said, "you're the only one with the Secrets."

That did matter. Matthias knew it did. He sighed. "Then get Denl and Jakib," he said. "We'll travel in a group."

"Yer na well enough to travel," Marly said.

"I'm well enough."

"No, yer na," she said. "The walk from Jahn, twas a strain on yer body n yer wounds. Ye act like yer made of stone, but yer na. Ye survived and twas a miracle. A man, even a man like ye, shouldna take miracles fer granted."

He shoved a water bladder still full from their trip into the pack. He didn't need lectures. There might be Fey here, and he had to see for himself. He couldn't hide in his house much longer.

"I'll take my own risks," he said.

"Aye," she said. "N leave the rest a us ta fend fer ourselves."

"You did fine before I showed up," he said.

"There were na thousands a Fey on the Isle then," she said softly.

"Matthias," Tri said, "she is right. You have some serious wounds. Maybe this can wait."

"It cannot wait," he snapped. He tied the pack closed, then tied it around his waist.

"It was my idea," Tri said. "I can warn them myself."

"You can't find them without me." Matthias stood completely upright and adjusted the pack. "Get Denl and Jakib. We'll go as a group. And that's the end of it, Marly. I won't have you arguing with me any more."

"N I will make me choices as ta if I'm gonna help ye when ye return, all tired and bloody and bruised," she said.

"You think that's how I'll come back?" he asked.

"Yer wounds are na healed yet," she said. "Ye'll be bloody na matter what happens."

"I haven't been yet," he said. "You've taken care of the wounds nicely."

"Tis na right," she said, "you goin off after more Fey. They near ta killed ye last time."

"I beg your pardon, ma'am," Tri said. "But I never said they were Fey."

"Ye said they were tall. Fey are tall. N he's only going with you because he believes they're Fey." She was frowning at Tri.

Her humor had been good since they arrived. Matthias was a bit startled by the change.

"Actually," Tri said, "Matthias is tall. It could simply be . . . outsiders, like him."

"N ye paused afore the word 'outsider' because why?"

Sharp woman. Matthias wished he could smile, but it wasn't worth the pain.

Tri glanced at Matthias.

"I dunna know how a man born in a place is an outsider," she said.

"You haven't been in Constant long enough," Tri said. "Matthias is lucky to be alive and so, I would wager, are you."

She frowned. "Ye told him?"

"That your family came from here?" Matthias asked. "I didn't have to. It's obvious in your coloring and height. You're unusual, Marly. You'll stand out."

"Like those tall ones yer hunting."

"Yes," he said. He didn't want to tell her the rest, didn't want her to know what life here was like. But he would. He had to.

He cleared his throat, then sighed. "Marly, it could just as easily be you and me that the locals are afraid of. We're tall enough to scare them. It doesn't matter if we're Fey or not. It doesn't matter if we were born here or not. They're terrified of people like us."

"Then why'd ye come here?" she asked.

"Because the Secrets were born here," he said.

"Secrets?" she asked. "Of the Tabernacle?"

He nodded. Tri was watching him with an intensity Matthias had never seen before.

"What do ye mean 'born' here?" she asked.

"They're recipes, most of them," he said, lying only a little. "The ingredients come from here."

"N this is important why?"

"Because one Secret, holy water, killed Fey. The others might, too."

She took a step toward him. "Yer telling me that our God gave us weapons agin the Fey?"

"Yes," he said.

"A loving n just God?"

"That's Tabernacle crap," Tri said, then turned to Matthias. "Sorry."

Matthias shrugged. It meant nothing to him. The Tabernacle had distorted the Words to its own end from the day it was built. It was gone now. Although he missed it, he didn't mourn it. There was a difference.

"N ye see yerself as some sort of general in some sort of holy war?" she asked.

"No," Matthias said. "But I do believe we should fight with whatever tools we have."

"It seems odd ta me," she said. "Ta worship with the tools a war."

"We've done it from the beginning," Tri said. "The sword is a tool of war, and the center of Rocaanism."

"Ye sound as if ye know of this stuff," she said to him. Matthias had been thinking the same thing. Had Tri learned more than the location of varin in his days as a Wise One?

He merely smiled. "You'll find the beliefs about the Tabernacle are different here," he said.

"All beliefs seem ta be different here," she said. She smoothed her hair back, leaving one arm crossed over her stomach. "What'll ye do with these 'tall ones' if they're na Fey?"

Matthias had some ideas. Perhaps they would recruit them, bring them back to the house. Or perhaps he would do nothing. He hadn't decided. "We'll see when we get there," he said.

She sighed, as if she knew he were holding back from her. "I'll get Denl and Jakib fer ye," she said and left the room.

"Difficult woman," Tri said.

Matthias shook his head. "She's strong and smart. She worries, that's all."

"I think she feels something for you," Tri said.

"Pity." Matthias twisted the pack around his waist until he was comfortable. "Do you think the tall ones are still here?"

"I have no doubt. Where would they go? Besides, the rumors say they have friends working in the quarry."

Matthias tightened the strings. The pack rubbed against his back. "This gets stranger all the time."

"Only if you think they're Fey. What if they're like your people? A few tall ones and the rest normal?"

Matthias winced at the word choice. He was beginning to like Tri up to that point. "You think I'm abnormal?"

"It's a fact of Constant," Tri said. "Anyone taller than me is abnormal. Anyone who's taller than me and survived his exile to the mountain is even stranger."

"They're still doing that here, aren't they?" Matthias asked.

"I was hoping to stop it," Tri said, "before circumstances made me leave the Wise Ones."

Then Denl stepped into the room. His round face was lined, his blond hair messed. He had been exhausted since before they arrived. Matthias attributed it to fear: Denl had been terrified since the Fey invaded. He had tried to hide it, but hadn't completely succeeded. It was only after they had been on the road for a few days that Matthias had learned about Denl. His entire family had been slaughtered in the first Fey invasion. He was taken in by some Auds and raised in Rocaanism. It was only his birth position, as the fifth in a family of six, that had kept him from becoming an Aud.

The Tabernacle had been strict about taking only second sons.

"If this trip is about murder, ye'll na have my help," Denl said, but he directed his comments to Tri, not to Matthias. Denl still saw Matthias as the Rocaan, and no amount of talking that Matthias would do could change Denl's mind.

A man canna stop bein Beloved a God, Denl would say.

"I simply want to talk to them," Tri said.

"N if they're Fey?" Denl asked.

Tri looked at Matthias. "I'll probably defer to Matthias's greater knowledge."

Matthias met his gaze. Did Tri know him well enough to understand that Matthias would kill a Fey on sight?

"I dunna understand why ye must go, Holy Sir," Denl said.

"These could be Fey," Matthias said. "I need to know."

"Why? It dinna make a difference to us. They're all over the Isle."

"It makes a difference to me," Matthias said. "I killed the woman whom they considered second only to their Black King."

"I thought God killed her," Denl said.

"Under my watch," Matthias said. And with his help. Only the strictest interpretations of the Words would allow anyone to believe that God killed Jewel. Matthias had put the holy water on the cloth. Matthias had put the cloth on Jewel's head.

She had survived a religious ceremony in the past—the joint wedding ceremony, performed by Matthias and the Fey's Shaman. God did not strike her down then. But then, God had not allowed the cloth Matthias had used to be stored with the holy water on that day.

"They've been after me ever since," Matthias said.

"I will na go if murder is the point," Denl said.

"Information is the point," Matthias said. "You can stay if you want. Marly wanted you along to protect me. I don't need protection."

"Aye, ye do," Marly spoke from behind Denl. Her brother Jakib stood beside her. Jakib, at least, didn't have the rumpled look that Denl did. If anything, he seemed stronger. He was definitely cleaner, having used some of the well water to wash. His hair, now that it was clean, was the same copper red that Marly's was. "N that's why yer na goin without these men."

"Since when do you order us about?" Matthias asked with a bit of humor.

"Since now. We canna lose ye, na now."

Jakib shrugged. "She's me sister. I canna fight it."

"But I can," Denl said. He turned.

Marly put a hand on his chest, stopping him. "Ye claim ta have faith," she said. "Ye claim a purity na offered the rest a us. If ye have it, then ye'll protect the Holy Sir."

"He says he's na the Holy Sir," Denl said.

"N ye say he is. Ye canna have it both ways, Denl. Either he is or he's na, but tis something ye must know in yer heart and na yer head."

Denl sighed. He ran a hand through his hair, then shook his shoulders as if easing tension out of them. Finally he looked over his shoulder at Matthias.

"Ye have enough snacks fer all a us in there or do we ha ta fix our own?"

"I have enough," he said. "I doubt this will take long."

"It may take the rest a our lives," Denl said under his breath.

Marly shoved him slightly. "It'd better na. I dunna want ta go through life witha the three a ye."

Matthias's heart rose at the fact that she included him.

She glared at Tri. "N ye," she said. "Ye see ta it that they come back."

"I will, ma'am," he said.

"I'll be holdin ye ta it," she said.

"You don't need to worry," Matthias said. "We'll be back."

She peered at him. Her look made him uncomfortable. It was as if she could see through him.

"I hope yer right," she said. "I hope yer right."

TWENTY-FOUR

SOMEONE had recently traveled this tunnel. Tuft stopped and landed on the floor. It was made of stone, as most of the tunnels were, but the stone was old. The mortar from above had crumbled and fallen. Some of the chunks were the size of boulders.

He knew, though, that was a reflection of his small size. If he grew to his full height, he wouldn't be able to walk upright in this tunnel. If he tried to crawl, his wings would catch on the rough ceiling and their thin membranes would rip.

The floor was also covered with moss, and so were the walls. The mortar had been brushed aside in the center of the floor and the moss was recently trampled. Someone had crawled through here.

A lot of someones had done so once. Tuft figured that was how the Black Robes had found their cavern. This narrow tunnel had to be built through the old stone bridges that crossed the Cardidas River. He could smell the tang of river water, feel the dampness in the stone. If he listened hard, he could almost hear the water moving below him.

This tunnel would lead him to the Black King's great-grandson, he knew it.

He got off the floor and flew again, relieved that so many someones had gone through this before him. He had hated the dirt and cobwebs he'd faced that morning. The unease he had felt then was still with him.

Some of that too had to be from seeing the Black King. Tuft had had perfunctory audiences before, usually with the other Wisps on this mission. In the past, Flurry had been Rugad's favorite. Whenever Rugad needed a Wisp to investigate something, he had sent Flurry. The gossip among the Wisps was that Flurry saw things others missed.

But Flurry hadn't returned from his mission to find the Black King's great-grandson two weeks before. Neither had Cinder. They had been hunting for him together.

Some suspected that the great-grandson had found them and murdered them to stay away from the Black King. Others speculated that the Islanders had found a new kind of poison, one that killed small Fey.

A badly burned Infantry man claimed that Flurry had found the great-grandson and that an Islander sent a fire spell into a corn field to kill all the Fey.

No one believed the story. Islanders didn't have those kinds of powers.

But the thought made Tuft uneasy. Especially the closer he got to finding the great-grandson.

Wisps were easy to kill. One of his ancestors had gotten caught in a jar of honey and drowned. Still another was eaten by a cat.

Tuft was scaring himself. He had to stop thinking about these things. The closer he got to his quarry, the more he had to protect himself.

He didn't have to get close.

All he had to do was spy them from a distance and then bring the troops in. He could escape long before anyone even knew he was there.

And there were no cobwebs. He had to remember that. This tunnel was clear.

A faint smell of smoke was mixing with the musk of river water. He was either getting close to the surface of the city or he was getting close to a burned-out area. There was another scent below the smoke smell, one that made his skin crawl.

Rotting flesh.

He hadn't smelled that since the last battles on Nye. The Nyeians were desperate and they continued fighting long into the night, going for days while the corpses of their compatriots rotted at their feet. It had been a week-long siege before the Fey had broken through. Thousands of dead, all left in the sun, in the heat, for days.

He never thought he'd get over that. He had to force himself to eat after that because the smell stayed on his tongue for months.

He flew out of the tunnel and into a wall of stench: rotting flesh, old smoke, and general decay assaulted him. He flipped over once, then caught himself, swallowing hard to keep the meager contents of his stomach down.

Smells were always harder when he was smaller.

The tunnel had ended in a large room. Bodies clustered near its opening, most of them weeks dead. Another fork dead-ended toward the side. There was only one way to go.

He kept toward the ceiling, one small hand over his mouth and nose. The bodies belonged to Black Robes. Suddenly the acrid smell of smoke made sense.

He had to be below the Islanders' holy place, the place that Rugad had destroyed. The layout of the tunnels must have made the place a horrible trap. The Black Robes that had managed to crawl to the other side were lucky—he was amazed they had survived at all.

One body in a doorway looked crushed, as if something had walked on it. He hovered near the corner where the ceiling met the wall and tried to hide his tiny light. He eased through the door, and saw, at the other end, Rugad's great-grandson holding a crate.

The great-grandson raised his head slowly, as if he sensed something. Tuft held his breath. Another man—a boy, really—in a dirty robe that had once been a light beige came out of a side room carrying a crate. The great-grandson said something and the boy shook his head.

The great-grandson could sense Tuft.

Tuft backed away slowly. The area they were in appeared to have many doors, but they didn't look like passageways. He couldn't really explore it. But if he got out of here quickly, he could get the Infantry below.

He could capture the Black King's great-grandson.

He flew back and stopped near the bridge tunnel. There had to be another way out. He hovered for a moment, considering.

But if there were, the Black Robes would have known.

They wouldn't have died inside the tunnels or crawled to the other side.

There were only two ways out. Either he had to go past the Black King's great-grandson, or he had to go back.

He would go back, but he had to hurry. He could fly fast. He had once held the Wisp record for traversing Nye the fastest. It had been years ago, but he could fly that fast again.

He had to.

He didn't dare lose his quarry now.

TWENTY-FIVE

CON carried the full crate down the catacomb. His back ached and he was covered in grime. The sword bumped against his leg as he moved, but he wanted to keep it beside him. He wasn't sure if that was because it had unusual properties or because it had taken the place of the swords he used to see around the Tabernacle. The religious swords, the ones that spoke to him of God.

Or perhaps he kept it as penance for all the lives he had taken.

He tried not to think of them, and indeed, he had avoided doing so for most of the last week. But every now and then, memory of that moment, the moment when the sword slid through flesh as easily as water, would return to him.

He made himself concentrate on his work. He had searched for another way out, but had found nothing. Sebastian couldn't sense anything either.

He'd even asked Sebastian if they should return to the cavern. Sebastian had shuddered and whispered, "No. . . ."

With the rope ladder gone and the staircase burned, they had to build a way to get out of the catacomb. Con figured if he could get the pile of crates high enough, he and Sebastian could reach the floor ledge. Then they could boost themselves out.

He didn't want to think about Sebastian trying that. With his solid stonelike weight and his nonathletic manner, it would be difficult at best.

But their only other choice was to go back under the bridge. And they couldn't do that.

They had pushed the bodies against the wall, using them to brace the crates. Con had done much of that distasteful task. Sebastian had started to cry, that awful rasping sound he made, and Con hadn't been able to take it. Certain things seemed to terrify Sebastian; death—and its most visible signs—was one of them. On other things, he seemed sensible and almost normal.

Con wasn't sure why he had gotten this Charge. Sometimes he wondered why, with the Tabernacle gone, he continued it. He tried to control the blasphemous thoughts, but they were hard, especially here, in its ruined bowels. How could a god, particularly the God he had encountered in his studies, have allowed this?

What point did it serve? Did it allow the Holy One to bring his followers closer to God's Ear? Or did it test the faith of the survivors?

He didn't know. He didn't have the answers for any of it. He was the lowest of the low, an Aud who had, until two weeks ago, done menial tasks that no one else wanted to do. Then the Rocaan had called him to his study and given him the Charge that had led him to Sebastian.

And Sebastian had been a trial in and of himself.

But over the last few days, Con had developed an affection for Sebastian. His quirks, his difficulties, his loyalties. If only he were more agile. If only he could help more.

Con's hands were filthy with the rotting flesh of his former comrades. His nose was clogged with the stink of decay, and he wasn't sure he would ever get clean. But he kept working, trusting Sebastian's instincts, the instincts that got them through the tunnel in the first place.

Sebastian carried a crate out of the room. He cocked his head as he stepped into the catacomb and then he shuddered once. Con set down his own crate on the bed they were making, and turned.

Sebastian was walking at double his usual pace—almost at normal speed.

It looked as if he were running.

He reached Con quicker than he ever had before. Con took the crate from Sebastian, grunting as he did so. Its weight was nearly double what he expected. Sebastian was slow, he was heavy, but he was strong.

"Did . . . you . . . see . . . that . . . light?"

Con frowned. Light? Except for the light pouring down the small tunnel near the bodies, the catacombs were in shadow. Fortunately his eyes were used to it, from being underground for so long.

"No," he said.

Sebastian held up a hand. "It . . . feels . . . different."

"What does?" Con asked, dreading the answer.

"The . . . magick."

Con swallowed. How could there be magick down here to feel? These catacombs were below the Tabernacle, the place where magick gave way to God.

"Is this like the last time?" Con asked.

Sebastian nodded. One slow movement, up and down. "The . . . same."

"So you want us to leave? We can go back," Con said.

"No!" Sebastian said. "The . . . light . . . came . . . from . . . there."

"Is it following us?"

Sebastian went completely still as if the thought had not occurred to him until this moment. "I . . . do . . . not . . . know. . . . But . . . we . . . must . . . leave."

"We're working as fast as we can," Con said. "We can't go any faster. There's only the two of us."

"You . . . can . . . go. . . . I . . . can . . . boost . . . you."

"No," Con said. "We stay together. Besides, if I left, you'd never get out of here."

"I . . . could . . . go . . . back."

"Into the strange magick? I don't think so."

"Con . . . it's . . . Fey. They . . . hate . . . peo-ple . . . like . . . you."

"They're not real fond of you, either from what I saw when I found you," Con said. "Let's just finish building this stairway and get out of here."

"I . . . hope . . . we . . . have . . . time."

"Me too," Con said, and felt his exhaustion in each word. He would have to work harder and faster.

And he would have to pray.

The Rocaan had given him this Charge for a reason. Con had defended Sebastian so far. He had guarded the King's only son. They had made it through several impossible situations.

Surely the Holy One would help him through one more.

TWENTY-SIX

MATTHIAS rarely went to the center of town. He hated being surrounded by the stone buildings, hated the press of people near him. He never felt that way in Jahn, but here, among people who stared at him because of his height, he felt it always.

Almost as if he could feel their enmity.

Almost as if he could feel the terror that had sent him, as an innocent, to a near-certain death on a mountainside.

"The tall ones left town around dawn," Tri said. He was as nervous about going into the main part of town with Matthias as Matthias was.

"I dunna know how ye believe ye can find em anaway," Denl said.

Jakib nodded. He seemed to pick up on Matthias's unease. None of the group that Matthias had traveled with here seemed comfortable in this place. They had been uneasy since they left Jahn. Yasep, their leader, had said it was because they had only lived in Jahn, but Matthias knew that to be a lie. Most of the group had accents from the Kenniland Marshes, and Jakib and Marly had looks that showed they had been born here.

Yasep was hiding something, as usual, only Matthias didn't know what it was.

And at the moment he didn't care.

What he did care about was the feeling deep in his belly, the feeling that the "tall ones" Tri had talked about were Fey.

And the even deeper feeling that Matthias knew how to find them.

He knew he had to go to the center of town, to the market, no matter what would happen to him there. That was where he had to start.

Once he reached it, he would know what to do.

If he hadn't been such a skeptic, if his religious days weren't behind him, he might have hoped that the still small voice was finally speaking to him, giving him its wisdom, wisdom he had hoped for as an Aud and even more so as the Rocaan.

But this didn't feel like a voice. This was a knowledge as sure and fine as the knowledge of his own name.

"If you don't want to go into the market with me," Matthias said, "I understand."

"Tis na that," Jakib said. "Tis like yer tryin to walk inta the face a the enemy."

"We don't know that," Matthias said.

"The market isn't a good idea," Tri said. "They'll be spooked from this morning's incident. A lot of people don't know you're back. And you don't . . . look like yourself any more."

Matthias smiled, then winced as pain lanced through his face. "They wouldn't care how I looked," he said. "They'll always be frightened of me."

Still, a shudder ran down his back. He didn't like to tempt the people here. For the most part they left him alone, but he had had bad moments in the years he lived here after he had left the Tabernacle. Some of the moments were so uncomfortable that he considered going elsewhere, but he didn't. He needed the information the mountain provided.

He also didn't like to be away from the mountain anymore. It drew him, even if he didn't go up its side.

Matthias led them down a slight hill into the marketplace. It was in the exact center of town, in a plaza that had been built for this purpose. Many of the booths were permanent, built at the same time as the plaza itself. Families owned the booths and the position, along with the small business itself, ran from generation to generation.

Matthias's stomach tightened as he came closer to the plaza. Every muscle in his body was taut. He hated coming here. When he had lived here before, he had hired someone to do his shopping until he ate some spoiled meat and was deathly ill. After that, he had only friends shop for him, and even then, he was leery.

The marketplace was not as busy as it would have been in the afternoon. Some of the merchants were wrapping up their wares. Others were pulling coverings over their booths. Still others were making sales—which, in this part of Blue Isle, often included barter. Matthias scanned the customers and saw no familiar faces. He recognized many of the merchants, however, although they didn't seem to recognize him.

He swallowed, and stepped forward, his feet brushing against the polished stone of the plaza.

All around him, conversation stopped.

"Demon-spawn," someone whispered.

"Tall ones again," someone else said.

Tri raised his hands. "Silence!" he said. "That's Matthias. Don't you recognize him?"

"Demon-spawn," a woman said. She stood near the edge of the crowd. As Matthias passed her, she spit at his feet.

He resisted the urge to look at her. If he did so, and something happened to her later, he would get the blame. Instead he kept his eyes downcast. He was looking at the stone, but watching people through the corner of his eyes.

"*Begone,*" someone whispered.

He could feel the word down to his feet. A panic built in him. He had to leave. He had to leave now.

"Stop," Tri said. "He's a member of our community. He was rejected by the mountain. You have no right."

"He has no right to be here," a man said. "He has never had a right to be here."

Matthias kept walking. Below him, the stone started to glow as if a small trail of fire as wide as his little finger were burning before him.

"Demon-spawn," another woman said as he passed. She too spit at him. The spittle landed on the tiny fire but did not sizzle.

Matthias's stomach jumped again.

"What do ye see?" Jakib asked.

"That light," Matthias said softly, pointing downward. "Do you see it?"

Another fiery trail appeared beside the first. This one burned silver. He crouched, touched it and felt—

Jewel. Nicholas. Standing beside the crib, their newborn son inside. Jewel hovered near it, not letting Matthias close. The baby cried once—

"Tis stone," Denl said, and Matthias thought he heard panic in Denl's voice.

The trail remained. The image had left.

Fey. This path was left by Fey. Why? To trap him? Had they placed the image in the small fiery path for him to find?

Why?

How had they known he was here?

"Demon-spawn."

"*Begone.*"

The panic rose in him again. He clenched a fist, took a deep breath, and pushed the panic away.

Beside him a woman gasped and clutched her chest. She shot him a wild-eyed look, then ran out of the marketplace.

Tri put his hands beneath Matthias's arms. "We need to leave."

"I found them," Matthias said.

"They're not here now," Tri said. He tugged on Matthias. "Let's go."

Denl had his hand on the hilt of his knife. So did Jakib. They were standing beside Matthias as if they were guarding him.

"I've changed my mind," Tri said. "I don't want to find them."

Matthias touched the other fire trail. He saw nothing special. The trail wrapped around his fingertip, but he felt no pain. The stone was smooth and cool beneath his skin.

Tri tugged again.

"Demon-spawn." This time several people said the word at once. Matthias saw even more feet around him. He glanced up, realized that everyone in the marketplace was watching him.

The trails burned ahead of him, thin lines glowing in the twilight.

He stood, shaking. The Blooders were staring at him, all of them, as if he were hideous, as if he could turn them into ash with the blink of an eye. His hand started to wander to his injuries, but he didn't let it. He held his fist to his side.

"Demon-spawn," several voices murmured.

Matthias held up his other hand. He was trembling. Tri had stepped slightly behind him. Jakib and Denl hadn't moved.

"You people have no compassion at all," Matthias said. This

time he did let his fingers brush his bandaged face. "I nearly died a few weeks ago, and you don't care."

"You shouldn't have lived, demon-spawn!" a man shouted from behind him.

Bile rose in Matthias's throat. He swallowed. "I'm from here. Someone, maybe even someone in this crowd, fathered me. Someone gave birth to me, and has never spoken to me, never even acknowledged that I exist. Instead, you let the so-called Wise Ones take me to that mountain, naked, and alone, and leave me on the snow."

"Matthias—" Tri's voice held a warning.

"I am here," Matthias said. "I was born here, and I live here, and you will have to accept that I am as much a part of this place as you are, tall as I am, disfigured as I am, hated as I am. I won't leave just because you tell me to."

"You should have died on that mountain," the man behind him said.

Matthias didn't turn. He didn't want to see who spoke to him that way.

"Maybe," Matthias said. "Or maybe the Roca had another plan for me."

"The Roca doesn't love tall ones," a woman said.

"Really?" Matthias asked. "Then maybe the plan was God's."

"Matthias—" Tri warned again.

"Or maybe it belonged to the demon you served."

"I served the Tabernacle," Matthias said.

"And do no longer," said the man.

"Oh, I still do in my way," Matthias said. "It's why I'm here."

The mountain's shadow was falling across the town. If he looked up, he would see the sun's light still glowing in the sky.

The trails before him were stronger in the growing darkness. They winked at him, as if beckoning him forward.

"I dunna think arguing with a mob is a good idea," Jakib said in an undertone.

"It would be better for all of us if you left," the man said.

"No," Matthias said, "it wouldn't. The Fey have taken over Blue Isle, and I'm one of the few people who know how to fight them."

"You're fighting nothing," said a small woman toward the front of the crowd. "You've come here to hide."

"Matthias—" Tri still had a grip on Matthias's arm. "Please. Let it go."

The trails flared slightly, then faded. He glanced at them, afraid they would go out.

"I came here because Rocaanism originated here. The Roca is from here."

"No religion was born here." The small woman came forward. She was younger than Matthias. He didn't recognize her. She had wavy dark hair and an unlined face. "A man was born here."

"The Beloved of God," said the man who had been taunting Matthias.

"The religion was created by people like you, for their own benefit, their own power."

"I'm not so sure," Matthias said.

"Please." Tri's voice had gone down to a whisper. "This is not for debate. These people cannot be swayed by your words."

"There is na enough a us ta fight, Holy Sir," Denl whispered. "Listen ta the man."

"What you believe doesn't matter," the woman said. "The truth is all that matters."

"And what is truth?" Matthias asked. His voice rose. He recognized a tone in it that he hadn't heard since he was Rocaan. Since he was supposed to make such pronouncements. "Truth is different for you than for me. For you, the truth is that because I am tall, I am to be feared. For me, the truth is that because I am tall—something I cannot control—I am hated. I am no different from the rest of you inside."

"Holy Sir," Denl whispered. He had moved closer to Matthias. So had Jakib. The crowd was closing around them. The trails, once blazing across stone, now disappeared into bodies.

"We were warned of the tall ones generations ago," the man said.

"By whom?" Matthias asked.

"The Roca," a woman said.

"Really?" Matthias asked. "Then study your own literature, your own history. Some of the old stories say the Roca was tall."

"And most say he was like us." Tri spoke as loudly as Matthias. "Please, Matthias, you are not welcome here. Let's go about our business."

Matthias glanced at him. Tri, in one small speech, had allied himself with the people of Constant, and yet somehow still remained allied with Matthias himself. The fear startled Matthias. It was so strong that even Tri, who had gone against the Wise Ones, was backing down.

"Like you," Matthias said, acknowledging Tri. "Some of the stories say he was short. Like you."

Tri stepped back as if he'd been slapped. Denl made a panicked sound in his throat. The crowd was getting closer.

Matthias stared at them. Familiar faces, old faces, faces he didn't recognize. They were a sea before him in the growing twilight. The lighted trails leading away from them did not illuminate their feet or the stone.

The trails were something other.

The trails were what he had come for.

Not to argue with people who, as Tri said, could not be swayed.

"I'm going to stay in Constant as long as I need to," Matthias said. "You may as well get used to me."

Then he walked forward, careful not to step on the trails, but to walk beside them. The crowd parted as he moved toward them, as if they were afraid to get near him, as if touching him would hurt them.

All around him there were rustles and whispers.

Demon-spawn.

Soulless one.

Tall one.

Begone.

Begone.

Begone.

The words pushed him forward, and he let them. The trail led away from the marketplace, and he followed it. Denl and Jakib stayed beside him. After a moment, Tri caught up to them.

The crowd let them go. Once Matthias glanced over his shoulder. The crowd remained, huddled together at the edge of the plaza, staring at him, their eyes reflecting the dying light.

They seemed to glow from within, and he shuddered, just once, before continuing forward.

The trail wound its way through the streets of Constant. He looked up, toward the mountain, and saw the lights faintly against its side. The mountain felt stronger this night. It was nearly a live thing, its presence as clear to him as Jewel's and Nicholas's had been a moment before.

Midway up the mountain, a light flared, then died away, almost as if a door had opened. He could sense the room: warm, inviting, like the Tabernacle used to be on a rainy evening.

And then the feeling was gone.

"Are ye all right, then?" Denl asked.

Matthias realized he had been standing still in the middle of the stone-covered road, staring with his mouth open at the mountainside.

He closed his mouth.

"I'm fine," he said.

But he wondered. Lights everywhere, beckoning, beckoning. They had to be traps laid by the Fey, traps that only he could see. He had no holy water on him, and even if he did, it no longer worked anyway.

And he was going unprotected.

Or did these lights mean something else, something only "tall ones" could see? Was that why the people of Constant feared him? Because he was part of the mountain in some way?

"Matthias," Tri said. "We can't stay here much longer. They'll come."

"I know," he said. "We're not staying." There was only one way to answer his own questions. He couldn't hide forever.

He took a deep breath and let it out. "We're going up the mountain," he said, and then walked forward, toward the beckoning light.

TWENTY-SEVEN

THE trail had disappeared far below them. Gift, Leen, and the Cap were scaling rocks and finding footholds in the crevices between them. Gift was actually glad that Leen had stopped him from bringing too much stuff. Climbing was awkward enough without being overbalanced by weight.

The Cap had the worst time of it. His small arms and stubby legs didn't allow him the reach that Gift had. Gift had looked back just once to see the Cap, arms wrapped around a boulder, struggling with tiny footholds that Gift couldn't even see. Gift had stepped right through that area.

The Cap had also insisted on bringing all of his weapons. They were tied to him as if he were a Beast Rider instead of a Red Cap. He was lucky he was strong. The average Fey couldn't carry that much equipment.

Gift had wondered how the Cap had done it for the bulk of their trip. Coulter had suggested that the Cap leave the weapons with him, and the Cap had refused. He seemed to think they gave him a protection he didn't otherwise possess.

At least the rock field was relatively flat. It sloped upward, but in a way that Gift could manage. Leen had said, as they started, that it looked as if there had once been a rock staircase going up here. After she pointed it out, Gift saw it too. Decades, maybe centuries ago, someone had placed flat rocks into the ground and worn them smooth. But landslides had come off the mountain, covering the area with large and small rocks, making the staircase unpassable.

Ahead of them, the blackness pulsed. It covered a small portion of the mountain, and looked, in some ways, like an unprotected entrance to Shadowlands. Leen and the Cap still said they couldn't see it.

Gift could see it and feel it and almost taste it. It was that close.

He refused to let himself look in any other direction. When they had started climbing, he had glanced at the valley beneath them. It was lost in mist, the buildings barely visible, the trees poking out like blades of grass. It looked so small that it terrified him, and once he had that thought, he slipped on the rock he was holding. He managed to catch himself, but he promised himself that he wouldn't look down again.

"How much farther?" the Cap asked. His breath was coming in small gasps. He was clearly winded.

Gift wasn't yet, but he didn't know how much of that was anticipation. As he grew closer to the blackness, he felt a wave of euphoria wash over him with each pulse. He hoped that it was not some kind of luring effect. His only salvation from that, he knew, was that Leen and the Cap couldn't feel it.

"Not too much farther," he said.

"You said that a long time ago," the Cap said. "I'm going to stop if we don't get there soon."

"It was your idea to come," Leen said.

"I didn't realize we'd need the magick of Beast Riders," the Cap said.

Gift's hands were growing cold. The ground between the rocks was covered with a faint dusting of snow.

"Careful," he said. "It's getting slick."

He glanced up again. The blackness pulsed. A few more rocks to cross and then they would be on a flat stone, almost like an entryway. He was getting tired too. He could feel it in his back and shoulders, in his legs and feet.

Then he saw an opening in the rocks. The stairs here were thin and broken, but they were walkable. He stopped on a small flat dirt area, and waited for the Cap and Leen.

Sometime during their passage, the Cap had gotten ahead of Leen. It was just like her to protect the weakest one in the troop without his knowledge, even if he was a Red Cap. Gift smiled at her. She nodded but didn't stop her work on the rocks. She was close enough to the Cap to catch him if he fell, far enough away that he wouldn't know she was protecting him if he didn't need it.

When he reached the small flat spot, he doubled over and breathed hard. "This is it?" he managed.

"No," Gift said. He pointed to the larger flat spot. The area was made of continuous stone as if someone had taken rocks, flattened them, and formed them into a floor. "We need to get there."

"At least we have stairs," Leen said as she reached them. She put a hand on the Cap's back. "Breathe slowly."

He did. Gift was surprised that the Cap listened to her. He didn't listen to anyone else. Gift was also surprised that Leen was being so kind to a Red Cap.

Maybe she had gotten used to him.

"What do you see up there?" Leen asked.

"Besides that ledge?" Gift asked.

She nodded.

"That same blackness I saw before," he said. He squinted, but it didn't change. "It's almost alive, you know? It moves, almost as if it's breathing."

The Cap stood slowly. He was still clutching his stomach. "And you want us to go there?"

"Yes," Gift said. Then he frowned. "What does it look like to you?"

Leen raised her head. "The sunlight's blocking it," she said.

"It can't be," Gift said. "This side of the mountain faces south."

"Besides," the Cap said without looking, "the sun is going down, and there are rocks blocking the western side."

"So you see a brightness?" Gift asked, wondering at the difference.

"No," she said. "I see a glare. There's a difference."

There was. He knew it, and it bothered him on a deep level. "How come I can see this and you can't?"

"Maybe you're the only one who's supposed to go there," Leen said.

"Or maybe you're seeing a type of magick," the Cap said. "Remember that Coulter could see it too."

"But what he saw was different," Leen said.

"And Leen will have magick one day. She just hasn't grown into it yet."

"That's right," the Cap said. "She can see a glare. I can't even see that." He raised his head, shaded his eyes with his free hand, and looked. "It looks like a mountainside. Nothing more, nothing less."

There was sadness in his voice.

"Steps leading to a rock ledge which ends in a mountainside?" Gift asked.

The Cap nodded.

"How very amazing," Gift said. "Maybe everyone who sees it sees something different."

"Maybe," Leen said, but she didn't sound so certain.

They both were losing their nerve, and Gift wanted to get up the mountainside. He wanted to see this dark thing.

"Let's go," he said. "We only have a short way."

"That's what worries me," the Cap said under his breath.

"You ready?" Gift asked him.

The Cap took a deep breath. He was still a bit flushed from the climb, but not seriously.

Gift nodded to him, then turned and mounted the first stair. It was broken off in the center so he had to step to the sides. He climbed it, then the next and the next, using the piles of rocks on either side as railings.

The Cap followed him, and Leen trailed behind, as she had before.

It only took Gift a few moments to reach the ledge.

It wasn't made of a continuous piece of stone at all. It was rock mortared together long enough ago that the rocks themselves had cracked. It was slightly uneven and rough beneath his feet.

This was a man-made structure, built to look like part of the mountain.

The hair on the back of Gift's neck rose.

The Cap came up beside him and immediately sat down. Some of his swords scraped the stone, but he didn't seem to notice. Leen had to go around him.

Gift looked up toward the blackness. It wasn't pulsating any more. In fact, it didn't look like a live thing. All he saw was a cave opening, as rounded and natural as the caves he had seen in other parts of the mountain.

Except for the swords outside.

Stone swords, carved out of rock. They were taller than Gift. Two of them were embedded into the rock, points down. Their hilts were in the air, as if waiting for giants to snatch them from the ground.

Another two were sticking out of the sides of the cave's mouth. The points were again embedded into the rock, their hilts waiting to be grabbed. The swords were several feet above Gift's head, and laid out flat.

A fifth sword balanced above the center of the cave's mouth. It stood on its point, but its back was pressed into the stone. It didn't look as if it were carved into the stone; it looked as if it were added later.

"That's their religious symbol," the Cap said. His voice shook. "We need to leave."

"No." Gift grabbed the Cap's arm. He couldn't explain it, but he didn't feel any threat here. Just the compelling need to go inside.

"It's got to be some kind of trap," Leen said.

"No," Gift said. "It's more than that."

He let go of the Cap and started for the swords. The Cap ran forward and wrapped his small body around Gift. Gift could feel the press of knife and sword hilts against his legs.

"You can't go," the Cap said. "You can't. If you die in there—"

"I won't," Gift said.

"At least let me go first," Leen said. She pushed past both of them, drew her knife and headed toward the swords.

"Can you see the opening?" Gift asked.

"Vividly," she said, her tone dry. She was frightened—he could tell from her posture—but she didn't stop. Gift freed himself from the Cap and stepped a bit forward.

Leen stopped between the two swords and touched the closest with her fingers. Her hand was trembling.

Gift held his breath—

And nothing happened.

She nodded. "I'm all right," she said. She stepped past the swords and into the cave's mouth.

"Wow!" she cried, and her voice echoed.

She came back out, past the standing swords as if they were no more than trees and grabbed Gift by the hand. "You have to come in there."

"No traps?" the Cap asked.

"If there are any, they're farther inside," Leen said. "But I don't think anyone's been here for centuries."

Gift didn't need a second invitation. He kept his hand in hers. Even though he had felt an urgency to get up here, the urgency was gone now. He wanted to take his time, see everything.

As he approached the swords, he forced Leen to slow down.

"They're carved," he said.

"Of course they're carved," the Cap snapped.

"No," Gift said. "Look at the scrollwork."

The blades were etched as if they were really made of metal. And the hilts were detailed as well. The etchings on the blades were swirls and symbols that Gift did not understand. The details on the hilt looked familiar.

He grabbed Leen's knife, stood on his tiptoes, and scraped. Dirt flaked off. Layers and layers of dirt.

Beneath it, a jewel gleamed dully, catching a bit of redness from the sun.

Jewel-encrusted hilts. He wondered if these swords were really made of stone or if the layers that covered them had formed to the metal itself.

"What is this place?" the Cap asked.

Gift stood flat-footed again, and handed Leen her knife. "I don't know," he said. But the elation he had felt earlier was growing. He had to be here.

He knew it.

It felt right.

"I don't like this," the Cap said. He shoved himself in front of Gift. "You go everywhere last. If there's some kind of trap in here, we'll find it first."

Leen stood in the cave's mouth, directly below the point of the sword above. She was bouncing, as if she couldn't contain her own excitement.

The air was cold and crisp, but Gift felt no chill. He glanced at the swords above him. They appeared to be braced on nothing. It was as if they were flung into the stone and then stuck there. He could almost imagine them vibrating with the initial impact, then settling into their current position.

The only sword that looked as if it had been placed there on purpose was the one above Leen.

"Come on," she said.

He thought it odd that her mood would shift so quickly. Perhaps the Cap's fears were grounded. Perhaps there was something here they didn't dare tamper with.

The Cap pushed ahead of Gift. When he reached Leen's position, he too stopped.

"By the Powers," he said. "What *is* this place?"

Gift came up beside them, and felt the breath leave his body.

The cave was full of light. It was as if a small sun shone from one corner, illuminating everything. The light was dazzling but not blinding, and it felt entirely natural.

The cold from the outside was at Gift's back. Before him was a dry, inviting warmth. Stairs went down almost as far as the eye could see. The floor below looked like it were made of white stone.

"Marble," the Cap said and pointed down.

The cave seemed to go on forever. It split off in sections—rooms—almost like Gift's father's palace.

And the walls . . .

The walls were covered with swords.

Real swords that gleamed in the light.

"I guess you didn't need all those weapons after all," Gift said to the Cap.

"These are mine," he said, hand on his swords. "Those could have some religious significance. They could hurt us."

"Look," Leen said, and pointed to a spot near Gift. The wall behind him—the wall beside the cave's mouth—was covered in chalices. They all sat on their own ledges, carved out of the same white stone.

The walls farther back seemed to have still other items on them, items that Gift couldn't identify from this distance.

It was, truly, one of the most miraculous places he'd ever seen.

He took a step down, and the Cap put out an arm, stopping him. "We still don't know what this place is," the Cap said. "Let us go first."

Leen seemed to shake herself from her awe and took a step down, followed by the Cap. Gift let them go first, knowing it would make little difference.

He still felt no threat from this place. Its warmth and light and fresh air made it seem like a haven. Its decor seemed to come alive, just for him.

The steps were chiseled into the white stone. It was slippery beneath his feet. He took each step at a time, waiting until the Cap and Leen had taken it before proceeding farther.

The floor below was flat. Pedestals rose, items on them unrecognizable in the soft light. Toward the back, a table had been carved out of the white stone, and where the room split, a fountain spewed water into a basin. The sound was faint and soothing.

And he was thirsty.

But he knew better than to drink it untested. He had been trained to stay away from water on Blue Isle, especially when it was surrounded by icons of the Isle's religion.

The other two reached the main floor and nothing happened.

Gift stepped down the last step. The floor, up close, was not pure white. It had swirls of gray running through it. He looked up. The ceiling was so high that he could barely see it. In the top center was the source of the light throughout the room. It was round and large and glowed beautifully.

Then he heard footsteps. He whirled.

No one stood in the cave's mouth.

No one stood at the opening to either corridor.

The Cap and Leen were staring at him as if he had suddenly gone mad.

"Did you hear that?" he asked.

The footsteps were drawing closer. They were light, barely audible above the bubble of the fountain.

He turned again. Sound was hard to pinpoint in this echoey space.

"I don't hear anything," Leen said.

"Me either," the Cap said.

Then a woman appeared behind the fountain. Gift squinted. There were stairs there, stairs he hadn't seen before. She was standing on the top of them.

She looked familiar.

She looked Fey.

When she saw him, she smiled. She ran down the steps lithely, like a woman who was still young.

He couldn't move. His heart was pounding.

She took a path around the fountain.

The Cap and Leen didn't see her. They were watching the other openings, looking as if they were trying to listen for something, something they couldn't hear.

"Gift," the woman said. She held out her arms. She was

wearing breeches, boots and a leather jerkin, Infantry clothes from his Grandfather's army. Her black hair was braided down her back.

Gift didn't move. He was staring at her face.

He had seen it twice, both times in a Vision.

In his first Vision:

She had been standing beside a man with yellow hair and pale skin. Then her face melted.

And then in the second Vision, the day he had nearly died. The day Coulter had saved him by Binding them both together.

The day she *had* died.

She ran toward him and put her arms around him.

She felt warm and real and very much alive.

"My Gift," she murmured.

"Mother?" he asked and let her pull him close.

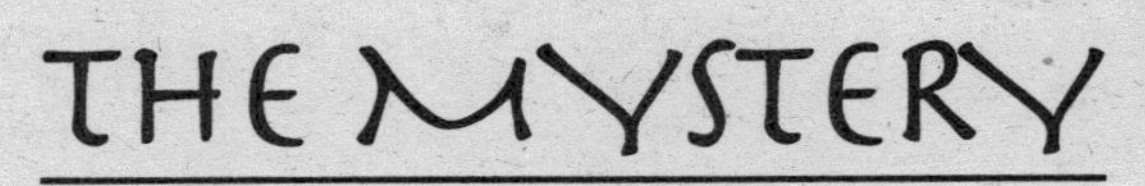
THE MYSTERY

TWENTY-EIGHT

ONE of the men shouted an all-clear.

Adrian laid down his pickax and almost groaned with relief. His blisters had burst in the middle of the morning, and now his hands were bleeding. He had kept working, though, through the meal break, the hot sun of the afternoon, and into the twilight. He had to remain after the discussion he'd had with the quarry owner and that strange man, the man from the village.

The man who was looking for Gift and Leen.

Adrian hoped Scavenger and Coulter made it back to the hiding place all right. After they had left, he worked this small section of the quarry by himself, breaking down the rocks into fist-sized stones that could then be polished and shaped for building materials. It was backbreaking, difficult work, and it didn't engage his mind at all. Farming always had, with its constant changes, the cooperation between man and soil, man and weather, man and crops.

Here there was nothing. Nothing except the muscles in his arms and back, in his shoulders and spine, in his legs and waist.

He ached everywhere.

And he was worried.

He'd had the entire day to worry. What if they hadn't made it? What if the townspeople had found their campsite?

Why did they hate the so-called tall ones, and what did it have to do with the Fey?

He stretched and heard the bones in his back crack. The pain was exquisite. He had done physical labor on his farm, but nothing like this, nothing this repetitive. Not even planting was this kind of work.

The other day workers were threading past the main table, picking up their mark and getting their pay for their day's work. He made his way slowly in that direction. If he hadn't known that people had worked the quarry all day, he would have thought nothing had changed.

Bits of broken stone lay across the ground, next to larger rocks and boulders. A few wheelbarrows were resting in the center of the quarry. Small bits of rock were piled in the center, to be broken down even farther later. The locals here used the tiny rocks as road covering, something Scavenger had called a travesty. *It hurts people's feet,* he had said as they were walking over the tiny rocks. *Better to have the flat dirt.*

But not better, Adrian supposed, in the rainy season. Here, where the land was naturally hilly, many roads trailed along hillsides. They would become impassable mud in the rainy season or slide away altogether. At least the gravel prevented the roads from becoming mud.

Nothing could stop them from sliding away.

The line moved slowly. None of the other workers looked as exhausted as he felt. Few of them, though, were newcomers. Most of them chose this day labor as a living. It had surprised him. He would have thought that most people would want to be their own masters. But then he had looked around. The rocky hillsides and the thin topsoil made farming difficult. Work here was for the hardy, and a lot of the food came from downriver. Adrian wondered how long that would last, now that the Fey were in power.

The townspeople here seemed blissfully unaware of that problem.

He wished he could be.

The entire day, the entire past week, he'd felt as if time were running out. He wasn't sure what kind of training the nonmagical Scavenger could do for Gift, and he knew that Gift and Coulter had to repair the rift between them. He still didn't completely understand it. They had tried to explain it to him, using words like Link and Binding, but he knew they had to be talking about a physical concept, and he only knew it as an emotional one.

Emotional ties were not severed by an outside party.

He finally made it to the long stone table that sat at the front of the quarry. He had to make a small mark in a bowl of dirt to prove which marker was his. The man behind the table handed Adrian his marker and three gold coins.

The owner was standing beside him.

"Good work today," the owner said. "Will we see you tomorrow?"

Adrian had no idea. He felt as if the question were a trick and he was too tired for tricks. But he made himself smile.

"Of course," he said.

He clutched the coins in his bleeding hands and walked to the gate, as straight as his aching back would allow. He could use some water and some food, but there was none here.

The sun had set behind the mountains, but the sky retained just a hint of color. That would be gone soon. It would be full dark by the time he had to go up the mountain.

But he could feel the owner's gaze on his back. If he went up the mountain, he would look even more suspicious.

Adrian sighed, and kept walking with the other workers, trudging down the main road, heading for town.

TWENTY-NINE

PAUSHO leaned against the boulder that marked the entrance to the quarry. She hated the quarry, even though it brought the bulk of the work in from the town. The quarry was old, and it had been cut deep into the mountainside as the years progressed. When she looked at the mountain from Constant, she could see the bowl the quarry made, the bowl where part of the mountain had once been.

It was as if they had cut from the mountain's living flesh.

She rarely climbed the path to the quarry, but she felt she had to this afternoon. She wore her darkest sweater, leggings, and heavy boots. Fyr was beside her, nearly hidden in the boulder's shadow. Zak stood even closer to Pausho, his hand on her shoulder.

The growing darkness helped keep them from view of the quarry workers. Not a one had glanced at them. They trudged down the hill, their bodies bent from their labor, their minds clearly focused on the evening ahead.

Quarry workers had some of the roughest jobs in Constant. They worked for days, sometimes weeks, and received a lot of pay. Then, when the needed rock was formed, they had no work until someone started building again.

Sometimes quarry workers were without jobs for months.

One of the Wise Ones had been a quarry worker. He had explained the system to Pausho with a touch of nostalgia. He had liked the hard work, and thought the decisions of the Wise Ones were simple compared with his day labor.

How she missed Wise Ones like that.

How she longed for such simple times.

Now that she had kicked Tri out of the group, she had the dilemma of finding someone to take his place.

But not until she found the tall ones.

She wasn't sure what she would do once she found them, but she had to know where they were. They couldn't lurk near Constant. If she allowed that, she was hurting her vows. She had to solve this problem first and get them as far away from the town as possible—by whatever means necessary.

Zak was watching the passing workers carefully. Most were their neighbors. The faces were familiar to Pausho, the stances, the hunched-over walks. A number of the older men had fathered tall children, and brought them to the Wise Ones, tears streaming down their faces. Those men couldn't look at her any more.

But she could look at them. They had put the good of the community ahead of their love for their children.

Some of the men had had other children, but most had not. They had left their families and lived off the land, finally returning to Constant and getting whatever work they could. Tall ones disrupted lives from the moment they took a breath.

And she hated it.

Finally, Zak's hand tightened on her shoulder. He was watching a man at the stone table. The man was sunburned and blond, no taller than the rest of the workers. But he was a stranger. Pausho did not recognize his face.

"That one," Zak whispered.

He had spoken to the stranger who had come to the quarry with the tall ones. Zak hadn't believed everything the stranger had told him. The man appeared to be too calm. A stranger being questioned like that, Zak reasoned, should have been nervous. But this man spoke as if nothing bothered him whatsoever.

The tall ones had been turned away the day before, and his other companions were missing, although Ome, the owner of the quarry, had sworn that they had arrived with the stranger that morning.

He would lead them to the tall ones. She knew it. Oh, he

had been cunning enough to fool a lot of people. They would have thought his calmness a sign of his innocence, and the fact that he alone remained in the quarry a sign of his lack of attachments, but she knew better.

Tall ones were cunning.

Wise Ones had to be even more so.

The stranger had taken his marker, and Ome's assistant had placed coins in the stranger's hand.

"You're sure?" Pausho whispered.

"Positive," Zak said.

She nodded and beckoned Fyr to come forward. Then she pointed at the stranger.

"That's the one we follow," she said.

"The one getting his coins?" Fyr asked softly, her voice trembling slightly. She was now the newest Wise One, now that Tri was gone. Pausho had brought her along because she was young and would be able to follow the stranger as far as he went.

"Yes," Zak said.

Pausho put a hand on Zak's. "You can go now," she said, "Fyr and I will take care of this."

"You'll need me with you."

Pausho smiled at him. They had been friends a long time, she and Zak. They had gone through more than any two people should have. But Zak was older and getting frail, even though he probably didn't realize it. He didn't need to spend a night trailing a man who might mean nothing to them.

"Fyr and I can do this," Pausho said.

"Actually," Fyr said. "I can do this alone."

"It's better to have two," Pausho said.

"It's better to have one," Fyr said. "Less noticeable."

The stranger had gone through the gate. He paused for a brief moment, his head almost turning toward the mountain. The movement was slight, and if Pausho hadn't been looking for it, she might not have seen it.

Then he trudged in the same direction as the rest of the workers.

"It's better to have a man," Zak said, watching him go.

Pausho understood his argument. All the other workers were men. A woman would be conspicuous.

If she were visible.

Which Pausho was not planning to be.

"All right," she said, knowing they had no real time to

squabble. "Zak, follow the workers down. Fyr and I will remain out of sight. If he veers away from Constant, we will follow him. If he goes into town, you will."

Zak's hand left her shoulder. He slipped past her without a word, and mingled with the men on the trail.

"He's not going to stay with the workers," Fyr said.

"I know," Pausho said.

"Let me go," Fyr said. "I'm more agile."

Pausho put an arm around Fyr's waist. "You're more agile, but I know how to treat tall ones. Let's share the danger."

"Do you think there will be danger?" Fyr whispered.

"Yes," Pausho said, and keeping to the shadows, followed the stranger down the hill.

THIRTY

CON stood on top of the platform of crates and placed another on the pile. His arms ached, and his back was sore. Sweat ran down his face and made his robe stick to his skin. He had never been so filthy and tired in all his life.

Sebastian was still agitated, forcing them to work faster than Con would have liked. Sebastian himself was moving at what seemed to be his fastest speed—almost the speed of a normal person's casual walk. Twice Sebastian had tripped over his own feet and fallen on the crate he carried. Once he'd smashed it open, sending potatoes skittering across the stone floor of the catacombs. He kept looking over his shoulder, making sure there was nothing behind him.

He did say the strange light was gone.

But he was afraid it would be back. He claimed that it was the magickal change he had felt on the other side of the bridge.

Con felt that the sooner they got out of the catacombs, the better. He was beginning to get nervous himself. A short time ago, he thought he heard thumps in the back tunnel, but Sebastian had said nothing. If there had been noises, Sebastian would have gotten even more nervous.

The darkness wasn't helping, either. When they had started work, light had filtered in from the hole above. Apparently that was where the doorway used to be, and since the Tabernacle had burned, the sunlight fell directly into the hole. Now the sunlight was gone. It hadn't provided a lot of illumination, but it had provided enough to make Con feel as if he was going somewhere.

Right now, he felt as if he were building a tower to the sky.

And an unstable one at that. The crates were different sizes, and they wobbled on top of each other. He had hoped that the higher up he got in the passage, he would discover that parts of the stairs remained. But none did. The fire must have burned very hot.

He knew they would get out, but he was discouraged just the same.

He didn't tell Sebastian of his discouragement, but he felt as if Sebastian knew. Sebastian was working as hard as he could. Every time he fell, he apologized profusely, and then tried to work even faster. Con had finally asked him to take his time. Sebastian's accidents were taking too much of Con's efforts, and much as Sebastian tried to help, Con was essentially building this stairway up alone.

He had gone back, just once, after Sebastian had mentioned seeing the tiny light. Sebastian had screamed after him, then burst into tears, but Con had continued. He had gone back as far as the bridge tunnel and gazed up. It would have taken very little effort—compared to building this monstrosity—to boost Sebastian back into that tunnel and to go back to the cavern. But as Con stood there, he had felt a distinct unease. It was almost palpable. He put a hand on the tunnel's ledge and a shudder went through him.

Perhaps that was the still small voice warning him away from that path. Perhaps he felt, on an entirely different level, the change in magick that Sebastian had talked about.

Or perhaps it was simply no longer safe to go back and he knew it deep down. There was nothing for them there, except to wait. The Fey would eventually discover the tunnels, and if Con and Sebastian stayed in the cavern they would be caught—again.

And this time, Con didn't think he could get them out of it.

He had returned, almost at a run, and found Sebastian lingering on the edge of the main corridor, tears streaking his grimy face. Dirt lodged in the cracks of his skin, making him look as if his features were etched in blood.

Con had reassured Sebastian that they weren't going back the way they came, and then they both turned their attention to getting out.

Fortunately, there were a lot of crates. The Auds had planned for their survival well. It was too bad that they had died down here anyway.

He climbed off the pile of crates and went back to one of the side rooms for another. There were crates stacked against the walls in each of the rooms, and he and Sebastian had been whittling them down, taking the closest rooms and working back to the farthest.

He was in the second room this time. Most of the crates were gone. He lifted one off the floor and stopped.

Someone had coughed.

Sebastian never coughed.

Con swallowed. He carried the crate out of the room and stopped in the corridor.

Nothing.

No sound at all.

Except Sebastian in the next room, shuffling across the floor.

Con waited until Sebastian emerged.

"Did you hear anything?" Con asked.

Sebastian shook his head slowly.

"Do you feel anything?"

"On-ly . . . the . . . chan-ge . . . from . . . be-fore," Sebastian said.

"It's still here."

"Once . . . chan-ged . . . it . . . stays . . . that . . . way," Sebastian said.

"Forever?" Con asked.

"No," Sebastian said. "Un-til . . . some-bod-y . . . else . . . chan-ges . . . it . . .again."

And no one had. So if the light or the magick shift had stayed, they had no way of knowing.

And they had no way of knowing if it had returned.

Con took a deep breath. The crate he was holding was getting heavy. And he still had some distance to go with it. He carried it to the crate pile, then balanced it carefully, and stepped onto the first layer of crates. He and Sebastian had built several layers, each angling toward the wall, and they shuddered as he stepped on them. They were sturdy enough, but just barely.

He was nearly to the highest layer when he heard another

coughlike sound. He made himself set the crate down, and he turned.

Sebastian was standing at the base of the crate pile, holding his crate like a statue. Only he was trembling.

He had heard the sound too.

Slowly Sebastian set the crate down. Con crouched and peered into the corridor behind them. It seemed darker than it had before. He heard a faint shuffling, as if clothing were rustling.

Then, all along the back, lights flared.

Eerie lights.

The lights the Fey had.

The lights that appeared to have tiny glowing bodies trapped inside glass.

There had to have been fifty lights. They scattered throughout the corridor. They flared as if people had pulled a cover off each simultaneously.

As his eyes adjusted, he saw a sea of faces staring at him.

Fey faces.

"Noooooo," Sebastian wailed.

Con wanted to join in. But he didn't.

He grabbed the hilt of his sword and pulled it out.

He didn't know how many Fey he could kill with this blade, but he knew he was about to find out.

THIRTY-ONE

WISDOM placed the meal on an ornate table near the embroidered couch. The smell of fresh bread enticed Rugad's nostrils. His stomach rumbled, but he made no move away from the window. He kept his hands clasped behind his back and continued to watch Wisdom through a reflection in the wavy glass.

Wisdom seemed solicitous. His braids fell along his back and sides, brushing his tattooed arms. He kept his hair out of the food. When he stood, he stared at Rugad for a moment, but his expression was neutral. Rugad half expected Wisdom to make a face.

"Forgive me, sir," Wisdom said, "but I do think you need to eat."

Rugad still did not move. The sun was setting over the city, sending waves of red light through the still-smoky air. He liked being on flat land, where the sun lingered longer than it did near mountains. The sunset was stunning, and he found himself longing to be outside, to be in a Shadowlands, to be anywhere but here.

"Sir?" Wisdom said.

He was going to force Rugad to speak. Rugad didn't want to waste any words, not now, not when he knew how speaking felt. He would save it for more important things.

He turned, glared at Wisdom, and then turned back toward the window. The light was mingling with the clouds, creating red smoke. Wisdom's image lay across that, staring at Rugad. Wisdom's expression was carefully neutral, as if he were trying to control some great emotion.

Finally he nodded once, even though he thought Rugad could not see him, and then left the room. Rugad waited until he heard the door snick closed before leaving his post at the window.

As he walked, the jar with his voice in it bumped against his hip. Sometimes he missed the range and power of that voice, the casual use he had put it to for so long. Nothing was casual about speaking now.

The meal prepared for him in the palace's kitchen used the palace's stores. Nicholas had eaten well, although his peasantry to the south had not. Rugad had respect for Nicholas as a warrior, but as a ruler, Rugad believed Nicholas tolerated too much poverty. Nicholas hadn't learned the first rule of leadership: unhappy people revolted.

The Fey knew that. The Fey knew that very well.

If Rugad couldn't kill Nicholas and make himself—or his great-grandchildren—into the rulers of Blue Isle, then he could do the next best thing. He could make those pockets of poverty believe that the loss of Nicholas the King's throne was the best thing that ever happened to them.

Rugad was already doing that to the south and in other parts of the country that he had conquered easily. There were still untamed sections of Blue Isle, and he would try to charm them, too.

There were several ways to make a country loyal. The simplest and easiest was by force. It was never the best. He hated having his people unhappy.

He did not want to be the king his countries revolted against.

Even Nye, which had been part of a prolonged battle, had eventually bowed to his will. And now, decades later, the citizens of that fine country had been sad to see him leave. He had worried about his exit: his grandson Bridge was the logical ruler, but Rugad had not officially appointed him. Bridge was a lousy Visionary and an even worse diplomat. Rugad had decided that it would be better to let Jewel's brothers fight out the position of leader on their own. If they failed—and someone else took their place—it wouldn't matter. Nye was one small country in the Fey Empire. It didn't need the Black family as rulers. It could survive any Visionary, and do so probably better without Bridge and his ilk than with them.

Rugad sat down on the embroidered couch. He took a slice of bread off the tray and frowned at the rest of the food. A bowl of soup, a slice of mutton—gathered from where he didn't know, since he hadn't seen any sheep near the city—and some cheese. More food than he would be able to eat, especially with his throat still sore.

He took a bite of bread because it smelled too good to resist. It tasted as good as it smelled, fresh and doughy and still slightly warm. The soup was good, too. It was made from a beef broth and had several vegetables as well as chunks of meat. The first bite he took warmed his throat. The second eased the ache. He ate so fast, he almost felt as if he were a young man on the battlefield again.

Almost.

When he finished, he took a sip of the honeyed mead that the Domestics had been preparing for him since his injury. It stayed warm until he drank it, no matter if he waited a matter of minutes or hours. It had healing properties that sped his recovery, and he found that he felt rejuvenated after each sip.

The sun had nearly set. The red glow on the horizon was fading. The room itself was growing dim. In a moment, he would have to get someone to bring him a torch and to light some candles.

But he didn't move. Not yet. He enjoyed these last few moments of every day, the moments just before the sun disappeared over the mountains to the west, moments just before the city became dark.

And it did become dark. The palace sat amid vast ruins. He hadn't had to level a city before, at least not like this one. His soldiers had set some fires of their own, but the burning of the Tabernacle had destroyed most of the buildings on the other side of the river. For the first few nights after Rugad had taken over Jahn, the still-hot embers glowed orange all evening. Since then, the fires had gone out completely, and at night the palace itself glowed like a lighthouse on a stormy seacoast. Desolation for miles. As far to the south as he could see, there were only ruins of buildings, but no buildings themselves.

A knock at the door made him set down the mead. He stood.

"Come," he said, the very word bringing back the ache that the liquid had eased.

The door opened.

Boteen stood outside, hunched slightly in the short hallway. Behind him stood a Domestic with a torch and a candle.

Rugad beckoned them with his hand. They came inside. The Domestic placed the torch in the torch holder near the door, then used the candle to light all the lamps on the room. The lamps gave the area a soft light, not the bright, almost unnatural light cast by the torches. Early on, the Domestics had brought in a Fey lamp, but the souls inside began to wail when they saw the room. The sound was soft, but persistent. Rugad had ordered it removed so that he could rest.

He had never heard Fey lamps wail like that one, although he had heard of such a thing in the old stories. The amount of power it took for the souls to make themselves heard was vast, and the Fey lamp had flickered and died a few days afterward.

Boteen waited until the Domestic left, then closed the door behind her. Rugad watched Boteen. He was so tall, so slender that he looked as if he could break. The tops of his boots were coated with ash and mud. The bottoms were clean so that he wouldn't track into the Black King's residence.

"I have found one Enchanter," Boteen said.

"Where?" Rugad still wasn't used to the rasp. He had expected his voice to be more powerful than it was.

"There is an area north of here, where the mountain range is called the Eyes of Roca. The northeastern end has some of the tallest cliffs in the world. Their stone is red, and therefore they're called the Cliffs of Blood."

Rugad knew all that. He knew the geography of Blue Isle as well as he knew the wrinkles on his skin.

"You have Seen him?"

Boteen's smile was tight. Only one Enchanter in the history of the Fey had ever had Visionary powers. Only one. And he had tried to overthrow the Black family six centuries before.

Tried, and failed.

The Black family's resources were greater than most knew. Even most Enchanters.

"I have felt him," Boteen said, that tight expression making his voice sound a bit constrained. "But more than that. I have found trails. He may be with your great-grandson, although I have my doubts. His energy mingled with that of your great-grandson on Jahn Bridge. I felt your great-grandson through the Enchanter, then mentally followed the Enchanter's trail to the Cliffs of Blood."

"But you didn't go there."

"I didn't have time. I could if you wanted me to."

Rugad shook his head. He had been meaning to send people to the Cliffs of Blood. He had been meaning to make some changes all over the Isle.

Now was the time to do so.

"You had said there was another," Rugad said. "Where is he?"

Boteen's gaze flickered onto Rugad's face, and then flicked away. "I am having trouble locating him."

"I thought Enchanters felt each other."

"They do," Boteen said, "up to a point. I knew there were two others on the Isle. I just didn't know where. Now I have found one."

"But not the other." Rugad ignored the pain in his voice. This was more important.

"Not the other," Boteen said.

"Then how do you know you have the right one?"

Boteen opened his mouth, closed it, then sighed. Not many people could read the emotions that flitted across his face, but Rugad could. Boteen took a deep breath. "Actually, I don't."

Rugad felt his shoulders slump. He had been hoping that Boteen was right. He didn't like hearing the doubt that Boteen expressed.

"There are some . . . strange things . . . about this Enchanter," Boteen said.

"Strange?" Rugad clasped his hands behind his back. He could listen more attentively this way. He could also ignore the discomfort in his throat.

"He hates Fey, and yet he has contact with your great-grandson."

"And you think they are together?" Rugad asked.

"I don't know if they're together," Boteen said. "I think it unlikely, and yet there is a possibility."

"Why?"

"They had contact on the bridge across the river the night that Flurry told their King of our arrival. That is the night your great-grandson left town."

"So you believe they left together."

"I do not know. The Enchanter nearly died that night, but someone took him away."

"Flurry did not report seeing my great-grandson with anyone injured."

"But Flurry would not have been looking at Islanders."

"He would have reported it if my great-grandson was with one."

"Perhaps."

"Why would an Islander Enchanter who hates Fey ally himself with my great-grandson? Why would he kill for him?"

"He killed Fey for him," Boteen said softly.

Rugad's hand went to his throat. Suddenly the pain was back, sharp and strong. The girl had also shown a willingness to kill Fey. Did their father have more of an influence on the boy than Rugad thought?

Rugad swallowed, remembering the relaxation techniques the healer had described for him. The pain subsided slightly. "I thought he was raised by Fey."

"Failures," Boteen said. "Who knows what they taught him to do when real Fey arrived."

Boteen had a point. But it wasn't good enough.

"I want you to find this second Enchanter," Rugad said. "I will send some of my people to the Cliffs of Blood. We will know if they have seen other Fey, since none of my troops have gone there before, and neither, so far as I know, had Rugar's."

Boteen bowed his head. "I am not certain I can do that," he said softly.

Boteen had never told him that he couldn't do the work before. "You must," Rugad said.

"This second Enchanter, he's shielded. He has been since we arrived. It is as if he felt me, and then made certain I couldn't find him."

An image flashed through Rugad's mind. It wasn't quite a Vision—more of a memory—and not a visual one. It was the way the Link felt when he was shoved out of his great-grandson's mind.

"If that is the case, the Enchanter you found has nothing to do with my great-grandson," Rugad said. "But it wouldn't hurt to find him anyway."

"What makes you suspect that?" Boteen asked. His voice was soft. He wasn't defensive, merely curious. "If I know, perhaps I can find him better."

"I met my great-grandson's protector," Rugad said. "Not directly, but when I had found Gift's mind, I encountered an angry force that shoved me back, then locked the door after me. I could travel along that Link again, but I was sealed out of Gift's mind. An Enchanter who does that would shield his trail."

"These Enchanters are not trained as Fey are trained," Boteen said. "You cannot make these assumptions."

"And you cannot assume that because they have different training, it is inferior," Rugad said. "My son's mistake here was that he underestimated these people. We will not. You will continue to search for the second Enchanter. I will send a team to the Cliffs of Blood."

"You'll need me to go as well," Boteen said.

Rugad stared at him.

Boteen shrugged. "I am the only one who can follow that trail," he said. "There are only three Enchanters on this Isle, and two of them are not Fey. No one else can read those trails."

Rugad sighed. Boteen was not entirely correct. Visionaries could be trained to read those trails. But Rugad didn't have the time or the inclination to travel across the northern half of Blue Isle. He had more pressing matters.

He sighed. "You will go on this mission," he said, "but you will not lead it. You will have a different agenda than the others. You do not want the Islanders to notice you. And you will follow the trails. Let the others do their work."

Boteen's eyes narrowed. He knew that Rugad did not make idle threats, but he clearly didn't know what Rugad was planning. "When do we leave?"

"As soon as I assemble the team," Rugad said. "I will contact you."

Boteen nodded, then started for the door. He stopped before opening it. "Rugad," he said, "if you are wrong, and I am right about which Enchanter protects your great-grandson, the boy might be in danger."

"I touched the essence of that Enchanter," Rugad said. "He loves my great-grandson, perhaps a bit too much."

"I hope you're right," Boteen said, and left.

Rugad knew he was right. But what Boteen didn't seem to understand was that sometimes love was as dangerous as hate.

THIRTY-TWO

SCAVENGER was standing on the marble stairs. He didn't like this place. It was warm when a mountain cave this high should be cold. It was bright when a cave with no openings should be dark. It was filled with the weapons from the Islanders' religion when it was clear no one had been here in centuries.

And now Gift was standing on the main floor, not moving, eyes glazed, and the last word he had said was "Mother."

Mother.

Both of his mothers were dead. His real mother had died fifteen years before. His other mother, Niche, had died only a few weeks ago, when Rugad had killed the rest of the Failures.

Leen was running down the remaining stairs. Scavenger started after her.

He grabbed her arm, and stopped her just before she reached Gift.

"Let me go," she snapped.

"No," he said. "It could be an enchantment."

"Here?" she asked. "From what?"

Scavenger looked around. In addition to the swords and chalices, there were bowls and tapestries hanging on back walls. A whole wall of vials glistened. Vials that held the holy poison.

Scavenger swallowed hard. Light flooded the place, and the marble floor extended as far as the eye could see. Beyond the fountain were stairs, and beside them, two corridors that continued a long way. He suspected there were caverns off those corridors, and something more up the stairs, all containing more paraphernalia from the Islanders' religion.

He shuddered.

"Scavenger?" she asked.

"This has something to do with their religion. And the water from their religion kills Fey. Imagine what the other parts of it might do. Something could have ensnared him when he walked in."

"But we're Fey," she said.

"You haven't come into your magick yet," he said. "And I don't have any."

"Oh." She glanced at Gift. So did Scavenger. The boy had taken a step back. His eyes were still glazed, though, as if he couldn't see what was right in front of him.

"What are you doing here?" he asked suddenly. But he wasn't addressing them. He was addressing the air.

"Maybe it's a Vision," Leen said, taking a step back herself so that she wouldn't touch him.

"Was his last Vision like that?" Scavenger asked, even though he knew the answer. Gift was like other Visionaries. He fell to the ground. He drooled. He writhed, sometimes in pain, and moaned. He didn't talk in complete sentences. Visionaries didn't act like people in a L'Nacin pretend story. They had what seemed like fits.

"No," she said softly. "It wasn't."

"You're not real," Gift said and reached out a hand. It stopped, fingers moving, as if he were touching something.

"See?" Leen asked. "He thinks he's looking at someone. Let me get him."

"No." Scavenger kept his grip on her.

"If someone were truly there, we'd see it," she said.

"Not necessarily," Scavenger said. "His brain is different from ours, and so are his talents."

"But if you're right about the religion, we have to get him out of here," Leen said.

Scavenger's mouth was dry. She had a point. She had a very valid point. But he wasn't sure what to do about it. In all his years, with all the magick he'd studied, he never heard of anything like this.

Had he?

Something niggled at the edge of his mind, but he couldn't remember it.

"Let me think," he said. "Let me think."

But the harder he concentrated, the farther away the feeling got. It was as if the feeling were a child who was scampering just out of reach.

"Maybe," Leen said, "he really sees something."

Her words broke his concentration. "I have no doubt he sees something," Scavenger snapped.

"No," she said, speaking quickly as if she were trying to placate him. "I mean, maybe something's really there."

"That's what I've been saying," Scavenger said. "Maybe something is."

"But maybe it has nothing to do with Fey magick," she said.

Scavenger froze. He hadn't considered that.

"I mean," she continued, "we are in a place where the Islanders' religion is. Gift is part Islander. Maybe this is something only Islanders see."

A chill ran down Scavenger's spine. When Scavenger had moved to Adrian's farm, he had learned as much as he could about the Islander religion. Knowledge, after all, was a protector. It would save him.

He had always believed that.

Gift wasn't just part Islander. He had the blood of their religious leader in his veins. The founder of the religion, the one that the Rocaanists called the Roca. The royal family was part of an unbroken line back to that man—centuries back. The amount of the Roca's blood running through his veins had to be small, but every Fey knew that blood told.

Blood told.

"This might be a religious vision," he said.

"Yes," Leen said, as if he were agreeing with her. He was actually just speaking aloud.

"Or it might be a warning," he said.

"A warning?"

"The cave is not well guarded. Why hasn't anyone come here in all this time? Because they knew what lay within?"

He glanced around at all the undisturbed wealth. If Fey had found this place, they would have plundered it. They would have sent the stones into the Empire, used the swords as weapons, and melted the chalices.

But the Islanders held the articles of their religion in high esteem. Even people who questioned the religion, like Adrian, respected the others who believed. Theft of these objects might be such a taboo that no one would even think of it.

"I don't understand," Gift said. "Why hasn't anyone explained this to me before?"

He sounded as if he were having a rational conversation. The hair on the back of Scavenger's neck rose. He didn't know what to do. For the first time since he'd learned all the Fey magick systems, he had run into a situation that he didn't recognize. He wasn't sure if they could tamper with it without hurting Gift, and he wasn't sure if they could leave him in the throes of whatever it was without hurting him as well.

Scavenger hated this feeling.

"Maybe one of us should go get Coulter," Leen said.

"What could he do?" Scavenger asked. He hadn't taken his gaze from Gift. Gift's arm dropped to his side, and he frowned, as if he were listening intently—to someone in front of him.

"Coulter's got Islander magick. He might know—"

"Coulter knows as much as I do. He was raised by the Fey until he was a small boy, and then Adrian taught him, alongside me. His magick comes from the Fey upbringing."

"If that were true," Leen said softly, "then you would be magick too. There's a wild magick here. You know it as well as I do."

He knew it. He knew it well. He just didn't like to admit it. Admitting it meant two things: It meant that he could never come into his own magick, and it meant that there was an entire magick system out there that he didn't understand—maybe that no one understood.

As much as he liked to pretend that he had accepted the fact he would never have magick, he hadn't. He figured that he would get it somehow, and Coulter had given him hope. If an Islander boy could have it, then Scavenger could, too.

Part of him knew that was wishful thinking. Part of him didn't care.

But the second thing, the second thing scared him.

It had taken him decades to learn all about Fey magick. Fey magick, in the hands of the inexperienced, could sometimes be deadly. And it could certainly be unpredictable.

To have a wild magick, or a magick system that no one

understood—well, that meant that the system was dangerous just by its very existence.

"Maybe we should shake him free," Scavenger said. He let go of Leen's arm. She glanced at him, her long face filled with uncertainty.

Then she reached out and slowly touched Gift.

He turned and glared at her with such ferocity that Scavenger's hand went, unbidden, to his knife.

"I'm fine," Gift said. "Now let me be."

"But—" Scavenger started.

"There's nothing in front of you," Leen said.

"You don't know that," Gift said.

"We can't see anything," Leen said.

"I heard you earlier." Gift sighed. He held up a single finger in front of him, as if he were asking someone to wait. "I'm all right," he continued, this time more gently, as if his words could calm them. "There's no need to send for Coulter. He'll be here soon enough. Why don't you two explore a little? But be careful of the items on the walls."

"And you'll keep talking to the air?" Scavenger asked.

"I'm not talking to the air," Gift said.

"Then who are you talking to?" Scavenger asked.

A look flickered across Gift's face, passing so quickly that Scavenger couldn't quite identify it. It felt like guilt, though, as if Gift were lying.

"I'm not certain," Gift said. "I'll tell you as soon as I find out."

"Be careful," Leen said. "You don't know what kind of place this is."

"I have a pretty good idea," Gift said, and turned away from them, smiling at his invisible companion as if in apology.

Scavenger watched him for a moment. Gift didn't say anything. He appeared to be listening.

"I don't like this," Scavenger said loudly, knowing Gift could hear him.

"You're not supposed to like it," Leen said.

"We're supposed to protect him," Scavenger said.

"And we are," Leen said. "We just don't know what we're protecting him from."

But Scavenger knew. Gift would look like that if he were talking to a Wisp in its small form, or if he were conversing with a Spy that had blended in. Islanders would see what Scavenger was seeing now.

Nothing.

Only Scavenger wasn't an Islander. He was Fey. He knew that magick took many forms.

He just didn't recognize this one.

And that frightened him.

THIRTY-THREE

CON gripped his sword tightly, but he felt completely overwhelmed. How, even with a powerful weapon like this one, could he defeat all those Fey?

The Fey filled the corridor, going all the way back to the entrance. They brushed against the soot-blackened walls, and had pushed aside the bodies of the dead.

"So you are the Black King's great-grandson," said the Fey woman nearest Sebastian. She was older than most Fey Con had seen, with a streak of white layering her black hair.

"No . . ." Sebastian said.

Con started down the pile. He'd fought off a number of Fey before with it. But never an army.

Never an army.

"The Black King wants to meet you," the woman said.

Sebastian stepped backward, into the pile, and the entire thing swayed. Con stopped, grabbed on, looking for a place to jump. He couldn't land wrong, though. He didn't dare lose the sword or hurt himself.

"Run . . . , Con." Sebastian shouted. "Run!"

"No," Con said, holding out the sword. "You won't take him as long as I'm here."

The swaying nearly stopped. Then Sebastian hit the pile again. Con suddenly realized Sebastian was doing that purposely.

But to what end?

The Fey were coming closer. Con couldn't wait for the swaying to stop. He took a step—

And the crates tumbled around him. He lost his footing, slipped, and fell backward, as crates fell in all directions. He wrapped his arms around his head, and something hit his fingers. The sword slipped from them. He heard it clatter through the crates. He could see it, cutting through the wood as if it were water.

It plunged through the bodies beneath him, disappearing into the pile of flesh.

Con saw all of that as he fell. He dropped quickly, crates scraping against him, splinters digging into his bare skin. The fall seemed to take forever, even though he knew it was only a matter of moments—

And then he landed, in soft goo and bones. Bodies. The stench covered him, and he fell into it, deep into it. His weight had broken through the rotting flesh.

Sebastian was screaming, that awful raspy sound that Con had only heard a few times before. It made his hair stand on end.

Then it ended abruptly, as if someone had placed a hand over Sebastian's mouth.

"Come on," the woman said. "Don't struggle. We won't hurt you."

"The Black King wants to see his great-grandson," a male Fey said.

Con struggled to get out of the goo. He pushed his face through and took a deep breath, nearly gagging at the stench. The crates were shattered around him, making an effective barrier between him and Sebastian.

Con couldn't reach his sword, either. He couldn't see it anymore. He wasn't sure where it was. All he knew was that he hadn't landed on it.

He shoved at the crates, trying to make them move. They were wedged pretty tight, and he was exhausted. He could barely move his arms. A pain ran through his lower back, a pain that didn't entirely feel natural.

"What about the other one?" a different woman asked.

"What about him?" the main woman said.

"Should we kill him?" And Con heard desire in her voice.

The female leader laughed. "Foot Soldiers," she said. "I thought you would have had your fill of carnage on the other side of the river."

"One can never have too much," she said primly.

"I suppose not," the first woman said, although she sounded doubtful.

"Well?" the Foot Soldier asked.

"No," the leader said. "Let him be. The Black King said he wanted to see this one right away. That's more important."

Con pushed against the crates with all his strength. They shifted, but they didn't part. He let out a little sob of air.

"No!" he screamed. "Take me!"

Maybe if they got him free, he could get the sword, and if he got the sword, he could fight them.

Someone laughed—he thought it was the woman again—and then he heard footsteps.

Walking away.

"No!" he screamed again. "Don't leave me here!"

But his voice echoed.

They had to be carrying Sebastian.

Because they were already gone.

THIRTY-FOUR

JAKIB and Denl had brought torches. Apparently Marly had given them a bit of food and some skins filled with water as well. By the time they were halfway up the mountain, Matthias was grateful for their preparation. He would have been both night-blinded and exhausted without their help.

The trails that only he could see were bright, though; they looked like fires burning through brush. The night was clear, but dark; there was no moon. The stars were faint glimmerings against the black velvet sky. The mountain loomed like a giant shadow before him.

Except for the glowing light in the center. It beckoned like a beloved room. The beckoning enticed him and made him shiver at the same time. He tried to ignore it as best he could, thinking that it was something else, something other, something that had nothing to do with the trails he followed.

He hoped.

"You cold?" Tri asked from beside him.

"No," Matthias said. Of all the discomforts he was suffering, cold was not one of them. The air had chilled since the sun went down, but the chill was expected: at least he had remembered to wear an extra sweater when he left.

"You plan to walk all night?" Tri asked.

"If that's what it takes," Matthias said.

"And what'll you do if you find them?"

Matthias didn't know the answer to that. He had no holy water with him, and it was worthless anyway. He had only his wits to fight the Fey.

And he wasn't sure he wanted to fight them at this time, anyway.

He found it interesting that Tri had asked the question. Apparently Tri's desire to warn the "tall ones" had disappeared with the sun.

Or maybe the Blooders they had seen in the center of town had chased it away.

Matthias didn't answer Tri. Instead, he kept walking, following the trails that etched themselves across the dirt path.

The trails were so odd. There were two of them, weaving back and forth across each other, burned into the ground as if they were meant to lead him forward. The panic they had raised in him when he was in Constant had faded—he wondered if some of that were caused by the town itself—but he still felt an odd prickling.

The others couldn't see the trail. Not Tri, not Jakib and Denl, not the townspeople.

Just Matthias.

Matthias had done so many things that were unusual, even impossible, and each time it bothered him.

The Fiftieth Rocaan, his predecessor, would have said that was because Matthias did not relax into God's will. The Fiftieth Rocaan had believed that Matthias had a special understanding of that will.

Matthias had discounted the Fiftieth Rocaan. Matthias's special understanding had come from his great scholarship. He had learned, in his early years in the Tabernacle, that he lacked the faith the Fiftieth Rocaan had. Many other members of the Tabernacle did as well—it was a profession more than anything else—but Matthias had respected the believers.

The Fiftieth Rocaan had been a believer.

And so had Titus, Matthias's successor.

Both of them had died at the hands of the Fey.

Matthias shivered, and looked up. The trails wound around a mountain path, illuminating it for him. They switched back and forth only a bit more, finally ending in a rock outcropping.

And as he looked at the outcropping, which was still some distance away, he felt the flicker of a presence.

He stopped. He had felt that presence before. Faintly. It had been there since just before he had become Rocaan. Only then he had felt it on the western side of Jahn, near the Daisy Stream. Soon the presence had become something he called wishful thinking, like a dream, like the shadow of a dead loved one looking over a man's shoulder.

And yet here it was on the mountainside, the mountainside where he was abandoned as a babe, so strong and clear that it seemed as if he could reach out and touch a person.

"Are ye all right, Holy Sir?" Denl asked.

Denl had stopped beside him. His torch flared brightly against the black sky. The fire almost looked unreal, as if it were drawn by one of the artists the Tabernacle used to hire.

"Yes, I am, thank you," Matthias said. The torch was distracting him from the trails. Something about them bothered him. They were different from the presence, and yet tied to it.

He shuddered again.

He couldn't go any farther without a plan.

And he wanted to go alone.

He turned to Tri. "Listen," Matthias said, "stay back here. If we do find Fey ahead, go to Constant. Tell the Wise Leaders you've found the tall ones, and tell them where."

"No," Tri said. "They're precisely the people we don't want up here. I came here to warn the tall ones to leave."

"I know," Matthias said. "And you can if the tall ones are Islander. If they're Fey, get the Wise Leaders. The Fey are more dangerous. They don't need protection. They will destroy the entire town."

"He's na makin it up," Jakib said. "They burned Jahn."

"N murdered most a the people in it," Denl said.

Tri shook his head. "You know what the Wise Ones will do. They'll come up here and murder those people."

"Yes," Matthias said. "I know."

Tri tilted his head back. "You'll murder people you've never met?"

"I've met Fey."

"But not these Fey."

"I don't know," Matthias said. "I have yet to meet a Fey who wasn't worth killing."

"Beg pardon," Denl said, "but the Holy Sir is right. Them

Fey is bloodthirsty, they is. They'll slice yer skin off soon as they'll talk to ye."

"Or capture ye alive n let one of their ghouls steal yer soul n put it in a box," Jakib said. He shuddered so visibly that the flame on his torch shimmered.

"You've all see this?" Tri asked.

"Aye," Denl said. "They've taken over mosta the Isle. They've burned Jahn. How many times do we gotta tell ye, man? They're here ta slaughter us all."

"You actually believe that," Tri said.

"No," Matthias said softly. "We know it."

He didn't like standing here. It made him feel exposed.

He turned to Tri. "Do I have to give the order to someone else?"

"I don't believe in killing," Tri said.

"What about in war?" Matthias asked.

"We're not at war," Tri said.

"Maybe Constant isn't," Matthias said, "but Blue Isle is. It's just your remoteness that's protected you all this time."

Tri took a shaky breath. Matthias didn't want to wait any longer.

"Well?" he asked. "Will you do it? Or should I send Denl?"

"They won't believe Denl," Tri said. "He travels with you."

"Then that leaves you, doesn't it?" Matthias asked.

Tri swallowed. "I guess it does."

Matthias nodded once and continued up the path. It forked sharply, and he followed it. The torches were behind him, casting his shadow along the trails. He loomed, looking even taller in the darkness than he imagined he did in person.

Or maybe the mountain was making him taller. He didn't actually know.

He could almost see the presence now. It was standing. He could sense its alarm. It felt him too.

Matthias jogged along the trail. Denl and Jakib tried to keep up with him, but the two men had shorter legs. They couldn't.

He wasn't sure he wanted them too. He wanted to see this presence alone.

The path was steep and his legs were aching with the strain. As he left the others behind, his eyes grew accustomed to the darkness. A third trail appeared, blending with the first two. It was fainter. Matthias blinked and looked up. What he had been calling an outcropping was instead a strange formation: several rock pillars topped by a flat stone ledge.

The presence was inside those pillars.

The trails Matthias was following littered the ground around the pillars. Then they continued on, upward toward the light that beckoned him.

But still he stopped just outside the rock pillars, hands shaking, breath coming in short gasps.

"I can feel you," he said. "There's no sense in hiding."

Behind him, he could hear the other three on the path. He hoped Tri would follow his orders. Tri was independent. That had been to Matthias's benefit before. He wasn't sure it was now.

Denl had come up behind Matthias, enough to create a circle of light around them.

A man stepped into the light. He was blond, round-faced, and blue-eyed.

And short.

He was very short. As short as Tri. Matthias towered over him.

The man was young, still a boy in his unlined face and his soft expression. Only those eyes made him a man. They held more sorrow than Matthias had ever seen.

The presence came from this man/boy. And with it, a sense of power like Matthias had never felt before.

"So you're the second one," the boy said.

Whatever greeting Matthias had expected, it wasn't this. "Second one?"

"I've felt you all my life," the boy said. "I thought you were Fey."

This, after the taunts in the town below, after all the reminders of the hatred around him.

"I'm not Fey," Matthias snapped.

"No," the boy said. "You're not. You're like me."

Jakib had joined them. His light mingled with Denl's. "Tis ana one else inside?" he asked.

"No," the boy and Matthias said in unison. Matthias clenched a fist. He had a sudden sense that his desire to see the boy alone had been the right one.

"Go back to Tri," Matthias said, taking the torch from Denl. "Wait for me."

"But Ho—"

"Do it," Matthias said, before Denl could use the honorific.

"Aye," Denl said.

Jakib glanced at him. "We promised Marly we'd look after ye."

"And you will," Matthias said. "Out of earshot."

"Ye know this lad?" Denl asked.

"I've been aware of him for a long time," Matthias said, and as he spoke the words he knew it was true. He had been aware of this boy every day of the boy's life, more than he had admitted to himself before. It was a natural feeling, like the feel of ground beneath him. One day the boy appeared, and Matthias felt him, like someone had just walked into a room.

"I dunna like this," Jakib said.

"You don't have to," Matthias said.

"She loves ye, ye know, If ye dunna come back—"

"I'll be back," he said, warming in spite of himself at Jakib's words. How could Marly love him? She had seen him only as an injured man, as one who needed help out of the tunnels, who, in the first days she knew him, could barely walk on his own.

"I won't hurt him," the boy said, and it felt as if he'd left off part of the sentence. *I won't hurt him—yet. I won't hurt him—ever. I won't hurt him—because he's like me.*

"If ye do, know we'll find ye," Jakib said. "We'll do the same to ye as ye do to him."

The boy nodded gravely, as if the threat meant something to him. But Matthias could feel the emotions running below the boy's surface. The boy did not believe they could harm him. And he certainly did not believe they could harm him as he could harm Matthias.

The cold surrounding Matthias grew stronger. He almost told the others not to leave. But he didn't. The boy had said too many things already—too many things that Matthias wasn't sure he wanted others to hear.

"It's all right," Matthias said. "Go."

Denl was still looking at the boy. "Ye realize this man holds the Secrets a—"

"Go," Matthias said. He knew what Denl was going to say. He was going to say that Matthias knew the Secrets of Rocaanism. That he knew how to kill Fey. But Matthias wasn't sure he wanted the boy to know that.

"Aye," Denl said. "But if ye die, we all do."

Matthias doubted that. He had seen the resiliency of his own people. But he did know that he was important to them, and to their survival against the Fey.

He had a feeling that this boy would help in that.

"I'll be all right," Matthias said.

Denl made a face, thrust the torch at him, and Matthias shook his head. He didn't want his hands full of anything. Denl waited a moment, then wedged the torch between two rocks. Then he headed back down the path.

"They protect you," the boy said, as if he found that unusual.

Matthias wasn't going to address it. He took a step closer to the boy, marveling still at how much taller he was. He could see the top of the boy's head, just as he could with other Islanders. Only this felt different.

"What do you mean we're alike?" he asked.

"You don't have to hide with me," the boy said. "Can't you feel it? I've known about you my whole life. I'll bet you've known about me."

"And the third," Matthias said softly.

"Yes," the boy said. "The third, who arrived with the Fey in this last invasion. But you're not Fey.

"No," Matthias said.

"And neither am I. Yet we have magick."

"I have no magick," Matthias snapped.

The boy smiled. His face was oddly pale in the torch light. "Of course you do," the boy said. "Otherwise I wouldn't be able to feel you."

You have a great magick, holy man.

Matthias had broken out of a Dream Rider's spell years ago, when the Fey said only the magick among them could do so. He had deflected a spell from another Fey, and killed him. He had woven a rope of blood and climbed out of the bottom of the Cardidas River.

"I have no magick," Matthias whispered.

"Sure you do," the boy said. "It's just not trained. Here. Try this."

He opened his hand and a fireball appeared in it. Then, as quickly as it appeared, it disappeared.

"I can't do that," Matthias said.

"You haven't tried."

"I can't," Matthias said.

The boy's smile widened. "Sure you can. Imagine it. Then feel it against your palm. We can create what we can imagine, you and I. Most people can't do that."

He remembered picking up the vials of holy water during

the first Fey invasion. Then flinging them at the Fey, hoping the bottles would stop them.

And they did.

They did.

But he hadn't imagined that kind of carnage.

Had he?

"Try it," the boy said.

Matthias held out his hand, palm up. He had to try this. If he didn't, he would wonder for the rest of his life. He imagined a fireball, like the one that boy had created in his hand, and then felt it against his skin. He looked down.

The ball was burning, a perfect circle of flame, red and orange and blue in the center, although cool to his touch.

He shouted and shook it away from his hand.

It fell toward the ground.

The boy snapped his fingers and the fireball flew to him. He crushed it between his palms, and the fire disappeared in a puff of smoke.

Matthias could still see the light from the flame etched against the darkness.

"When you create them," the boy said with caution in his voice. "They're real. You have to be careful of them."

"I didn't do that. You did that," Matthias said. "I can't do that."

The boy studied him a moment. "Is that how you survived all this time without believing in your own skills? Did you do that by denying your powers? Blaming someone else?"

"You did it," Matthias said, backing away.

"Then try something else," the boy said. "Something you didn't tell me about. Imagine that, and see what happens."

"No." Matthias nearly tripped on the rocks holding the torch. He gripped them for security. The torch shook, making the light waver. "What are you?"

"The Fey call me an Enchanter. I don't know what the Islander word for me is. I suspect it's lost."

"The Fey made you into this?"

"No." The boy sounded sad. "They wanted to believe that too, but they did tests. I have their magick ability and I was born before the first invasion. I'm real Islander. Just like you."

"You must be a Fey. Sometimes they can look like Islanders." Matthias remembered when one invaded the Tabernacle.

"Test me," the boy said.

"Holy water doesn't work any more." Matthias stood carefully. "You're Fey and you're trying to play with my mind."

"No," the boy said. "I'm Coulter. I'm an Islander just like you are. At some point you're going to have to believe in what you can do."

You have a great magick, holy man.

"Why are you telling me this?" Matthias asked.

"Because I've never met anyone else like me who wasn't Fey," Coulter said. "If we work together, think about what we can do. We have as much power as their most powerful people. If we use it—"

"Who are you traveling with?" Matthias asked. "Who do these lines belong to?"

To his surprise, young Coulter looked directly at the trails that Matthias had been following. "Two of my friends," Coulter said.

"How come I can see their lines and not the lines from my friends?" Matthias asked.

"You could see those if you wanted. But you have no need to. If we let ourselves see all the trails from everyone who has walked on this ground, we would go blind. So we isolate." The boy took a step closer. "Maybe you should look for your friends' trails."

Matthias shook his head. "And have you make them appear?"

"You can't blame me for all this," the boy said. "Imagine what you could do if you harness that power instead of deny it."

Matthias was shaking. "Your friends are tall. They went into Constant today and were driven out. Are your friends Fey?"

The boy swallowed. "Two of them are."

"You travel with Fey?"

"They're not what you think," the boy said. "They are running from the Black King like everyone else. He'll kill them if he finds them."

Matthias crossed his arms. "So will I, if I find them."

"You can't," the boy said. "They have nothing to do with this invasion. They're trying to stop the Black King."

"And I have only your word for it," Matthias said. "The word of a magick boy who may or may not be Fey himself."

"I'm not Fey," they boy said. "I told you. My name is Coulter. I am just like you."

"No, you're not," Matthias said. "I would never travel with Fey. Fey are evil creatures, abominations."

"Because they're magick?" the boy asked.

Matthias felt a shudder run through him.

"You deny your magick. Is that because it makes you too much like them? Does that make you an abomination?"

Demon-spawn.

"Does that make you evil?"

"I have no magick," Matthias said.

"But you do," the boy said.

"Why is it you Fey are so determined to make me one of you?" Matthias felt the killing rage rise up in him. He hadn't felt it since that night on the Jahn bridge, the night he almost died. "I am not one of you."

"And I am not Fey," the boy said.

"*You lie!*" Matthias screamed. He reached to the rocks behind him, grabbed the torch and flung it at the boy. The boy reached out with one hand and stopped the torch in midair.

"You try to kill me because I tell you the truth?" the boy asked. "You hate yourself that much?"

"I don't hate myself," Matthias said.

"You deny what you are. And when confronted with it, you get so angry, the mountain shakes. If you relax and believe me, you'll be much happier. We'll work together—"

"You don't look happy," Matthias snapped. "If you're so happy, why are you here on this mountainside alone? Did your friends abandon you up here?"

"No," the boy said. "But sometimes, with great power—" his voice broke.

"Comes great responsibility. I know," Matthias said. "Believe me, I know."

And he always felt he used that responsibility poorly as Rocaan. He had never asked for the position. He had been wrong for it. He lacked the faith. He could simply not believe in things Seen and Unseen, any more than he could believe in Islander magick.

"What do you want from me?" he asked softly. He felt as if he'd been asking that question his whole life. "Why did you lure me up here?"

"I didn't lure you," the boy said. "You came, following my friends."

"Where are they?"

The boy's smile was sad now. "I should tell you? After you just said you'd kill them?"

The torch hung between them, floating in the open air. Matthias stared at it for a moment, resisting the urge to see if it would fly back into his own hand.

"Tell them to leave here," he said. He may as well do what Tri had intended all along. "Tell them they won't get another warning."

Then he turned, with military precision, and walked back down the path, toward Denl, Jakib, and Tri. People who knew who he was.

People whose presences he couldn't feel.

THIRTY-FIVE

ADRIAN crouched behind a pile of rocks. He felt exposed, even though the darkness on the mountain was complete. He felt as if he were being watched.

The three men had come down from the hiding place, and they had come alone. Coulter, Gift, Leen, and Scavenger weren't with them. And neither was the fourth man. The tall one who appeared to be their leader.

Adrian hadn't been able to get a good glimpse of him in the dark. His companions were clearly Islanders, but the leader was tall enough to be Fey. His face was bandaged, a good disguise for Fey features.

A very good disguise.

But the man hadn't acted Fey. He had barked out orders to his men in Islander as they trudged up the mountain, and he appeared to be following a trail.

Was he one of the tall ones that the villagers were so terrified of? Was that something different yet from Fey, from Islanders? Was there a third kind of being on this Isle, one Adrian had never heard of?

He was almost ready to believe anything in this deep darkness.

He braced himself against the rock before him. His hands

were sore, and his back still ached, but these were minor inconveniences now. He had hoped for water and food, but he had known that would be an impossibility the moment he had seen those four men head up the mountain.

He had almost run into them.

He had been conducting his own ruse, pretending he was going elsewhere as he left the rock quarry, going down the mountain so that the quarry's owners didn't think Adrian was going to warn his friends.

Gift and Leen.

It seemed as if the entire town were after Gift and Leen. This fear of tall people seemed almost pathological to Adrian, and that made it all the more frightening. If he didn't understand it, he didn't know how to fight it.

And even worse, he didn't know how to warn them about it.

He shouldn't have listened to Scavenger. He shouldn't have allowed them to come to this place, so far from things he knew. He should have trusted his own instincts. In all his years on Blue Isle, he had heard nothing good about the Cliffs of Blood. In fact, the people who had left there refused to speak of it, shaking their heads and changing the subject each time it was brought up.

And now he was beginning to understand why.

The three men were crouched at the edge of the trail. They now had one torch between them. They must have left the other one with the leader, near the top.

The leader, who had to be with Coulter.

"I dunna like it," one of the men said. "He has na protection."

"Aye," another said. "But he told us ta leave."

"He did," the third said. "He seemed ta know what he was doin."

"He wasna actin like himself," the first man said. "Did ye see the look in his eye? Twas odd, I think. Ever since town."

"Since all them people yelled at him."

"I ken still hear em," the first man said. "*Begone*. The word gives me the shudders, it does."

"Twas like it had a push in it," the second man said. "Ye'd think they'd not treat one a their own that way."

"Things aren't as ye'd expect here," the third man said.

There was a pause. Adrian leaned farther forward, trying to see if they were still talking. Their faces were partially illuminated by the torch. It made their skin glow orange. They looked ordinary enough: three men, dirt covering their faces, but not so badly that he couldn't see the shape of their features. Their features were round, almost fat, like baby faces. Islander faces. After all his years with the Fey, he'd know the difference, even in the dark. Fey faces had no softness to them at all. They were all angles and lines and anger.

"What do ye think that man wants with him?"

"Nothin," the second man said. "Twas his idea ta stay."

"It was a bad idea," the third man said. "I don't like waiting here."

"Ye dunna like it? Ye were ready a give him up from the start," the first man said.

"Denl," the second man cautioned.

"Well, tis true," this Denl said, indignation in his town. "Ye'd even sided with that mob below. Makes me wonder if ye'd ha given him up if we hadn't been there."

"You don't know me very well," the first man said.

"Aye, I dinna, and after taday, I do na."

"Denl—"

Then, from above, a voice screamed, "*You lie!*"

It wasn't a voice that Adrian was familiar with, yet it was filled with such anger, such pain, that it made him shudder. What was going on up there?

"Tis him," Denl breathed. "They have him."

"What they?" the third man said. "It's just a boy."

"I dunna care," the second man said. "I promised my sister he'd come back alive." And then he started up the path.

The others followed, arguing as they went.

A boy. It was just a boy. No "they." Just a boy.

But which boy? Gift? Coulter? Or did they mistake Scavenger for an Islander child?

It didn't matter. All three of them were important to Adrian—and important to the Isle itself.

He was running before he knew it. Those three men were scared, and scared men did not think. They acted. They might hurt whichever member of Adrian's party was above. They might even kill that person.

And if it was Gift, he couldn't protect himself. Not like Coulter could. Not even like Scavenger could.

The numbers would still be off—two against four—but Adrian's presence would level the field somewhat. And besides, those four men would never expect an attack from behind.

He was only one person, but he could be a ferocious person when one of his friends was in trouble.

Those men would see.

They would learn.

And they might even die.

THIRTY-SIX

PAUSHO clung to her hiding place in the rocks. Fyr moaned beside her. So far neither the group at the base of the trail nor the stranger behind another set of rocks had noticed her.

That was good. She had had a difficult time following the trail in the darkness. The stranger had been good; he had gone into town, then veered behind some buildings, and backtracked up a side trail. If Zak hadn't pointed the stranger out, Pausho would have missed him.

Fyr would have missed it altogether. She hadn't even seen Zak. Pausho was questioning bringing Fyr along until she realized that Fyr hadn't tired yet. There was something to be said for young legs.

The stranger had followed the first group up the mountain. She had recognized two members of that first group: Matthias and Tri. Seeing Tri made a wave of anger surge through her. How could she have been so fooled by him? How could she have missed his tie with Matthias? Matthias was a demon-spawn, tolerated only because his foster mother seemed to have a lot of townspeople in her sway, even now, after her death. But Tri had seemed so normal, so like his father, so willing to be a part of the Wise Ones.

The willingness should have tipped her off. No one who

understood what the Wise Ones did was willing to join them. No one.

She and Fyr had stopped when the stranger stopped. Matthias and his group had gone farther up the mountain, and then three members of the group had come back down. She could see their faces reflected dimly in the torchlight. Tri looked exhausted and almost frightened. The other two were not familiar to her, but they seemed agitated. She couldn't hear their conversation, but it was animated.

The stranger could hear it, though. He appeared to be listening intently.

Had Matthias discovered the tall ones?

Was he going to join them?

The very idea made a shiver run down her spine. Matthias was dangerous in ways few people understood. She wasn't even sure he understood it. Tri had no idea who he had hooked up with, and he hadn't been part of the Wise Ones enough to learn all of their ways.

Besides, he had refused to read the texts. Fool that he was, he didn't avail himself to any of the learning open to him.

She was relieved about that now. There were things no one outside the sacred circle should know. At first she had feared that Tri knew them. Then she realized that he hadn't bothered to discover them.

It was good for the Wise Ones and bad for them at the same time. She had been the only one who hadn't trusted him. She had been the one to oppose him. All the others had thought him fine.

The others would feel betrayed, and they might somehow blame her. Blame her for her animosity toward him from the beginning.

Then a voice screamed from above: "*You lie!*"

It echoed clear and pure through the mountain range. She heard rage and pain and betrayal in that voice, an anguish equivalent to the anguish she heard whenever she placed a newborn in the snow. Even newborns seemed to understand what this adult was doing to them. Even newborns recognized betrayal.

The cry made the men up front erupt into action. They ran up the path. The stranger watched for only a moment, then he too ran.

"Should we go?" Fyr asked.

"We may as well," Pausho said. But she wouldn't run. Let the three groups—the tall ones above, Tri's friends, and the stranger—have their fight before Pausho arrived. Let them kill each other.

It would make her job so much easier.

She stood slowly, and listened as she did, hoping to hear more cries from the mountainside. The silence that greeted her was somehow much more ominous.

She made her way carefully to the path. The darkness was more severe now that the torch was gone. Fyr stayed beside her, comforting in her warmth and bulk.

"What's happening, do you think?" Fyr whispered.

Pausho shook her head. She hadn't even a guess.

The path got suddenly steep. Ahead, she heard voices. The sky glowed with torchlight—more than torchlight. It was almost like a bonfire.

Her mouth went dry. Ahead she heard voices, yelling. She could barely make out the words—something about attacking the Holy Sir. Another voice rose in denial, and yet another urging someone to stop. Then four voices rose in a single scream.

She hurried up the path. When she reached the top, she saw four men standing at the edge of the path. Matthias was most visible because of his wretched height. The stranger had moved closer to them, but he had stopped as well. In front of all of them was a man whose body was on fire. Two torches floated beside him as if they were balanced in wall sconces. Even though the fire engulfed him, he didn't seem to be burning.

"Keep away," he said. "Don't touch me."

"I was leaving," Matthias said.

"Your friends were trying to kill me," the burning man said.

The stranger made his way to the group. He held out a hand. "Coulter—" he started.

A ball of fire dislodged itself from the man's hand. It flew through the air and landed in the center of the men. Flames splashed like water. One of the men—Tri? she couldn't tell with all the light and shadows—slapped a flame off his leg.

"Stay back," the burning man cautioned.

"We're leaving," Matthias said again.

Another flame ball flew off the man and landed nearer to Pausho this time.

"I'm not the one who lies," the burning man said. "You are.

You said you were leaving, but you're going to find my friends and kill them. Aren't you?"

"I didn't lie to you about that," Matthias said.

"And you tried to kill me."

"I did nothing of the sort."

"No," the burning man said. "Your friends did."

A third fireball flew through the air and landed on the path. Pausho moved to the side, near some rocks. She could feel Fyr beside her, breathing sharply. the air smelled of smoke. Tiny fires were burning on the ground.

The stranger had moved even closer. "Coulter—" he said again.

A fourth fireball erupted, nearly blinding Pausho.

"Stay back!" the burning man said.

"It's me," the stranger said. "Adrian."

"Adrian," the burning man said, and suddenly the stranger was enveloped in light. It pulled the stranger toward the burning man, then past him, and into a protected area formed by rock pillars and a flat top. The light went out as the stranger disappeared.

"Let us go," Matthias said.

"Why should I?" the burning man asked. "You lied to me. You tried to kill me, and now you're going to kill my friends."

"What is this?" Fyr whispered, and Pausho could hear terror in her voice. Pausho didn't know the answer, but Fyr's terror ignited her own. They were facing something they had never seen before. Something beyond them.

Another fireball flew past them, and landed on the steep slope of the path, tumbling down, igniting small grasses as it went.

"Stop this," Matthias said. "You'll kill us all."

"Coulter, please," the stranger said from the blackness behind the burning man. "Let them go."

On the third mention, Pausho heard the name. She shuddered.

"What is it?" Fyr whispered.

"Let them go?" the burning man asked. "So that they can join those women below and then attack us? I don't think so. They want to kill Leen and—"

"I know," the stranger said, "but this isn't the way to stop them. Let them go."

"You don't understand," the burning man said, and in his voice, Pausho heard youth.

And panic.

"If I let them go"— did she hear a sob, too?—"you don't know what I've unleashed."

Coulter. She covered her head. *Begone,* she whispered. *Begone.* There was panic in her voice as well. Fyr put a hand on her shoulder.

"That thing knows we're here," Fyr said.

"I know," Pausho said. But she knew somehow that the burning man's knowledge of her was the least of her worries. This was the thing that the Wise Ones had always feared.

And she had allowed it to happen.

Coulter.

She closed her eyes.

It was her fault.

And somehow, she had to stop it.

THIRTY-SEVEN

CON had lost all sense of time.

The world had narrowed into stench and goo and sharp wooden edges. He was scraped and bleeding, and the decay had gotten into his skin, and he had heard somewhere that such things caused rot and death. Still he pushed through the mess and the darkness, getting splinters in his hands, and having more crates tumble on him, as he tried to get out.

He had found the sword a while back, but he hadn't had enough room to use the blade. He tied it to his side and continued pushing his way out.

The catacombs were strangely silent. He had been alone a long time.

He had stopped screaming as soon as he could no longer hear their footsteps. And then he tried to imagine those Fey as he had seen them, ever so briefly, before Sebastian had pushed him out of the way.

It took him a while to figure out why Sebastian had done it. Then Sebastian's words from earlier in the day had come back to him.

Con . . . it's . . . Fey. . . . They . . . hate . . . peo-ple . . . like . . . you.

Sebastian thought he had saved Con's life. And maybe he had. Con had been preparing to use his special sword to do battle with them, to fight them as best he could, as long as he could, until he was either dead or incapacitated.

Or the Fey were gone.

And he had thought that last an unlikely possibility.

But they had taken Sebastian, and Sebastian had been his Charge.

Sebastian had been his friend.

Con shoved on a crate with all his strength, and it toppled forward, shattering when it hit the stone.

It hit the stone.

He waved his hand in front of his face and felt nothing.

Nothing at all.

Nothing blocked him any more.

He was free.

He climbed over the last few crates. The darkness in the catacombs was complete. The Fey had taken the torch with them, just as they had taken Sebastian. No light filtered down from above.

It was still night, then.

He felt as if he had been imprisoned in that mess for days, and it had only been hours.

Hours.

He was so filthy. His robe was matted against his skin. He could feel bits of wood embedded in his fingers and his arms. He had to get clean; he had never felt such a strong urge to get clean before.

But he knew that would take time.

Finally his feet touched stone. It felt cool against his skin. Cool and welcome. He took a deep breath. At least the air away from the crates wasn't quite as fetid.

But Sebastian was gone.

Con had half hoped that the Fey would have left him behind. They had moved out so quickly that he was certain Sebastian wasn't walking with them. They had to have been carrying him.

And they were going to take him to the Black King.

The leader of all Fey.

What would that monster do to an innocent like Sebastian?

Con felt along the stone, finding pieces of shattered crate, whole potatoes, turnips and carrots, and bits of cloth. He explored the entire area around the crates and even farther into the catacombs.

Nothing.

Nothing except dead bodies and ruined crates.

Not even a Fey lamp remained.

Con sat down on the stone floor, the energy that had sustained him since the Fey left dissipated. This was his darkest moment, darker even than when he learned that the Tabernacle had been destroyed. Darker than falling through the crates and being buried in the stack of wood and corpses.

He had failed his Charge. He had allowed the gentlest person he knew to be captured by the most ruthless in the entire world. The Black King would crush Sebastian with a single sentence. Perhaps the Black King already had.

"I'm sorry," Con whispered, but he wasn't certain if he was speaking to himself, to the Holy One, or to Sebastian.

He put his head in his hands. He was just a boy, when it came down to it. Ever since he found Sebastian he had felt like a grown-up, only because he was so far ahead of Sebastian in so many ways. But he was just a boy. He hadn't lived two dozen years yet, hadn't even reached the age where Auds were considered candidates for promotion. Very few Auds at his age even had a Charge. He only knew of one other: The Fifty-second Rocaan had had a Charge when he was this young. The Fifty-second Rocaan had gone into the Fey's secret hiding place with a message, without weapons and without anyone beside him.

And the Fifty-second Rocaan had come out alive.

But someone had given the Fifty-second Rocaan that Charge. Con's original Charge had been to warn King Nicholas that the Fey had invaded Jahn. Con had never achieved that Charge. The King was fleeing the palace when Con arrived. But Con had found the King's son and protected him.

Protected him until tonight, until a few hours ago, when the King's son had protected Con.

Sebastian had suspected this separation might happen. Perhaps Sebastian had been planning to give himself to the Fey ever since he felt that first "difference" in the magick. He had given Con the instructions to find his friends after all, insisting that Con repeat the instructions back.

Where are your friends?

South. . . . A . . . day's . . . walk . . . for . . . you.

What about for you?

Sebastian had never answered that question. Had he

known? What kind of magick did that half-Fey stone boy have, anyway? And would it help him in the Black King's hands?

Or would God help him? Sebastian did have the blood of the Roca in him after all.

Con bowed his head and said a small prayer for his friend, sending it with his whole heart and mind to the Holy One, hoping it would reach God's Ear.

God couldn't abandon Sebastian now. Not after he and Con had been through so much.

Could he?

The Words said that God liked an active man. Con had done what he could for Sebastian by praying, but he couldn't leave it all in God's hands. If the Words were true—and Con knew they were—then it would also be up to Con to save Sebastian.

Con had seen the palace. He had seen the Fey all over the lower floors. Sebastian was right; the Fey hated the Rocaanists. They would kill Con as quickly as they would listen to him.

He needed help, and the people in the cavern behind him wouldn't be of much use at all. Besides, the Fey had to have come from that direction. There was no other way into the catacomb.

The Fey had come from that direction.

Con shuddered.

They were probably dead in there. He was lucky to be alive. Alive, thanks to Sebastian.

He couldn't leave Sebastian in the hands of the Black King.

But he couldn't go to the palace alone.

Where are your friends?

South. . . . A . . . day's . . . walk . . . for . . . you.

A day's walk. And then time to return. Two days, minimum. Could Sebastian survive the Black King for two days?

Would the Black King kill one of his own, even one as odd as Sebastian?

Con didn't know. But he did know this: If he went alone to the palace, he would die. If he went with help, he might have a chance of survival.

And if he survived, he might be able to rescue Sebastian.

Con bowed his head one more time. He said a short prayer for Sebastian, asking God to protect him while Con brought help. He tried not to ask anything for himself. He tried not to ask forgiveness for failing his Charge.

He tried, but he could feel the emotion of it beneath the prayer. He knew he wasn't fooling God any more than he was fooling himself.

His hands were shaking. He finished the prayer, then stood. He glanced at the pile of tumbled crates. They looked like shattered toys sticking out of the mud. Like a child's sculpture gone awry.

He couldn't rebuild it. That would take even longer.

He would have to go back.

He would have to get out of the tunnels on the other side of the river.

He could only hope that the Fey were already gone from the cavern.

He couldn't fight them. He needed his wits, now more than he ever had.

"Please, God," he whispered. "Please." And he wasn't sure whether he was asking for help for himself, for Sebastian, or for both of them.

Then he knew: He was asking that he and his new friend would make it through this crisis together—alive.

THIRTY-EIGHT

"THEY will distract you," Gift's mother said, looking at the Cap and Leen. They were standing a bit farther up the stairs, watching him. Leen had her arms crossed. The Cap was frowning as if he were trying to figure something out. "Come with me where we can talk in private."

Gift hadn't moved since he told the Cap to back off. He was watching his mother—or the shade of his mother—or the image of his mother—with a deep attention to detail. Her braided hair moved when her head did. Her eyes, dark and black like any pure Fey, glistened with tears when she saw him. She had no lines on her face, and her skin had the resiliency of youth.

She had been older than that when he saw her in his Visions. And older yet when he saw her through Sebastian's eyes. He had a vague memory of her, too, a memory that was rising as he spoke to her. A memory of her face looming over his, of her voice in the next room, laughing with his real father. And then the arrival of tiny people above him, wrapping him in a blanket, cocooning him as they floated him out the window, telling him he was going home—

"Gift," she said again, as if she knew his attention was wandering. "Please, come with me."

No matter who she looked like, he knew better than to go off with her.

"They won't distract me," he said.

"They already have. And they're afraid of me. Look at that Red Cap"— she spat the word, as if she hated Red Caps. Maybe she was his mother. Maybe she really was here. "He's staring at me as if he thinks he should be able to see me."

"Why can't he?" Gift asked.

She reached out and touched his face. Her calloused fingers rubbed against his slightly pointed ears, then caressed his rounded cheeks, and finally touched his blue eyes.

"You look like your father," she said softly, in wonder, as if she couldn't believe it. "Like your father if he were Fey."

Gift stepped back so that she couldn't touch him any more. "Why can't Scavenger see you?"

The Cap looked up at the mention of his name. Leen froze too. They were watching Gift intently. Even though he had snapped at them, their presence reassured him. They wouldn't let anything harm him.

At least, not anything they could see.

"No one educated you at all, did they? My father took you to Shadowlands and gave you no education whatsoever."

That judgmental tone again. Gift wasn't sure he liked it. And he especially didn't like the implication against his adoptive parents, Niche and Wind. The very thought of their names sent pain through him.

"I was raised Fey," he said.

"But not a warrior."

Another sore spot. How was she finding all of them? "What has that to do with you?"

She smiled and tugged on her jerkin. "I preferred being a warrior. Those Visions at the end were merely confusing." Then her smile faded. "You have Visions, don't you?"

"I'm not going with you anywhere nor am I telling you anything until I know what you are," he said.

The Cap crossed his arms. Leen moved closer. Her hand remained on her knife's hilt.

Gift could see them move through the corner of his eye. And so could his mother. Her eyes flickered toward both of them, and then she smiled.

"They're so protective of you. That's good, but not necessary."

"It's becoming more and more necessary," he said. "The

longer you delay in telling me what you are, the less credence I'm going to give you."

She sighed. "You, of all Fey, should know what I am. That you do not shows a failure in your education on the part of your grandfather."

"I never spoke to him."

"That's clear," she said. "I don't know why he had to take you when he didn't treat you as befits a Black Heir."

"He didn't tell me anything," Gift said.

"And neither did the Shaman?" His mother sighed. "She should have Seen your Vision. She should have nurtured it."

Gift said nothing. He had no idea why the Shaman hadn't helped him more. He had rarely seen her when he was a boy, and when he did, she had studied him as if he were something she had never seen before.

Still, she had given him advice about a great number of things.

But only when he asked.

And he didn't ask a lot.

He wasn't going to ask what this woman before him was again. If she didn't tell him, he would take the Cap and Leen and leave this place. He would assume she was a Vision conjured by the strangeness of this cave. Or he would guess that she was a manifestation of Islander magick, something that his mixed heritage allowed him to see.

She tilted her head back. Her eyes shone, as if he had done something to make her proud. "You're stubborn, too. Of course you are. Your father and I were both stubborn. We were so stubborn that when we clashed swords neither of us wanted to give. And you don't want to give, either. You really won't come with me, will you, unless you know what I am."

"And maybe not even then."

She sighed. Then she looked up and spread her hands. A light shone across her face. He couldn't see the source of it. It bathed her, flushed her skin, made her seem even more alive. He felt another presence in it, or a thousand other presences. The cave itself grew warmer. The water in the fountain splashed higher. The swords swung on their pegs, and the chalices rattled on the shelves.

The Cap stared at the swords. Leen looked at the chalices. Those manifestations, then, were real. It appeared to be only his mother that they couldn't see.

Finally she lowered her hands. The light faded. The swords stopped swinging, and the chalices stopped rattling.

"What was that?" the Cap whispered. His voice echoed throughout the cave.

"I don't like it here, Gift," Leen said.

He ignored her. He was watching his mother. The flush still warmed her cheeks. She looked even younger yet.

"I have to break the rules for you," she said. "And I don't know what magickal demand breaking them will cause. You understand that for every deliberate change in magick, there is an equal and unpredictable change?"

He had never heard that. He raised his chin slightly. "Are you warning me?" he asked.

Leen's hand seemed to tighten on the knife.

"I have to," his mother sounded plaintive, as if she too were frightened. "To talk to you freely breaks the bonds of my form. If I don't warn you, I could do even more harm."

"And you want me to accept the risk?"

"Or to accept me without question," she said.

He stared at her. His mother. Jewel. The wife to his father, King Nicholas. The woman who was murdered the day his sister was born. The woman whose name no one spoke in his presence, except Sebastian, who had mourned her until he died.

"Accepting without question is foolish," he said.

"For that would be faith," she said. "And only Islanders believe in faith. But you are half Islander, Gift."

"I was raised Fey," he said.

That comment made her blink and move away from him. She tugged on her jerkin, then glanced around the cave, as if she were seeing it for the first time.

"Yes," she said. And he thought he heard sorrow in her voice. "You were raised Fey."

He didn't care how she felt. He wasn't even sure she really existed, and if she did exist, if she was his mother or some other manifestation, something Islander or worse, something from their religion.

"So you have to tell me."

She nodded. Once. Then appeared to take a deep breath. He didn't even know if she breathed. If she existed. All he knew was that she was invisible to the others.

The two who did not have magick.

Or Islander blood.

"I am a Mystery," she said softly.

"Obviously." He was in no mood for games.

"No, Gift," she said. She turned toward him, and her gaze met his. Her eyes were dark, intense, as if she could will him to understand. "I am a Mystery. I became one of the Mysteries. You should know what they are. And I had to consult a Power before I could tell you."

By the Mysteries, Fey sometimes said. *By the Powers.*

And to explain unusual events: *That must be one of the Mysteries,* or *That was sent by one of the Powers.*

He felt cold.

"I've never heard of this," he said.

"I have protected you since you were three," she said. "I showed you how to rebuild Shadowlands as it collapsed around you."

"I didn't see you then," he said.

"Something about this place makes me visible," she said.

"What, exactly, about this place?" he asked.

She bit her lower lip. "I cannot tell you."

"Then I cannot believe you," he said.

She shook her head. "I am restricted in what I can do. I will lose all my powers if I do too much, and it will damage you as well."

"How convenient," he said.

She ran a hand along the side of her face, as if she were checking to see if her hair remained in place. "Someone will be here shortly," she said. "Someone you know and trust. She will explain to you what this place is."

"She?" he asked. He didn't know any women that he trusted.

Except Leen.

And she was already here.

"You asked to hear me out, Gift," his mother said. "We have already touched the magick. We may as well finish what we can."

"You are a Mystery," he repeated.

The Cap looked at Gift sharply. The Cap's small face flushed, and then he looked at the air where Gift's mother was, as if he could will himself to see her.

"Yes," she said.

"Why you?" Gift asked. "Why not my real parents, Niche or Wind?"

"They weren't your real parents," she said softly.

"They raised me." He hadn't meant to yell at her. But the words came out that strong. They echoed through the cave, resounding back at him.

They (they) . . .

Raised (raised) . . .

Me (me) . . .

She nodded, her gaze not meeting his. "They did," she said.

"You didn't even know I was gone," he said.

"Oh, I did," she said. "I just didn't understand it."

The Cap had moved closer. He started to reach toward the air where Gift's mother was, and Leen grabbed his hand.

"Let them talk," Leen said.

Apparently she believed now that Gift saw something. She may even have had an inkling as to what it was.

"Small comfort," Gift said.

"You were such a bright baby," she said as if she hadn't heard him. "And then, one day, you weren't. I thought it was me. I thought I had made the wrong choice. I thought the old wisdom was wrong. It said that Fey blood mixed with non-Fey blood produced talented children. It kept the magick fresh. I thought maybe something didn't work with the Islanders."

"It worked," Gift said. All the cooing about his amazing abilities as a child. His sister's ability to Shift so easily. He still remembered her bird form flapping over him, its blue eyes beady, intent on his. She had wanted to kill him that day. She would have, too, if other Fey had not intervened.

"But I didn't know that then. I was taking such risks—" She waved a hand, as if she were speaking out of turn, as if it were inconsequential. "It was another life."

"You're beyond that now," he said, unable to contain the sarcasm.

She shook her head, as if she couldn't quite believe what she heard. "No," she said. "No. I am not done with that life yet. It is one reason I'm here."

"Oh?" he asked. "And my parents, they're done?"

"I don't know about them," she said. "I only know that I have never seen them. I know that not every Fey becomes a Mystery."

"Some become Powers?" he asked.

She put a hand on his mouth. Her fingers were cool, but not

too cool. If he hadn't known, he would have thought she was still alive.

"Do not speak lightly of things you do not know," she said.

She was apparently waiting for his agreement. When he nodded, she removed her fingers.

"Not every Fey has a Mystery, and not every Fey becomes one. Some Fey have many, and all Mysteries guard more than one Fey," she said. "A Mystery is granted its greatest love and its greatest hate. And then we get to choose another living being. I chose you."

"So I am not your greatest love," Gift said.

She smiled, as if his comment did not bother her. "Nor my greatest hate," she said.

She could be flip about it, but he was not pleased. Deep down, the fact that he was not the most important person to his mother, even though she hadn't known him, hurt.

It hurt.

"Why choose me?" he asked, and he tried to keep his voice neutral. He thought he heard vestiges of the hurt in it, but he suspected that she didn't. She wouldn't.

Because she didn't know him.

Leen heard it, though. She frowned as she looked at Gift. Her hand was still on the Cap's wrist. He seemed to be waiting, waiting for her to let go so that he could investigate what was going on.

"Because you needed me then," she said. "Because of my ignorance, you nearly died."

"You saved me?" he asked.

She shook her head. "I wasn't a Mystery yet. Your friend saved you. Watch him. He's important."

"How?"

"Just watch him," she said.

"So I needed you then." Gift said, trying to get her to continue.

"You still do." She crossed her arms as if she knew he wouldn't like what she had to say next. "The urge you felt to come here, I gave to you. I wanted you to see me. I wanted to talk to you. I needed to talk to you."

"Why?" he asked.

"Because this is a crucial time, Gift, and you need my help."

He crossed his arms. So many people had been telling him he needed help, *their* help, as if he weren't capable of doing things on his own. Coulter had helped him and had cut off Gift's Links to others, resulting in Sebastian's death.

Sebastian's death hurt the worst because it could have been prevented. That live Vision of Sebastian exploding—

Gift shook his head. "And just how do I need your help?" he asked.

"You have powers," she said, "that you've never used. No one has trained you in your Vision. No one has taught you how to be a Visionary of the Black Throne. I can do that."

"From my understanding," he said, "my mother had not reached her full powers when she was near the Black Throne. She didn't know these things either."

She smiled. The expression was small and tight and pain-filled. "You understand well. But I'm—"

"A Mystery now," he said. "All-wise, all-knowing, and yet so unable to share. Forgive me if I don't believe you. Forgive me for thinking you're too convenient."

"You need me, Gift."

"And you appear here, in this bastion of the Islanders' religion, a religion that kills Fey, to tell me that you are one of the greatest of the Fey."

"So you do know of the Mysteries."

"I was raised Fey," he said. "I *told* you that. But then, being a Mystery, you should have known it."

"I did know it," she said.

"What are you really?" he asked. "Something only Islanders can see? Some spirit that haunts this cave that attracts those most attuned to it?"

"I am what I said I am," she said.

"Oh, a Mystery, then. And you decide to appear to me now. You couldn't help me when I was three and dying, so Coulter had to do that. You couldn't help me when Shadowlands exploded—oh, wait. You said you did. Only I didn't know it. You didn't help me save my parents. You didn't save me when the Fey soldiers found us in the hayfield. Coulter had to do that again. Forgive me for not understanding what you've told me. Forgive me for believing that you want something else—"

"Gift," she said and her voice mingled with the Cap's.

Gift turned to the Cap, half afraid that she had somehow tried to speak through him.

"What?" Gift asked.

"If she is a Mystery, you need to listen," the Cap said.

Gift rolled his eyes. He couldn't help it. This had gone too far for him. "And if she isn't?"

"You'll know," the Cap said.

"Well, I don't know," Gift said. "And it's too convenient, here in this Islander cave."

"Convenient?" the Cap asked. "You were the only one who could see this place. We had to travel days to get here. This is not convenient."

"I could see it, and Coulter could see it. He is not Fey," Gift said.

"But he has magick," the woman said. "And it is equal to that of any Fey."

"And I suppose you know why that is," Gift snapped at her. "And I suppose you can't reveal it."

She didn't respond. She stared at him. "I'm here for you, Gift," she said. "And for you only."

But I thought you could help your greatest love and your greatest hate, too."

"I said we were granted them," she said. "I did not say help. I chose to help you. I could have chosen many things. I could have chosen to hinder someone. I could have chosen to observe."

"So why did you wait until now to help me?" Gift asked.

"I did not wait," she said.

He frowned. She would nearly convince him, and then she would turn everything on its head. But how could a person—or even the shade of a person—convince him that it was a Mystery? He did not know. His training had not prepared him for this.

And he knew so little of the Islanders. Most of what he knew he learned from Sebastian, who understood things imperfectly. And he could not travel across the Link anymore. He couldn't even ask Sebastian if he wanted to.

But Adrian would be coming soon. And Adrian, even though he did not practice the Islanders' religion, was raised in it. Adrian knew more about it than Sebastian would.

He would reserve judgment about this woman apparition until then. He would wait to see if Adrian could see her. Adrian would be the test. He was Islander, but he had no magick.

Adrian would help him figure this out.

She was studying Gift. He wondered if she could read his thoughts. She didn't seem to be able to, but he couldn't completely tell.

"You don't understand the nature of my intervention, do you?" she said finally, since he had not spoken. "I helped you rebuild Shadowlands. Do you think you learned in an instant what most Visionaries take years to learn?"

"I don't remember you," he said. "I was alone then."

"And who do you think got you out of Shadowlands before your great-grandfather came? You would have died there, when he killed the Failures."

"I thought Black Blood couldn't kill Black Blood."

"That's right," she said. "But accidents happen. And he didn't go with his troops into your Shadowlands. His hands would not have been on it."

"They say he came for me."

"And he might have killed you, if I hadn't gotten you out in time."

Now he knew she was lying. He had had two Visions. Two Visions so clear that they made him leave Shadowlands. He could still see them as if he had had them moments ago:

In the first, he was standing in front of a Fey he had never seen before. They appeared to be in the Islander palace, in a large room. The room had a lot of Fey guards. Behind them, the walls were covered with spears. A throne rested on a dais, but no one sat on the throne. On the wall behind it was a crest: two swords crossed over a heart.

He had never been there before, but he recognized the crest. It belonged to his father's family.

The Fey was a man with the leathered skin of a fighter. His eyes were dark and empty, his hands gnarled with age. He had the look of Gift's long-dead grandfather. He was staring at Gift, hands out, eyes bright, as if Gift were an oddity, almost a religious curiosity.

Then Gift felt a sharp shattering pain in his back. The Fey man yelled—his words blurring as his face blurred, as the room blurred, and then the Vision disappeared into darkness.

The second Vision was somehow more disturbing, even though it felt impersonal. He wasn't in his body. He floated above it, as if he were looking through a spy hole or were a spider on the ceiling. His body stood below, taller than the strange Fey man. His body was exactly the same age it was now; it belonged to a teenager, not a full-grown Fey. The man and Gift's body stood close together. Fey guards circled the room. Two guarded the door. The Fey carried no weapons, but some of them looked like Foot Soldiers, with slender, deadly knife-sharp fingers.

No one seemed to see him.

The older Fey wasn't speaking. He was examining Gift's body as if it were a precious and rare commodity. The body—and Gift—were studying the man in return.

Then someone in a hooded cloak slipped through the door. The Fey guards stepped aside, and the old man didn't see the intruder. A gloved hand holding a long knife appeared from inside the cloak, and with two quick steps, the intruder had crossed the room, and shoved the knife into the body's back.

Gift was screaming, but he couldn't get inside the body. The old man was yelling, the door was open, and the intruder was gone.

The body lay on the floor, eyes wide, blood trailing from the corner of the mouth. It coughed once, then its breath wheezed through its throat. The wheeze ended in a sigh, and all the life disappeared from the face.

Gift's face.

And then the Vision ended.

Two versions of his own death. One from inside his body—where he felt the final death-blow—and one from out. They had confused him, and so he had gone to the Shaman as she had taught him to do with difficult Visions long ago. She had looked at him with compassion.

Did you know that each Visionary sees his own death? she had asked.

He had nodded. *So this is mine?*

She had shaken her head. *Two Visions, two paths. In the second, you do not die. Someone else does.*

Sebastian did. Sebastian, good, innocent, and childlike. Sebastian, the golem who should not live and did. Sebastian, whom Gift loved like a brother. Sebastian, who had so much of Gift inside of him that Gift wasn't certain if one could survive without the other.

How do I stop it? Gift had asked.

You must change the path.

But how?

The Shaman had shrugged. *I have not seen this path. We cannot compare. The future is too murky. Everything is changing now. By next week, our lives will have a different meaning.*

He had changed the Vision. Or at least, he had changed

part of it. Sebastian had died, from a stab to the back. But it had not been by someone in a hood. It had been by Gift's great-grandfather's guards, and Sebastian had chosen to sacrifice himself, to save Nicholas.

Gift has Seen that too. He had Seen Sebastian, light pouring out of each hole in his body, just before that body shattered.

"I had a Vision," he said to his mother's apparition. "You didn't help me out of Shadowlands. I had a Vision."

She smiled at him. "Where do you think Visions come from, young Gift?"

"They are sent . . ." he said, starting to recite the catechism of a Visionary, the catechism taught him by the Shaman. But he let his voice trail off before he could finish.

"They are sent," his mother said, "by the Mysteries and the Powers."

"So you know the future."

She shook her head.

"You must, if you can send Visions," Gift said.

"The future is always changing. You should know that, too."

"But you know one version of it."

"Perhaps," she said, "and perhaps I do not."

"But you could help me. If you truly have the power you say you do, you could show me the right path," he said.

"I could," she said. "And tomorrow I could show you a different path, equally right. And the next day, I could show you yet another."

"So you won't help me."

"This is an uncertain time," she said. "You had a string of Visions only a week or so ago. It showed different futures, all coming from the same event. It was a warning, young Gift, that each action you make will have an effect right now. Each decision—"

"Even talking to you?"

"Coming here was an important choice," she said. "Accepting my help will be another."

"Why are you pressuring me?" he asked. "If what you tell me is true, you've been here my whole life. Why now? Why can't I decide tomorrow or the day after that?"

"This is the place where three points converge, Gift," she said. "Soon I may not have a choice as to what I do."

"Explain that," he said.

"I don't have to," she said. "In less than a day, you'll know."

"I want to know now," he said.

She brushed a soft hand across his cheek. Her smile was gentle. "You are my son. And Nicholas's. Neither of us had much patience. You seem to have even less."

"So what I choose now dictates your future," Gift said.

His mother shook her head. "What you choose now dictates the future of all the Fey," she said.

THIRTY-NINE

THE Shaman insisted that they walk through the dark. She had a small torch and she carried it gingerly, as if she were afraid that it would burn her fingers. It cast a very thin light on the trail.

Nicholas had never seen darkness like this, not in all his life. He had rarely gone outside of Jahn. The city always had lights. Or it had always had lights before the Black King burned it.

The thought sent a shaft of pain through his heart. One day he would learn his own limits. He would learn how many losses he could endure before his heart burst from the strain of it all. First his father, then Jewel, then Sebastian, and then his kingship, maybe even Blue Isle itself.

And still he kept moving. Still he kept trying. He wasn't always sure why.

Except for Arianna. She was ahead of him, her tall, slender frame outlined by the light of the Shaman's torch. They had walked farther down the mountainside. They were in the trees now, tall pine trees that smelled fresh. The snow was above them, but the night was cold, even here.

The mountains, the Shaman said, were always cold.

She insisted on traveling in silence. She said there were

beasts here that could hurt people. And even though she was not native to the Isle, she seemed to know.

She knew much more than he expected. But she wouldn't tell him how long it would take to reach Gift. All she said was that they had to hurry.

Nicholas was moving by rote now. He had passed exhaustion miles back. Arianna had been exhausted when they started. He didn't know what kind of energy she used to keep going. Sometimes he thought she was so far gone that she didn't even know what she was doing. If the Shaman had found the edge of a cliff and said to jump, Arianna just might without a single question asked.

He was so worried about her. She was different now. Less, somehow. The loss of Sebastian had taken something from her. It didn't seem to matter that he wasn't her blood brother. He had been more to her than that. He had been the brother of her heart.

Nicholas understood that.

Sebastian had been a child of his heart.

The pain flared through him again. He took a deep breath. As long as he felt pain, he was alive.

The trail was a narrow path that wound around trees and boulders. He could barely see it in the dark. Mostly he walked where Arianna had walked. He was thankful for the boots she had stolen for him. He was thankful for small things now.

Small things were all he had.

Small things: Arianna, and the hope of Gift.

The hope of Gift, and the equal and almost greater hope of getting the Isle back. Of giving the Isle to his children, without the Black King's interference.

Sometimes Nicholas wished he had shoved harder. He couldn't believe that the Black King had lived through that sword through the neck. Nicholas had thought that Fey were easier to kill.

Jewel had been.

At least for Matthias.

All it had taken was a touch of holy water to a cloth Matthias had placed on her head.

And then she had died.

Horribly.

He took two greater steps. If Jewel had lived, Arianna would not have. Jewel had not known how to bring a Shape-Shifter into the world, particularly one as powerful as Arianna. And no Fey would have come into the palace voluntarily at that time.

Although Nicholas had once wondered if the Shaman would have come when Jewel had her first birth pains. She had come as Jewel was dying. She might have come to save Arianna at birth.

And then again, she might not have. The Shaman was a firm believer in the way that things should go. She believed that the Fey Mysteries and Powers would make things right.

He suspected that was what forced her to lead them in this darkness, what gave her the direction to find his real son.

Gift.

He liked the name. It was so very Fey, and yet not Fey. It was, like Jewel's name, in the L'Nacin tradition. In the tradition of other peoples that the Fey had captured.

Jewel had been well named. She was his jewel. She had been from the moment he saw her, even though they were at opposite points of a blade.

And Gift was well named. He was the son that Nicholas wanted, the son that would replace the son he had lost.

At least Nicholas hoped that would be the case.

He hoped Gift would accept him.

So much depended on this son he had never met. An entire Kingdom rested on their interaction. The future of the Fey Empire as well. The Shaman was helping them because she did not want the Black King to continue his rule.

Nicholas's thoughts had run like this the entire night. As they walked, his mind had worked around and around each topic, ending, as always, with Gift. He saw nothing beyond this meeting with his son. He had no plans yet, felt he could not have any plans until he met this first child, the hope he and Jewel once had of uniting their two races.

Ahead of him, the Shaman stopped. Her hand was shaking. The light from the torch wavered across the ground. It made the world itself look as if it were moving.

"Take this, Arianna," the Shaman said. Her voice sounded thick, as if she could barely speak.

Arianna didn't move. Nicholas sprinted ahead, grabbing the torch from the Shaman. She looked at him, her button brown eyes filling with tears, and then she collapsed in a heap at his feet.

He handed the torch to Arianna and was about to pick up

the Shaman when his daughter placed her free hand on his shoulder.

"Don't," she said. "It's a Vision."

He peered at the Shaman. Her eyes were open, but unseeing. She was breathing. She looked like Ari had looked in the tower, shortly after the troops had routed the Fey.

"But you're not—"

"Visions are personal things," Arianna said. "She told me."

Nicholas crouched beside the Shaman. Her hands were clenching and unclenching, her lower body twitching as if she were trying to run. Her mouth worked. Only her eyes remained unmoving. Staring straight ahead as if they were seeing into the darkness itself.

She looked as if she were dying. He had only seen eyes that lifeless on bodies.

On Jewel.

He wanted to touch the Shaman, to wake her, to make her stop this.

"How long can this continue?" he asked Ari, although he knew her understanding of Visions was less than his.

"Until it's done," she said, and he looked up at her. Apparently the Shaman had been talking to her. And apparently Arianna had been listening.

"I don't like this," Nicholas said.

"Imagine what it's like from the inside," Ari said. Her voice was dry. She hadn't crouched beside the Shaman. She stood tall, almost as if she were a light, a column herself.

As if she didn't want to face this.

"Have you had another one?" he asked.

"No," Arianna said. "Sometimes, the Shaman said, they don't come again for years."

She didn't sound happy about it. She didn't sound happy about this ability at all. She had reveled in her ability to Shift, so much so that she had Shifted without help, without Solanda's permission, for years.

And she had done it well.

Nicholas would not be alive if his daughter hadn't disobeyed those rules almost from the beginning of her life.

The Shaman let out a deep sigh, then she slowly brought a hand to her face. Her eyes closed.

"Now?" Nicholas asked Arianna.

"If you want," Arianna said. She sounded as if she would

never help someone who had just had a Vision. Or perhaps she would never help the Shaman.

Nicholas put his arms under the Shaman's shoulders and helped her up. He cradled her against him. He had never really held her before, not like this, and he hadn't realized how frail she was. She was tall and large, like his daughter, but she lacked the firmness Arianna's young body had. She felt as if she could break if he squeezed too hard.

"Are you all right?" Nicholas asked.

"As right as I can be," the Shaman said. Her voice was shaky. She wiped the sides of her mouth with her thumb and forefinger, then sighed again.

"What was it?" Nicholas asked.

"I'm not sure," the Shaman said. "Did you See anything?"

"I don't have Vision," Nicholas said.

"I know," the Shaman said. "But sometimes there's an open Vision, especially when it's happening now or if it's really powerful—" she shook her head as if she didn't want to say any more.

"I didn't See anything," Nicholas repeated, half disappointed that he hadn't.

The Shaman looked over her shoulder at Arianna. "Did you?" she asked.

"I had no Vision," Arianna said. She sounded relieved.

"Oh, dear," the Shaman said. Then added softly, "This one's mine."

"Yours?" Nicholas asked.

"Help me up," the Shaman said. "We have to hurry. We don't have much time."

"What's happening?" Nicholas asked.

"Help me up," the Shaman said again.

He braced her against him, then lifted her slowly. Her entire body was shaking. If he didn't know better, he would think she was trying not to cry.

She moved away from him slightly and brushed off her robe. Then she took the torch back from Arianna.

"We have to keep walking," the Shaman said.

"You'll tell us what you saw as we go," Nicholas said, and it felt like an order. He'd never given the Shaman an order before.

She started down the path. She walked hunched over, and he wondered if the fall had hurt her.

"Is she all right?" Arianna whispered.

"I don't know," Nicholas said.

"*Come on,*" the Shaman said.

They hurried to catch up. Nicholas's heart was beating. He could still feel her frailness in his arms.

"What did you See?" he asked again.

The Shaman let out a small breath. "According to Fey tradition," she said, "there are three Places of Power in the world. The first is in the Eccrasian Mountains. That's where the Fey are from. It is said that a goatherder one day discovered this place and brought his family inside. When they came out, they were Fey."

She didn't look at them as she spoke. Her voice was shaking.

"How could that be?" Arianna asked.

"Just listen, child," the Shaman said. It was the closest she had ever come to yelling at Arianna.

Arianna glanced at Nicholas. In the light of the torch, he could see the fear lines on her thin face.

"I do not know how much of that early myth is true," the Shaman said, "but it is part of a Shaman's training to visit the Eccrasian Mountains, to go to the Place of Power."

"Have you been there?" Arianna asked.

Nicholas was listening closely, not yet sure why the Shaman was telling them this.

"Yes," she said. "I was only recently returned when I was assigned to Rugar's fleet. I am young, as Shamans go. Very young."

She didn't say anything for a moment. She brought her other hand up and smoothed her wild white hair. It wouldn't tame. It never had. Her movements seemed odd, jerky, slow. As if something in the Vision had disturbed her greatly.

"What did you See?" Nicholas asked again.

"Nicholas, please, let me tell this as I can," the Shaman said. "There isn't much time."

"You've said that before." Arianna's voice rose slightly. "What's going to happen?"

"It's not Black Blood against Black Blood, is it?" Nicholas asked. She had had a Vision like that, shortly after Arianna had had her series of Visions. The Shaman had told him of that one. It had terrified her so.

"Nothing so vast as that," she said, "at least I don't think so."

She let her hand drop.

"Although I might want it to be that way," she said, and then smiled at them over her shoulder. It was a sad smile.

"You'd want total destruction?" Arianna asked.

"No," the Shaman said. "I'd want this Vision to be as important as the one about Black Blood. But it is not. I know it is not."

"Then you can tell us," Nicholas said.

"There is no point in telling all of it," the Shaman said. "And there is much I have to sort out. But you need to know part of it."

The trail widened. They were keeping a good clip, maybe even faster than the pace they had walked earlier. Arianna seemed to be doing fine. She seemed to be better than she had before the Shaman's Vision. Perhaps keeping her mind on the Shaman's problem was keeping Arianna from concentrating on her own.

Perhaps they shouldn't have been walking in silence. Perhaps Nicholas should have been trying to talk with his daughter, to ease her pain, at least little.

"Fey mythology says there are three Places of Power," the Shaman said. "Three. We have only discovered one, and that was in the Eccrasian Mountains. Some say that the Fey's thirst for conquest is merely a cover for the search for the other two Places of Power."

"I thought it was to bring fresh blood into the Fey lines," Nicholas said.

"It is that," the Shaman said. "It is clearly that, and has been since the first Fey mated with a non-Fey. But the Places of Power have been a driving force in the Fey from the start."

"Then why didn't Jewel say anything to me?" Nicholas asked.

"So many Fey believe the other two Places of Power to be myth. If they were more than that, then there would be other races like the Fey, attempting to conquer the entire world, right?" The Shaman's question needed no answer.

But Arianna spoke up anyway. "Not if the races were different," she said.

"Races aren't that different, child," the Shaman said softly. "If they were, we wouldn't have so much in common, any of us. I have traveled half the world, and I've seen a lot of differences, but not the kind that you talk of."

"This has something to do with your Vision, though," Nicholas said. "The Places of Power."

"Yes," the Shaman said. "This morning, I Saw a Place of Power. I Saw—"

She shook her head, as if she didn't want to finish.

"You Saw?" Nicholas prompted.

She glanced at him, and he got the distinct impression that she wasn't going to finish the sentence, at least not in the way she had been planning to before.

"Your son has found a Place of Power," the Shaman said.

"Gift?" Nicholas said.

"If he hasn't already found it, he will before we arrive. But it's in the Cliffs of Blood. Did you know of it?"

A Place of Power in the Cliffs of Blood? Nicholas had never been there. He had heard that the people there were headstrong. He had even met the Wise Ones on occasion and found them to be a bit off. Their beliefs were ancient. The Tabernacle hated them, and thought them to be a weird sect of Rocaanism. Several generations earlier, the Tabernacle had petitioned the palace to rid the Cliffs of Blood of the "blasphemers," but it had never happened. The Wise Ones never left their small towns, and only the most adventurous Auds traveled there. The Cliffs of Blood remained, as did many of the remote sections of Blue Isle, entities in and of themselves.

"No," Nicholas said. "I've never heard of one."

"Are you certain?" the Shaman asked.

"The Roca was from there," Arianna said. "Right, Daddy?"

Nicholas frowned at his daughter. He had given her rudimentary training in Rocaanism, but had not done much more. He figured he owed her that much, since she had the Roca's blood in her veins. She needed to know a bit about the religion to rule the Isle. But, knowing Arianna, she had probably done more study on her own.

The thought sent a shiver of fear through him. Learning about Rocaanism could have been deadly for her.

"That's hard to answer, sweetheart," he said. "There are many legends that say the Roca was from the Cliffs of Blood. But there are others that say he was from the Snow Mountains, and still more that say he was from the Kenniland Marshes. Every region of Blue Isle wanted to claim him."

"Except Jahn," Arianna said.

"It was the Roca's sons that built Jahn," Nicholas said. "The city did not exist until well after his Absorption."

"Legends have a basis in truth," the Shaman said.

"I know," Nicholas said. "But with the Roca it's hard to know what's true and what's not. So many places claimed him that I often wonder if he weren't more than one person."

The Shaman was quiet. She kept her head bowed. He had learned over the years that her silences spoke louder than her words.

"You think this Place of Power is important."

"I know it is," she said.

"You think it has something to do with the Roca."

"I think," she said slowly, "that it has something to do with the wild magick on the Isle. The magick we could never account for."

"The Fey got their magick from the Place of Power," Arianna said. "You think I did too?"

"She's never left my sight," Nicholas said. "You know that."

"I do," the Shaman said. "I also know that two types of blood flow through her veins. Black Blood—the most potent of all Fey blood—and the Blood of your Roca. I think the power of your children is no coincidence, Nicholas. I think it is the logical extension of the merging of two peoples who come from Places of Power."

"If there is such a place here, I should know of it," Nicholas said.

"Perhaps," the Shaman said. "I think it is typical Fey arrogance that says because there are no other races like the Fey, therefore the legend of the three Places of Power is false."

"This Place of Power on the Isle, you don't think it was just created, do you?" Arianna asked.

The Shaman looked at her sharply, dark eyes intense, then she turned her attention back to the trail. It was still wider, as if it were used more. That made Nicholas nervous.

"Fey mythology says that the Places of Power are as old as time itself, child," the Shaman said. "The Place of Power came first. Then the Fey discovered theirs."

"If there is no other Place of Power between the Eccrasian Mountains and Blue Isle," Nicholas said, "then how do the Fey know there are three of them?"

"Magick is pure in the Place of Power," the Shaman said. "And questions can be answered, for a price."

"What does that mean?" Arianna asked.

"It means," Nicholas said. "Someone asked if there were others and discovered that there were two more. But not their locations, I gather."

"The locations were mentioned," the Shaman said. "The legend says this: 'There are three Points of Power. Link through them, and the Triangle of Might will reform the world.' "

"That doesn't mean anything to me," Arianna said.

"But it does mean something," Nicholas said. "It means that the Places of Power are points, and if you connect them somehow, you have a triangle. If you find two, you should be able to find the third."

"Yes," the Shaman said. She made her way around a boulder that had fallen in the middle of the path. "And there's more than that. It is part of the Fey legacy. The word 'Link' is crucial."

"This is what Sebastian was upset about, isn't it," Nicholas asked. "He said he lost his Link with Gift."

"He said it was broken," Arianna said softly.

"We are all Linked," the Shaman said. "You, Nicholas, are Linked with Arianna. I can See that Link if I try. It hums between you, a multicolored thread. Visionaries can not only see the Links; they can travel across them. If I could find a way to penetrate your Link, I would be able to go from you to Arianna."

Nicholas nodded. He had understood this before, only less perfectly. The Shaman was good at explaining Fey concepts. He had relied on her more than once.

"Penetrating the Link is the key. It is more difficult than it sounds," the Shaman said. "Just because I can See your Link does not mean that I can travel it. I need a point of entry, a way to get through to you."

Another boulder was in the middle of the path. Nicholas walked around it. He put out a hand and then scraped a shin against a rock he couldn't see. The darkness was still full. Dawn was only a figment of his imagination. He wondered, vaguely, how long this night would last.

"And these Links are what this legend talks about?" Nicholas asked.

"Yes," the Shaman said. "It is why Visionaries search, and why there is always a Fey Shaman at the original Place of Power. If the second place is discovered, the Fey plan to Link the Shaman with a Shaman in the second Place of Power. If the third is discovered, all three Shamans will Link, and then we will have the Triangle of Might."

"Which is?" Arianna asked. She sounded calm, as if this meant nothing to her. Perhaps it did. But it meant something to Nicholas. No wonder the Shaman had wanted the Black King out of the picture. If the Fey had a way of becoming even stronger than they were, of dominating even more than they did, it would be better for the entire world if the Fey were not so bloodthirsty, if instead they had some compassion.

"We don't know what the Triangle is, child," the Shaman said. "We only know that these things are usually well named. Places of Power are that. And 'Might' is a pretty inclusive term."

Nicholas shuddered. He grabbed onto a tree as the path veered to the left and started down again. He wished the darkness would ease, even slightly.

"I'm sorry," he said. "I can't believe that the Black Family would allow Shamans to control the Triangle of Might."

The Shaman glanced at him, and on her wizened face, he saw traces of a smile. "I like you, Nicholas," she said. "Nothing gets past you."

"What?" Arianna asked. She sounded irritated. "What does my dad see that I don't?"

"It is not by order of the Black Throne that the Shamans keep one of their number in the Place of Power," the Shaman said. "It is Shamanic decree. Fey magick is split, as Nicholas knows, between Domestic magick and Warrior magick. The Black Throne specializes in Warrior magick. It has little respect for Domestic magick."

"Why?" Arianna asked.

"Because Domestic magick is quiet," the Shaman said. "And because it has respect for all things. Warrior magick does not. It dominates all things."

"Are you saying that because I'm of Black Blood I have Warrior magick? I'm a Visionary, same as you."

"No," the Shaman said. "You are not the same as me. Your Vision is different, darker, and your magick has the potential for greater power. There is no calmness in you, Arianna. If you were to come to the Shamans with your Vision and ask for a position among us, we would turn you down."

"Because of my Black Blood," she said, head down. Nicholas

wanted to put an arm around her, but the trail was not yet wide enough for them to walk side by side.

"Because of your ferocity. I do not know if that is entirely a product of Black Blood. I think, at times, it might be a product of your Shifting. I have never known a passive Shifter."

"What about my brother?" Arianna asked. Nicholas heard the venom in her voice. She had decided long ago to hate her brother. The fact that they were traveling to see him seemed to make that feeling stronger. "Would you let him become a Shaman?"

"He is one of the gentler creatures of Black Blood I have ever met," the Shaman said. "He reminds me of your father, Nicholas. He is an unwilling participant in all of this."

"Is that a yes?" Arianna asked.

"That is conditional," the Shaman said. "He is the first member of the Black Throne I have ever met who has this feature. I am concerned about it, frankly. I worry that he is not strong enough for the tasks ahead."

"Yet you dislike those features in those of us with Black Blood. You do not trust us in the Places of Power."

Nicholas shuddered. He wasn't sure he liked to hear his daughter identify herself as someone with Black Blood. She was his. She had been raised an Islander. And she was. A special one.

With wild magick.

"I did not say that," the Shaman said. "We do not trust you with the Triangle of Might."

"Why would Shamans be better?"

"We might not be," the Shaman said.

"But you say my son has found the Place of Power," Nicholas said, wanting them to end this discussion. "Does that mean you know where it is?"

"I will be able to find him," the Shaman said. "We have a small Link. I can trace him through it."

"And somehow this discovery has disturbed you?"

"Oh," she said, and then she sighed. "It is not the discovery that disturbs me. It is the Vision."

"What did you See?" Nicholas asked again.

"It pertains only to me, Nicholas," she said.

"You Saw your death," he said, and that pain in his heart, the one that had been there since Jewel died, the one that had been growing steadily since, expanded again.

"I have Seen my death many times," she said. "Each time, it has been averted."

"You didn't answer me directly," Nicholas said.

"The future is always in flux," she said.

"Tell me," he said. "I'll help you avoid it."

She stopped. Arianna almost walked into her. The Shaman turned around so that she could face him.

She put her hand on his arm. "Nicholas," she said. "You cannot stop this. There are greater forces at work here than our friendship."

"Our friendship has benefited both the Fey and the Islanders," he said.

"And so it will continue," she said. "But promise me that you will remember this. Promise me that you will always remember the larger picture."

"I won't allow you to die," he said.

"My death is my choice," she said. "Just remember that when I do die, I will do so to help make things right. Think on this conversation. It will be hard for you."

"Your death is not something I want to face," Nicholas said softly.

"It is not my death that will be hard," she said and squeezed his arm. "It is the life that lives in my stead that you will object to."

"And whose life is that?" Nicholas asked.

"You will see soon enough," she said as she turned away from him, and headed down the path.

FORTY

MATTHIAS stared at the burning boy. He could feel the boy's fear—or was it his own? He wasn't certain. The boy was arguing with the man he had pulled closer to him, a man whose presence Matthias hadn't even been aware of.

Things wouldn't have gotten so out of hand if Denl, Jakib, and Tri hadn't come up here, knives drawn, to attack the boy. They had thought somehow that Matthias was in danger. They had gotten within a few feet of the boy and he had turned into a fireball. Matthias had tried to calm him and to leave, and the boy had gotten even angrier.

He was protecting Fey.

Matthias shuddered.

The boy burned brightly against the dark night. The fireballs were smoldering on the mountainside—fortunately, there wasn't much grass—and the air smelled of smoke.

"If you don't want us to leave," Matthias said, "you have to tell us what to do."

He wasn't sure he wanted to give the boy that much power, but it didn't really matter. The boy might ask him to work with him again, and Matthias would refuse. He didn't like this meeting, didn't like this boy, didn't like the fear that rolled through the air like waves.

Another fireball launched. Matthias ducked as it whistled overhead. It landed behind him with a thump.

"Coulter!" the new Islander said. "Stop."

But he couldn't stop. Matthias knew that. The fireballs were out of his control. They seemed to be coming from his fear.

"What do you want us to do?" Matthias asked again.

"Leave my friends alone."

"Fer godsakes, Holy Sir," Denl whispered, "Promise ye'll do that."

"All right," Matthias said.

"And don't lie!" the boy shouted.

"I'm not," Matthias said, even though he was.

Another fireball shot through the air, this one coming directly toward him. Denl and Jakib jumped away. Tri crouched, his hands over his head.

Matthias had had enough. He stood as tall as he could, and he held up a hand. The fireball hit a spot about three feet from his hand and bounced back toward the burning boy. The boy caught the ball and extinguished it.

"Stop this now," Matthias said. "This has gone on long enough."

The boy shot another fireball at Matthias. This one didn't feel out of control. It felt deliberate, as if the boy were aiming at him. Matthias kept his hand up, and the ball bounced against the unseen barrier, flaring against it for a moment. It was almost as if it had hit glass.

Like the opaque wall that had formed inches from his hand in the cell with Burden, all those years ago. The opaque wall that acted as a shield, that had protected him from Fey attacks—

Matthias brought his hand down. His heart was pounding, and not from the fireball attack.

—The Fey call me an Enchanter. I don't know what the Islander word for me is. I suspect it's lost.

—You have a great magick, holy man.

—Someday you're going to have to believe in what you can do.

—If a person squints, he can see magick energy flickering off another person. It crackles off you.

—I have their magick ability and I was born before the first Invasion. I'm real Islander. Just like you.

—You have a great magick, holy man.

—I'm a real Islander. Just like you.

—Just

—like

—you.

"This is a trick," Matthias said. His voice echoed throughout the area. "You're doing this so that I feel like I'm like you. You're trying to make me into something I'm not."

The fears he felt, the changes, were all an act.

The burning boy flared out. The torches beside him fell to the ground and were extinguished. The small flames from the fireballs still burned, but the light in the area dimmed greatly. Red and green colors danced in front of Matthias's eyes. He could still see a reflection of the burning boy's flame, although it didn't exist.

"It worked, too," the boy said. "You defended yourself. And it seems like you've done that before."

The man beside him glanced at him in surprise. Tri brought his arms down. Denl and Jakib sat up. There was movement beside Matthias, barely within the range of his peripheral vision. Two women stood up. They looked familiar, but he didn't have time to figure out who they were.

"You did this," Matthias said. He was shaking.

"I did the fires, yes. But you defended. I aimed for you or your friends every time."

"You have bad aim, Fey."

"I'm not Fey," the boy said.

"He's not," the Islander man behind the boy said. "He was born before the Fey invasion."

"I need to take the word of two Islanders I've never met before."

"No." That was a woman's voice. It shook. Matthias turned. It was one of the Wise Ones. Her face was half in shadow. The flames from the fireball beside her cast a golden light on her right side only.

Pausho.

"That boy is a Coulter. His father is one of the survivors of the mountain. Like you, Matthias."

Her words made him cold. He clenched his fists, and they grew warm. He looked down. Small tongues of flame flickered between his fingers.

"Stop that!" he shouted at the boy.

"I'm doing nothing," the boy said. "The magick is trying to break free. I wonder how many times it has, over the years. I wonder how much damage you've done by not letting it go."

Matthias unclenched his fists, and the flames faded. The smell of smoke was giving him a headache. Tri hadn't gotten up. Denl and Jakib were still sitting in their places, watching him.

The boy was clever, he'd give him that. Making it seem as if Matthias had magick, like the Fey. The Fey knew in some inexplicable way how crazy that made him.

"You're his father?" Matthias asked the stranger beside the boy.

"No," the man said. "Not his real one. We've sort of adopted each other."

"I don't have a real father," the boy snapped.

"But you did," Pausho said, "if your name is Coulter. It's a family name. It comes from here. Your father left here as a young man, saying he'd never return. That was twenty-some years ago. Shortly before you were born, I'd guess."

"I don't have a real father," the boy said. He sounded uncertain now.

"But you did." His friend spoke softly. "Remember Solanda. She told you how she found you."

"She kidnapped me," the boy said, his voice crackling with anger.

"Yes, she did," his friend said, "but the old woman wasn't your mother. She had adopted you, remember? From a couple that was murdered by the Fey. She kept your name for you. It was Coulter. Like your father's. You told me that. Remember?"

"No," the boy said.

Matthias didn't like the way this was going. It felt like a show put on for him. How did that boy know he was coming? How did the boy know that Matthias had created such barriers before? What kind of system did the Fey have and why were they after him?

"You can stop," Matthias said. "You will never convince me that I'm like the Fey."

"I'm not trying to convince you," Pausho said. "I simply know the name Coulter. I remember bringing the boy up here."

"What does that mean?" the boy asked. "'Bringing him up here'?"

"They kill babies," Matthias said, "If the babies don't meet their standards."

The strange Islander flinched. Tri shook his head. Denl and Jakib looked at him, and he wasn't sure what kind of look they were giving him, whether it was surprise or shock or both. They had heard of this before, there had been talk of it in the village below. Apparently it hadn't sunken in.

"And now you see why we bring those children here," Pausho said. She indicated the boy with her hand. "See how dangerous they are left untended?"

"You didn't bring him here. You brought his father here."

"And he was saved. And in saving him, it allowed him to procreate, to father this creature. Of course you're like him, Matthias. You're just like him. Demon-spawn. And you should have died all those years ago."

She said it so calmly, so rationally, as if she weren't talking about his life, as if she were talking about a weed she didn't want in her garden.

Matthias's stomach turned. His headache grew. "No," he said. "I'm nothing like that."

"You're exactly like that. Most tall children are."

"He's not tall," Matthias said.

"His father was," she said. "The rule doesn't always work, but it usually does. It's rare that someone as normal as that boy has the powers he has. It makes me wonder about his mother. Was she from here too?"

"You talk about people I've never met!" the boy said, and there was anguish in his voice.

"You met them," Pausho said. "They're your parents. Whether or not you remember them is another thing."

"You're saying that there are others like Coulter?" the strange Islander asked.

"I don't know," Pausho said. "Not many. Most of the children that we put here die as they're supposed to. Or disappear. And not all of the ones the mountain rejects have great powers. Sometimes they have simple abilities."

"The Wise Ones have been killing babies because they have extraordinary powers?" Tri asked. He was even paler than he had been. In fact, in the firelight, he looked almost green.

"Killing out of fear," the strange Islander said.

"No," she said. "Out of necessity. If you had read the Words—"

"I canna believe the Roca wants ye ta kill innocents," Denl said.

"Then you know nothing of the man you call Beloved of God," Pausho said. "It is the Roca's instruction."

"Not even I believe that," Matthias said. The headache was

pounding now. He had never felt quite so odd in his life. He couldn't absorb everything Pausho was saying. She had never met the boy before. Had she? And would she work with Fey to entrap him? It made no sense.

Although the Fey wanted him. They wanted him badly.

For discovering the properties of holy water.

For killing Jewel.

For murdering Burden.

They did want him. He just didn't believe they'd go to such lengths to get him.

"We have the real Words in Constant," she said. "The Roca had two sons. One became King of Blue Isle, the other the spiritual leader. The Roca wanted all the power to remain in his sons. He did not want any of the other powerful ones to live."

Matthias felt a shudder run through him. He had always suspected the Tabernacle's process of choosing a Rocaan was wrong. After his studies, he had concluded that the Rocaan had initially been meant as an hereditary title, like the King.

"You're saying that Nicholas has these powers?" Matthias asked.

"If he is the blood of the Roca," Pausho said. "It is why we have never contested the royal family's rule. They are an unbroken line."

"That explains Gift," the boy said.

"Gift?" Matthias asked.

The boy started to answer, but the strange Islander put a hand on his arm. "I think we've had enough tonight," his friend said.

"What's Gift?" Matthias asked.

"It doesn't matter," the boy said. "But now maybe you'll believe me."

"I don't see why I should," Matthias said. "Nor do I see why you are trying so hard to convince me."

The boy stared at him for a moment, then sighed. "You know," he said. "Now that I know what you are, I wonder the same thing. I had a hope that we would be able to work together. But you can't even work with yourself. Come on, Adrian. Let's find the others."

The boy took his friend's hand and they started up the path. Matthias watched them go. He was too unsettled to follow them. And too exhausted. He needed rest. He needed to tend this headache.

He needed to think.

They disappeared into the darkness.

"Where are they going?" Pausho asked.

But no one answered her.

No one knew.

But they would be easy enough to trace. And Matthias would trace them.

As soon as he figured out what he had just learned.

FORTY-ONE

RUGAD could not sleep. He sat on his balcony and stared across the dark city at the river. The night was black. There was no moon. The stars were faint flickers in the sky. He could barely see the river, and only because it was a ribbon of darkness in the ruins of the city. He could hear the river as well, gurgling as it moved on its course to the Infrin Sea.

He hadn't even changed for bed. He still wore his clothing—and the jar with his voice inside. He didn't sleep with it tied to him, too afraid the jar would open somehow in his sleep, but he carried it with him whenever he was awake.

He had stopped keeping track of time, but he knew it hadn't been too long ago that Tuft had come to him. The Wisp had brought news of the golem's capture. Only the Wisp had thought that the Fey had captured Rugad's great-grandson. Either way, Rugad did not want the rest of his troops to know. He had sworn Tuft to secrecy, promised him a promotion and extra responsibility, then sent the Wisp on his way.

Rugad wanted to meet the golem alone. A golem, especially one over two years old, was a rare thing. This one was eighteen, and it had shattered once. It had powers of its own that enabled it to stay alive this long.

Powers of its own.

Rugad would discover what those powers were. With luck, not even the golem knew. That would give Rugad more of an advantage than he already had.

But he was impatient. He had seen the golem just once, when it had saved the life of King Nicholas and in the confusion of its explosion had allowed Nicholas to escape. Odd that the creature was not with Nicholas now. There was a story in that. A story he would discover.

He had discovered other things, though, in the weeks that he had been recuperating. He had learned the golem's place in Islander society. The Islanders believed the golem was the King's true son.

Islander culture was patriarchal, like so many of the cultures he had encountered in his years as Black King. The Islanders had not been enlightened enough to allow a woman to rule at any point in their history. The royal line had always been carried through the male. The royal issue had always come from the male.

Even if his great-granddaughter—she of the clear eyes and the incredible determination—even if she wanted to rule, she could not.

She could not.

Nicholas would have let the golem rule in her place rather than let his Fey-raised son rule.

And that was telling as well.

As he had lain in his bed, Rugad had wondered how Nicholas planned to reconcile the royal line with a golem in charge. A golem was quite literally made of stone. If it had its own magick, as this one seemed to, it could have a long life span, but even that would not make up for lack of issue.

Would the daughter's children have been passed off as the golem's? Was that even possible with all the servants in the palace?

Not that it mattered now.

Now Blue Isle was Rugad's, and Nicholas's convoluted plans regarding his children played into Rugad's hands. Rugad had captured what the Islanders considered to be the heir to the throne.

The heir.

And a golem, depending on how much of his magick was based in the Mysteries and the Powers, was most likely a blank slate. Rugad knew better than to hope this one was, and yet,

Nicholas had abandoned it. A person rarely did that with an active golem, one with a personality of its own.

The golem had been found with a Black Robe near the city's burned Tabernacle. Its "family" was nowhere around. The Black Robe had been the one to rescue it, and the Black Robe had taken it away.

Perhaps the golem was not a Fey creation after all. Perhaps it had started as one, but perhaps it got most of its power from the Black Robes.

Rugad would have to find out.

Even that might work in his favor. Most of the Black Robes were dead. In fact, he had just slaughtered another group of them that morning. When he had determined that the golem was no longer with those Black Robes, he let his still-bloodthirsty troops loose. The slaughter had been quick, but not merciful.

He suspected it was the last gathering of Black Robes in Jahn.

The remaining Black Robes, if there were any, would be killed when they were found in the countryside or when they tried to revive their religion, as these types so often did.

He would stop them and they would die, and their construct would be used for his purposes, not theirs.

He smiled and leaned back in his chair.

He almost wished he had ordered the Infantry to bring the golem through the streets of Jahn. Then, at least, he could see their progress. Instead they were proceeding through the maze of tunnels beneath the city.

Those tunnels had proven useful. He suspected they would be even more useful as time went on.

He didn't like the setback of losing Nicholas or being unable to locate his great-grandchildren. But he knew it for what it was. A setback, and a setback only.

A knock on the door made his smile widen. He could not speak loud enough to bid the person to enter. He stood slowly and went inside. From there, he said as loud as he could, "Come."

The door opened. A contingent of guards filled the hall, with Wisdom in front of them.

"We have your prisoner," Wisdom said.

"Bring him in," Rugad said. He was beginning to get used to the pain of speaking. It no longer surprised him, and so he did not think that much of it any more. He knew what price he was going to pay each time he opened his mouth.

Wisdom reached behind him and pushed the golem forward. It was as Rugad remembered, tall and slender and Fey-like, with the look of Nicholas about his face. Its eyes told of its stone-nature, however. They were slate gray, as all golem eyes were. And if the eyes hadn't given it away, the cracks in its skin did. Anyone who had seen a golem before would recognize this one for what it was: a golem that had shattered at least once, although Rugad would have guessed that it nearly had lost itself one other time before.

The golem was staring at him, its face expressionless. It did not show any honor to its betters, which did not surprise Rugad. It had been raised among Islanders and probably did not know what it was in its first few years of existence. It might not even know that Rugad was its better.

Wisdom brought it into the center of the room. It stood near a pair of ornate chairs behind the embroidered couch. Guards started to follow, but Rugad held up his hand.

"I want five guards posted at this door," he said, "two other groups of five at the end of the hall, and another group of five on the balcony. I need five more near the main entrance, and several at the tunnel openings."

The leader of the guards, a woman by the name of Blade, nodded at him. Silently she indicated which guards would go to the balcony, and they did, making their way around him with a nod as they went outside. The remaining guards split up, a well-functioning team that made him smile at Blade with approval.

She did not smile back, something he approved of even more. She remained outside his door, arms crossed.

"Close the balcony doors, Wisdom," Rugad said.

Wisdom released his grip on the golem and went to the doors. Rugad used that moment to walk around the golem.

It was cracked and filthy. It smelled of rotting flesh. If time were not of the essence, he would have had it cleaned before it was brought here.

But Rugad had been prepared for the smell. Tuft had explained the circumstances of discovery. Rugad had been appalled. In Fey culture, only those extracting magick touched dead bodies. Those extracting magick—or Red Caps, who always smelled this foul.

Wisdom had returned. He crossed his arms and stood in alert position beside the golem.

"Thank you, Wisdom," Rugad said. "You are excused."

"I don't think you should be alone with it, sir," Wisdom said.

"I will not be," Rugad said. "If I have any trouble, I will contact the guards."

"Sir—"

"You seem to have gained a habit of contradicting me, Wisdom," Rugad said. "Is this left over from my injury or does this indicate a desire for the Black Throne?"

Panic flared in Wisdom's eyes. Rugad now knew he would have to make an example of the man.

"It is habit, sir," Wisdom said, "from the days when you could not speak."

Rugad smiled. "I could not speak, but I could always communicate. It seems you forgot that as well."

"I was concerned for you," Wisdom said.

"And I value that concern," Rugad lied. "As I do now. But it is misplaced. I will be all right."

"As you wish," Wisdom said, and bowed. He must have been panicked. Bowing was something he rarely did.

He let himself out after leveling a warning glance at the golem. As if the golem would be afraid of Wisdom. It had much more to fear from the Black King. And judging from the light in those slate gray eyes, it knew that fact.

"What do they call you?" Rugad asked. He might have known, but he had forgotten. Golems were usually not this important, in the scheme of things.

"Se-bas-tian," the Golem said. It spoke slowly, its voice the rumble of stone against stone. How could anyone think it Fey? How could anyone believe it to be a living creature and not a magickal construct? Perhaps the Islanders were easily fooled, but his granddaughter should not have been. Jewel was usually brighter. Had she expected her noble experiment to fail this badly?

"Sebastian. It is an Islander name."

"My . . . fa ther . . . is . . . Is-land-er," the golem said.

Ah, and perhaps in that answer lay the proof. The golem had a brain. Rugad had suspected it earlier, when it had saved Nicholas's life, but this proved it. The golem claimed not the blood connection, but the emotional one.

"Where is your father?"

"I . . . do . . . not . . . know," the golem said.

Rugad smiled. "Would you tell me if you did?"

"I . . . do . . . not . . . know . . . that . . . either."

And there he saw the true golemness of its nature. It hadn't confronted the problem, therefore it did not need a solution.

"Where were you going when we found you?"

"A-way . . . from . . . the . . . Fey," the golem said.

"There is no away," Rugad said. "We have taken the Isle."

"The . . . tun-nels . . . were . . . a-way."

"For a time," Rugad said. "And then we found you."

"You . . . kil-led . . . all . . . those . . . peo-ple . . . be-cause . . . of . . . me?" Its voice shook. Compassion in a golem. How very rare. And a clue, Rugad thought, to the secret of its long life. Either the one who created it had compassion, or it served another purpose.

Or both.

"I discovered them because of you," Rugad said. "You can determine if that's the same thing."

The golem turned away from him. Rugad took a step closer. He would have to approach this thing with caution. As with all magicks on Blue Isle, he didn't dare underestimate it.

"You . . . have . . . kil-led . . . a . . . lot . . . of . . . peo-ple."

"More than you know," Rugad said.

"Why?"

"It's called war, little creature," Rugad said, suppressing a smile.

"No . . ." The golem raised its head. Its gray eyes met Rugad's and Rugad had the distinct impression the creature had known of his approach. "It . . . is . . . con-quest."

"Yes," Rugad said. "It is."

"But . . . peo-ple . . . die. . . . It . . . is . . . not . . . worth . . . my . . . fa-ther's . . . life, . . . my . . . fri-end's . . . life, . . . the . . . lives . . . of . . . peo-ple . . . I . . . do-n't . . . even . . . know."

Rugad tilted his head. What a fascinating creature. He hadn't heard such sophistication from a golem before. It was trying to argue philosophy with him.

The question, of course, was why. Was it trying to distract him? Or did it sincerely want to know?

Perhaps it was trying to put off what it saw as its upcoming death.

But golems were amazingly hard to kill. Surely it knew that much.

"We kill as few people as possible," Rugad said. "We need workers for the Empire."

"But . . . they . . . are . . . not . . . just . . . work-ers. . . . They . . . have—"

"Lives, loves, people who care for them. I know." Rugad waved a hand. He had heard this before from other sources, and intrigued as he was by this golem's curiosity, he didn't want to explain what was essentially unexplainable. There were so many layers to what he did. The expansion of the Fey empire was not done just for conquest, nor was it done for the thrill. The Fey were meant to rule the world, but they had to conquer it one place at a time.

And just as the Fey were meant to rule the world, Rugad's family was meant to rule the Fey. If the golem were truly Fey, he would understand this. It was as simple as the type of magick a Fey was born with. If he had no magick, he became a Red Cap. If he had Shifting magick, he became one of the most pampered of all Fey.

Yet there was even more than that, things Rugad would not ever speak of for fear his own people wouldn't understand. He was getting older, and the thrill of creating violent death had left him as a young man. He would retire to one of the large estates in Nye if he had his way, or perhaps see the Eccrasian Mountains before he died. But he might not have that choice. He had brought the Fey this far. He needed to bring them as far as he could while training his successor. And Jewel's brother Bridge was not a worthy successor. Rugad had left so many trusted advisors in Nye with Bridge primarily because he was afraid that Bridge would make a serious—and costly—mistake.

"You . . . do . . . not . . . know . . . why . . . you . . . do . . . this," the golem said.

This time, Rugad did smile. "Of course I know," he said. "I simply will not debate it with a creature like you."

He reached across the short space between them and grabbed the golem's wrist. The skin was cold and barely pliable. A rough approximation of skin. He could feel the cracks beneath his fingers.

The golem looked down, then started to pull away. Rugad grabbed its other hand. He squinted. He could see the faint lines of Links through the cracks in the golem's face.

"Let's see what you're really made of," Rugad said, and stuck a finger in the golem's ear.

There were four strong Links flaring inside. Two of them were severed, one a long time ago, its strands black and flat, decayed. The second had the vibrancy of Rugad's great-grandson—it was still yellow, although the yellow was fading. This one was not severed permanently. It just looked as if the door had closed.

Rugad remembered—

—the force that had appeared inside Gift, the whirling force that had seized him and thrown him out of Gift's body as if he were nothing more than a bit of soul for a Fey lamp.

So that was what it had done, that Enchanter. It—*he*—had closed all of Gift's Links and made him inaccessible.

But this creature had lived with the royal family. And it had two other Links.

Rugad could not step inside the golem's body—he needed a Link of his own to do that—but he could invade an existing Link. He had taught himself how to do that years ago, and he had done it several times, the last using Gift's Link to Shadowlands to take him to his great-grandson.

And getting thrown out.

He could feel the golem pulling at his hand, flapping at him ineffectually. The golem probably did not understand what he was doing. The only Link that looked traveled was Gift's. The others existed but had not had any internal visitors.

But the golem was smart, and Rugad had vowed not to underestimate it. He plunged his finger into the first still established Link he found. It was the largest, a white Link with a trace of purple in the middle.

Then he slid himself into it, the part of himself that was not attached to his body. His essence. What so many cultures called his soul.

The Link was wide and full of great affection, and easily traveled even though the path felt new.

And as he moved along it, he learned who it belonged to.

Arianna.

His great-granddaughter.

He would learn where Nicholas had taken her.

Rugad had not expected it to be so easy.

He had succeeded on his very first try.

FORTY-TWO

IT had been years since Boteen had ridden in a carriage. It had been even longer since he'd ridden in one guided by Horse Riders. A majestic team, husband and wife, allowed themselves to be strapped into the conventional horse riggings at the front of the carriage. Then they had trotted along, as if they were simply dumb beasts, instead of leaders of their own troop, great Fey in their own right.

The things Rugad could get his people to do.

Boteen stretched out inside the carriage. He was not alone: there were several other Fey in the troop, but he was the only one in this carriage. Some Wisps and Bird Riders flew overhead, and an entire Infantry troop marched behind. The Infantry was the backup, as they were in any mission of this kind. If diplomacy did not work—and diplomacy in this instance would be quite simple, something Rugad called "Surrender or Die" diplomacy—then the Infantry would be called in while the Wisps sent for the Foot Soldiers.

Another carriage, also pulled by a team of Horse Riders, followed along behind him. In it was one of Rugad's favorite Charmers, a Domestic (for reasons Boteen had yet to fathom), and a Scribe. The Scribe was unusual. Rugad had brought three of them along on this trip, and they were, for the most part, useless. But Rugad believed in keeping himself informed, and also in sending messages back to the entire Empire. He used the Scribes for that.

Boteen thought it silly. Scribes had very little magick and almost as little brain. That was, Rugad said, what made them excellent recorders. Sometimes they recorded things on precious paper, but most often they reported meetings back word for word, a tedious process that could take hours, even, in cases like this, days. Boteen had had to sit through several Scribe recountings, and each one had made him, by the end, want to rip those scrawny little beings' voices right out of their throats.

He hadn't, of course. Enchanters were perceived as dangerous enough. If they didn't handle their magick properly, they lost their very precarious hold on sanity. He had watched himself closely for that. Too many magick systems running through him, too many to manage, and too many stressors had often led him to be unreasonable. If unreasonable was the worst that happened to him, then he would be all right.

He shivered. The night air was cool, and he had the carriage windows open. They were traveling along a cobblestone road that ran beside the Cardidas River. They had left Jahn hours ago and were heading northeast. He had seen the maps. The trip would take them along main roads until they got into the foothills of the Eyes of Roca. There the roads were less passable—sometimes impassable in the winter—and the towns were few and far between. He was not relishing disappearing into pure Islander country with only a handful of Fey to back him up and an Infantry troop in case someone got into trouble. Most of them wouldn't even know if he were in trouble. Enchanters had ways of hurting each other that weren't visible, that weren't even comprehensible to normal Fey.

But this Enchanter wasn't really Fey. He was Islander. And he probably hadn't had the training that Boteen had. From the impressions Boteen took of the man, he'd had no training at all. That made him difficult on the one hand, and an easy mark on the other.

Boteen only hoped that this Enchanter would lead him to the Black King's great-grandson. To have Rugad in Boteen's debt, well, that would be the biggest coup of all.

It would certainly make this trip worthwhile. Boteen leaned back in the carriage seat. He didn't want to sleep in here. He felt odd enough traveling in the contraption. He had learned from the Domestics who'd prepared it that this carriage had been owned by the Tabernacle. They claimed they had cleaned it of all anti-Fey spells, but he had Cleansed the thing himself before getting in. Actually, he had performed three small spells: a Cleansing of all harmful things; a Repellent, so that any remaining harmful things could not touch him; and a Charm, so that even if they remained and tried to touch him, they would be favorably disposed to him.

He had never used quite so much protection before, but he had never been so leery of a vehicle before. He had been willing to use the energy before this trip to safeguard his own life.

The carriage was large and black. Several other people could easily have fit inside. The seats were made of velvet, and Boteen could still see the outlines of the tiny swords that had once been embroidered into the material. There had been tiny swords on all the outside corners of the carriage as well. The Domestics had removed them, but no matter how many spells had been done on the vehicle, small ghost swords remained.

Through the first hour of his journey, he had stared at the ones inside, trying to fathom them. He had seen religious symbols in many other countries, but never had he seen one quite like this. A sword. A weapon of death.

It made no sense to him.

He had studied them until he could stand it no longer, and then he had ordered the Fey lamp to extinguish itself.

He had been sitting in darkness ever since.

He had nothing else to do. He knew they were heading on the right path. He had sensed the Enchanter in the Cliffs of Blood. Boteen had not felt it necessary to follow the Enchanter's trail. That trail was convoluted. It had crossed and recrossed several boundaries. It had doubled back on itself and it had faded twice. He had seen that much inside Jahn. He didn't want to lead this entire troop in circles. Time, as Rugad noted, was the most important thing here.

Time, and finding the boy.

Boteen wasn't sure what he would do with the other Enchanter. The man's hatred of Fey was a serious problem. Boteen doubted he could negotiate.

He would probably have to kill the Enchanter, which was a shame. The Fey could learn so much from him.

But there was a second: he knew that. And maybe the second would be more reasonable. Right now, Boteen did not have the luxury for niceties.

He leaned deeper into the seat and put up his feet. His skin crawled as the velvet moved slightly. He was imagining spells where there were none, but he knew it was better to be alert.

Rugad had warned him repeatedly not to underestimate the Islanders.

Boteen would not. He would assume that even if the other Enchanter were not trained, he would be powerful. Boteen could only hope for the advantage of surprise. After that, he figured, it would be a contest of equals.

Or near-equals.

Experience in battle always counted for something.

In the end.

FORTY-THREE

LUKE hadn't traveled at night since the second Fey invasion. This night, though, he was moving through his cornfield, traveling as silently as possible.

He had heard that one of the farms to the south of his had become a Fey base. He wanted to check out the rumor in broad daylight, but he couldn't think of an excuse. He knew he wasn't the best liar, anyway, and that to risk it might show the Fey that he was plotting against them.

He wanted them to become complacent. He had seen the signs already.

The guards that had visited the farms every day for the past two weeks didn't come as often now. They still visited daily—but only once a day instead of twice or three times. Luke's neighbors said the same thing.

He crouched in the cornfield and finished his preparations. He had a lot to do. He needed to pick a target and then assemble some men to harm that target. He had ideas on how to do that as well.

He knew the one thing he had to avoid: the appearance of a resistance to the Fey. If he caught them by surprise, he would do more good.

That meant no meetings, no secret rendezvous, and very little explanation of the plans beforehand. He felt like he had when he was a boy, when he had been on that attack where he and his father had been captured by the Fey. His father had known what the plan was, but Luke hadn't. He was just a teenager then, and had come along because he begged.

His father had regretted giving in ever since. Their lives certainly would have been different if Luke had stayed home.

He wouldn't be crouched in the cornfield, using soft dirt to cover his pale skin.

The dirt on his father's farm was the darkest Luke had ever seen. He had gotten the idea in the afternoon while Jona's girls helped him work the farm. They were solid workers, and they would make certain that he got everything done, despite his work against the Fey.

He couldn't thank Jona enough for that. The best thing Luke could do was make certain that his plans against the Fey worked.

What he had come to was this: He needed to create a weakness in their army, a hole in their strength that couldn't be covered up. If he succeeded, he hoped the word would get around to other Fey garrisons and the Fey would worry about the Islanders.

The Islanders had an advantage: Even though the Black King had arrived with thousands of Fey, the Islanders still outnumbered them. The key was to get those Islanders to resist all at the same time.

It wouldn't happen overnight. It might not even happen while Luke was alive—he fully expected to die in his resistance to the Fey—but it would happen. And he had to be the one to start it.

He had special knowledge.

He knew that even if Nicholas was dead, Gift lived. And in Gift flowed the blood of the Roca. Gift might not know the traditions of Blue Isle, but he could learn—and Luke's father could teach him. Gift was part Fey, but Coulter loved him. And Coulter would not love someone who had only the Fey Empire in mind. At worst, Gift could unite the Fey Empire and Blue Isle.

At best, he could drive the Black King out.

Luke needed to provide the opportunity for Gift to drive his great-grandfather out. He needed to make it possible for the Fey to leave Blue Isle. Very few people knew how to do that.

But Luke did.

He hadn't lived among them, but his father had. His father had often said that the Fey's greatest flaw was their belief that no one could be better than they were.

It was how the Islanders had kept the first invasion at bay. The Fey had conquered so many other countries, using small armies and more intimidation. But the Islanders had stopped the Fey, using fear and holy water, something not every Islander had.

Holy water no longer worked, but Luke was willing to bet his life that fear would.

Fear would.

And he was going to begin that tonight.

Alone.

He finished rubbing the dirt on his arms and face. He rubbed some extra on his blond hair and on his clothing. If someone were looking for him, they'd be able to see him.

But they had to be looking.

He slowly made his way out of the cornfield. It was on the southern reaches of his father's land. The farm that the Fey supposedly held wasn't too far if Luke stayed off the roads and in the fields. His problem was that he couldn't damage crops as he went. Too many irate farmers might report the damage to the Fey, thinking the Fey had done it, and the Fey would get wise.

There was no moon. The stars winked above him but provided little light. That was good. He couldn't have planned this better if he had tried.

He crossed an unplanted field that separated his father's farm from the nearest neighbor's and noted that someone had been tilling the soil. This field was uneven and rock-strewn. The soil had played out long ago. His father and the neighbor had been trying, over the last few years, to figure out how to revive the soil. Either the Fey had ideas or they didn't care.

They wanted all the land planted.

Luke saw how the years ahead would work: The Fey would demand more and more produce from the Islanders. The produce would be shipped off Blue Isle or used for ships that passed by on their way to Leut. Islanders would get less and less of the food, and some would die off. Then the Fey would realize they were losing their forces, and relax a little. This interconnected relationship would go on until the Islanders couldn't remember a time without the Fey directing their every move.

He saw it so clearly, and he wasn't sure why. Maybe it was because of his father. Maybe it was the stories Scavenger told about the life the Fey had created for the conquered in other countries.

Maybe it was just Luke's fear, building on itself.

He had reached the farmhouse. It was quiet. No one stirred and no lights burned. He had hoped he had waited until the right time to travel unseen. He was moving about late enough. Now all he had to do was hope that it wasn't too late, that he would get back before sunrise.

He crossed behind the house, past the well, and on the outside of the nearest field. This neighbor planted hay, although he still had hay bales rotting in his field from the year before. King Nicholas's policies hadn't always been good for farmers, and so many had suffered when trade with Nye was cut off. His neighbor had hoped to sell the hay as feed to stables in Jahn, but obviously that wasn't going to work.

Luke had heard that Jahn was gone.

He couldn't quite believe that. He couldn't wrap his mind around the destruction of an entire city. But he also knew the Fey were capable of it. Scavenger once said the Fey saw cities as places that caused dissent, and were better off destroyed, leaving the outlying areas where men couldn't gather and resist.

Little did the Fey know.

Luke worked his way silently around the hay bales. They smelled sharp and pungent, and beneath the hay odor was the scent of rot. The smell tickled his nose, and he felt a sneeze building. He put a hand over his mouth, hoping to hold it off, but to no avail. The sneeze came. He managed to stifle it with his hand and throat, but the sound still seemed explosive in the quiet night.

He crouched against the bale. Nothing moved. No lights were lit in the farmhouse, and he heard nothing on the nearby road. Maybe no one had heard him.

Maybe if they had they had thought it something else.

He let his breath out slowly. Another urge to sneeze came over him, and he moved away from the hay. The strong smell was causing the problem. If he got far enough away, he wouldn't sneeze again.

The hay field seemed huge in the darkness, the bales rising like small hills against the black night. His heart was pounding hard against his chest. He didn't know what he would say if the Fey found him. That he was stealing his neighbor's hay? That he was sabotaging his neighbor's crops? That he couldn't sleep?

They would believe none of those responses.

And neither would he, in their place.

The only thing he could do was not get caught.

He finally crossed a small drainage ditch that separated his neighbor's property from the one that the Fey had confiscated. That neighbor, Antoni, had planted a series of small trees as a border between the properties. The trees were bushy and not much taller than Luke. He used them for cover, careful not to shake the branches.

He had no idea what kind of the magick the Fey here had.

He used the trees until he could see the farmhouse. There were lights inside, and Fey guards on each door. He didn't see the telltale dirt circle or the floating lights that indicated a secret hiding place—the kind the Fey called Shadowlands. He had been inside one of those places just once. It had been like being in a box that floated on air. Everything was gray inside, and unchanging.

His father had lived like that for years.

Luke never wanted to be captured in a place like that again.

The third captive, Ort, had been tortured to death there.

Luke shuddered. He stayed within the shelter of the trees and made himself think.

He needed a strike against the Fey, something that would surprise them and damage their psyches.

He had no magick and neither did his friends. Also, he had to make sure that none of them got caught. A flat-out attack would not work. The Fey probably expected it.

He needed something more subtle.

He had to find that here.

There didn't appear to be any other Fey about besides the guards and the ones inside the farmhouse. Apparently the Fey had somewhere else that they were keeping the troops. This had to be an outpost, a garrison in charge of keeping the farmers in line.

It would be vulnerable to things most farms were vulnerable to: fire, flood, pestilence. The Fey themselves could be killed. But all of this would have to be accomplished without a direct attack.

He squared his shoulders. He had to explore the grounds. Even something small would upset them. Maybe something small would upset them more than something large.

But he had to find the right thing. Attacking a guard would

be expected. So would seizing weapons. He had to hit them in a way that would profoundly affect them and would show them that he understood how they operated.

He needed a perfect strike.

And he wouldn't be able to find it from the trees.

He slipped onto the edge of the untilled field. He had never felt so vulnerable in his life. The darkness didn't feel as thick here. He could see the dirt, see the house itself, with the light coming from the windows, sense the guards.

The guards. He didn't know what kind of equipment they had.

He didn't know what kind of magick they had.

Could they sense him, too?

Scavenger had never told him about any Fey with that sort of ability, but then Scavenger didn't talk about all aspects of the Fey. His father hadn't mentioned that either. In fact, his father had said the Fey usually relied on magickal constructs to keep them protected: the charmed opening to the Circle Door into Shadowlands for example, or Shadowlands itself.

The Fey were rarely in situations where they needed guards. The leader of a troop was usually a Visionary who could create a Shadowlands. But the Black King had probably arrived with too many troops for him to create Shadowlands for all of them. And Luke doubted that the smaller units, the ones guarding the rural regions, had Visionaries in charge.

He was sure there weren't that many Visionaries.

In fact, Scavenger had said that Visionaries were rare.

Rare.

Luke swallowed and crossed the back of the field, moving closer to the house. He had lived on farms all his life: he knew how to get from one place to another without making much noise. He was thankful that Antoni didn't have any animals, because animals always stirred. He hoped that there were no Beast Riders among the Fey either, because they might stir as well.

There were two tall trees at the back of the house. They served as a windbreak. Antoni had planted others near the front, but they weren't nearly as tall. Luke might be able to use the trees somehow, but he wasn't certain how. Climb them and listen to the Fey plan? They usually didn't discuss plans in groups. Throw something from the branch to start a problem inside the house? Attack from the trees?

He didn't like any of those ideas.

He stopped behind the first, and gripped the rough bark. His heart was pounding. He'd never reconnoitered Fey before. He'd approached them only that one time, twenty years before, and then attacked.

And the attack had resulted in his capture.

His fingers dug into the bark.

He couldn't think about that. Thinking about that would distract him.

He had to find something.

The barn was to the south of the trees. A guard stood in front of its door as well. Were there troops sleeping inside? No one seemed to be sleeping in the house. What else did the Fey have to guard? Infantry carried weapons, but they usually carried them on their own persons. Many of the other kinds of Fey *were* weapons.

Prisoners? Were there prisoners in the barn? Prisoners like his father had been?

Luke's heart started beating harder. He knew of no one missing from his local circle. Even Antoni and his family were working another farm. The Fey had killed no one around here, and captured no one so far as Luke had heard.

But he didn't know the fate of his father and Coulter and Scavenger. Could they have been captured again? He had thought they got free, from the stories he had heard. They had attacked an entire Infantry troop two weeks ago. Somehow Coulter had stopped them, and they had fled.

Luke had assumed they were safe.

But what if the Fey had captured them? Would they bring them back here, this close?

Or were there other prisoners?

And why would the Fey take prisoners at this late date?

To make them work? To experiment on them like they had on Ort? To turn them into weapons like they had with Luke himself?

Suddenly his fear turned into anger. They had no right to mess with innocents.

Freeing prisoners would be precisely the kind of hit he had been looking for.

Precisely.

But it would take work.

And before he could even make the plan, he had to make sure the barn held prisoners. The last thing he wanted to do was to bring in a small untrained group of farmers and have them walk into a meeting with the Black King.

He had to get past that guard. He had to see inside the barn before he made a decision.

The tough part wouldn't be sneaking inside the barn; he'd done that many times as a child. The tough part would be crossing another open expanse of ground, this one closer to the farmhouse, with guards on both sides.

But he could do it.

He knew he could.

FORTY-FOUR

ADRIAN was shaking as they went up the trail. His eyes still hadn't adjusted to the dark. He could only follow the black shape that was Coulter ahead of him.

Still, Adrian glanced behind him to see if the others followed. He wasn't sure why they would; Coulter had attacked them quite hard. But he didn't trust them. And he should have.

Oddly enough, he should have.

His feet kept slipping on rocks. This trail, if indeed it was a trail, was thin. Coulter was moving fast, too, as if he felt that something were pursuing them.

"Coulter," Adrian said. "I can't see well enough to keep up with you."

"Sorry," Coulter said. He immediately slowed down. Adrian caught up, close enough to feel the warmth of Coulter's body and smell the slightly sulfuric odor that had accompanied the fireballs.

"You worried me down there," Adrian said, and then frowned. The words had come out before he'd had a chance to think about them. But now that he'd spoken then, he felt that he should go on. "I've never seen you act like that."

Coulter shrugged. Adrian could see his shoulders move

against the darkness. Black against black. What an interesting sight.

"What were you doing?" Adrian asked.

"Trying to recruit him to our side."

Adrian felt cold. Coulter had never done anything like that before. Coulter had been a loner all of his life. It had taken Adrian months to get Coulter to warm to him, and then years to get Coulter to trust him. And even then, Adrian wasn't certain how close Coulter felt to him. Yes, they did talk, and yes, Adrian felt like Coulter's father in many ways, but not in all ways.

And Coulter had kept the distance, not Adrian.

"Gift would never have stood for that," Adrian said. "You know what this man has done."

Although Adrian wasn't sure he disapproved. He wasn't sure at all. Jewel, even though she had been King Nicholas's wife, had been as evil as the other Fey. More so, in fact, as far as Adrian was concerned. She had imprisoned him, sent Ort away for torture, and used his son as a weapon.

"Gift would approve," Coulter said, his voice tight, as if Adrian's criticism had hurt him. He made his way around a boulder, then put out a hand to help Adrian. Adrian took it. "He needs all the help he can get in fighting his great-grandfather."

Coulter's hand was not hot, as Adrian had expected. It felt cool. Coulter's magick had always baffled him.

"Fighting his great-grandfather?" Adrian was confused. Of course, the former Rocaan would fight the Fey. There was no question of that. But to that man, Gift was Fey. "Do you know who that man was?"

"Yes," Coulter said. They had made it around the boulder. He dropped Adrian's hand. "He's the other one."

"The other—?" Adrian's frown deepened, and then he remembered the conversation. It had seemed so long ago, even though it had been less than a month. It had been the night that Gift had shown up on the farm. Coulter had felt him coming.

Coulter had also felt something else. He had been staring at the ground, and he had said something strange:

"Instead of two of us here, there are three."

"Of course there are three," Luke said. "You, me, and—"

"No," Coulter said before Adrian could shush his son. "It's all energy. It's like Links or trails. The energy holds things together, too. I can feel it, like you can feel sunlight."

Adrian tightened his grip on Luke's shoulder. "Three what?"

"I can feel the Isle," Coulter said. "There's always been me, and someone else like me."

"Who?" Adrian said.

Coulter shrugged, his shoulders moving against the night sky. "I don't know. Someone far from here."

"And now there's a third?" Luke asked.

Coulter nodded. "To the south. Where the Wisp came from."

"What does it mean?" Luke asked.

But Adrian knew. It was all the Fey ever really talked about, all they thought about. The reinforcements had finally come, and somehow they had breached the mountains in the south.

With an Enchanter.

What had Rugar called Enchanters?

The most powerful of all Fey.

"The former Rocaan is an Enchanter?" Adrian asked.

Coulter stopped. He stopped so fast that Adrian bumped into him.

"That's the former Rocaan?"

"Yes," Adrian said.

"How do you know? You weren't religious."

"I didn't recognize him," Adrian said. "It's just that one of those men called him Holy Sir, and the old woman called him Matthias. The honorific title for the Rocaan is Holy Sir, and the name of the Fifty-first Rocaan, the one who abdicated, is Matthias. He disappeared. What better place to hide than here?"

"And he hates Fey," Coulter said softly.

"He does that," Adrian said. "So much so that he murdered Gift's mother."

"I should have recognized him." Coulter shivered. They were standing shoulder to shoulder, and Adrian felt the shudders run through him.

"How?" Adrian asked. "He left the Tabernacle before you came to the farm. There's no way you could have seen him."

Before that, Coulter had been in Shadowlands. Adrian was one of the few Islanders Coulter had ever seen.

"When I—saved Gift," Coulter said, and in that simple phrase he had left out so much. He hadn't just saved Gift. He had repaired Gift, bound Gift to him, and made sure that Gift remained alive. "I saw him. Gift saw what was happening to his mother. I saw that man put the poison on her head."

Poison. The Fey term. There was so much that Coulter got from the Fey. So many of his perspectives, so much of his world.

"But his face was bandaged below," Adrian said. "How could you have known?"

"Bandaged because Leen attacked him," Coulter said.

And then Adrian remembered. Leen had said something about killing the Islander who had killed Gift's mother.

They hadn't realized he had lived. Adrian wondered how that was so. What had happened on that bridge?

That was the same night that Coulter had said he had felt a third Enchanter. Coulter had known that the Rocaan wasn't dead, but Coulter hadn't realized that the Rocaan was the second Enchanter.

Coulter's shaking had moved to Adrian. "You said he was just like you," Adrian said. He had to make certain he was clear about this.

"He is."

"He's an Enchanter?" Adrian asked.

"That's a Fey word," Coulter said.

"But he is, isn't he?"

Coulter nodded. "I thought we could use him. I thought two Enchanters against the Black King's one. It would be perfect."

"So you brought him to you?"

"No," Coulter said. "He just showed up."

The chills Adrian had felt earlier had returned. "He just showed up?" Adrian asked.

"Yes," Coulter said. Then he leaned his head down. He rested the edge of his skull against Adrian's. It was a small touch, but it showed that Coulter needed comfort. "He said he was searching for the Fey. He was looking for Gift."

"But he didn't know who Gift was," Adrian said. "Not when you said Gift's name."

Coulter brought his head up. Adrian felt the sudden lack of pressure, the removal of the small warmth. "That's right," he said. "He didn't."

"But he knew that there were Fey about. He had heard about it?"

"He was following their trails. Like I can do. That's what I was doing on the farm the night Gift arrived. Remember? I was looking at new trails."

Coulter's voice had a ragged edge.

"I remember," Adrian said. He glanced over his shoulder.

His eyes had become more accustomed to the dark. Shadows had become more distinct. But there still wasn't enough light to see clearly. If someone were following them, he wouldn't be able to see until they were close.

"We need to keep walking," Coulter said, and his words echoed Adrian's thoughts exactly. "We need to get away from them."

"They'll follow," Adrian said.

"And we'll be ready," Coulter said.

"You can keep them back?" Adrian asked. He didn't want them near Gift or Leen. He didn't like the way the group had talked about "tall ones" or the Fey.

"For now," Coulter said.

He sighed deeply and then started up the trail again, going slowly enough for Adrian to follow. He glanced over his shoulder. There was no one behind him.

At least, no one he could see.

"How far do we have to go?"

"Not far," Coulter said.

Adrian was glad. He was exhausted. Between the work he had done during the day and the tension he had felt on the mountainside, he wasn't sure how far he could go without either food or sleep. He was learning to get by with less of both, but he wasn't a boy any longer. His recuperative powers weren't what they had once been.

He thought of what Coulter had told him, and shuddered. The Rocaan, the former Rocaan, with Coulter's powers. Did that mean all Rocaan, had such powers? And if so, why hadn't they used them before?

What had Rocaan said to Coulter?

You're trying to make me into something I'm not.

And Coulter had said, *It worked, too.*

It worked, too.

Adrian tripped over a small rock, righted himself and kept going.

"What were you doing when I found you?" Adrian asked. "Why were you attacking him?"

Coulter didn't stop. "His friends came after me."

"But it sounded like you were forcing him to do something."

"I was." Coulter's voice had gotten soft. "I was forcing him to use his magick."

"Why?" Adrian asked.

"Because I thought he'd work with us. We needed him to know what he could do."

Adrian felt the hair rise on the back of his neck. "You mean he didn't know how before?"

"No," Coulter said. "I'm sure he did things, but not consciously."

"And you made it conscious."

Coulter scrambled over another boulder, then glanced up as if he could see where they were going.

"Coulter?" Adrian asked. "Did you make him conscious of his magick?"

"I don't know how he couldn't have been," Coulter said. He wouldn't look at Adrian.

Adrian climbed over the boulder as well. The rock was cool on the sides but still warm on top from the day's sun.

"But he wasn't, was he?" Adrian asked as he got to the other side. "He didn't know what he could do."

"No," Coulter said. "He didn't know."

"And you showed him." Adrian let out a slight breath. He didn't know how to feel about this. Matthias had killed Jewel. He would go after all Fey.

But that also meant he would go after Gift.

"I showed him," Coulter said. And then he stopped, put a hand to his head, and shook it. Just once "But I might have done something worse."

"Worse?" Adrian asked, not quite understanding.

"Yes," Coulter said.

"What could be worse than learning how to use magick you didn't know you had?" Adrian asked.

Coulter brought his hand down. His eyes glittered in the darkness. "Learning how to control it," he said.

FORTY-FIVE

THE fireballs were burning out. But they still cast an eerie light over the mountainside. The stone columns looked like they were man-made, and the flat rock on top appeared to be a roof. Denl and Jakib went into the structure to investigate, but Matthias remained outside. He sat on a boulder, one hand on his skull, wishing the pain would go away. Pausho and the other woman were watching him, almost as if they were afraid of him.

Almost as if they were waiting for him to dismiss them.

"Are we going after them?" Tri asked. He meant that boy and his friend. They had disappeared up the mountain, looking for their Fey friends.

Matthias nodded. He didn't move. He wasn't ready to. He didn't quite know how to proceed.

There was no doubt he had created that small barrier. There was no doubt that he had done so before. Or that he had created the blood rope that he had used to get out of the river the night he nearly drowned.

No doubt that flame had just licked his fingers. Flame he had created.

He held up his hand. It looked like his. The fingers were long and supple, their shape familiar. They didn't seem like they could do anything different.

But they had.

He had magick.

Just like the Fey.

God, his head hurt. He raised it slowly and looked at Pausho.

"You tell me," he said, deciding to use her fear against her. "You tell me what you know."

"There's too much," she said.

He made himself smile. The movement tugged on the wounds on his face. "I don't care."

"It would take all night."

"You're making excuses. You don't want me to know everything, do you?" he asked. "Then you would lose your power."

She crossed her arms. She was old, but she had the look of strength to her. "The mountain returned you. I must live with that. But that doesn't mean I have to tell you anything."

"How many babies have you brought up here over the years?"

"Not many," she said softly.

"Compared to what?" Tri asked. He had moved to Matthias's side. Matthias couldn't tell, but it seemed, in the grayish orange light of the dying fires, that Tri was paler than usual. How much had he done as a Wise One? Had he brought a newborn up this mountainside too?

"Compared to before." She pursed her lips, as if she wanted to say more, but couldn't.

"Before?" Matthias asked.

She nodded.

"Before what?"

"When the Roca ordered it," she said.

He spun away from her, turning his back rapidly. Whatever his beliefs had been, however he had felt about the existence of God or lack thereof, the depth of his own faith or lack thereof, he had a respect for the religion.

And she clearly had not.

The Roca he knew, the Roca he studied, would never have behaved that way.

"You justify murder so easily," he said.

"The Roca was the Beloved of God," she said from behind him. Her voice remained strong. As if she believed every word she said.

"Are you saying that putting babies on mountainsides is a religious act?"

She didn't answer him. He turned. She was watching him. He had seen that look before. The old Danite who had taught him the Words Written and Unwritten used to look at him that way when he missed the point of something.

When it was obvious.

She did believe it was a religious act.

Murder as a religious act.

And that was an abomination.

Are you telling me you killed my wife on purpose? Nicholas had asked him the last time they met.

No, Matthias had said. *It was God's will.*

It was God's will.

He shook his head, as if to get his own words out of it. In the past fifteen years, he had done nothing wrong. He still wasn't sure if killing Jewel was wrong.

Or Burden?

Killing Burden had not been a religious act. Matthias had flung holy water on a defenseless man, a man behind bars, a man who couldn't touch him.

A Fey.

Who might have had enough magick to attack him, even with the bars between them.

If you thought of God, Nicholas had said, *you wouldn't use him as an excuse for murder.*

An excuse for murder.

For murder.

Matthias put his hands back to his skull. It hurt so bad that he thought it was going to explode.

"When did the Roca tell you that?" he asked. "When did he tell the people of Constant to kill their babies? He ordered his sons to split the rule just before he was Absorbed. How could he have ordered such an abomination during that small bit of time? And how could it have been followed?"

"You are the Rocaan, and you do not know the history of your own religion?" she asked.

She smiled at him, as if he were crazy. He winced at the pain in his head. It throbbed with each beat of his heart.

"I know everything the Tabernacle taught," he said, "and more. I know many of the old stories."

"But you never saw the original Words," she said.

He frowned. "They were destroyed in one of the schisms."

She shook her head. "They've been here all along."

"They still exist," Tri said. He had been watching this closely, but he had remained near Matthias. As if he were protecting Matthias. As if Matthias needed protection.

"You've seen them?" Matthias asked him.

"I was supposed to read them as a Wise One. I never got around to it."

Matthias swallowed. The light from the fires was fading into a soft orange. The smoke was clearing a bit. The wind had picked up.

"You had an opportunity to read a historic document and you never got around to it?"

Tri shrugged. Matthias frowned at him. Could Tri read? Was that what stopped him?

It didn't matter. What mattered was settling his swinging emotions, clearing the headache, and getting up that mountainside.

"The Words you studied are incomplete," she said. "We have all of them. The Roca was Absorbed. But twenty years later, he returned."

Then Matthias laughed. She had played with him after all.

She didn't move. Her look returned to the one the old Danite used to give him. Mixed with another—the one that his history instructor used to give in the special school the Tabernacle had sent him to.

The school where he had met Nicholas's father, Alexander. It had been attached to the Tabernacle, and there he and Alexander had become friends.

Good friends.

The Fey had murdered Alexander, too.

"The Roca returned," she repeated.

"A dead man does not return," Matthias said.

"The Roca did. He came to the place of his birth and instructed the people of Constant. That's when he wrote the Words."

A chill ran up Matthias's back, although the mountainside was warm from the fires. That had been one of the questions that had plagued his scholarship. He had always wondered who wrote down the Words.

And why.

"You lie," he whispered. "You lie to confuse me. You like because you've always hated me."

"I do not hate you, Matthias," she said. "I believe you are evil. And I believe it is part of your nature. It is the magick that burning boy tried to call up in you. It corrupts. You are corrupted."

"But you said the Roca had these powers. That means he was evil, too," Matthias said.

"He was sent from God," she said.

"But I have the same powers, you said." Matthias was not understanding her. Was it his headache? "If I do, then you're saying I was sent from God also."

"There was the Roca," she said in a singsong teaching voice. She had clearly said this a thousand times before, but to whom he did not know. "There were the Soldiers of the Enemy. And then, when they were gone, there was the Enemy from Within. It pretended to be of God, but it was not of God. It used the powers of God's Beloved for evil. You descend from the Enemy from Within, Matthias."

"How do you know that?" he asked.

"Because you are tall," she whispered.

Matthias's headache grew. He pressed against the sides of his head. He wasn't ready for this argument. He couldn't think about what she was saying.

What the boy had said.

Matthias turned away from all of them, cupped his right hand against his chest and thought about fire sparking from one finger to another.

A tiny flame flared at the end of his thumb, just as if it were a candle that someone had lit. Cradling his hand closer to his chest, he touched his thumb to his forefinger.

The flame moved.

Just as he imagined it would.

Then it leapt from his forefinger to his middle finger, from his middle finger to his ring finger, from his ring finger to his little finger.

He crushed the flame with his left hand.

No one else was here who could do this.

No one knew he had thought of it.

Pausho was afraid of the magick.

The boy—Coulter—was long gone.

Matthias's mouth was dry. He could barely breathe. His headache was growing worse.

"Holy Sir?" Denl was in front of him. How had Denl gotten there? Matthias hadn't seen him come up. "Are ye all right?"

"Fine," Matthias said.

"For a moment twas flame I thought I saw on ye."

Matthias swallowed. It was hard against the dryness of his throat. "A reflection. I thought I saw the same thing, and realized it was a reflection." And then he smiled.

Denl smiled back at him. "Twas nothing inside. But they did camp there, twould seem."

Jakib approached, more slowly. He had an odd expression on his face. Had he been watching?

If he had seen anything, had he understood it?

"Are we goin ta go up the mountainside now or wait until dawn?"

The tall ones. That boy. The Fey.

So much to think about.

So much had changed within the last few hours.

And yet nothing had. If the boy was right (and how could he be?—how could he not be?), then Matthias had had these powers all along.

All along.

That night, the night the Fey had covered his face and given him nightmares. The night that he had nearly died in the Tabernacle, the night they had caught Burden, Matthias had awakened from that Fey spell. He had broken out of it.

Burden had been shocked.

Only magickal beings can break a Dream Rider's spell, he had said.

Only magickal beings.

"Holy Sir?"

"I really don't want you to call me that," Matthias said. He didn't even have to think about the response. It emerged from him, as part of him. Denying he was the Rocaan, even though he had been, because—why?

Because he had killed someone?

Because he had lacked belief?

Or because he had been called demon-spawn all his life, and he had been raised Islander: taught to believe that demons could not serve God?

But maybe they could.

Pausho had said the Roca himself had the same powers.

Matthias turned to her. He felt detached from himself, his headache the only live thing inside his body.

"What's up there?" he asked.

She frowned at him, clearly not understanding.

He waved a hand toward the trail where the boy and his friend had disappeared. "What's up there?"

"Look for yourself," she said.

He turned his head before he realized what she meant: She meant him to go up there. Which meant that there probably was a trap.

But as he gazed at the mountainside, he saw a shimmer against the darkness, as if the darkness itself had turned silver. Like moonlight on water.

Like fog rising against the lights of a house on a dark night.

He could feel it, faint and shimmering inside him. He had always felt it near these mountains. Like he had felt sunlight on his skin.

Only he was used to it. He rarely thought about it. It had just been part of the world for him.

But he hadn't known where it had come from before. He hadn't seen it.

Seeing it made it feel stronger.

"What is that?" he asked again, almost to himself. He felt as if the answer were inside himself.

Then he turned back to Pausho. He had seen a lot of Fey magick. He knew this wasn't theirs. But he also knew the Fey had gone up there. Had they known something he hadn't?

"Tell me what it is."

"Go see for yourself."

"I will," he said. "But I want to know first. I want to know what I'm walking into so that they can't trap me."

"They won't trap you," she said. "They'll be too busy."

"With what?" he asked.

"The icons," she said.

He frowned.

She sighed. "The Tabernacle lost everything, didn't it?" she asked. "All knowledge, gone."

"I know of nothing up on that mountainside," Matthias said. "And I was one of the Tabernacle's greatest scholars."

She raised her chin. "It is the holiest place on Blue Isle. Some say the Roca was born there. Some say he died there. But the Wise Ones know he was reborn there. He came back through the cave, and gave us the Words there."

"It's a cave?" Matthias asked.

"It's a holy place. It is filled with the Spirit of the Holy One."

"N the Roca came from there?" Denl asked. "Are ye sure?"

"According to the Words," Pausho said. "And if you go inside, you'll understand."

"But the Fey—"

"If the tall ones are there, they're busy," Pausho said. "There is much to see. There is much to learn."

"Have you been there?" Matthias asked.

"Once," she said. She looked down as she spoke. "I was a girl."

She swallowed and he thought she wasn't going to say any more.

"Because of that, I was designated a Wise One. I became one, when one of the older ones died. Because of that place."

"And you never went back?" Tri asked.

"I didn't want to," she said.

"What happened there?" Matthias asked. "What could happen in that place to make you become a Wise One?"

She shook her head, then raised it, the woman he had known—and hated—once more. "I vowed never to speak of it."

"I don't care," Matthias said. "I want to know what I'm going to see."

"I don't know what you'll see," she said. "But you were once Beloved by God. Surely you of all people can see the holiest spot on the Isle."

"You call me demon-spawn," he said.

"You're that too." She smiled. "I suspect your visit will be very unusual. Very unusual indeed."

"Should he stay away?" Jakib asked.

"You're asking her?" Matthias asked. "The woman who tried to kill me when I was a few hours old?"

But she was looking beyond him at the shimmer on the mountainside. And when she spoke, her voice was dreamy.

"I discourage no one," she said, "from touching the Hand of God."

FORTY-SIX

GOD was punishing him.

Someone was punishing him for failing his Charge.

For letting them capture Sebastian.

For failing to tell the King that the Fey had arrived.

Con sat in the darkness near the opening to the bridge tunnel, his arms wrapped around his knees. His robe was filthy, his hands were still covered in stuff he couldn't identify, and he smelled so bad that he could no longer smell himself. He was bruised from his fall, and the side of his leg was raw where the sword kept brushing against it.

He had made it through the bridge. He was on the other side, and now, things were even worse.

The Fey had murdered everyone.

All the people who remained from the Tabernacle.

The other Auds, the Danites, the Officiates, and the Elders.

They were gone.

He was the only one left.

And the Fey would catch him soon.

They hadn't heard him, nor had they seen him. But he could see them, from his position near the opening of the cavern.

Nearly a dozen Fey worked in the large room. They were small Fey, shorter than any he had ever seen, and they were working on bodies. First they had carried the bodies to the walls and then they had stacked them, one on top of the other. They had separated the bodies according to those with clothes and those without; those with flesh and those without.

Those without flesh were tossed into a pile. He couldn't tell what it was, but they worked that pile differently. They weren't as careful with those bodies as they were with the others.

While some Fey continued to carry and sort bodies, others were working over bodies on the piles. They were stripping flesh and placing it in pouches. One Fey, smaller and younger than the rest, seemed to be in charge of removing the religious icons. He touched the filigree sword necklaces by their chains, holding them between a thumb and forefinger as if they would burn him.

They just might.

Near the doors, other Fey stood. Taller Fey. They held swords and they watched from all directions. The Fey guarding Con's door hadn't seen him yet. Hadn't heard him slide into the area from the bridge, either, for which he had been very lucky.

The Fey in the cavern were carrying on loud conversations, complaining and arguing over prime specimens. One Fey, a woman, was goading them into fast action. She claimed the bodies would rot if they didn't move quickly enough.

And the Black King would be angry at them.

That comment of hers had frightened him. At first he had thought the Black King had to be nearby. Then he realized that somehow the Black King used or demanded the flesh that the small Fey were pulling off the bodies.

Off the people Con had spoken with just the day before.

If Sebastian hadn't warned him, Con's body would be there now—naked or clothed, skin-covered or skinned, he didn't know. But he did know that he would be there.

And he would have died a horrible death.

The thing his eye kept going to was not the bodies lining the cavern, nor the small Fey working around him, but the lamps they had hung from the torch pegs. It had taken him a while, but he had realized that the lights weren't flames, but small and people-shaped. He thought for a moment he had recognized the movements inside the glass—recognized them as belonging to someone he knew. But he was too far away to tell who it was.

To get out of here, he had to go through that mess.

He had to get past all the Fey guards, past the small hardworking Fey.

Past the bodies of the people he had known.

He had the sword, but he didn't believe it could help him through that many Fey. He had survived the other time he used it because his back was against the wall and Servis helped him keep the Fey occupied.

This time, he would have to go through the Fey army, and his back would be unprotected.

He had no companion.

He had never been so alone in his life.

He wasn't even sure he had God on his side any longer. He had failed at everything. He had lost Sebastian and lost all the people he had known.

The Tabernacle was gone.

The Rocaan was gone.

The religion was dead now.

Except for him. One small Aud with no training. One small Aud whose God might be angry at him for letting everyone down.

He bowed his head. He had no prayer inside him. The only thing he knew how to ask for was his own survival. And that was a selfish prayer. The Roca, in the Words Written and Unwritten, had cautioned that God liked an active man, that a man's strength lay in his ability to rescue himself and others.

God did not like to rescue people. Apparently He did not see it as His duty.

So Con thought before he prayed. He thought for a long time. Then he thought of the Holy One, whose duty it was to wing the prayers to God's Ear, and whispered:

"Grant me clarity."

It was the only thing he could think of. He needed to be clear enough to see what was ahead. And he hadn't slept in a long, long time. At least he had eaten. God had provided food below the Tabernacle, and Con had stashed some in his robe. He didn't want to think of the filth that covered the food, but it didn't matter. At this stage, food was not only nourishment. It was sleep. It was the only thing that kept him sane.

The small Fey were the same size as he was, maybe a little shorter.

He had never seen Fey that short.

He crept closer to the opening, then squinted. Their skin was dark, their ears were upturned, and their eyebrows upswept.

They were Fey, but they appeared to be as small as Islanders.

And they were covered in dirt.

The Fey guard had moved away from the passageway. He was standing near a pile of bodies, staring at them, clearly bored. Apparently, he didn't think anyone would come down here.

But Con didn't know how to get past him.

Then the guard picked up a robe and asked a question in Fey. Con understood only a little of the language; it hadn't yet been required by the Tabernacle, although he had learned a few words before he left home as a young boy.

He believed the guard was asking what they were going to do with the clothing.

Another Fey yelled at the guard from across the cavern. The guard dropped the cloak as if he had been burned.

Con's heart dropped. He hadn't realized how he had been thinking. He had been hoping that the Fey would put on the robe. Con could have pretended to be one of their number and sneak across.

But now his clothing would be suspicious.

He held out a hand. He could barely see it in the dim light. But from here, it looked as dark as a Fey hand.

He was filthy.

He probably smelled as bad, or worse, than they did.

His clothing was wrong, but he could change that.

He needed to look like a Fey.

He glanced at his robe, tugged the sleeves, pulled on the skirt. He could rip it, try to mold it into Fey clothing. He peered out again. The short Fey were wearing long sleeves and britches. The guards were wearing leather jerkins and britches as well. Their boots went to their knees.

Con was barefoot. He had no way to tie his robe to make it look like britches. No way to sew it to a new form.

He had to steal clothes.

Or wait.

If he waited, he might not get out. Or they might catch him. Or Sebastian would die.

Sebastian might die anyway.

Con's only other option was to try to sneak across.

If he snuck across and they caught him, he could fight them with the sword. He could hope that the sword's power would be enough.

But he didn't think it would be.

If he snuck across, and the sword failed him, he would die. If he brazened his way across and they caught him, he would die. But if he made it . . .

If he made it, he had another problem. He had to go through the ruins of Jahn. He had to go to Sebastian's friend.

Fey clothing would make it easier. Especially if Con didn't clean up.

He swallowed, hard.

He could kill the guard. That would not be a problem. He had the sword and it would make short work of that Fey. But the idea of facing all the others, unprotected, terrified him.

And made him feel vaguely ill.

He had killed Fey before, using that magickal weapon. And it had bothered him. It had given him nightmares. It had made him wonder about his own commitment to God. And he had managed to blame it on the situation. He had stumbled into that situation, and had no choice.

This time the choice was his.

This time, it would be his idea to kill.

He sighed. He had no other choice. Surely God would forgive him. A man had to kill if his survival depended on it. Con would die in these tunnels if he didn't do something now.

The key was to catch the guard by surprise, and kill him quickly. Quietly. And then to sneak through the Fey.

Somehow.

Con wiped a hand over his face. That cavern was awfully big. And filled with Fey.

If Con died, he would be of no use to Sebastian.

He would be of no use to anyone.

He took a deep breath.

He would wait. There would have to be a time where the guards weren't paying attention. Or where the numbers of Fey were fewer.

Or when they left. They couldn't stay here forever, could they?

He took a small breath. He would go to one of the side tunnels that led nowhere, and he would curl up.

He would sleep. And if they saw him, maybe they would think he was dead.

It was his only choice.

It was his only chance.

"I'm sorry, Sebastian," he whispered, and bowed his head. Then he began to crawl away from the cavern, away from the Fey, in a direction he had never gone before.

FORTY-SEVEN

RUGAD traveled the Link. He flowed through the white, along the purple, moving swiftly along a great distance.

This Link, between the golem and Arianna, Rugad's great-granddaughter, was fine and thick and solid. They loved each other.

Rugad had not realized that golems could feel such affection. He had not realized they could feel anything at all.

He got closer to the end of the Link. He felt his great-granddaughter's presence more strongly than he would have if she had been in the same room with him. She was mercurial, this child, and emotional, and smart. But she had not yet learned how to tame the emotions so that she could use her intelligence better.

She was young.

So very young.

If he could have smiled, he would have.

He slowed. She would have this end of the Link protected. As he neared the area, he imagined a body for himself. Always the body was his young body, strong and vibrant. He put his hands in front of himself, braced for impact—

—and fell into the girl's unprotected body. He tumbled for a moment inside her mind until he remembered that he had no body and didn't need to fall. Then he stopped.

The girl screamed—physically screamed. Her entire body shook.

This would not do.

He shoved her essence aside, pushing it into a corner of her mind. The essence was fluid. As he pushed it, it became a cat, then a horse, then a man, then a girl, and then a flat piece of flesh before becoming a girl again. He held her against her own mind with the power of his, and looked out her eyes.

It was dark. He was on a mountainside and it was cold. The girl's physical body was exhausted and hungry. He had never felt someone quite so fragile before. He doubted he had ever been that way.

And it was not an fragility of essence. Her essence was strong. It still fought him from the corner he had shoved it to. Her essence became a bird and pecked at his imaginary hand. Then it became a knife and cut him, but he willed himself to feel nothing. She didn't yet understand what he was. Then she became a woman again and bit and scratched and fought, and fought, and fought.

All in silence.

Poor thing. She didn't realize that one of the few weapons she had here was sound.

He held her in place with one part of himself. Then he extended his hand, brushed her mind with his little finger, and let a piece of skin fall off. She struggled again. He shoved her back harder.

Then he stepped closer to her eyes.

Rugad forced himself to concentrate on what he saw through them.

The darkness. The mountainside.

The cold.

Ahead of him, the old woman. The girl's eyes were adjusted to the dark. He squinted, just a little.

The old woman, as the girl thought of her.

The old woman.

He recognized her.

The Shaman he had sent with Rugar. She did live, just as Rugad thought.

She did live. She had survived somehow. A Failure who had made it.

And she was with his great-granddaughter.

Rugad felt a hand on the girl's shoulder. He glanced at it. It was a male hand, Islander from its paleness and its short stubby fingers. He looked directly at the person the hand belonged to—

—and almost smiled in triumph.

The Islander King.

Nicholas.

"Are you all right?" Nicholas asked. "You screamed."

Rugad didn't know the girl. He didn't know how she would normally respond to such a question.

Behind him, trapped in her own mind, the girl froze when she heard her father's voice.

Then she shouted, *Daddy! I'm in here! I'm trapped! Daddy!*

But Rugad controlled her mouth. The words never emerged.

He was in complete control of her body. He made it smile weakly as it looked at Nicholas.

"I tripped," Rugad said, hoping he got the inflections right. "It surprised me."

"Are you sure you didn't injure yourself?"

"I'm sure," Rugad said.

Nicholas did not take his hand off her shoulder. "I wish we could stop," he said.

"Me too," Rugad said. "But we can't."

Daddy! Arianna shouted. Her voice was loud inside herself. It was all Rugad could do to prevent himself from pulling out of her body's eyes, turning to her essence and make her shut up.

The Shaman had stopped. She was looking at him. At *her*. He had to remember who he was now. The Shaman was too far away from him to see her expression.

He stopped too. He craned his neck, looked around him as much as possible.

Mountains. Tall, treeless, a trail that was heading east. Snow above him. He wished there were more light so that he could see what lay beyond.

"Arianna," the Shaman said, and in her voice, he heard caution.

She stayed a few feet from him. Nicholas's hand tightened on his shoulder.

"Is there something ahead?" Nicholas asked the Shaman.

The body felt different. Liquid suddenly. Fluid. Almost like it was water instead of flesh and bone. Rugad had never felt anything like that before.

He had to risk a look at the girl.

She was sitting in her corner of her own brain, her imaginary knees drawn to her imaginary chin. She had stopped shouting. She wasn't even looking at him. She appeared to be like most people whose Links he had traveled across, into whose minds he had come to rest.

Passive.

Terrified.

Unable to fight.

It was an act.

He had seen this girl in action. He had seen how coolly she fought under such strange odds.

"Something *is* wrong," Nicholas said and his voice sounded far away.

"I don't think you should be so close," the Shaman said.

The fluidity grew. The body no longer felt stable.

Too late he remembered that the girl was a Shifter.

Rugad had never heard of anyone invading a Shifter's body. He knew that Doppelgängers could take over other Fey, but never replicate their magick. Did that work for Visionaries as well?

Girl—he started, and then his feet disappeared from underneath him. The body was changing. He clung to it and could find nothing familiar.

Nothing he recognized.

Except the girl herself, sitting in the corner of her brain. As he struggled within her shifting body, she raised her head, and smiled at him.

He cursed her.

She had outthought him.

Again.

FORTY-EIGHT

ARIANNA could feel him. His presence completely dominated hers. It was powerful, commanding, strong. He held her inside herself with a mere thought. And then he manipulated her body as if it were his own.

She tried everything. Becoming anything she could think of to make him let her go.

It wasn't until she spoke that she had realized that she didn't have a body. She was Shifting, but only in her mind. It was almost like make-believe. It had no effect on him at all.

Then she had screamed for her father, and he hadn't heard her.

Then the man—her great-grandfather—the Black King—had spoken with her voice.

And her father believed it.

Like he used to believe it when Arianna Shifted into one of the grooms, or into Sebastian's shape.

Her father was too easily fooled.

But the Shaman was not. She seemed to hear the difference. Only Arianna couldn't communicate.

So she had reached into a part of herself that almost no one else had, certainly no Visionary. He wouldn't know how to stand in it, like he had stood in her eyes. He wouldn't know how to feel like she did.

How to Shift.

It had taken her a while.

But she had the Shift now, and it had caught him by surprise. He was swimming in the Shift, in that moment when her body was a mass of flesh without really having any skeletal structure at all.

She could almost feel her own skin, but not quite. Still she could control the Shift.

First she shrunk herself.

First she became a cat.

She watched him get his grounding, find the eyes, look out them. She waited until he saw through them, and she Shifted again, this time going large, a horse, her limbs stretching, her fur becoming a coat, her four paws becoming four hooves.

He turned toward her then, inside her mind, and he took a firmer shape than he'd had before. Before he'd been vaguely Fey, a body that had gone by her and then lost its definition, except for the hand that held her in place.

Now he had a full Fey body. It was younger than the one she had seen before, with a full head of hair that went down his back to his thighs, a hawklike nose, and Fey features that were so sharp they looked as if they were drawn with charcoal.

But his eyes were the same. Dark and menacing, and without any warmth at all.

He grabbed her shoulders and pulled her forward. For a moment, she felt as if she had lost her grip on that Shifting part of herself, and then she remembered: she had no physical body inside her mind. Her arm could reach as long as she wanted.

Or she could do it without an arm at all.

She Shifted again, and he fell over as the body rocked. This time she went as small as she could: a lizard, like the kind she used to see in the garden. She would hold that shape because it would unnerve him. The eyes did not see in the same way, and the body did not move like a mammal's. It had taken her two days to learn how to move inside a lizard's body.

He wouldn't have the time.

He got up, and came back to her, gripping her shoulders again.

Make it stop, he said.

Get out! she spat at him. *It's my body.*

It's mine now, he said.

Get out!

Shift back.

No, she said. *If you stay here, you do what I want.*

Then tell me where you are. Where we are.

Get out, old man. I tell you nothing. If you come to me physically, I will kill you.

You can't do that, girl. I'm flesh of your flesh, blood of your blood. You kill me and everyone will die.

It's a story, she said.

It's the truth, he said. *The only truth you need believe.*

Get out.

No.

She could feel his determination as if it were her own. As if they were the same person in some odd and undefinable way. He would not leave, and she believed the story just enough to worry about it.

He climbed to the eyes and looked out. The world was multifaceted, the rock before them several rocks, the air temperature affecting the temperature of their skin.

Shift, he said.

No. She sent back the same determination he had sent to her. *As long as you're in me, I will control what we do.*

They'll step on us. There was no fear in him, only fact.

She shrugged. If they did, they did. It was a risk she had to take.

He came back to her. This time, she did not flinch. *Shift back.*

No. Then she smiled. *You Shift us.*

He shook his head. His magnificent hair swayed as he did so. The form he had taken inside her was as young as her form. He hadn't been that young in decades. Her great-grandfather, looking foreign and exotic and very, very familiar.

She had his features. Buried in a face shaped like her father's. She had her great-grandfather's features.

She shuddered. She couldn't stop it. Her smile faded, and she wondered if the recognition had come from him or from her.

He had gone back to the eyes. He hadn't tried to find a way to control the Shifting. Was he trying to control her mind? If so, why did he let her know he was here? Why didn't he just manipulate her?

Because he couldn't. If he could, he would. She knew that of him, and she hadn't really spent much time with him. She recognized the ruthlessness, had felt a small part of it within herself.

She stepped closer to him, then kicked his leg. He turned, those dark menacing eyes glaring at her.

You're not Shifting us because you can't. She smiled again.

He frowned at her. *Is your knowledge so limited that you don't know the Fey ways?*

She didn't answer it. He knew that she had been raised by her father. He knew that she had limitations.

But she also had more power than he thought.

If you don't get out, she said, *I'll force you out.*

Big talk, little one, he said. *I will not leave until you let me know where you are.*

She shook her head and crossed her arms. *Get out.*

No.

She studied him for a moment. *You've never done this to a Shifter before.*

His eyes widened slightly and she felt the surprise before he buried it. The bleed of emotion went both ways, then. He could feel hers, and she could feel his, even if he didn't want her to.

So you don't know what I can do.

I know, child, he said. The Shaman's endearment for her sounded odd on his lips. He didn't mean it kindly. He didn't think of anyone kindly.

Except her mother.

He had thought that way of her mother.

You forget, he was saying. *I know everything of the Fey.*

I'm not just Fey, she said, and Shifted again. This time she went from lizard to robin, feeling the snout change to a beak, the eyes move from multifaceted to binocular, the scales change to feathers. She held the shape for just a moment, and then Shifted again, back to the lizard because the shape trapped her great-grandfather so well.

Already her body was tiring. She had had no reserves when she started this, and she had even less now. Soon it would simply collapse from sheer exhaustion.

Understanding dawned on his face.

Her smile grew. *I'll do this as much as I have to. You'd better leave.*

Eventually, you'll have to stop, he said.

She shook her head. *I can do this forever.*

His eyes narrowed. *You'll run out of energy.*

Yes, she said, *but I won't stop.*

We'll freeze in one shape until the energy comes back, he said. *It is no great threat. I can wait.*

I got stuck once, she said. *Many years ago, and I think I know how to avoid it now.*

You think?

She shrugged. *It doesn't matter. I'll Shift until I can't any more.*

It will kill you, he said.

If you stay, she said calmly, feeling no fear at all, *it will kill us both.*

FORTY-NINE

GIFT rolled his eyes. He was beginning to have enough of this. The cave was cold. The water was still splashing out of the fountain, and he was getting hungry. The Cap and Leen were beside him, looking worried. Leen still had her hand on the hilt of her knife, but the Cap hadn't touched his weapons.

That bothered Gift most of all.

His mother—or the thing that purported to be her—stood in front of him, watching him, as if everything depended on his next sentence.

"The future of all the Fey," he said, and shook his head. "The future of all the Fey. That's been thrown at me since I was a boy. 'You're the future of the Fey, Gift. You belong to the Black King's family. You're the heir to the Black Throne.' Year after year, I had to do things for the future of the Fey. My grandfather used to say that all the time before he died. Then the Shaman. I had to watch what I did because it might affect the future of the Fey."

He took a step toward his mother. "Now you," he said. "Now you say you are a Mystery, and Mysteries control Visions and Visions are scenes from the future, and you tell me that *I* must chose one future, that you can't advise me, and that I must choose what's best for the future of the Fey."

"That's right," she said softly.

"Then what good are you?" he asked. "What good at all?"

"You'll see," she said.

"I'll see? I'll *see*? I don't want to see." His voice was echoing off the cave walls. Vials of holy water shook, the water inside reflecting the cavern's odd light. "If you're going to help me, help me. Otherwise leave me alone."

She cocked her head to one side, as if she were listening to something he couldn't hear, and then she closed her eyes and sighed.

"Interesting timing, my son," she said, and vanished.

He hadn't expected her to go away. He reached out, into the space she had been, and felt nothing. "Mother?" he said. "Mother?" He took another step toward the spot where she had stood. "Jewel? Stranger? Please?"

"You told her to go away," the Cap said. "Did she?"

Gift ignored him. He glanced around the cavern, back to the fountain where he had first seen her. She was gone. He had felt her presence earlier, and now even that was gone.

He stood, hand out, feeling that same strange separation he had felt the day Coulter had saved his life. No, that wasn't quite right. He felt as he had felt when he learned that the Black King had murdered everyone in Shadowlands.

Everyone.

Including his adopted mother.

He sat down abruptly and let the feelings wash over him. He had *told* her to leave, but he hadn't *meant* her to leave. He had just been so frustrated by her unwillingness to tell him everything. And he had been a bit frightened, too. Just a bit.

No Fey had made it this far north. At least, not Fey that his grandfather had led. He doubted that any of his great-grandfather's soldiers had been here either.

His mother had been a Visionary, like he was, only her powers hadn't been as great. She hadn't escaped. The Shaman had told him later of his mother's death just after his father's coronation, during his sister's birth.

The Shaman had told him, and he had Seen it.

And nearly died because of it.

"All right," he said. "You've made your point. Now come back."

His words no longer echoed. The place seemed to have more

substance than it had had before, as if the walls had gotten somehow closer together. But his eyes didn't see that. Only his ears knew it. It was as if a door had closed, a door to somewhere else.

She was gone.

"You shouldn't have challenged her like that," the Cap said. "Mysteries are capricious."

"I thought you didn't know about the Mysteries," Gift snapped. He wasn't angry at the Cap, not really. He wanted to yell at his mother or that thing that had called itself his mother. He wanted to slap her, scream at her, and cry in her arms.

He wanted her help.

He wanted her comfort.

He wanted her back.

"No one knows about the Mysteries," the Cap said. "Except maybe Shamans. It's said they meet with the Mysteries before they begin their service."

"The Shaman's dead," Gift said.

The Cap shrugged.

Leen sighed. She let go of her knife, then shook her shoulders, as if holding them in readiness had made the muscles tense. "I don't think that she's the issue anymore. She's gone now, and this place terrifies me. I'd like to leave."

"Not until Coulter and Adrian come," the Cap said.

"When Gift was yelling, those bottles moved," Leen said. "I've seen what they can do, those vials. Cover died when one of those got poured on her. I don't want to be here when those things shatter."

"They won't shatter," Gift said.

"Still," Leen said. "This place is full of *their* religious stuff. It could be harmful."

"To you and me," the Cap said. "But Gift is part of them. It might not hurt him at all."

"You think that's why I saw her, don't you?" Gift said. "You think she wasn't a Mystery. You think she was just part of their religion."

"Possible," the Cap said. "But from what you said, she sounds like a Mystery. I am not quite as frightened by this place as Leen. I think we're safe as long as we're smart."

"Smart?" Leen said. "You mean like not touching any of the religious artifacts? Staying away from the fountain?"

The Cap nodded.

"We don't know anything about their religion. For all we

know, this floor is part of it, and we're taking a risk just sitting on it."

"Adrian will know," the Cap said.

Gift cleared his throat. He'd had enough of this arguing. He was still shaking from his mother's disappearance. "We said we'd wait here. Let's. You can wait outside if you want, Leen."

"Beneath all those swords?" she asked. "Oh, no, Gift. I don't trust anything about this place."

She crossed her arms over her chest and stood beside him as if she were standing guard. Gift felt as if he should move, but he didn't have the energy to do so. He wanted to remain where he was, to hold the hollowness his mother's disappearance had created in him close to his heart. Her disappearance was important somehow. Maybe she had done it to teach him that he shouldn't play with her, that he shouldn't question her.

She had said there would a price for questioning her—actually, for her answers—earlier.

He sighed. He was tired of paying prices. He was tired of being the future of the Fey. He was tired of it all. He wasn't Fey, and he wasn't Islander. He didn't want anything to do with the man who had murdered his family and friends, and he didn't know what to do about his real father.

Maybe he should find him. Maybe that was why she had come.

But none of his Visions had shown that. His Visions had always shown him dying in the palace.

Him or Sebastian.

And Sebastian had died.

Gift winced.

Pick a Vision, she had said. Go in that direction. But how did he know which one was the right one? He had tried to stop a Vision before, and it had still resulted in Sebastian's death.

Maybe he shouldn't follow a Vision at all. Maybe he should chose his own path. But he didn't know what that would be. Find his father, if his father was still alive? Rule Blue Isle? Find a way to kill the Black King without actually doing so himself, in the tradition of the Black Throne? That was what the Cap wanted. He would even volunteer his services.

Gift knew that much.

Or should he stay in hiding forever, becoming his own person, and leaving the future of the Fey to the Fey themselves?

"Come back," he whispered to his mother. "I promise I won't yell again. Just please, come back."

FIFTY

NICHOLAS crouched over his daughter, hands wide. The Shaman was coming this way, but he needed to guard Arianna. He needed to see what happened to her next.

He hadn't thought she was in any danger. He had been so concerned with the Places of Power, with her speech, with his son, that he hadn't been watching Arianna.

Then she had screamed, and it had sent a wave of terror through him. He had caught up to her, and touched her shoulder. She had reassured him that she was all right in the oddest voice he had ever heard from her, and then she had Shifted.

The Shaman had warned him to pull his hand away just in time.

He had never seen his daughter Shift so rapidly. Cat, horse, lizard, robin, and then back to the lizard. If he hadn't been watching, if she hadn't screamed, he might have stepped on her.

"What is this?" the Shaman asked, and the question was not one he could answer. She stopped beside him, and stared at the spot where Arianna had been.

"What's going on?" Nicholas asked. "Do Shifters do this when they're tired?"

"No," the Shaman said. She moved up beside him and

stared at the spot where Arianna had been. "I've never seen this before. But something is not right."

She waved a hand in front of her, then sighed. Nicholas's heart was pounding. The Shaman took a sharp breath.

"You see something," Nicholas said.

"Rugad is here," the Shaman said.

"Here?" Nicholas looked around. He couldn't see the Black King anywhere.

"No," the Shaman said. "Inside Arianna. He traveled across a Link."

"How do you know?"

"I can see his trail inside one of her Links."

"He's making her Shift?" Nicholas asked.

"No," the Shaman said. "He doesn't have that kind of magick. She's fighting him."

At that moment, the air near Arianna changed. A bird flew up slightly, then landed on a rock.

It was Ari. She was a robin again.

Nicholas moved toward her. The Shaman followed. As he got close, he saw Arianna Shift a seventh time. That elongated face reappeared before it shrank, the tail grew long and spindly. Forelegs grew out of the robin's breast, and back legs splayed, all while Arianna grew smaller.

A lizard.

A lizard he could barely see on a boulder before him.

"Arianna," Nicholas said and started to crouch.

The Shaman grabbed his arm. She pulled him up, put both hands on his shoulders, and turned him toward her. She was trembling. He could feel it through her fingers and arms.

"You said to me before we left on this trip that you could be the only one to kill the Black King."

"And you said I failed before because it might turn the Blood against the Blood."

His mouth was dry. He had never seen the Shaman like this, terrified and excited at the same time. He didn't know what she was thinking, and he wasn't sure he wanted to.

"If we are to take him," she said, "this is our chance. He's vulnerable. We would have to kill the lizard."

Nicholas shoved her away from him. He had never felt a revulsion like this.

"That's Arianna!"

"I know," the Shaman said.

"I thought you said Domestic magick is peaceful."

"It is," she said. "I couldn't do it. You would have to."

"I can't kill my daughter, no matter what's inside her. I can't do it. You have no right to ask me."

"I have every right," the Shaman said. "You said you would do anything to save Blue Isle and get rid of the Fey. This is how you do it."

"By killing Arianna?"

"By killing the Black King."

The Shaman was watching Nicholas intently, as if she were trying to gauge his response. As if she expected him to take her seriously.

The lizard hadn't moved. Nicholas wondered if Arianna could hear them arguing. If the Black King could hear.

"She's fighting for her life, and you want me to kill her." Nicholas shook his head. "That's my daughter. I can't kill my daughter."

"A Fey would," the Shaman said.

"'I am not Fey," Nicholas snapped.

The Shaman folded her hands in front of her. She let out a small breath. "I thought you would refuse. But I had to offer it."

"Offer it?"

"One life in exchange for a safe future. It is logical."

"It's my daughter," Nicholas said. "You said my killing the Black King might cause the Blood against Blood. Surely killing my daughter would."

"Not if it were an accident," the Shaman said.

She sounded to calm. She sounded like no one he'd ever known. The Fey were ruthless, he knew that, but he didn't think she was. He had trusted her with his life.

He had trusted her with Arianna's life.

"I will not touch her," Nicholas said.

The Shaman let out a small breath. "Then there is one other way."

Nicholas glanced at the lizard. It had not moved. Arianna had not moved. Was she fighting her great-grandfather? Was she winning? He hated Fey magick. He hated its secret ways, its paths.

He wished Jewel were here to guide him through. Not the Shaman.

Jewel.

Arianna was her daughter, too.

Then he felt her, almost as if she were standing beside him. Illusion. It was a cruel illusion.

As his daughter was fighting for her life.

"There is one other way," the Shaman said. "I could travel through your Link to her. I could try to get the Black King out."

"No," Nicholas backed away. He wrapped his arms around himself. He didn't know where his Link to Arianna was visible, and he didn't want to know. He just didn't want the Shaman to touch it.

"You can trust me," the Shaman said. "You've always been able to."

"And you just suggested killing my daughter as a way to get us out of this predicament," Nicholas said. "I can't let you near her."

"You said no, Nicholas," the Shaman said, "and I cannot do it. I would lose my magick. But I can travel through your Link, find the Black King and see if I can eject him."

"Without killing him."

The Shaman did not answer.

He hated her silences. They were terrifying.

"Would you kill him?" Nicholas asked again.

"I can do it," she said. "I am not of Black Blood."

"But you would lose your magick."

"I would," she said.

"While you were Linked through me to Arianna. What would happen then?"

The Shaman bowed her head.

"You would stay, wouldn't you? Or do you know? Would you die? Would Ari die?"

"This has never been tried, Nicholas," the Shaman said.

"And you want me to try it now?" he asked. "Now, after you suggested *killing* my daughter?"

"It may save her."

"Save her." He glanced at the lizard that was Arianna. She hadn't moved. He wanted to go see if she was dead, but he didn't dare. Not yet. "Save the Fey, you mean."

"No," the Shaman said. "Save her. You don't understand what's happening to her."

He took a deep breath. The Shaman was right. He didn't know. And it was driving him mad. Ari had Shifted before. She had stopped Shifting. Did that mean the Black King had won? Did it mean she had lost control of herself? Did it mean she had won?

He didn't know.

"What is happening?" he asked and managed to somehow sound calm.

"When someone travels uninvited through a Link, they often do it to observe. But Arianna caught Rugad. Or he hadn't come to observe."

Her tone sounded ominous. Nicholas was in such a habit of trusting her, such a habit of believing her, of listening to each nuance in her voice, that he did so again.

Even though she had suggested killing Arianna.

He realized, at that moment, that the Shaman—who had brought Arianna into the world, who had enabled Arianna to survive—might have had her reasons for saying what she did. And, he realized, the Shaman was probably the only person he knew whom he would listen to after such a monstrous suggestion.

"If he hadn't come to observe—"

"He would take her over," the Shaman said. "He would, as best he could, become her. And we wouldn't have known. But Arianna's a Shifter. She's doing the Shifts. And she's controlling the body. For now."

For now.

"And if she loses, he could stay there forever?"

The Shaman didn't move. "There's no record of that. And it might not be wise for him to do so."

"Or maybe it would," Nicholas said softly.

If the Black King died—and if Gift were out of the way—Arianna would be the head of the Black family. She was a direct heir to the throne. The Black King could continue to rule, using her body as a pawn.

"No, Nicholas," the Shaman said. "For his own body would be vulnerable. And when his body dies, he dies."

"So right now, his body is in danger because he's not in it."

"Yes," the Shaman said.

"And all we have to do is find it."

"He's probably not here," the Shaman said. "Links have no geographic boundaries. I thought I had explained that to you before."

She had. He just hadn't completely understood. "So we don't have to kill her," Nicholas said. "We just have to find him."

"It won't be that easy."

"Neither will killing my daughter," Nicholas snapped.

The Shaman backed away from him. "I had to tell you that option," she said.

"Because it's logical?" he asked.

"Because," she said, "the decision was yours, Nicholas, and you needed all the facts."

"But you knew I wouldn't do that."

He couldn't see her eyes in the darkness, but he could feel them, looking at him with that compassion that she had always had.

"You are the closest to Fey of any non-Fey I have ever met," she said. "I do not know what you would choose to do. I only know that I had to give you the option. The decision is the decision a leader must make, not a father."

"This leader is a father," Nicholas said. "You can't separate us."

"I know that now," the Shaman said. "And I will forever remember it." She came closer, her movements tentative, and then she took his arm.

"It is," she said, "what makes you different from us."

"You're saying a Fey would kill Arianna. You're saying Jewel would have killed her own daughter in this situation."

"Rules are not made idly, Nicholas," the Shaman said. "The injunction of Black Blood against Black Blood is a necessary one because Fey will kill if they have to. They will even kill the ones they love."

Nicholas glanced at the lizard. It—she—it still hadn't moved. He crouched beside it but did not touch it.

"That is a rule you need to remember, Nicholas," the Shaman said. "You have raised a child who is pure Fey."

"She has Islander in her."

"But it may not be enough," the Shaman said.

"What does that mean?" Nicholas asked.

"It means," the Shaman said softly, "that someday you might have to watch your own back."

"That Arianna might kill me?"

"If it gives her this kind of advantage."

Nicholas shook his head. "She loves me."

"I know," the Shaman said.

He felt the anger flare again at her calmness. "If you're telling me this to get me to take action against the Black King, it won't work."

"I know," the Shaman said again. "But remember this moment. You might live to regret it."

FIFTY-ONE

ARIANNA stood beside her great-grandfather. He was staring at her. Outside, faraway, her father and the Shaman were talking, but she couldn't make out the words.

She didn't try.

Her great-grandfather was watching her. She had never seen eyes like that. She had never seen a face like his, all narrow and angular, and so powerfully handsome. The man she had met—decades older—was striking, but the handsomeness was gone. It had been replaced by a cruelty that had etched itself into his features, a toughness to the skin and body that spoke of strength and age and power.

You cannot kill me, little girl, without destroying everything.

She smiled.

I can, she said, *and I nearly did. The last time we met.*

Then her great-grandfather turned, as if he heard something. She didn't hear anything, but she felt something. A presence. Another one. A different one.

She looked up too, as her great-grandfather floated across the open space toward some doors she had never seen before. The doors opened before he could reach them and he cursed in a tongue she had heard all her life but did not understand.

A boy burst through the doors. A boy who was not really a

boy, but a man. A young man. One who looked like her and like her great-grandfather. Only his eyes were light-colored and his face shaped like her father's.

Gift.

She growled deep in her throat. She did not want that boy here as well as her great-grandfather. Had they teamed up?

Her great-grandfather didn't think so. He shoved at the boy, who shoved back. Her great-grandfather fell aside with a look of surprise. The boy started to reach for him, then stopped and looked at Arianna.

His eyes weren't just light, they were gray. Gray, not blue, and there were lines on his face that no young man should have.

Sebastian? she asked, and her voice came out in a whisper.

Ari. She felt joy like she hadn't felt in a long, long time. His joy. He reached for her, then her great-grandfather stood. He ran for Sebastian and shoved him at the door, but Sebastian held on. Here, in this place, Sebastian moved quickly. There was no stutter in his speech or hesitation in his manner. And he seemed to know how to function.

It was as if he had been born to live in a place like this.

Help me, Ari, he said. *Help me help you.*

She ran to his side and yanked on her great-grandfather's shoulders. Sebastian pushed at the same time, and her great-grandfather fell back, landing on top of her.

She felt the air rush from her body, then she remembered she had none. She pushed him off, and Sebastian stood on him, holding him down for a brief half moment.

You're alive, she said. *Where are you?*

With him, Sebastian said. Her great-grandfather grabbed his foot and pushed, but Sebastian couldn't be moved. *Ari, when you find me, realize that Con will know what to do.*

Con?

He saved me before. And then Sebastian grabbed her great-grandfather and shoved him through the door.

Close this! Sebastian shouted. She could feel him float away. He had rescued her. He had known what to do. A place where Sebastian was stronger, more alive than she was.

But her great-grandfather was wily and powerful. No matter what Sebastian was in here, he might not be able to outthink her great-grandfather. Arianna peered through the door. She couldn't see them, but she could feel them, struggling ahead of her.

What she did see was light. Multicolored light that opened into a tunnel. He had come through this. Both of them had. It was part of her and she hadn't even know it was there. What had her great-grandfather called it? A Link.

She had others. Other Links. And people could invade her through them.

How had Sebastian known and she hadn't?

And then she remembered that time she first saw Gift, standing beside Sebastian, eyes blank. They had been traveling along their Links. She had gathered that from what Sebastian had said in the tower room that horrible day the Fey burned Jahn.

I'm . . . all . . . by . . . my-self, he had said in a very small voice.

And she had tried to correct him. She had said, *You're not alone, I'm with you.*

But . . . not . . . in-side.

But not inside.

Gift and Sebastian had shared this from the beginning.

And someone had cut it off. For a moment, Sebastian had said, he had felt four presences inside himself.

Me . . . , Gift . . . , and . . . two . . . others. A . . . big . . . presence . . . and . . . then . . . the . . . snip-per.

A big presence. Her great-grandfather?

And someone to cut the Link. Was that what Sebastian wanted her to do? To close the door?

But if she went through it, and traveled on this trail, she would find her brother, the brother of her heart, and her great-grandfather.

And maybe she could stop him, once and for all.

Maybe she could surprise him, and stop him with Sebastian's help.

Without invoking the Black Blood curse.

Maybe.

It was worth a try.

She stepped into the tunnel of light, and hoped she was making the right decision.

FIFTY-TWO

THE golem knew how to travel a Link. And how to work it. The golem had him by an imaginary grip that felt real even to Rugad. No matter how much Rugad fought it, he couldn't seem to get away.

He wanted to get away.

But the golem had a hold on his imagination, on his real self, and that worried Rugad.

Twice the golem and the girl had outwitted him.

Twice.

Rugad struggled, but the golem kept tugging him forward. Halfway there, Rugad figured what was happening. They were traveling *inside* the golem's Link, not along it as Rugad had. The golem had complete control here.

And it knew it.

Rugad had to get to the outer rims of the Link. He had to move beyond it, had to fight it somehow. But he had never encountered this before. He didn't know if anyone else had either.

If they had, they hadn't lived to tell about it.

The golem would take him inside its body, and then what? Trap him there? It was conceivable. Rugad had no Link to it. And if the golem moved away from Rugad's body, then Rugad had no way of escape at all.

What had it said to his great-granddaughter?

Ari, when you find me, realize that Con will know what to do.

Con?

He saved me before.

He had saved the golem before.

The golem had exploded before. Con must have been the name of the Black Robe who had reassembled him. Con.

Exploded.

If the golem exploded with Rugad inside, and no Link to jump through, Rugad would truly die.

He felt something that was not quite fear. It was excitement, and an odd euphoria. A challenge. A brain that really could challenge his. In combination, his great-granddaughter and her stone man could defeat him.

Only if he let them.

He could feel himself moving at a rapid clip, sliding through the Link. If he pulled back, he would reenter the girl, but he would be trapped there. And the Shaman knew it. The girl hadn't paid attention to what they were saying, but Rugad had. The Shaman wanted to kill him, and she would.

With or without that sentimental fool of a King. The Shaman would kill Arianna, and thus kill Rugad.

He would not be able to hide in the girl well enough to fool the Shaman. And he would not be able to control the girl's magick.

But if he went into the golem, and the golem exploded, he would die.

He would die.

Or he might be trapped in the creature. It was made of stone. It moved slowly and it had no real power.

Except the power it had created for itself. And there was no way to know what that power really was.

Its arm had lengthened. It was keeping Rugad back as it sped to its own body. He could feel the pull now, the pull of a soul to a body, its own body. He was reaching the end.

He had to decide.

He had to decide now.

He only had one choice really. Only one option that would allow him to survive.

And not even that was guaranteed.

An open-air leap.

He would have to leap from the Link to his own body, exposing himself, his consciousness, his soul to the air itself before it slipped into its own body.

There were so many risks: they flashed before him as he considered it.

He could miss entirely, leap too early and end up landing on ground miles away from his body.

He could leap into someone else, someone standing too close, and he would be trapped there.

His body could reject him.

So many possibilities, and no time to prepare for any of them.

He wasn't even sure he could break through this Link.

The key would be not to separate himself from the golem. Let the golem think it had Rugad, and then, at the last minute, just before entering the golem's body, Rugad would break through. The Link was always weakest at the attachments.

He would use that. He would ram through the light of the Link as if he had stuck a finger in it.

He could open a Link with his finger. Surely he could break into one with his mind.

After all, Links were created by the magickal brain, and used only by magickal brains.

He would be able to do it.

The pull had grown even stronger. He could feel himself spiraling. He let himself get tugged, felt himself move faster.

Then the golem disappeared before him. He could feel it, feel the coldness of the stone. He felt the golem's stone self envelop him—

—and then he pushed off the entrance with all his strength.

The light of the Link was like glass. He bounced off it. Part of the golem was tugging at him. The other part had moved inside. He could feel it, getting ready to destroy itself. The golem's thoughts were leaking into his, so therefore his had to be leaking into the golem's.

He tried to shut off his mind and push away at the same time. He imagined himself breaking through. His hands—his imaginary hands—slapped the glass.

And then he realized he was close enough to his own body. He had to time it right. He would have to slip into the golem's head, escape the golem's grasp, and find the golem's ear. His own finger would be there, and he would be able to slip into it, return to himself.

He let the golem pull him. Light was pouring inside the golem, filling him. Rugad flashed on the golem's previous shattering:

The golem's eyes glowed, and light streamed out of all the cracks in its body. For a moment it looked like a man who'd swallowed the sun.

King Nicholas pushed himself up, and reached for the golem. It extended its hand—it was glowing too—and then it mouthed something Rugad didn't understand.

Rugad's eyes were nearly closed. He could feel the sword in his body, the pain the King had caused. Through his half-closed eyelids, he could see Nicholas take the golem's hand. Light traveled up Nicholas's body.

Then the light grew even more. It was blinding. Too much. Nicholas tried to pull the golem away from it—

And the golem exploded.

From the inside, the light felt like a pressure, like the sun the golem had swallowed was growing, about to burst. Rugad could barely move with it, could barely feel himself. He couldn't see the golem's ear.

The golem held him tightly. Rugad kicked at it, pushing as hard as he could. The light was crushing down on him. He knew it had to be breaking through the cracks like before, seeking a way to escape. The first time, the golem hadn't planned the explosion.

This time it had.

It was sentient.

If Rugad had ever thought otherwise before, he knew he was wrong now.

It was sentient, and it wanted to trap him.

But not kill him.

It hated killing.

That was the weakness. Rugad pushed through it, through the golem's doubts, past the light and to the ear.

The pressure continued to grow. He could see his finger, but he wasn't sure how to enter it. He had never done this before. The finger looked large, a foreign object in the delicate workings of the stone ear.

Light was pouring out around it, sliding past the finger, pushing Rugad in that direction. He felt smaller, as if the light were crushing him. If he needed to breathe in this form, he wouldn't be able to. It was crushing him against the stone walls of the ear.

He would have to leap, just as he had thought.
He would have to try.
He braced his foot against the eardrum and shoved.
The light grew—
He soared toward his own finger—
And the golem exploded.

FIFTY-THREE

ARIANNA stepped into the tunnel of light. She had never been in a place like this before. It was warm and inviting and as familiar as an old shoe. And yet it felt strange.

She could still feel the remnants of her great-grandfather here. Almost hear him shouting as Sebastian dragged him along.

Sebastian.

He was still alive.

And he was planning something.

She had never seen him so mobile, so active. He had never spoken so clearly. Oh, she had missed him.

She had missed this place, even though she had never been here.

At least not consciously.

She could feel them both here, though, herself and Sebastian. It was as if this place had existed in her dreams and she was entering it now, awake. This was their bond, their heart connection. It radiated the affection they felt for each other. The affection they had shared since she was born.

Her memories were buried here, her first glimpse of Sebastian's face. His struggle to say her name. His hand, cool and hard and comforting as he held her.

And ahead, their great-grandfather—thinking?

Of escape.

She started down the tunnel. Behind her, she could feel her body Shift. Of course. She wasn't there to hold it in its lizard form any more. She wasn't there to guide it.

She turned, torn. Would it pick a real form or would it pick a variety of forms, like a child's?

Ahead, she could feel her great-grandfather's anger, and beneath it, Sebastian's desperation. He was thinking—of killing?—her great-grandfather.

Sebastian?

Who cried at the death of Fey who'd been trying to kill them?

Sebastian?

The Shift rocked the Link.

Her great-grandfather was afraid of not making it to his own body. So here was a danger in remaining unprotected.

She had to return to her own body, to guide the Shift, and then she could move forward, and help Sebastian. It wouldn't work if something happened to her first.

She started back through the light. She could feel a pressure building behind her. It felt familiar. The light grew brighter, and brighter. The hair on the back of her neck—her imaginary neck—stood up. She glanced over her shoulder and saw nothing but brightness.

Her great-grandfather wasn't panicked—he was too smart to panic—but he was worried. He was remaining calm, and trying to find a way out. A way out before—

Before—

Before Sebastian shattered.

No! she cried and started to run toward Sebastian, toward the brightness. It blinded her, and then she realized that she could take anything in here. She could survive anything because she had no physical body.

The brightness was crushing her. It was too intense.

It got closer and closer, holding her back, holding her in place. No matter how hard she tried, she could get no closer.

Sebastian! she shouted, hoping he could hear her.

The light was too hot, too bright, to contain. It was coming from Sebastian. She recognized it, and she remembered it. She remembered it seeping out of the cracks in his skin. Out of his eyes, out of his mouth, and she remembered what happened next.

He shattered.

No! she shouted again.

He was doing this for her. He was trying to get their great-grandfather for her. Just as he had protected their father only a few short weeks before.

Sebastian!

But her cries kept coming back to her, as if the intense light were some kind of barrier. She pushed against it, and then it pushed back at her.

She shoved again—

—and the light grew as bright as sunlight on water, blinding, so white that she didn't believe anything could be whiter. And in the center of it, she saw Sebastian, his gray eyes closed, his face squinted, his fists clenched.

And then the light exploded around her, sending her back into herself with such force that she flew past her eyes, past the part of her brain where she had fought with her great-grandfather, past the Links, past everything into a darkness so deep that it was the opposite of the light she had seen a moment before.

She was tumbling, head over heels, and she couldn't stop herself. It didn't matter that she had no physical body. Her mental one had been pushed by a force she had never encountered before. She kept tumbling backwards, into the growing darkness, until she slammed against a wall.

Pain radiated through her, and she saw Sebastian, faintly, eyes open, smiling, before the light vanished altogether.

Con knows, he said, and then his voice faded.

Con knows.

Con, she whispered, and lost herself to the darkness.

FIFTY-FOUR

THE silence in the cave was overwhelming. Only the gurgle of the fountain made any sound at all. The light had grown brighter, even though it had to be dark outside.

Gift felt the step against his thighs. The marble was cool even though the cave was comfortable. The Cap was watching him. Leen was, too, her body stiff with fear.

Gift was waiting.

He kept expecting his mother to reappear. She couldn't leave him now. He needed her. Or he thought he did. He wanted her here when Coulter arrived. Together, he and Coulter could figure her out.

Together, he and Coulter could solve it.

"Has she come back?" the Cap asked.

Gift shook his head. He was shaky. He hadn't been this shaky in days. Not since he realized that everyone he had known, everyone he had grown up with, everyone he had loved, was dead.

"Maybe she wasn't real," Leen said. "Maybe she was a hallucination, and it finally ended."

"It was too responsive to be an hallucination."

"How do you know?" Leen asked. "Have you ever had one before?"

"No," Gift said. "But I've had Visions. And they weren't like this either."

Leen sighed. "I wish Coulter would get here."

"Me too," Gift said. "What do you think is keeping them?"

"Adrian had to get back from the quarry," the Cap said. He ran a hand over his face. "They were pretty suspicious of him. Maybe something happened."

Gift felt his heart lurch. He couldn't lose more friends. "Should we send someone down for him?"

"No," the Cap said. "We'll wait. That's what we said we'd do. That's what we should do."

"Coulter's down there alone," Leen said. "You could spare me. I don't want to be here anyway. I could wait with him."

But Gift didn't want her to go. He didn't want be alone with the Cap in this place.

He didn't want to be alone with the Cap at all. The Cap had threatened him two weeks ago. That had been terrifying. The Cap had held a knife to Gift's throat and tried to kill him. His explanation had seemed logical, too.

The Black King is here for his great-grandchildren. What'll he do when he gets them? He'll make them into him. Although Gift and his sister will be better than the Black King because they have more power. Only they don't know how to use it yet. I can solve this once and for all. I can kill this boy. And if I can get to the girl, I'll take away the Black King's reason for being here.

Gift frowned. The Cap had let him go, and then had saved Gift's life twice. By the time they got to the Eyes of Roca, the Cap had offered to teach Gift how to become as powerful as the Black King.

As if a Red Cap knew how.

I can solve this once and for all. I can kill this boy. And if I can get to the girl, I'll take away the Black King's reason for being here.

Gift wrapped his arms around his legs. "Scavenger," he said slowly, "can Fey send other Fey Visions?"

The Cap turned. "What do you mean?"

"I mean what I asked. Can Fey send other Fey Visions?"

"The Mysteries do. Visions come from the Mysteries."

"No," Gift said. "I mean living Fey. Like my great-grandfather."

"Why?" Leen asked. She came closer, concern in her voice. "Did you just See something?"

"Of course not," the Cap snapped. "Does he look like a man who just had a Vision?"

Gift groaned with exasperation. "Scavenger?"

"No," the Cap said. "I don't think Fey can give each other Visions. I've never heard of it. But then, I don't know everything about Fey magick." He waved a hand. "And I know nothing about places like this. Islander Magick. Their religion must come from here. Why? Do you think your mother was some kind of sending?"

Gift scratched his neck. He didn't know what to think. "Maybe," he said. "Maybe the Black King sent her to make me trust her. Maybe she's not a Mystery at all. Maybe he sent her to make me calmer about him, to eventually make me accept him."

The Cap sat beside him and adopted the same position. Gift could feel the smaller Fey's body heat in the coolness of the cavern. "Maybe," the Cap said, "but that doesn't seem like the Black King's way."

"How would he know where we are?" Leen asked.

"And if he did," the Cap said, "why wouldn't he capture us?"

"Because you said it," Gift said. "You said he came to make me and my sister his heirs. He couldn't treat us badly in that case."

"He might," Leen said. "He might figure you have the same desire for power that he has."

The Cap rested his forehead on his knees. "It doesn't make sense," he said. "If the Black King were trying to coerce you to his point of view, or even to seduce you to it, and he knew where we were, why wouldn't he send a Doppelgänger who looked like someone you loved? Or why wouldn't he try to do the job himself? He's a crafty man, and a subtle one, but he's direct when he needs to be. And he often works alone. A man like him can't trust many people."

The Cap brought his head up as if he were thinking this through and had come to a realization.

"No," the Cap said. "The Black King wouldn't trust you with anyone. He'd want to convert you himself. You're of his blood. He doesn't know you. He'd assume that you'd be like him. That you could coerce smaller minds into following you."

Gift smiled in spite of himself. He'd never thought of himself in those terms. He'd never lived in those terms.

"I'm not a smaller mind," Leen said.

"To the Black King you are," the Cap said.

Gift sighed. He looked at the Cap. "You said that you'd kill me before you'd let the Black King get me. Did you mean that?"

The Cap looked at Gift sideways. The Cap's eyes were dark,

unreadable, a bit wild. His mouth was turned sideways as if he were about to say something distasteful.

"I would hope," he said softly, "that you now have enough sense to kill yourself."

"By the Powers," Leen said. "Gift is strong enough. He could fight the Black King."

"Strong enough to fight decades of training? Decades of manipulation? I don't think so," the Cap said.

"So you would kill me," Gift said.

"If I thought you'd become his plaything, I would," the Cap said. "You know that about me. Why bring it up now?"

"Because," Gift said. "I was thinking of letting Leen go back to Coulter. I was thinking of being alone with you. I guess I'm still not willing to do that."

"It's not personal," the Cap said. "It has nothing to do with you. It has much more to do with your great-grandfather—"

The Cap's words faded, even though Gift knew that the Cap was still speaking. The room tilted, and Gift felt oddly dizzy. He was in the palace again. He was floating above the floor, above ornate chairs like the ones that used to be in Sebastian's suite. Only the room was bigger. The doors to the balcony were closed. The main doors were closed.

His great-grandfather stood at Sebastian's left side, his hand on the side of Sebastian's head. Light poured out of Sebastian's body. Sebastian was smiling, and tears were running down his face.

"Ari," Sebastian whispered.

Then he looked up. With his right hand, he reached toward the ceiling. "It's all right," he said, and Gift thought he was speaking directly to him.

"No," Gift said. He'd seen this before. This very thing. And it was happening again. How could it be happening again?

The light filled the room. His great-grandfather fell backwards, crashing against the ornate chairs, shattering one. His great-grandfather's eyes were open—

—and blank.

The light grew so bright that Gift wanted to shield his eyes. It filled the room, made everything white. Sebastian seemed to be sucked inside of it, the cracks in his body growing wider and wider.

Gift reached toward him—

And Sebastian shattered.

Again.

FIFTY-FIVE

NICHOLAS was still crouched beside the lizard that was his daughter. He held a hand over her, longing to touch her, to help her in some way. The Shaman had to be wrong. Arianna's Fey nature was strong—he knew it was strong—but it couldn't rule her. She had to have some of him.

She had to have some of his father.

Some of Alexander, the man who was so tender that he had trouble waging war.

But Nicholas knew deep down that Arianna would have no trouble. She was a fighter—he was a fighter, and Jewel had been as well. Their daughter had that trait from both of them, and it made her reckless. The Shaman said she had Seen a Vision of Black Blood against Black Blood.

Was the cause happening here, inside this small lizard?

Inside his daughter?

Suddenly the lizard's head whipped around and its tail swished. Its tongue darted out and its eyes rolled, then it Shifted. A hand grew out of its side, and a hoof off the other side. Its back arched, but its small head remained the same.

"Hey!" Nicholas cried.

The Shaman was beside him almost as quickly as he spoke.

The lizard's head kept turning, its tail flicking. He wished he could see its eyes better, not that it mattered. He wasn't sure he would see Arianna in them anyway.

The hand clenched. The hoof beat against the ground. The lizard's body convulsed.

Instantly he flashed back to those days of Arianna's babyhood where she had to have someone watch her at all times. She had gotten stuck in her Shifts so many times that he had been afraid she would die that way.

"What's happening?" he asked. "Do we help her?"

The tail shrank and absorbed into the body. The hoof grew out farther, followed by a bit of leg. Fey leg.

"Grab her," the Shaman said. "She's not controlling the Shift."

The fear he had felt earlier rose in him. He hadn't done this in years. He touched the lizard's cool skin, imagining his daughter, using his hands on the hand in front of him.

It was her hand. He recognized its long, slim fingers, its once well-manicured nails. They were dirty now, and a bit ragged, but still Arianna's.

"Come on, baby," he whispered. "Come on."

The Shaman was stroking Arianna's body. Pieces of other forms appeared: a feather, which the Shaman pushed until it disappeared behind a scale; cat whiskers, which the Shaman tugged slightly; a cracked bit of gray skin that reminded Nicholas of Sebastian, which the Shaman caressed until it disappeared.

Nicholas held the hand. The head kept whipping back and forth, the tongue appearing and disappearing. The hoof disappeared completely and a leg shot out. A girl's leg, long and slim and naked. It kicked and Nicholas held it too. He had forgotten this, this guiding of a Shift. He had no magick to help it move, but he could show the magick one—his daughter—which parts were right and which ones weren't.

"What's going on?" Nicholas whispered. "Do you think this is the Black King?"

"He can't use her magick," the Shaman said. She didn't sound panicked, but she did have a concern in her voice, a concern he didn't entirely understand.

"Then what is it?" Nicholas asked. A wrist appeared, followed by a forearm, then an elbow, and finally a shoulder. From the shoulder to the leg, Arianna's torso appeared, but only on the left side. The right side remained tiny and lizard-shaped.

"She'll die if this continues," the Shaman said. "We'll worry about the cause later."

"Can you do anything?"

"Only what you can do," she said. "I can't use Arianna's magick any more than Rugad can."

"If she dies and he's with her—?" Nicholas couldn't finish the question.

"He'll die too."

Just as they had talked about. Had his daughter heard? Was she trying to kill the Black King, sacrificing her own life in the process?

He felt hands on his, guiding them toward her shoulder and back, touching the half skin, half scales. Each place his fingers touched the scales turned to skin. The Shaman watched, then did the same thing, working her way up the neck.

The two of them, together, might make this work. He concentrated on his daughter, his tall Fey daughter. He wouldn't let her die. Not for any reason.

He suddenly felt hands on his left. Not the Shaman's hands, not his hands, not Arianna's hands. Someone else's. He glanced up, half expecting to see someone but not being surprised when he didn't. He had never had the sensation quite like this before, but he had felt others around him from time to time. He'd always thought it was because he had suffered so many losses so fast in his life: his father, his wife, and now, perhaps, his daughter.

The Shaman's hands had helped Arianna create a neck, but the head was too small. The lizard's eyes were bulging.

"It's as if she's not there," the Shaman said softly, almost to herself. And Nicholas understood. No Shifter would get herself in that position. Not an adult Shifter, not one who controlled her actions. If a Shifter got stuck between Shifts, with a neck the wrong size or a heart too small, she could die.

She could die.

"Come on, baby," he whispered. He wasn't going to get her through childhood just so that she would die here, in the middle of nowhere, with her whole life ahead of her.

"Ari, please."

The Shaman's hands were beneath the lizard's jaw. A chin started to form. A Fey chin complete with birthmark. Nicholas smiled to see it. Arianna hated that birthmark.

The eyes were bulging. The body was rigid. He wasn't sure it was breathing.

Then the Shaman cried out. She turned toward him, her eyes blind. "Nicholas—" she said, and fell across Arianna.

He didn't know what it was, but he did know he didn't have time to help her. He had to save his daughter first.

He shoved the Shaman off her, and moved his hands to Ari's chin. He couldn't look at the Shaman. He concentrated on skin, on turning scales into smooth skin, on turning a lizard's features into his daughter.

"Please," he whispered, and this time he wasn't speaking to his daughter; he was talking to the Holy One for the first time in years, hoping his voice would reach God's Ear. "Please, don't let her die. I'll do anything. Please."

And all the while he talked, his fingers moved, skin formed, and his daughter's half-lizard body remained still.

FIFTY-SIX

SHE was working on Arianna, guiding the Shift, feeling the body beneath her fingers flow and change. Nicholas was worried—the only time he seemed to feel any fear was for his daughter—and he wasn't working quite as efficiently as he should. The Shaman hoped he understood the need to work quickly.

She was working on Arianna—and trying not to think of the causes of this, not yet—concerned that the Black King had taken Ari from her own body to somewhere else—perhaps imprisoned her in his—when the Shaman felt the odd dizziness that usually preceded a Vision.

"Nicholas—" she warned—

And then the world Shifted. She Saw the palace: Alexander's rooms, only they weren't Alexander's any more. The furniture was no longer dusty, the balcony doors, though closed, had the look of recent use. A food tray sat on one of the tables.

Rugad stood in the center of the room, his finger in the ear of the golem. Sebastian.

It lived, and she hadn't realized it.

A thread of fear ran along her back.

The magick in this place was very, very powerful.

Gift was very, very powerful.

Light was pouring through the cracks in the golem's face, pouring out of his mouth, his eyes, his ears. Rugad's eyes were glazed, blank. He was gone, too.

What was happening? Arianna wasn't with him. Was this a future Vision? It had the feeling of a now Vision. Were they both inside the golem?

And the golem was about to explode.

She went toward it, even though she had no real form. Perhaps she could see them in its light-filled eyes. But as she got close, the golem raised its unencumbered hand. She looked up, and saw a shadow against the ceiling.

Someone else.

Someone with Vision.

Someone on the Isle?

Gift?

"Child," she said, not certain if she was talking to Gift or to the golem itself.

Or to Arianna, if she were trapped inside.

The light grew brighter.

The golem said something she didn't understand, and then smiled. The Black King fell backward, smashing a chair, the sound echoing through the room. There would be guards here soon.

And it was so far away.

She could do nothing.

She peered at Rugad's face. It was empty.

Empty.

She turned to the golem. It was smiling, but tears were running down the cracks on its cheeks. It knew what it was doing.

It knew.

It saw her, spoke again—

And shattered.

The rock sprayed everywhere. Instinctively, she ducked—

And the world shifted again.

She was dying outside the cavern door, a burn mark on her chest. Above her, one of the Islanders' holy swords stuck out of a rock. She tried to sit up, tried to reach Gift. He had to know how to use the Place of Power. That was her only mistake.

Her biggest mistake.

She thought of him, wishing her Link with him was stronger—

And the world shifted a third time.

She saw Rugad's grandson Bridge, Jewel's brother, in Nye, sitting in one of those banker's chairs, talking with his advisors.

"Maybe he died there," Bridge said.

She surfaced for a moment, felt the drool on her lips and chin, felt the ground digging into her chest. Nicholas was sitting beside Arianna, murmuring words the Shaman couldn't quite hear. She tried to sit up—

And saw blood. Rivers of it, flowing all over the Isle. Bodies lying in the streets, and Fey circling, circling, like demented animals.

A woman sat on the Black Throne.

No, a man.

A woman.

The images flashed, changing as something else changed.

And then everything stopped.

Two Enchanters stood in the Place of Power, near a fountain, about to put their hands in the water.

Two Enchanters.

Only one would live.

Around her, the Powers floated, circling and laughing. She couldn't see their faces. She couldn't see their bodies. She could only feel them, and hear the laughter. It was loud, but not as loud as the voice:

This is not your Place, it said. *Turn back.*

Turn back.

"I can't," she said. "I have changed my allegiance."

You don't know what your allegiance is to, the voice said.

But she did.

She did.

Her allegiance was to that man who huddled over his daughter. That man who tried to save a girl's life. Her allegiance was to that man and one of his children.

Only the Shaman didn't know which one.

"Help us," she said.

What do you think we're doing? the voice said, as the Vision let her go.

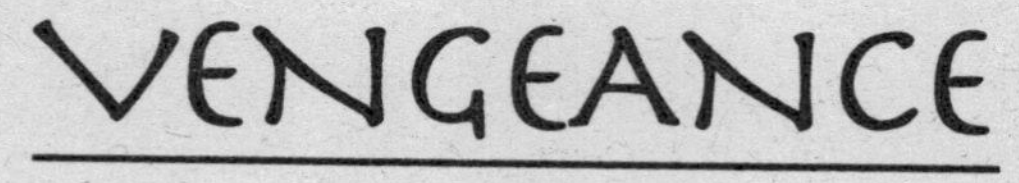
VENGEANCE

FIFTY-SEVEN

RUGAD soared through the air. He felt vulnerable, more exposed than he had ever been. Nothing protected him, not his guards, not his troops, not even his body. He was merely a blip of light traveling through space.

The beginnings of the explosion had dislodged his body. It fell backward, shattering a chair. Its eyes were open, blank, and no expression crossed its face as it fell. The sound of the shattered chair would bring someone quickly. He had to get back to himself before anyone arrived. The essence, the soul, searched for a warm, inviting host. His own body might be too far away.

Or too empty.

He dove.

Behind him, the golem's explosion rang throughout the room.

He touched his shoulder, crawled up his own face, across the craggy skin, the high cheekbones, and pressed against the eye. All of this happened so fast, and yet it seemed so slow. But the bits of rock from the golem's explosion weren't even airborne yet. Rugad had to be slightly out of time, a phenomenon he'd heard about but never felt, something that usually only Shamans achieved.

The eye's liquid layer was a barrier. He could feel it, slimy against his imaginary fingers. The rocks overhead were reflected in the eye's shiny surface. He crawled along the side of the face, and slipped into the ear.

And suddenly, he was inside himself.

His back ached, his head ached, and the pain in his throat from his wound was intense. He looked out his eyes and saw the rocks coming down toward him.

He tucked into a fetal position, protecting his head as he did so, and the rocks pelted him. Dozens of them, large and small, stinging and slamming into him. The jar on his hip shattered, and with a cry, his voice floated free.

The rocks landed all around him, sounding like hail.

The doors to the balcony burst open. The guards he had placed outside hurried in. The suite's main door opened as well, and the remaining guards came inside. They crouched around him, pushing rock off him, helping him sit up.

He hated seeming so vulnerable.

Hated it.

He shook them off, despite the pain. A small drop of blood flowed into his eye. He probably had a cut on his forehead.

More guards entered the room. He had posted twenty guards around the suite, and they all seemed to have come inside.

"I suppose you all designated new guards to watch the hallway?" he snapped, hating the way his voice was barely more than a whisper. His old voice had not lodged within his throat. It was gone.

He spoke with the raspy voice the Healers had given him.

No one moved.

"I'm fine," he said again. "Now get out of here."

Ten of the guards left, returning to their posts. The other ten remained, huddled around him, taking his air.

He stood on his own. He had a powerful headache. Clouds of dust were floating in the room. Rubble was everywhere. Rocks on tables, on chairs, on the floor.

"Where's the boy?" Blade asked. She was close to Rugad, eyes wild.

"It was no boy," Rugad said. "It was a golem."

Her eyes narrowed. "You knew that."

He nodded.

Then she smiled. He liked her. Even if her guards lacked some of the discipline he wanted.

"Gather up this mess and dispose of it. Don't put the pieces in the same place," Rugad said. "The creature has already reassembled once. We don't need it to reassemble again."

"As you wish," Blade said.

Rugad brushed the dust from his hair. He was slightly dizzy, whether from the fall or the blood loss, he didn't know. He was still weak from the first injury the golem, the girl, and the Islander King had inflicted on him.

He had had enough. They had bested him twice and in different ways.

They would not best him again.

"Send for my generals. Have them meet me in the Audience Room," Rugad said to Blade.

"Would you like a Healer?"

No sense in letting the wounds fester. And he didn't know what would happen if the rock of the golem got inside him. Would it make the wounds worse?

"Yes, send one down to the Audience Room as well." Then he stepped across the rubble, away from the shattered chair, and out of the suite.

There was nothing he could do about his voice. Once gone, he could not recapture it.

All he could hope for was that someone else would not take it.

And they wouldn't, if no one knew it was missing.

The hallway's air was clear. Except for the guards at either end, it was empty.

He had been easy on these Islanders, even though they had forced him to destroy a whole troop of his, even though they had cost him his son and his granddaughter. His great-grandchildren fought him, and he couldn't have that, not for the future of the Fey, and not for the Black Blood.

He had to take care of it, and he had to do so now. If he waited too long, his grandson Bridge would think something wrong and attempt to come here on his own.

This Isle would eat Bridge alive. Bridge was barely capable of running Nye.

And there had been peace in Nye for twenty years.

Rugad had allowed too much to slide past him. He needed to take care of all the business.

His great-granddaughter was showing him that.

As he passed the guards on the stairs, he touched one on the shoulder. "Send Wisdom to the Audience Chamber. I also want seven Foot Soldiers to meet me there, and I want a Lamplighter."

"Aye, sir," the guard said, bowing his head and running down the stairs before Rugad.

Rugad followed more slowly. He resisted the urge to use the railing, and he made himself take deep breaths. A half second more and he would have been dead. Destroyed inside the golem, unable to protect himself against the pain of the explosion.

Or would he?

The golem didn't die the first time it exploded.

Perhaps it didn't die the second time, either.

Not that it mattered. If no one knew where the rubble was, no one could resurrect it.

He smiled for the first time since he had returned to his own body. Now he only had four Islanders to deal with: the Shaman, the King, and his own great-grandchildren.

By the end, the Shaman and the King would be dead, and the great-grandchildren would belong to Rugad, body and soul.

FIFTY-EIGHT

LUKE crouched low as he crossed the open expanse of field. He tried to keep his eye on the guards near the house and the guards near the barn. He figured if he couldn't see them, they couldn't see him.

He hoped that was right.

He kept his face in shadow as best he could. His skin was so fair that it reflected light, despite the dirt he had coated himself with. Fortunately, there was no moon tonight. It was one of the darkest nights in his memory.

His feet shushed against the ground. His breath was coming in small rasps. He was trying to be as quiet as he could, and so each noise he made seemed louder than it normally was.

He wasn't going to get captured by Fey again.

He wasn't.

And no one else would, either.

He would free the prisoners in that barn—if, indeed, there were prisoners inside—even if he had to take on the guards himself.

He knew that wasn't entirely wise, but he saw no other choice. The Fey were unpredictable, and they worked fast. By the time he could put a rescue team together, the Fey might have done something with the prisoners.

He was halfway across the field now. Voices echoed in the darkness. He stopped and slowly sank into a crouch. From that position, as low as he could get without actually sitting and losing mobility, he scanned the area. The guards in front of the house were talking in Fey.

He still couldn't see the guards around the barn.

He assumed the guards he heard were the ones by the house, but sound played tricks on nights like this. He made himself look at all parts of the field. He wanted to get this over with as quickly as possible, but it would do no good if he moved too fast and got caught.

Better to take his time.

Better to be sure.

Over his left shoulder, he could see the field that he had just walked. If someone were looking, they would see the slight damage from his feet. But only if they looked for it.

That pleased him. He hadn't forgotten how to move surreptitiously through a field. Who'd have thought that boyhood skills would come in so handy?

Then he made himself scan all the way across again. The guards near the house were still talking. The guards near the barn still weren't visible. He moved slowly enough so that he glimpsed the field in front of him before he looked over his right shoulder.

One of the hay bales before him rustled. He froze. The Fey weren't all tall and slender. Some could turn themselves into animals. Others could be small sparks on the wind.

And some were small enough to hide in hay bales.

His mouth was dry.

It would take so little to catch him here. One small mistake on his part.

But he couldn't imagine Fey in every noise. If he did, he wouldn't try anything.

What he needed was a story. If he were caught, he needed something to tell them. Perhaps he could try to pass himself off as one of those Fey who could make themselves look like Islanders.

Doppelgängers.

It was too dark for the Fey to see his eyes, and Scavenger had said that only the eyes revealed a Doppelgänger. Luke knew enough about Fey systems to bluff. And maybe if he bluffed, he would be able to get away.

The thought soothed him. He had a plan now, even if he were captured.

He stared again at that hay bale, but it didn't rustle. The field was quiet, except for the faint hum of the night: the familiar chirp of the crickets, the regular soft noises of a breeze-filled field. He continued scanning until he looked behind him again.

Nothing.

And the Fey near the house were laughing.

He took a deep breath and continued. As he passed the noisy hay bale, he shot a look at it. Nothing was out of place. If someone hid in it, he would be able to tell.

He was safe, so far.

The farther toward the barn he went, the less he could see the Fey guarding the house. They were still talking and laughing, though. They had to feel pretty secure to do that. Scavenger said that most Fey guards were stoic unless they were certain there was no danger.

Luke smiled.

Little did they know.

He reached the end of the field.

The two guards in front of the barn were silent. They stood very straight, staring before them at nothing. If he hadn't known better, he would have thought they were asleep on their feet.

But he couldn't tell if they were silent because they felt his presence or because they had no choice. The barn doors were huge, and they really couldn't talk to each other without shouting.

He smiled again.

Fey clearly weren't farmers. If they were, they would have known there were a dozen ways to enter a barn. People—and animals—didn't go in just by the front doors.

He wove around to the side. The wood was pretty good here, and he bit his lower lip as he moved. He hoped that Antoni hadn't just recently rebuilt the barn. If that were the case, Luke might have to find another way in.

But in the back, he found what he was looking for: a rotted board that was half peeled away. He wondered if an animal had done it, and if so, what kind. This sort of barn rarely held anything more than shelter for foxes or other small animals. The chickens and gardens were on the other side of the house.

Horses were usually too big for other animals to concern themselves with.

There was a small dug-out area beneath the rotted board. He would have to slide through sideways. He glanced around him, saw nothing, and then crawled into the hole.

He slid and caught the faint scent of dog as he did so. Fur clung to parts of the board in front of him, and tickled his nose as he went through. His shoulders fit, but his leg banged against the barn's wooden side as he kept moving. It was hard to push himself and fit through at the same time.

Still, he made it all the way in, and sat for a moment, catching his breath. The darkness was complete in here. He had to wait until his eyes adjusted.

The barn smelled odd. He never been in a barn that smelled like this. Most barns smelled of horseflesh, if the farmer was lucky enough to own a horse, or of cows if he had cattle, or of hay and grains if he didn't keep animals inside.

The faint smell of dog continued, but over it was a danker odor, one he associated with the days of the first Fey invasion.

Rot.

The inside of this barn smelled faintly of rot.

A shudder ran down his back.

He stood slowly, wishing his eyes would adjust quicker. His hearing seemed even more sensitive than before. He could no longer hear the Fey guards at the house talking, but he could still hear the crickets and the soft noises of the field. The barn made no noises of its own.

He could feel the guards' presence on the far side of the barn.

He hoped they couldn't feel his.

His head hit something and immediately the barn flooded with light. Pain radiated from his skull to his temple. He put a hand to the crown of his head as he staggered forward and turned.

At head level was a Fey lamp. Only this one looked new. It was made of wood, with glass casings, and a braided hanger. Inside—

Inside were Antoni, his wife, and their children. He had heard that they had been reassigned, that they were working on another farm. But now that he thought of it, he realized the Fey had told him that piece of information.

It was Antoni and his family, all right, except they didn't look like themselves. They were white light, with their own features, their bodies glowing and the glow creating the same effect torches had. They were pressed up against the glass, tiny figures with their hands palm out, their noses and chins flattened. They were staring at him. Antoni was speaking, but Luke couldn't hear him.

Luke's stomach turned. Scavenger had told him about Fey lamps. He had said that the most fascinating thing about them was that the souls inside didn't know they were dead. Their bodies were gone. The souls gave off light until they had nothing left to give.

Luke closed his eyes for a moment. He couldn't help them. They were already dead, and they just didn't know it.

He didn't want to be the one to tell them.

And he didn't have time. Someone would notice the light. And he didn't know how to shut it off.

He took a deep breath, opened his eyes, and turned around. He had expected to see prisoners, asleep or in various stages of torture, so it took a moment for what he actually saw to register.

Pouches.

Hundreds of pouches, stacked like bricks against the walls and columns in the barn. The hay had been pushed to the side. The dog was gone—or at least, it wasn't here—and the floor was literally covered with pouches, except for small trails so that people could get through.

This was where the smell of decay came from. Scavenger had explained those pouches, too.

They came from people the Fey had killed. The Fey filled them with skin from bodies and with other parts, and used the remains to create new magick.

More magick.

Luke's stomach turned again, and he had to swallow hard to keep his last meal down. Parts of Antoni and his family were probably here. Parts of other people he knew as well.

Parts of him, if he wasn't careful.

He clenched his fists. He knew what his first mission would be. He would burn this place. He would make sure the Fey never had use of these pouches.

It wasn't like rescuing prisoners. But it would do.

It might even be better.

It might save more lives.

The doors up front rattled. The guards had seen the light,

and they were coming in. Luke glanced around. He had triggered that light by bumping it. They needed to believe that something else hit it.

He grabbed a pitchfork off the wall, and moved it near the light, tilting it, so that the handle leaned against the lamp. Then he put a finger to his lips. Antoni nodded.

Luke smiled faintly, wishing he could do more, then he got down on his stomach and slithered to the hole. Before crawling out of it, he glanced through, and saw nothing.

Safe so far.

He crawled out, careful not to hit anything.

He would head for the fields, and then for home.

His heart was pounding, but he felt lighter. He had a plan now. He had a mission.

And he would succeed.

FIFTY-NINE

THE Shaman opened her eyes. She was lying on the path, her face embedded in the dirt. Drool ran down her chin and her left cheek. She was dizzy and exhausted.

And frightened.

She had seen Powers, and perhaps had heard from a Mystery, and Seen another whole slew of Visions. The only thing it had in common with the last slew was the Blood against Blood.

A warning.

It was a warning.

She sat up slowly. Nicholas was still bent over Arianna, but her upper half looked like a girl again. He had gotten her to Shift at least partially, and now he was working on the lower half.

Thank the Powers that the Shaman had awakened when she did. He didn't know the rest. She would have to tell him.

She ran a hand over her mouth, wiping off the dirt and saliva. She brushed off the front of her robe, then got up and made her way to Arianna.

"Keep touching her," the Shaman said. "She might Shift again if you don't."

Nicholas looked up. His face seemed more visible than it had before. Did that mean this horrible night was ending? Was the sky lightening? She couldn't really tell yet. There weren't birds this far up, nothing to herald the dawn.

He looked haggard and old. Losing this child might kill whatever spirit he had left.

And the Shaman had suggested it. She knew Nicholas. He would never forgive her for that, even if it was something he had to consider.

Perhaps she should have said nothing.

"How long will this go on?" he asked.

"I don't know," the Shaman said. She crouched beside him.

"You had a Vision."

She nodded. "I had several."

"Was Arianna in any of them?"

"I don't know," she said.

"Please." His voice was ragged. "No games."

"No games," she said. "I saw one of your children. I'm not sure which one."

He let out a soft sigh. His hands worked Arianna's right knee. The rest of the leg was horseflesh. He was working his way down to the hoof.

"What's happening?" he asked.

He had to know. The Shaman put her hand on Arianna's leg. Together they would work this last piece of her into Fey form. "She's gone."

"Gone?" Nicholas's voice shook.

"From her body. It's the only thing that would cause this."

"The Black King has her?"

"I don't know," the Shaman said. The horse's coat was warm against her hands. "I don't think so. I Saw—"

She closed her eyes. She would have to tell him about the golem.

Nicholas had stopped moving. "Yes?"

"I Saw the Black King, and the golem, your Sebastian. I think the golem tried to kill the Black King."

"Sebastian?" Nicholas raised his head. "I saw Sebastian die."

"He's not like you or me," the Shaman said. "He's not flesh and blood. He's stone. Some golems, rare golems, can reassemble. Those golems have a life of their own. It's part of the Mysteries, the things we don't understand. There have been others in our history."

"He reassembled?" Nicholas's hands stopped moving. The Shaman placed her own on top of them, and forced them to knead the spot where Arianna's skin had turned to horseflesh. The Shift still occurred beneath his fingers, slowly, but steadily.

"Apparently," the Shaman said. "It was through his Link that Rugad found Arianna."

"Sebastian was captured by the Black King?"

"And Sebastian lured Rugad into the stone, shattering again. I don't know if it worked, Nicholas." Even the attempt showed that the golem had intelligence she had not suspected. She wasn't sure if she liked it or not.

"And Arianna? Was she with him?"

"I couldn't tell." The Shaman took a deep breath. This was the hard part. "I have a Link with Arianna, but it's not strong enough to travel on. You have a stronger Link. I'd like to use it. I'd like to find her. You can't hold her forever. Her body will Shift again, and then it will get stuck. It'll die, and when it dies, so shall she."

"You wanted to kill her earlier," Nicholas said. His fingers kept moving, but they seemed to be the only part of him that was. The rest of him seemed rigid, more rigid that she had ever seen him.

"I wanted you to know the option," the Shaman said. "If you had been Fey, you would have made a different choice."

"A choice you would make."

"It's not mine to make, Nicholas. It was yours."

"And now I should trust you with my daughter's life?"

"There is no one else." The Shaman felt an urgency that was foreign to her. She knew some of it had been brought on by her Visions, but some of it had to do with Arianna. This situation was odd, and she couldn't pinpoint quite how. She had to make Nicholas understand.

Beneath his fingers, an ankle had formed. All that remained of Arianna's uncontrolled Shift was a single hoof.

"I would travel your Link," the Shaman said, "and I would search for her. Somehow Arianna has become disassociated from herself. She might be with Rugad, but I doubt it. If she had been, the golem would not have tried to kill him."

Nicholas nodded. "Sebastian would never harm her. Unless his personality changed. Would that—shattering—change who he is?"

"No," the Shaman said. "He is even less of his body than we are."

"Then, if what you say is true, she wasn't with the Black King. Could she have been with Sebastian?"

The Shaman shook her head. "He wouldn't have shattered then, either. It would have killed her. No. I fear that Rugad trapped her somewhere, somewhere that she can't get out of without help. If he's dead, then we'll have to find her, or she'll remain trapped."

"And if he's not dead, he'll come back for her."

"He can't," the Shaman said, "not without someone else's Link. He has no way to get to Arianna. She wasn't Linked with many people. You, the golem, maybe her real brother by blood tie. Her mother through a natural Link. Me, through an old Link, formed the day she was born. And that's it. No one else. Jewel is dead. He doesn't have Gift, and he doesn't have us."

"And Sebastian is gone."

"Physical access to him is gone," the Shaman said. "As long as his body remains disassembled, Rugad has no way to reach Arianna."

"Would he reassemble Sebastian to get to her?"

"I doubt it. Rugad is smart. He knows the golem can't be controlled. He's had proof of that twice. He doesn't need to experience it again."

Nicholas ran his hand over the hoof. A heel had appeared, a Fey heel, but the front part of the foot was still hoof.

He said nothing.

"You've trusted me for two decades, Nicholas. I won't turn on you now," the Shaman said. She wasn't used to begging. She couldn't believe her hasty words, her accurate words, would provoke this response in him.

"You turned on me earlier," he said.

The Shaman sat back on her heels. "I saved Arianna's life. She wouldn't exist if I hadn't come to the palace that day."

"And you have refused to help at other times. Why would you help now?"

"Because the situation has changed," the Shaman said. "I will do anything to get rid of Rugad. You'd best remember that. But he's gone now. Your golem has removed him somehow from Arianna. She's the same girl she was"—at least the Shaman hoped she was; she wasn't going to tell Nicholas her other fears—"and we need her."

She put a hand on Nicholas's arm. He flinched but did not move away. "I have a deep affection for you, Nicholas. More than I've had for anyone since I became Shaman. But if the Black King took you over somehow, I would not hesitate in killing you to get to him."

"Even if it caused you to lose your powers."

"Even if," she said.

"Then why didn't you go for Arianna? Why did you ask me?"

"Because she's of Black Blood," the Shaman said, "and she might be able to save all of us. The choice wasn't as clear-cut then."

"Are all lives expendable to you people?" he asked. His fingers had eased an arch out of the hoof. All he had left were Arianna's toes.

The Shaman swallowed hard. She had always been as honest with Nicholas as possible. It was not wise to change now.

"In the right circumstance," she said softly, "all lives are expendable. Even our own."

"And how am I supposed to know which circumstance is which?" Nicholas asked.

"I have never lied to you, Nicholas."

"But you haven't always answered my questions."

"I will tell you if lives are forfeit." She was breaking an oath. Complete honesty was not the way of Shamans. They were too close to the Mysteries to tell all. But she had to, to regain Nicholas's trust.

"So it all boils down to trusting you." He held his daughter's foot. If it had changed back, the Shaman couldn't see it. His hand covered the last of the hoof.

"It does," she said.

"Can't I just wait?" he asked. "Can't we see if Arianna will come back on her own?"

"You can," the Shaman said. "It may never happen, or it might happen an instant from now. It is another risk you can take."

"And you're the only one who can help her?"

"No," The Shaman said. She hadn't wanted to tell him this, but she would. "Anyone with Vision can help her. Visionaries and Enchanters both have the ability to ride the Link."

"So my son could do it," Nicholas said.

"Your son could," the Shaman said, "if you trust him."

Nicholas bowed his head. She knew what he was thinking. She could almost read his thoughts. Nicholas had always been this clear to her. She often wondered why there was such a bond between them when they had come from such different places, and she wondered if Nicholas felt the same way. She knew he had affection for her, but she doubted it went as deep as her affection for him.

He was thinking. He was thinking carefully about who should save his daughter. Logically, it should be his son, but he had never met his son—not as an adult. And his son had been raised by Fey. No, it was better that he trust the Shaman, whom he knew, rather than his son, whom he did not.

Nicholas would find sadness in that thought, she knew, and it didn't bother her. She had come to expect it. The man had suffered many losses, many strange losses, in his life. The fact that he didn't know his son was only one of them.

"I guess you'll have to do it," he said, and there was even more doubt in his voice than she expected.

"I will not harm Arianna," the Shaman said.

"You'd better not." There was fierceness in his tone. Fierce protectiveness. Woe to anyone who intentionally harmed his daughter. Nicholas would not hesitate to retaliate.

"We will all be caught up in the Link," she said. "This is not the place to do it. Anyone could sneak up on us. We all could die."

"I thought you said this has to be done quickly."

"It does," the Shaman said. "But we need to be in a place of safety first. The Place of Power is not far. It will be safe there, and it will give me a chance to have help of the Mysteries, should I need it."

"I thought you said my son is there."

"He is."

"If we are unprotected—"

"He can't touch Arianna," the Shaman said. "If anything happens to one of us, it might happen to her. He'll know that. He'll understand the risk."

"And the companions?"

"Will do as he says."

"I hope you're right," Nicholas said. He slid his hands under Arianna's back. "Grab her clothing. We don't have time to put it on her, but we will cover her with it until we get to that Place of Power."

"Then you'll do this?" the Shaman asked, picking up Arianna's shirt, pants, and cloak. She took the boots and the bundle as well.

"I have no other choice."

As she laid the clothing on Arianna, Nicholas watched her. The Shaman could still feel the distrust emanating from him.

"I'll do the best I can," the Shaman said, "for you, for Arianna, and for the Fey."

"That's what I'm afraid of," Nicholas said, and started down the trail.

SIXTY

THE tunnel Con crawled through was going uphill. He frowned as he went. His exhaustion was still there, but he suddenly didn't feel the burning need to sleep any more.

Uphill.

And out?

The tunnel had some fresh cobwebs, small ones. The tunnel had been used in the past, but apparently not since the Fey had arrived.

Behind him, he could hear the Fey talking as they worked. The small Fey were discussing things like body placement, worrying about decay. He tried not to listen.

The farther he crawled, the quieter they got.

He put a hand on the wall and stood. The tunnel had become high-ceilinged, and now no one could see him. It veered sharply to the left and continued to go up. He felt the strain on his calves. He had to touch the wall to maintain his balance.

The stone was damp and cold. He kept walking. The tunnel echoed, but the echoes seemed dulled, somehow. And then he realized why.

It was a dead end.

The stone before him turned into brick. Someone had bricked this part of the tunnel closed.

That seemed strange. He leaned against it, sighing. At least he could sleep here. No one would see him. He could rest and then surprise the Fey. Maybe if he rested long enough, they'd be gone.

Vain hope. But he needed some kind of hope. Any kind.

He sank down, using the brick to brace himself. His left hand found a bit of cloth, and he turned it over in his fingers.

Cloth.

This tunnel had been used until the Fey arrived.

No one had had time to brick anything. Besides, the mortar felt old.

Grant me clarity.

Clarity.

He swallowed, not quite believing what he was thinking.

This was a passage. A secret one, like the one he and Servis had used to enter the palace all those weeks ago. Like the one he and Sebastian had escaped through.

But he wasn't too far from the waterfront. There were no important buildings this close to the water, not on this side of Jahn. On the other side, he might have believed that this were part of the Tabernacle. But it wasn't.

It led somewhere else.

Probably somewhere burned, although the smoke smell seemed fainter here. Or perhaps there were Fey above, waiting for him.

Grant me clarity.

He sighed. He'd had a clear thought. Now he had to act on it.

He turned, felt the space between the brick and the stone. Mortar crumbled between his fingers and fell like soft rain onto the stone floor. He crouched closer, hoping the Fey wouldn't hear him, and leaned on the brick as he worked. His work was slow and methodical, his fingertips growing sore.

Maybe people could only enter from the other side. Maybe he was trapped here.

Maybe he would have to go back and face the Fey.

He sighed, closed his eyes, and murmured, "Whatever God wishes."

And he meant it. Whatever God wished. Con had tried. He had tried to warn the King. He had tried to save Sebastian. He had tried to fulfill his Charge.

It was his fault that he had failed, but he would continue to try.

That much he could promise himself.

And God.

The brick at the base stopped about an inch above the floor. Con's heart beat harder. That meant he was right. This was a secret passage. No one would stop brick this close to the floor and not go all the way down. It didn't make sense.

Unless the brick was a door instead of a wall.

He held his breath, and felt along the base of the brick. It was rough against his fingertips, scraping unevenly. The mortar fell in small chunks that surely had to be audible on the other side. In the middle, he felt a small depression.

He pushed it.

With a slight grinding sound, a panel to his left slid open. He let out the air he'd been holding and glanced over his shoulder.

Even if the Fey did hear it, it would take them a while to find him.

He leaned forward.

The panel opened into a room. If people were inside, they would have already heard him. He would be better using the surprise he had just gained than running away.

He stepped inside. He was about to feel for the way to close the panel, then changed his mind. The quicker he was done, the better off he would be.

The room was small and smelled faintly of sweat. A fireplace was to his right, and it was cold. A pallet was spread on the floor, and several wooden chests surrounded it. On the nearby chairs were Fey leathers, and in the room beyond, a small pile of swords.

The Fey were using this place as a barracks.

He caught his lower lip.

There were only the two rooms, and for the moment, they were empty. If he hurried, he would be able to use the place to his own benefit.

The front room had been tossed before the Fey took residence. Fabric and threads still littered the floor. Embroidery hoops were stacked against the wall. A needle and pins had been placed on a small table, out of the way of bare feet.

A woman's place, then. One of the women who had sewn tapestries for the Tabernacle and for the palace.

She was long gone, dead or worse.

He sighed.

He touched one of the leathers. It had been a good idea below to be wearing Fey clothing, but not here. If he walked through town, with his pale skin and short bearing, he would only attract attention.

But he couldn't continued, stinking like he was. The robe was ruined.

He crouched near the chests and pulled one open, hoping to find clothing. He did. Women's clothing. He pulled open the next one, and found men's garments. So she had been a seamstress as well. He had hoped for as much.

He turned, grabbed a pitcher from one of the tables, then took off his sword. He peeled off his robe and kicked it into the secret corridor. He hadn't taken that robe off in weeks. He left on his filigree sword, hoping the chain would hide the jewelry beneath his shirt. It was hard enough to lose the appearance of a Rocaanist. He didn't want to get rid of all trappings of his faith.

He poured water over himself, scrubbing with one of the Fey leathers. Let them punish him. They had murdered his companions. The least he could do was ruin their clothing.

He scrubbed the stench off, and dried off with more leathers. Then he slipped on a linen shirt and trousers, obviously made for gentry. There were no shoes, so he took the extra pair of Fey boots. They were large. He stuffed some of the loose pieces of fabric in the toes.

All the while he worked, he moved quickly and kept an eye on the main door. He had to get out. The last thing he wanted to do was get caught.

Once he was dressed, he grabbed his sword. He made certain that he had the sword he had come in with, not one of the swords lying in the cache. Then he again debated closing the panel. But he didn't need to keep it secret. He had no idea why the woman had. He gave it one last look—apparently the Fey below hadn't heard him—and he headed for the main door.

As he passed through the main room, he took some tak from the side table, and the remaining piece of a loaf of bread. He stuffed it in his shirt.

Then he pulled the door open. The street was empty, and the buildings still stood. Apparently this was one of the parts of Jahn that had not been touched by all the horrible fires on that awful day.

The street was empty, but he wasn't sure it would be for long. He scurried outside, and headed toward the river. He had to cross the bridge.

He had to get to Sebastian's friend's place.

Con stopped for just a moment. He glanced at the palace, which still stood. Sebastian had to be in there, alone and frightened. Con could try to go to him. He had no weapons, though, and even though he no longer looked like an Aud—a fact that bothered him so deeply that he tried not to think about it—he might still be recognized as one. The large boots hurt his feet. He hadn't worn shoes since he had sworn to the Tabernacle, years ago.

He shook his head. It would do no good to get killed in a rescue attempt. Better to gain the help of Sebastian's friend.

Sebastian estimated that it would take Con a day at least to this friend's place. Con hoped the directions were good ones. He also hoped that he would be able to make it without being stopped by the Fey.

Grant me clarity, he prayed again.

With clarity, he could think of reasons to be on the road. With clarity, he could talk his way out of any situation.

And then he remembered what he had forgotten. He put his fingers around the tiny filigree sword.

Thank you for the help so far, he added. Then he took a deep breath and ran for the river.

SIXTY-ONE

ARIANNA huddled in the darkness. She had never been in a place like this before. It had no real walls, although she had crashed into one; no real floor, although she was standing on something; and no light at all.

It took her a while to remember that she had no body either. Her body was so much a part of her. Its Shifting ability defined who she was. Now she was bereft, alone, without the familiar ability to change with her environment.

She wasn't even sure what her environment was.

Something had happened. Sebastian—who was alive—had shattered again, and when he did so, he sent her clattering backward. He had done it for her. He had been planning it when he had come for the Black King.

If he had shattered before and come back, then he could do so this time.

He was still alive.

Wasn't he?

And then there was the Black King. She shuddered, a feeling so strong that she touched her imaginary arms to see if they had become real. He had been inside her, touching her mind, trying to control her.

But between her Shifting and Sebastian's quick thinking, they had forced the Black King out.

Maybe even killed him.

She shuddered. Was this what the darkness was? The result of killing the Black King? Of Black Blood warring on Black Blood? She had told the Shaman she didn't believe in the ancient superstition. She had said the same thing to her great-grandfather. But now that she was alone, more alone than she had ever been in her life, she wondered. Had she done this?

She made herself sit still, take some deep breaths. It felt odd to breathe, since she knew she didn't need to. There was no air in here, at least none that she could feel. No real temperatures either. No hot, no cold. She could shiver if she had to, and she could feel too hot, but it was all controlled by her mind.

Or her self. Perhaps that was more accurate.

She had to think. She had been going through the tunnel—that had been real—and then the force of the explosion had sent her spinning backward. She had gone through herself, past her eyes, her ears, and into this darkness.

Maybe she had been wrong. Maybe this darkness was part of her.

But where was it? And how exactly had she gotten here?

If she could imagine temperature, perhaps she could conjure light.

She frowned, thinking of sunlight, but the darkness didn't change. She tried to turn on an imaginary light, but that didn't work either.

She bit back frustration and made herself think.

Temperature indicated how she felt. Her imaginary body could change with her thoughts. But light exposed the outside world, which could not change with her thoughts.

Light was beyond her.

She sighed.

She had to do something.

She closed her eyes. She had to stop believing she had regular limitations. It was like Shifting. Most people's bodies remained the same all their lives. They had two arms, two legs, a head, and a torso. She had had wings and no arms; she had had four legs; she had even had a tail. She could think in ways other than a regular body.

And that's what would help her now.

She would keep her feet here. And then she would stretch

her torso, looking with her head until she found light. She would never have to leave this place, but she could go as far as she needed to. She could look for the escape.

No matter how long it took.

She sighed again.

Once she was out, she would deal with the feelings her great-grandfather had left her with. She could still feel him beside her, as if he were still there, even though she knew he was long gone. And Sebastian. Somehow they had found a vulnerable place in her, a place she hadn't even known existed.

Her great-grandfather had used it to control her. If she had been a regular Fey, if she had been an Islander, her great-grandfather would have controlled her. Arianna would have been stuffed in a corner of her own body, watching as someone else controlled it.

But he hadn't. In the end, she had kept control from him, and Sebastian had forced him out.

Sebastian.

When she got back to herself, she would find him. She hadn't known he was alive. If she had, she never would have left him in the palace.

It must have taken the Black King the past two weeks to reassemble Sebastian. And when he did, he used Sebastian to find Arianna. But Sebastian hadn't allowed it.

Sebastian had saved her.

Again.

Oh, she missed him.

And her father.

And even the Shaman.

When she got out of here, she'd be kinder to them. She hadn't realized how much she needed them until now.

When she got out.

She clenched her imaginary fists. It was time. If she failed to find a way out, she could sit here and think forever.

But now she had to find a way to save herself.

She imagined the darkness as mud, and she planted a foot deep within it. The foot felt stuck. She smiled. That was what she had hoped would happen. Then she pushed forward against the darkness, as if it were water and she were a fish. She swam in it, feeling her leg stretch as her foot remained stuck.

She had no idea how far she could stretch.

All she knew was that she had to try.

She moved in a straight line and then stopped and bounced as if a rope had pulled tight. Her leg stretched no farther. She was still in deep darkness. She felt a surge of panic, and then made herself slow down again.

She had just thought about limits.

What had Solanda told her all those years ago?

The only limits you have are in your mind.

It wasn't entirely true, not in life, anyway. But here it might be. Each time she thought of them, she might be creating new limits.

She didn't want to do that.

But how to unthink them?

She tugged.

Her leg remained taut.

Amazing that it didn't hurt.

Pain flooded through her.

Cursing, she went back in the direction she came. When she reached her foot, she stopped and caressed her leg. The pain slowly eased.

She had done that. She had caused the pain by a single thought, and that thought had stopped her. She had prevented her own escape.

She knew it, and she didn't know how to change it.

Somehow she had to stop the negative thoughts.

Somehow she had to control her own mind.

She had never really done that before.

But she had almost perfect control over her own body. That had been hard to learn, but she had done it.

She would learn this, too.

She freed her foot from the darkness/mud. Then she stuck the other foot in that same place, feeling the sucking power of the darkness against her toes.

This time, she would go as far as she needed to. This leg could stretch forever, if it had to. And the stretch would feel good.

She hoped.

She pushed off the darkness and swam forward.

This time, she wouldn't stop until she found light.

Until she found a way out.

SIXTY-TWO

ADRIAN kept looking over his shoulder as he trudged the last part of the path. They sky was lightening. Dawn was coming, and not a moment too soon. He wanted this night to be over.

He was trying not to think about what Coulter had told him. Coulter believed he had taught Matthias how to use his powers, powers Adrian hadn't known Matthias possessed.

And now Matthias knew where Gift was.

The trail had disappeared, at least as far as Adrian was concerned. But Coulter kept moving in a surefooted way, as if he knew where to go. Adrian could see nothing ahead, nothing except large red rocks and a faint dusting of snow.

The air had grown colder. They were getting higher. He felt slightly light-headed. Part of that was due to the exhaustion he felt. He hadn't slept in over twenty-four hours, and he'd put in a lot of work since then. He'd also been terribly frightened, first by Coulter and then by Coulter's news.

Matthias, here.

With Coulter's powers, only untrained.

Adrian couldn't quite imagine that. He had been there while Coulter observed the Fey, as Coulter learned how such powers worked. What would it be like to have those powers and not know why?

Was that how Matthias killed Jewel? Maybe it had had nothing to do with holy water, as they had said. Maybe it had more to do with him.

Adrian shuddered. He hoped Gift was ahead. He didn't think that the Fifty-first Rocaan had gotten ahead of him, but now that he knew the extent of the man's powers, he would put nothing past him.

Gift, Leen and Scavenger all had to be warned. The man had killed Fey in the past, and he would do so again. He was probably out to get Leen for hurting him in Jahn. And he certainly hated King Nicholas's half-breed children.

Adrian felt a slight tightness in his stomach. Things were not getting easier. Somehow he had thought once they reached this part of Blue Isle, they would have a bit of time to rest. But it didn't look that way.

If anything, it looked as if things had grown worse.

It took him a moment to realize that Coulter was leading him up a staircase. The rocks had been worn flat over time, but Adrian doubted if they'd been used recently. Landslides had tumbled small rocks and large boulders in their path. In the paleness of the growing dawn, he could at least see where he was going. He was pleased about that.

In the dark, he might have hurt himself.

Coulter scrambled over the rocks as if they were not there. Adrian had to struggle. His hands were so sore from the day's work that he could barely grip the stones. He thought of calling Coulter for help, but then stopped. As long as he could see Coulter ahead of him, his own comfort didn't matter.

It was better to get protection for Gift, whether Gift wanted it or not.

Adrian had reached the beginning of the snow. It made the rocks even more slippery, but the chill felt good on his face. He had gotten too warm during the fireball siege, and it hadn't left him. Not until he came here.

Coulter reached the top of the rock pile and stopped on a flat stone. It almost looked as if he had frozen there, as if he had seen something that prevented him from going on.

Adrian's mouth went dry.

He scrambled over the last few rocks, ignoring the slippery feeling beneath his feet, ignoring the pain in his hands. Coulter turned as Adrian clambered over the last rock and gripped Adrian's wrist, pulling him onto a ledge.

The ledge was made of several flat stones laid out together. It was man-made, as the staircase had been.

"What's wrong?" Adrian asked.

Coulter pointed.

Adrian followed the direction of Coulter's finger.

Ahead, he saw a cave opening, as rounded as other cave openings. But this one seemed man-made too. He could see the sharper edges, unblunted with time.

Someone had made the effort to carve this opening into the mountain's face.

But that wasn't what had caught Coulter's attention.

It was the swords.

They were carved out of rock. Two of them were embedded in the ledge, points down. The other two were sticking out of the sides of the cave's mouth, their hilts facing Adrian. They were huge. They appeared to be giants' swords, left in the dirt, waiting to be used.

But he recognized the designs on them. The carvings that he had seen ever since his childhood.

These weren't weapons.

These were Rocaanist swords.

Coulter pointed higher.

Above the cave opening with a fifth sword. Its point faced the ground as well, but it appeared to be attached to the mountain itself. It reminded Adrian of the sword inside the Tabernacle's main chapel, the one where Absorption Day services were held. He had gone several times as a boy, but never as a man. He'd hated the way the sword dangled from the ceiling, as if the Hand of God were about to come down and release the sword, killing some hapless worshipper who didn't really believe.

"What is this place?" Coulter asked.

"I don't know," Adrian said. He hadn't even heard of it. Not that he was greatly religious, but he would have thought he'd known of a place like this. "How did you find it?"

"It reflected darkness," Coulter said.

Adrian didn't ask any more. Obviously Coulter had seen it with the Vision that Adrian didn't have. The magick Vision.

"Is Gift inside?"

"If so, he has a lot more courage than I do," Coulter said.

A shiver ran down Adrian's back. "You don't think that going in killed him?"

"I don't know what to think," Coulter said. "This place has a presence. I've never felt anything like it before, at least not from a place. From a person, yes. But never from a place."

Adrian had learned long ago not to ignore Coulter when he made strange statements like that.

"What kind of people feel like this?"

"Most Fey," Coulter said. "That Rocaan—Matthias?—he feels like this. Only as if he were trying to bottle the feeling inside. This place, it spews the feeling out, as if the feeling were water and this were the mouth of the stream."

"Did the Tabernacle feel like this?" Adrian asked.

Coulter shook his head. "Shadowlands didn't either, although it had an echo of the feeling. But the echo came from Shadowlands' creation, not from its existence."

"So this is a magick place?"

Coulter smiled at Adrian, but the look was distracted, rather like a man who was participating in one conversation while listening to another. "It would seem so," Coulter said.

Adrian swallowed. Magick places made his skin crawl. Any thought of magick made him uncomfortable. It reminded him of his days in Shadowlands, when Luke had been Charmed by the Fey, Coulter had been attacked by them, and Ort had died because of them.

"Well," he said, knowing he could do little about this now, "perhaps I should go in first."

"No," Coulter said. "We'll go together."

Adrian put a hand on Coulter's arm. "Before we do, tell me. Can you see Gift's—trail? Are he and the others here?"

"They were," Coulter said. "I'm not sure what happened to them inside."

Adrian nodded. His light-headed feeling was growing. But he would go in. He would take the same risks that the others had. It was actually a lesser risk, because he wasn't Fey. If whatever had built this place had something to do with Rocaanism, it couldn't harm him.

It could kill Fey.

Suddenly Adrian couldn't wait any longer. He needed to know what had happened to his friends.

He crossed the ledge and walked past the swords. They were so perfectly formed he felt that if he touched them, he would set the blades to vibrating. The hilts were covered in dirt, but someone had scraped some of it away.

A small jewel was visible beneath.

That fact disturbed him somehow, but he wasn't certain how. He took a moment to analyze. He had to. He had to pay attention to all his feelings here.

It was the only way to be safe.

The jewel disturbed him the way that the Tabernacle used to disturb him; all the wealth inside wasted on men who had taken a vow to serve only the Lord.

He stepped past the swords to the cave's mouth.

And he stopped there.

Soft white light flooded him. It was as if he had stepped into the sun. For a moment, he saw nothing. He felt a chill at his back, and warmth before him, the dry warmth of a fire on a frosty night.

The warmth and the light were inviting. His feet moved of their own accord, but he noticed the compulsion and stopped.

Coulter stepped up beside him.

"Wow," Coulter said softly.

Adrian's eyes adjusted. The change was swift, sudden, and dizzying. One moment he saw only light, the next the interior of the cave itself.

Marble stairs were carved out of the cave's floor. They went down farther than he could see. The walls were covered in swords of varying shapes and sizes. All were older than any he had seen before, and he had seen his family's sword from the Peasant Uprising. But unlike his family's sword, these gleamed in the strange light.

Water was running somewhere. He heard the flowing sound, as if he had stumbled onto a waterfall or a gurgling stream. He searched for the source, but couldn't see it.

Coulter grabbed his arm, and pointed. Beyond the swords were more ledges, these covered with bowls. Silver bowls. And beyond the bowls were tapestries that seemed to cover other openings.

He got the sense the cave went on forever.

Adrian took a step down and nearly slid on the marble. No dust, no fallen rocks here. The place almost seemed as if it had been kept up.

He had to go down several steps before he could see the end of the staircase. The last step slid into a marble floor. Pedestals rose off the floor, covered with carvings and other items that so reflected the light that he couldn't make them out from here.

Toward the back of the cave, if there was such a place, in a growing darkness, a table had been carved out of white stone.

The room split near that table, and a fountain spewed water at the juncture. The fountain was tall and beautiful, and the water smelled fresh, like a mountain stream.

"Gift," Coulter said beside Adrian, and Adrian heard relief in his voice.

Gift sat at the base of the stairs. Leen stood on the floor beside him, and Scavenger sat close to him. Adrian frowned, uncertain why he hadn't seen them right from the start.

Gift looked up. His expression was wary, almost hurt.

"Coulter!" Leen said, and bounded up the stairs toward them.

Gift's hurt expression shifted suddenly. His features softened, and Adrian recognized relief.

"It's about time," Scavenger said, but his voice, which Adrian was very familiar with, also registered relief. And it took a lot to worry the little Fey.

"It took me a while to get away from the quarry," Adrian said.

"And we ran into a problem on the mountainside," Coulter said. Then Leen rushed into his arms and hugged him. Coulter glanced over his shoulder, surprise in his face, eyebrows raised. Leen had never shown affection with him. She had been wary of him before, worried that he would do something to hurt Gift.

She stepped back as if she had the same thought at the same moment. "Sorry," she said, brushing off her uniform. "This place is terrifying."

It was awe-inspiring to Adrian, but he could imagine how it would seem to a Fey. Being surrounded by icons of another religion, a religion that had items that killed Fey.

And the water, the bubbling water, was it holy?

He hoped they had the sense to leave it alone.

"We weren't sure what had happened to you," Scavenger said. He hadn't moved.

Coulter was standing rigidly, watching Leen as if she had burned him. Adrian suppressed a smile. The boy didn't deal well with shocks.

"We ran into some old friends of yours," Adrian said. "They might be coming here."

"Of ours?" Gift asked. That wary expression had returned. Something had happened to them here. Something that had them all spooked.

Adrian took a breath. He wanted to tell this, not Coulter. If

Coulter confessed to adding to Matthias's power, then Gift might never forgive him.

Coulter opened his mouth, but Adrian put a hand on his arm. "We saw the Fifty-first Rocaan," he said. "Matthias."

The looks which greeted him were blank.

"The man," Adrian said softly and as gently as he could, "who killed your mother, Gift."

Gift moaned and put his face in his hands.

"That's impossible," Leen said. "I killed him. I stabbed him two dozen times, and shoved him so deep in that river that he would drown if he didn't bleed to death."

"He's alive," Adrian said. "His face is bandaged. Obviously someone rescued him."

"Or he rescued himself." Coulter's voice sounded bitter. "He's not the average Islander."

"Thank the Powers for that," Scavenger said.

"No," Coulter said. Adrian tightened his grip on Coulter's arm, but Coulter didn't stop. "He's like me."

Gift raised his head out of his hands. "What do you mean he's like you?"

"He has the same powers," Adrian said. "He has magick. Coulter thinks the magick might have saved him, more than once."

"Stab me two dozen times and shove me in a bottomless well, and I could get out," Coulter said. "I could use several spells to get me out of that water. Eventually I would need help, but I could postpone death for hours, maybe days."

"And he clearly had help," Adrian said. "He had bandages on the side of his face, and he was traveling with several people."

Leen frowned and shook her head. "I can't believe this. I killed him."

"I wish you had," Scavenger said. "But you didn't. The question is, how did he get here?"

"That's not the question," Adrian said. "The question is how long will it take him to find this place?"

"Or maybe he already knows of it." Leen swept a hand toward the walls. The chalices gleamed. "You say he used to be the head of the Islander religion. This is their spot."

"Maybe," Gift said.

Adrian glanced at him. It was clearly a religious place. What would make Gift doubt it?

"He said he was following the trail of two Fey," Coulter said.

"He knew Gift and Leen had been in the village. He followed them using Enchanter powers. Only he didn't know that's what he had—"

"But Coulter figured it out," Adrian interrupted. He wasn't going to let Coulter tell Gift any more than necessary.

"Why would he track Fey?" Scavenger asked.

"To kill them," Gift said softly. "Like he killed my mother."

"I'm afraid so," Adrian said. "We have a couple of choices. It's dawn now. We might be able to make it down the mountain—"

"Back into that town?" Gift said. "No thank you. They weren't really happy with us either."

"Or we can backtrack and get out of these mountains, avoiding the site where we saw the Fifty-first Rocaan—"

"Possible," Scavenger said.

"Or we can defend this place." Adrian glanced around. The swords reassured him, while the chalices made him nervous. And the running water. If it were holy water, all Gift or Leen or Scavenger had to do was accidentally back into the fountain and they would die.

They might die if a drop splashed on them.

"We'll stay here," Gift said.

"We might not be safe here either," Adrian said. "All the symbols of Rocaanism here could be a warning to you. If any of them affect you the way holy water does, one mistake would kill you."

"And that Matthias might know how to use this place," Leen said. "It might have a religious magick we don't know about."

Adrian looked at her. Her eyes were narrow, her lips pulled back tight. She clenched her fists, and her right hand rested near her sword. She was frightened. He'd seen her angry, he'd seen her fight her own people, but he'd never seen her like this.

"I don't think the magick here is religious," Gift said.

"Then you're denying what's before your eyes, boy," Scavenger said.

"You didn't think so before," Gift snapped.

"I never said that," Scavenger said.

"What happened?" Coulter asked before Adrian could. Something had happened here, something that frightened Leen and set Gift and Scavenger into this verbal debate.

"Gift thinks he saw his mother," Scavenger said with a slight sneer.

"Niche?" Coulter asked.

Gift shook his head.

"Your real mother?" Coulter sounded breathless.

"She said she was a Mystery. Some Fey, when they die, don't pass on. They become spirits," Gift said.

"That's not it," Scavenger said. "And I don't think a Mystery would tell you she's one, do you? Then she's not a Mystery."

"You thought so before," Gift said.

"I was willing to listen before. I've been thinking about this. What better way to woo you deeper into the cave? Who knows what deadly stuff lurks beyond that fountain?"

Adrian had heard of the Mysteries. The Fey often discussed them in the same breath as something called the Powers. The Fey spoke of them with awe, and in the same way the Rocaanists spoke of God, the Roca, and the Holy One.

"Did she try to do that?" Adrian asked. "Try to lure you beyond that fountain?"

"No," Gift said.

"She wanted to talk to him alone," Leen said.

"Did you see her?" Coulter asked.

"No," Scavenger said. "*She* said only people with magick could see her."

"No," Gift said. "She said that she could appear to three people: the person she had loved the most, the person she had hated the most, and a third person of her choice. I was the one she chose."

"Why would she show up here?"Adrian asked. "She's been dead a long time. Why not show up before?"

"She said she had, only I couldn't see her. She's visible here. Not in other places."

"Is she here now?" Coulter asked.

"No," Gift said. He wouldn't meet their gaze, suddenly.

"Gift told her to go away, and she did."

"At least she listens," Adrian said.

"It's not funny," Gift said.

He sounded like a hurt child. If this Mystery was indeed Jewel, then she might be good for him. But it sounded to Adrian as if something in the cave knew where Gift was vulnerable and sought to touch him there.

But that wasn't part of Rocaanism. Rocaanism strove for self-sufficiency. It taught its followers to believe in the Roca, but not to call on the Holy One unless all other avenues had been thwarted. Yet there were parts of the religion he didn't know, and more parts he didn't understand. He had never understood why holy water was deadly to Fey, and why a just God would allow the tools of his religion to kill.

The very symbol of the religion was a sword, something that had seemed natural to Adrian as a boy, but had never made sense to him as an adult. Why glorify something designed only to kill or maim another? What kind of religion was this, anyway?

"I'd like to stay here," Gift said into the silence.

"It doesn't make sense, boy," Scavenger said.

"It makes the most sense," Gift said. "If we go to town, they'll try to kill me and Leen. If we backtrack, we run the risk of finding those villagers who seem to be searching for us in the mountains. If we stay here, we have only one door to defend and a lot of weaponry."

"We don't know if you can touch it," Adrian said.

"But you can. And so can Coulter."

"What if Scavenger's right?" Coulter said. "What if that woman isn't a Mystery? What if she's something put here, to lure you into part of the cave and kill you?"

"I won't let her," Gift said.

"You might not have a choice," Scavenger said. "Some magicks make you believe you're doing what's best for yourself when actually you're hurting yourself."

"I'll take the risk," Gift said.

"It's a risk we'd all take," Adrian said. "You are the heir to Blue Isle's throne. We can't lose you now."

"And to the Black Throne," Leen said.

"For whatever that's worth," Gift said. He sighed. "This might not even be important. We don't even know if this Rocaan is coming."

"Oh, he's coming," Coulter said. He turned toward the entrance. "He'll be here, sooner or later."

"We act like that man's all-powerful," Leen said. "He's not. I nearly killed him."

"And he doesn't have a very strong group with him," Adrian said. "I only counted five others, and I'm not sure that two were with him."

He thought for a moment. Gift hadn't moved from the step below. Leen had her arms crossed. Scavenger had turned on his step so that he could see them more clearly. Coulter had backed away from Leen until he was almost pressed against Adrian.

"Six against five, or maybe four against five," Leen said. "That's reasonable."

"Especially since you've defeated him before," Adrian said.

"He's got slop," Coulter said. It sounded like a warning.

"What does that mean?" Gift said.

"He didn't always know about his own powers. He tried to repress the magick. It slops over, it always does," Coulter said, "and he still has residue from that. It'll make him even more powerful."

"Are you afraid of him?" Gift asked. There was still a coolness about him when he dealt with Coulter, almost as if he were hoping to find Coulter in a misstep, in feeling something wrong.

"I'm cautious," Coulter said. "We can't balance odds like we would in a normal fight. Just because he has the same label I do doesn't mean we have the same abilities. He's older."

"And you're more practiced," Adrian said.

"But I'm not as desperate," Coulter said.

"He does hate Fey," Leen said. "That much was clear."

"It seems to be part of the culture here," Gift said.

"Not Fey," Adrian said. "Tall ones."

"Matthias is tall," Coulter said.

"Maybe the locals' fear comes from an understandable place then," Gift said.

"Maybe," Scavenger said, but he sounded unconvinced.

"We have more weapons," Adrian said, trying to get the conversation back on track. "We also have seasoned fighters. The Fey never made it this far north in the first Invasion, and I don't think this area was involved in the Peasant Uprising. There are no current soldiers and no history of war-making here. I think that too gives us an advantage."

"Are we prepared for a siege?" Scavenger asked.

"You can't lay a siege with only six people," Leen said.

"He hasn't come up here directly, has he?" Scavenger said. "Maybe he's getting help."

"Or maybe he's afraid of this place," Coulter said. "I could feel the magick pulsing out of here. If I could, he can. And he's not as accepting of it as I am."

Adrian felt himself grow cold. What was this place?

"We can use that," Gift said.

"What do you mean?" Scavenger asked. "Use what?"

"His fear of magick, of this place. If he doesn't know what's in here, we could make it seem more terrifying than it is." Gift stood up. "We could use his fear against him."

Coulter smiled slowly. "And he'd never get inside."

"That's right." Gift grinned back, then apparently caught himself, and stopped.

Coulter didn't seem to notice Gift's withdrawal. "We can plan this. We could scare him away from here for good."

"That'll help," Adrian said. "I really don't want to make that trek through those mountains any time soon."

"We might have to anyway," Leen said. "This man doesn't give up. If he did, he'd have died weeks ago."

"What are you saying?" Coulter asked.

"I'm saying," Leen said, "that if we scare him away from here, he might come back with more people. He might not ever give up."

"He left the Tabernacle," Adrian said. He looked at Gift. "There were two rumors. The first was that your father met with him and killed him in retaliation for your mother's death. The second was that your father *threatened* to kill him, and he ran."

"He clearly ran," Gift said.

"Or your father tried to kill him, and failed, just like I did," Leen said.

"The point is," Adrian said, "he never went back to Jahn."

"He was there when we met him," Gift said.

"Twenty years later."

"Twenty years," Scavenger murmured. "Isn't it odd how this man turns up when the Fey reappear?"

"It's the magick," Coulter said.

"So maybe the magick will draw him here," Leen said.

"Or," Adrian said, "it'll convince him to stay away."

"Or maybe we should just kill him," Scavenger said.

"It won't be easy," Leen said.

"For you, maybe. But Coulter can do it."

Adrian looked at him. The killing weeks ago had damaged something inside Coulter, created a wound that hadn't healed yet.

"If I have to," Coulter said, "I'll kill him."

"I hope it doesn't come to that," Adrian said, not wanting Coulter hurt further.

"Oh, I do," Gift said from the cave's floor.

They all turned to look at him. Gift, the one who seemed to

have the most trouble with leadership and the difficulties it entailed. Gift, who was gentle and the least warlike among them.

He shrugged. "Sometimes," he said, "people need to pay for the evil they've done. He murdered my mother and prevented any hope of avoiding the war we're in now. His action cost hundreds, maybe thousands of lives. Don't worry about killing him, Coulter. If you don't, I will."

Adrian had seen that darkness only once before in Gift. That was the night they had met, the night Gift had learned what the Black King had done to his adopted family and his friends.

The darkness disturbed Adrian, on a deep level. It was as if there were a part of Gift that was as yet untapped, a part that was—as Coulter put it—slop, which might affect them all.

Might harm them all.

Or maybe it would save them.

Adrian didn't know. But he was sure he was going to find out.

SIXTY-THREE

THE Audience Chamber no longer had the fripperies of the ruling house of Blue Isle. Gone was their coat of arms. Gone was their gaudy and fairly ugly throne. Gone were the suits of armor and the weaponry decorating the walls.

Gone too was the bloodstain from Rugad's near-fatal wound.

Instead the room had been transformed into a working war room. A long table, brought in from the banquet hall, stood in the exact center. Maps of Blue Isle, some found in the secret war room upstairs, others made by Wisps, Bird Riders, and Domestics working together, covered the walls. Rugad had them color in the areas held by his troops.

The only places his troops had yet to go were the mountains on the country's east, north, and northwestern sides.

Mountains.

His great-granddaughter had been in the mountains.

He had concentrated his troops on the highly populated areas. Those areas were secure now. He could afford to move troops to the mountains, to take care of the rebels, see what was in the villages there, and to discover any treasures that the Isle might be hiding.

He clasped his hands behind his back. Of course, he would have to send to Nye for reinforcements. And he would have to be careful about how he worded the order. The last thing he wanted was for his grandson Bridge to think that the great Black King of the Fey could not conquer Blue Isle.

Instead, he would have to let Bridge think that Rugad was preparing to go to Leut, to the next continent over. Rugad had readied Bridge for this; he had even chosen the secondary invasion force before he left. Bridge could make a few modifications on the Infantry level, but he could not touch the upper echelons. The last thing Rugad wanted was his not-so-sly grandson to try to strip the secondary force of its power.

If only Bridge had had the brains of his sister Jewel. Then he and Rugad would have come to Blue Isle together.

The door to the audience chamber opened, and seven Foot Soldiers entered. They were in uniform, but the uniforms were clean. It was clear that the Fey had not seen fighting for weeks. Their hands hung at their sides, and their fingers, with the extra set of fingernails, were curved. Four women and three men, loyalists all.

They nodded to him, and he nodded back. None of them looked at him long enough to note the cuts on his face or the rips on his clothing. If they did, they were too professional to let their gaze linger.

He indicated the back of the room with his head, and they walked there, climbing the dais, then lining up against the wall, single file.

Rugad continued studying the maps. Behind them, in the listening booths, were trusted guards. He wouldn't need them. His people were well trained, and none of them would dare cross him.

Especially after this afternoon.

The door opened a second time, and some of Rugad's generals entered. First Onha, head of the Beast Riders, promoted after her successful attack on the Tabernacle. She had a long nose and short, bristly hair. Her eyes were a bit too close together, and her walk was stiff. Her alternate form was as a mastiff, and she had some of that breed's characteristics.

Behind her was Slaughter. He headed the Foot Soldiers. He had risen to that position rather young. He had a L'Nacin name, like Rugad's grandchildren, but unlike the surviving grandchildren, he had an understanding of war. Rugad had promoted him as a very young man, at the conclusion of the conquering of Nye. Like other Foot Solders, he let his arms fall to his sides, and kept his hands cupped. He was as tall as Rugad, with lips that turned down and dark eyes that glowed.

The third general, the last in this group, was Kendrad, head of the Infantry. She was the oldest and highest ranking general he had brought on this trip. Only a few years younger than he was, Kendrad had taken her first blood beside him in the Battle of Hiere. She commanded the most troops, and had done so with an even hand for more than fifty years. He had thought of leaving her on Nye to watch over Bridge, but he hadn't fought without her since he was a boy, and he didn't want to leave her behind now.

She looked no older. Her body was still trim and muscular, her face unlined. The only sign of her growing age were the strands of silver woven into her black braid.

She took a seat against the wall. The others did as well.

Rugad didn't acknowledge them. They were here on his whim, and they knew it. He would wait until the others arrived before talking with them.

The other seven generals entered piecemeal, as they received the word. Frad'l slipped in, unnoticed by the Foot Soldiers, but all of the generals saw him. Frad'l led Rugad's Spies, and had the same shimmering, changing appearance as most of them.

An Islander wearing chef's clothing and carrying a small apron entered. Without looking at his eyes, Rugad knew it was Dimar, the head of the Doppelgängers. Rugad had brought so few Doppelgängers that he really didn't need a general to lead them, but Dimar was one of the very best, and had always been beside Rugad. Rugad did not want to change that either.

A shadow slipped across the wall, and the Foot Soldiers in the back stirred but did not move. Even the most courageous of the Fey were uneasy in the presence of a Dream Rider. Black, the shadow, led a troop of over a hundred Dream Riders. Rugad had brought more than usual, knowing he would need them as time progressed. They were the best at keeping populations in line or causing unexpected—and seemingly natural—deaths. Occasionally a Fey would pay a Dream Rider to kill another Fey. Such murders were rarely obvious. If they were, the procurer and the Dream Rider were brought before the Black King. Eight times in his reign, Rugad had ordered an execution based on evidence of such crimes.

Five times he had set the couples free.

The shadow made its way across the wall, slithered onto the

floor, then became a full Fey, standing among them. Even then, Black seemed darker than the rest. A Dream Rider's body absorbed light, and even without flattening itself could pass for a shadow to someone who wasn't paying attention. He sat next to Kendrad, who patted his hand. Of all the Fey Rugad had known, only Kendrad accepted Dream Riders as normal.

The Healer Seger entered. Her eyes widened when she saw Rugad's face. He waved her to the wall, out of the way. She would have to wait until he was through with some of his business.

Landre, head of Rugad's Spell Warders, entered, ducking his head as he came through the door. He wasn't as tall and lean as Boteen, but they were built similarly enough to be brothers. Landre wasn't a general, not in the military sense, but Rugad had learned in earlier campaigns to keep the Spell Warders on top of military procedures. They often had suggestions that made campaigns smoother.

Behind Landre came Ife, the Wisp in charge of the troops. Rugad had toyed with making Tuft leader after his courageous discovery of the golem, but then canceled the idea. Ife, for all his prissiness, had a military mind. He did not like to fly, and was not as useful in battle as he was in consultation. He had hurt a wing in one of the Nye campaigns and it obviously pained him. It curled against his back like a small child in need of comfort and it made him walk hunched.

Quata, one of the ship's captains, also entered. He was short for a magickal Fey, and stocky. Rugad had heard that Quata had a Red Cap in the family tree. But he was a good man, and he kept the Sailors informed. It was time to use the ships again instead of leaving them idle in the Infrin Sea.

And finally, behind him was a Charmer, Selia. She was slight for a Fey, but tall, with a beauty that was uncommon even among the her race. She had rarely spoken to Rugad, and probably had no idea why she had been summoned.

She would understand shortly.

She was the only one he smiled at. As she walked into the room, he pulled out a chair for her. She looked at him in confusion.

The others watched. They knew something was about to change.

Finally Wisdom entered the open door, and pulled it closed behind him. Rugad wondered if he had deliberately waited until everyone had arrived. He must have quizzed the guard who had summoned him. But Wisdom wouldn't have determined everything through that guard. In fact, he didn't seem to know that one member of their party was still missing.

He started to take a chair, when Rugad said, "I prefer it if you stand."

Wisdom turned to him. His hair was newly braided, and his scarification stood out against his skin. He had oiled it. He had guessed that this was somehow a crucial moment.

He would have had to have been blind not to see it.

He raised his chin slightly, so that he could look Rugad directly in the eye.

He had courage. Rugad had always liked that about Wisdom. It was the misplaced ambition that he had disliked. It had become a habit since Rugad's injury, and for the benefit of the generals, for the benefit of Selia, he would prove it.

Rugad spoke slowly, letting his voice sound fainter than it actually was. "You have been my adjunct since—?"

"The beginning of the Nye Campaign, Sir."

"And you have spoken for me when you had to, always seen to my needs, and made certain everything ran smoothly?"

"Yes, sir," Wisdom said.

"And since my injury, this power became, in your mind, yours. You spoke for the Black King who could not speak, so therefore you were the Black King. Your Charm magick made things seem so much easier. People scrambled to do your bidding, did they not?"

Wisdom's eyes narrowed. He was smart. He realized quickly that this was not a session in which he would be praised, or rewarded for his service.

"Did they not?" Rugad repeated, letting all the strength he had come into his voice. It still wasn't more than a rasp, but it would do.

"It was your bidding, sir," Wisdom said. He held his position, chin up, back straight.

"Was it?" Rugad whispered. "Was it indeed?"

The silence in the room was unnatural. Usually when a group this large gathered, there was stirring, an occasional cough, the sound of someone breathing.

No one made a single noise. It was as if they were afraid to move, afraid to be noticed.

Good.

"You have countermanded me in private no fewer than

twenty-five times. I have since discovered that you 'augmented' my orders on at least fifteen occasions, all while we were waiting for my throat to heal. You have told the Domestics that you are the voice of the Black King, and they should react accordingly. Haven't you?"

Wisdom did not move.

"*Haven't you?*" It was the closest Rugad could get to a yell. The words sounded like a harsh cough. Seger, the Healer, took a step toward him, then seemed to think the better of it.

"I have only done what is best for the Empire," Wisdom said.

Rugad took a step closer to him. Wisdom did not move anything except his eyes. They widened slightly. Even though he hid it well, Wisdom was afraid. He smelled of it.

"Have you now?" Rugad said.

"Yes." Wisdom swallowed. "Someone had to maintain order while you healed."

"I maintain order. I was never ill enough to stop giving orders. Just because I couldn't speak didn't mean I couldn't think." Rugad took another step toward Wisdom. Now there were only a few feet between them. Wisdom had to adjust his head slightly so that he could continue looking Rugad in the eye.

"I carried out your orders," Wisdom said.

"And augmented them."

"The paper—the written orders—weren't always explicit. People had questions—"

"Which you never referred to me."

"They were simple questions—"

"There are never any simple questions," Rugad said.

"I beg pardon, sir, but—"

"*There are never any simple questions,*" Rugad repeated, and then smiled. With that smile, he looked at his generals. They were watching, eyes wide. Rugad's gaze fell on Selia. She looked like a trapped rabbit who was pretending to be a lion. Her posture was rigid, her face expressionless, but her eyes were too wide, and her nostrils quivered.

"Do you see how he contradicts me?" Rugad asked her.

She swallowed. Then nodded. Once.

Rugad clasped his hands behind his back, and paced around Wisdom in a wide circle. When he reached his starting point, he went around again, and then again, each time making the circle smaller.

Wisdom tried to watch at first, then must have realized how

ridiculous he looked, and stared straight ahead. His mouth was so compressed that his lips were turning white.

Finally Rugad stopped before him, standing less than a hand's length away. "You have sullied the chain of command. You have undermined my authority. You have tried to take the power of the Black Throne as your own. Do you deny any of this?"

"I was acting in the best interests of the Fey Empire," Wisdom said. "I—"

"So," Rugad said softly, "it is in the best interest of the Fey Empire to have someone not of Black Blood sitting on the Black Throne?"

"No," Wisdom said. "I wasn't saying that. I was just trying to help. I was trying to do what you wanted."

"Had I told you I wanted that?" Rugad asked.

"No," Wisdom whispered, and for the first time bowed his head.

"What did I tell you at the beginning of the Nye Campaign, when I replaced my previous adjunct with you?"

Wisdom turned his head slightly, as if silently cursing. He had forgotten. Rugad knew he had, and now Wisdom had just realized that he had. He had forgotten to abide by the most important admonition.

"What did I tell you?" Rugad repeated.

"That from henceforth I was to stop thinking for myself. That if I had questions, large or small, I should come to you. If I had any doubts at all, it would be better to clear them with you. If I encountered problems, questions, or difficulties with my fellow Fey, I was to bring those items to you." Wisdom spoke in a whisper. He closed his eyes midway through his small speech as if he were just beginning to realize the magnitude of his failure.

"And?" Rugad asked.

"If I should ever fail in these duties, my sanity, my health or my life could be forfeit."

"Because?"

"There is and always shall be only one ruler of the Fey Empire." Wisdom dropped his head so far that his chin rested against his chest.

"Your reasons for your disobedience?" Rugad asked.

Wisdom shook his head.

"Your reasons?"

"I have none," Wisdom whispered.

"You disobeyed me without reason," Rugad said.

"Yes, sir."

"The truth is that you forgot," Rugad said, making his voice gentle. The rasp left when he spoke gently.

Wisdom raised his head slightly. He was as easy to lull as a victim of a Charmer. The Charmers were as susceptible to easy words as the rest of the Fey.

"Yes, sir. I did."

"You forgot the most important injunction I had given you," Rugad said. He glanced over his shoulder. Three of the seven Foot Soldiers had their hands hidden under their armpits. They understood what Rugad had been thinking. They knew that Wisdom might be theirs to kill.

Through the corner of his eye, Rugad watched Wisdom. His gaze followed Rugad's and the mask fell off his features. Beneath it, was total panic. Wisdom managed to cover it before Rugad turned to face him again.

"I had thought to let the Foot Soldiers take you and kill you. But that seems a bit too kind. Traitors deserve to die most of the time, but your crime is subtle."

Wisdom was shivering.

"A subtle crime deserves a subtle punishment, don't you agree?" Rugad asked.

Wisdom said nothing. There was nothing he could say. He knew that Rugad had him.

"I am not always a bloodthirsty man," Rugad said. "In fact, I do not like shedding blood, but it is part of my job. I would be remiss if I didn't shed a bit of blood here."

He smiled. Wisdom kept his head down, as if that would prevent his punishment. Or perhaps he didn't want to see Rugad's face.

"I trusted you," Rugad said. "I trusted you more than I trusted most. And in betraying that trust, you have made it that much harder for the Fey in general. Never again will I trust someone the way I trusted you. Never again will I treat someone as well as I treated you."

Rugad snapped his fingers. The Foot Soldiers came forward. Wisdom hunched in on himself, as if he were protecting his own skin.

"You are dismissed," Rugad said to the Foot Soldiers. "Except for you."

He caught the arm of Gêlo, who had been with him when

Solanda died. Gêlo had served him well then, and had not flinched at executing another Fey. He would not flinch here either.

"You will stay," Rugad said.

Wisdom raised his head slightly.

"You are a Charmer," Rugad said to him. "You make your magick with your tongue. It is your weapon to woo others to your bidding. They listen to the magick you speak."

A flush built in Wisdom's cheeks. He was not a dumb man. He caught the implications immediately.

"You also betrayed me with that tongue," Rugad said. "For that, and your subsequent crimes, it shall be removed."

"No!" Wisdom said. "You—"

Rugad held up a hand. "Charms do not work on Visionaries," he said. "Do you want your last words to be remembered as failed magick?"

He turned to Gêlo. "The tongue is yours to do what you will," Rugad said. "But take it quickly. I have other business to attend to."

Gêlo nodded. He approached Wisdom, who took a step back.

"It would be better for you," Gêlo said, "if you did not fight me. My fingertips are precision tools, but even precision tools slip."

Wisdom held still. He opened his mouth enough for Gêlo to stick his fingers inside. The generals watched, some with great interest, some with only mild curiosity. Seger had her arms crossed and her face averted.

There was a scratching sound, then a rip, and a moan from Wisdom. Gêlo removed his hand, cupping it, blood dripping onto the polished floor.

"Well done," Rugad said. "You are dismissed."

Gêlo nodded, then left the Audience Chamber. Wisdom still held his position, mouth closed now, blood dripping out the left side.

Rugad beckoned Seger to come forward. "You may stop the bleeding but not the pain," he said. "You nor any of your kind may not now nor ever replace the tongue. Is that clear?"

"Yes," she said, disgust evident in her voice.

"Before you treat him," Rugad said, "I have one more thing to say to him."

She sighed, but stayed back.

"Wisdom," Rugad said, "You are no longer my adjunct. You no longer have a place at my side. In fact, you no longer have a home among the upper echelon of the Fey. You shall leave your possessions here, and go out in the world, to live off the kindness of strangers."

Wisdom brought one hand to his mouth, then seemed to think the better of it. The fingers came away bloody.

"If you write anything, I shall know of it, and you shall be punished. If you ever invoke my name or my power in any way, you shall be punished. If you return to the headquarters of the Black Throne, wherever that may be, you shall be punished. If you repair your tongue, you shall be punished. Do you understand?"

Wisdom nodded.

"Good," Rugad said. "I want you to note that I have said you will be punished. You will not be killed. Do not do any of these things in the hope that you will be executed. You will not. Your death sentence has been set aside. Look on that as a sign of my lenience."

Rugad turned to Seger. "Take him outside, treat him, and then let him go. When you're through with him, come back to me. And make certain you have washed his stench off you. I never want to think of him again."

"As you wish," Seger said tightly. She put a gentle hand on Wisdom's arm, and led him out the door.

When the door closed, Slaughter laughed. "Such fear on such a proud face."

"He expected you to kill him," Kendrad said.

"Killing him would have been too kind," Rugad said.

"There is no living off the kindness of strangers, at least among the Fey," Black said.

"Fortunately for Wisdom, we are on Blue Isle," Frad'l said. "The Islanders pride themselves on their charity. It is part of their religion."

"The religion we destroyed," Onha said smugly.

Rugad smiled. He liked this group of generals. They understood him. They knew as well as he did that Wisdom would survive, but that was all. His life would never again be comfortable, easy, or pleasant.

He turned to Selia. She was listening to the comments, the look of the trapped hare still in her eyes. Her back was rigid, and her mouth was tight, as if she were preventing herself from speaking.

Rugad nodded his head slightly at her. "Selia," he said softly.

She started, then clenched her fists together as if her own jumpiness bothered her.

"I have heard that you can convince a Foot Soldier in the midst of blood lust to forgo its victim."

"I've done that once," she said.

"I have heard that you can make Red Caps laugh."

She shrugged. "It's not hard."

"I have heard that you can make Islanders believe the touch of a knife's blade is the caress of a lover."

A smile tugged at the corner of her mouth. "It was an experiment," she said. "It worked."

"Successful members of the Black Throne have always had Charmers at their side, to make certain things run smoothly, to be the eyes of the Throne, and the voice of the Throne when so ordered. You have just seen what happens to a Charmer who fails in this duty."

She nodded, her eyes wide.

"Are you willing to become my new adjunct? To serve me with diligence and to never once take the power of the Black Throne as your own?"

She swallowed so hard he could hear it from where he was standing.

"Yes, sir," she said softly.

He smiled at her. "Good," he said. "I shall tell you the rest of your duties after this meeting. Until then, listen and observe. And remember what will happen if you fail."

"Yes, sir," she said again.

There was a knock on the Audience Chamber door.

"Come," Rugad said, thinking it was Seger, back from treating Wisdom.

Instead it was an elderly Fey, his body shrunken into a question mark, his skin so wrinkled that his eyes were barely visible.

"Sir," the man said. "I am Xet'n. I was told you needed a Lamplighter."

"Yes," Rugad said. In the distraction of dealing with Wisdom, he had forgotten that he had ordered a Lamplighter. "In my chambers upstairs, I destroyed a golem. I have reason to believe that his soul is still there. Can you capture it?"

"If it hasn't left the premises," the Lamplighter said. "A living soul would remain for hours, maybe days, but a golem, sir, a golem is different. If it has life of its own, then it has a different understanding of mobility than we do. It might have moved on already."

"I understand the difficulties," Rugad said. "If you succeed, there's a reward for you. If it is not there, and you can track it, you shall also be rewarded. If you cannot find it, I will not hold that against you."

"If I cannot find it," the Lamplighter said, "it will be searching for its stone, or some other empty vessel. I will leave the lamp inside the suite, and if it returns, it may simply crawl in there. Should it do so, contact me, and I'll make sure we get some use from its magick."

"Excellent," Rugad said. "Have one of the guards show you to the suite."

The Lamplighter nodded, then backed out of the room. He had clearly never been in the presence of the Black Throne before. Rugad had been worried that the golem would not be tied to the space where it shattered. But he also believed this golem would not know its options. It had stayed in this chamber after it shattered the first time. It would stay in Rugad's.

When the Lamplighter had closed the door behind him, Rugad turned to his generals. They were watching him closely. They were scattered along the big table. Some of them used a lot of room, like Onha, the Beast Rider, and others, like Black the Dream Rider, used almost none. Dimar, the Doppelgänger, looked out of place with his Islander face and his cook's whites.

Selia was gripping the arms of her chair tightly, probably regretting her decision to become his adjunct, and Quata, the ship's captain, was looking a bit confused about the proceedings. Quata had expressed confusion before, when Rugad first insisted that he climb the mountain like the rest of the invading Fey. Quata had thought he was going to remain with his ship. He probably hadn't been on land this long since he received his captaincy.

"I have had word," Rugad said with no preamble, "That the Islander King and my great-granddaughter are in the mountains. I do not know their precise location; the word I received was not specific enough. Since we have a firm hold in the mountains to the south, we can be assured they have not gone there. We have needed to consolidate our power in the mountains in the northern part of Blue Isle. Now, I believe, is the time to do so."

Kendrad stirred, as did Onha. They looked even more interested than they had before. So their attention had been, in part, an act. Of course. They had both seen Rugad administer discipline many times. It was not new to them.

"We shall operate as usual," he said. "I shall give you my overall plan, then excuse you. You will develop strategy and report back to me within the hour. Any questions?"

He scanned the faces. They were attentive, but not filled with questions. Not yet. Perhaps not at all. This was an experienced group.

"All right then," he said. He moved toward the maps. "I want you to remove the bulk of your people from this country's heartland. I want you to leave small forces, enough so that these inexperienced Islanders believe they will still be punished, and punished heavily, for any infractions. I want you to send your troops to the mountains here"—he pointed to the Stone Guardians—"here"—his hand moved to the Eyes of Roca directly north of the city—"and here." He tapped the part of the map marked Cliffs of Blood.

Around the table, the generals nodded. Landre leaned back in his chair, his hands templed beneath his chin, as if studying the maps more closely than he had before.

"I understand there are small towns and villages along this route, and that they had given the Islander Kings a bit of trouble." He glanced at Dimar.

Dimar smiled. Doppelgängers were so useful. They had access to the knowledge of their host bodies. "The Wise Leaders of the Cliffs of Blood have refused to acknowledge the authority of religious group, the Rocaanists. They do acknowledge the *religious* authority of the King, but not his ruling authority. That religious authority is based on the King's direct lineage to the supreme religious leader, the Islander's Roca. It's odd that the King and his daughter would be hiding anywhere near these people, since there is so much strife. The other villages have historical opposition to the throne, some of which dates back half a millennium. I could go into more detail if you want."

"I think that's enough," Rugad said. "We might be able to use that attitude and turn it to our advantage. If we convince the Islanders, like we did with the group in the Kenniland Marshes to the south, that the Fey will be better for Blue Isle than its traditional ruling family, we might be able to take over the mountains with a minimum of bloodshed."

"I'm not opposed to bloodshed," Slaughter said.

"I prefer to leave as much of this Isle intact as possible," Rugad said. "We don't know what kind of valuables lurk in those mountains. Perhaps none. Perhaps a lot. I suspect the mountains have much to offer us. We might even have to bring over some of our mining domestics from Galinas." He leaned against the maps. "But I get ahead of myself. There are two objectives to this mountain campaign. First, we must find my great-granddaughter. And second, we must secure those mountain villages by any means necessary."

"What of the Islander King?" Ife asked in his lisping light voice.

"Kill him and bring the body back to me," Rugad said.

"Won't that alienate his daughter?"

Rugad shrugged. "I will work on the girl here. The key is to get her here. She is a fighter and quite cunning, as you all know." He brought a hand to his throat. Then he smiled. "But I would expect nothing less from a member of my family."

There was light laughter around the table.

Landre didn't participate. He was still leaning back in his chair, staring at the map. "I have spent the last week gathering information about this place," he said. "There is a wild magick here. And much of it seems to be preserved among the mountain people."

"Are you saying they will be a match for us?" Rugad asked.

"I do not know," Landre said. "It would not surprise me if some of their attack came from magickal weaponry. We've already experienced magickal weaponry here. The first invasion force"—he spit out the words as if they were distasteful—"succumbed to a liquid weapon. The day we took over this palace, a young Black Robe slaughtered several of our people with a single sword."

"We need to recover that sword," Rugad said.

"I was told he removed it from the wall in the Great Hall," Kendrad said.

"I would like it or others like it for study," Landre said.

"We will examine the swords on that wall," Rugad said. "After I determine which to take."

Landre nodded once.

"You sidetracked us. What was your original point?" Rugad asked.

"My point is this: None of the previous magickal attacks came in a form with which we were familiar. What may look to you like a simple stick might in fact be a wand. Be forewarned." Landre's voice wobbled on the last, as if he were trying to make a pronouncement.

"Prepare your troops as Landre suggests," Rugad said. "His point is a good one. We must never underestimate these Islanders."

The generals nodded. Then Quata cleared his throat. Rugad looked at him.

"Am I to understand, sir, that the ships you brought on this invasion are to take part in the attack on the northern mountains?" Quata asked.

"No," Rugad said. "I brought you here for another reason. I'm sending you back to your ship."

Quata let out a small breath of air. His relief was palpable.

"I want you to choose a ship, not the *Ycyno*, but one of the smaller ships, probably the *Lime Hill*, but you can see which one is more seaworthy, and send it back to Nye."

Quata nodded.

"I will have you meet with one of the Domestics. You'll load the ship with supplies from Blue Isle, things that can only be found here, things the Nyeians haven't seen since Blue Isle cut off trade twenty years before."

Kendrad smiled. She knew, as Rugad did, that long-missed goods would do a lot to repair the Fey's reputation among the Nyeians. It would also keep Rugad in the forefront of their consciousness, since he would be the giver of such bounty.

Rugad smiled down at her, then continued. "I also want you to take this order to my grandson Bridge. Tell him I want the second team and their ships sent to Blue Isle. They will approach the Isle as we did."

Landre leaned back in his chair. The temple of his fingers collapsed and he held his hands together tightly. He obviously didn't approve.

"The message you will send to Bridge is this," Rugad said. "You will tell him that we are preparing to go to Leut, and that we will need additional troops as we conquer a new continent. I will have a list prepared for you this evening of the names I want on the third team. Tell him to have that team ready in two months. I will probably need them then."

"All right, sir," Quata said. "When do I leave?"

"This evening. I will have a horse for you. It's a bit of a journey to the southern part of Blue Isle."

Quata smiled. He had already made the journey once. He knew how difficult it was.

"When are we planning to go to Leut?" Landre asked. His

question was laconic; it almost seemed as if he didn't care. But Rugad knew better. Landre always had a reason for his questions. Unlike Wisdom, he knew how to couch his objections in more acceptable terms.

"As soon as we have my great-grandchildren."

"You do not care if you've molded them by the time we head for Leut," Landre said.

"Not everyone shall go to Leut," Rugad said. He knew Landre had spoken up so that Rugad would tell them the entire plan. He didn't mind. He would tell them just enough so that they thought they knew what he was going to do. "Blue Isle is an interesting and captivating place, as my son discovered. We can't leave it untended as we did, say, L'Nacin, when we went on through Galinas. I did not know that when I left Nye. Some of these things must be discovered in the field. Now I know. And we need more troops."

Landre nodded. "I would appreciate extra Spell Warders if they can be spared," he said. "This place provides a challenge we have not seen in my lifetime."

"I will make certain we have some," Rugad said. He paused. No one else seemed inclined to say anything, so he nodded. "You're dismissed, then. I shall see you back here in one hour with a detailed battle plan."

They stood and started out of the room. Selia came up to him. "You were going to tell me my duties, Sir."

She was terrified of him. He could see it in her eyes. That was good; it would keep her honest. She would always remember the day she saw Wisdom lose his tongue.

"I will," he said. "In a moment. Take a break with the others. I have a few things to finish first."

She bent her head, then backed out of the room, showing complete respect. He smiled as he watched her go. She would be a nice change from Wisdom, whom Rugad had let get out of hand.

When she closed the door, he sank into a chair. He was shaking with the strain of keeping a good facade before his generals. The bleeding had stopped on most of his cuts, but not on all of them. It was taking Seger much too long to repair Wisdom. Rugad needed her, and soon. His body had lacked resiliency since he was attacked weeks before. The pressure he had put upon it, first abandoning it as he found his great-granddaughter, and then fleeing into it when he was escaping that golem, had left him weak and dizzy. He suspected some of that was from the blood loss.

But it might also be a warning. When he had come to Blue Isle, he had been a healthy man of ninety-two years. He still had fifty years of life ahead of him if he lived his normal lifespan. But warriors often didn't. Many died in battle. Others died young due to the stresses they had put their bodies through.

This last month had aged him. He hoped the feeling would leave as his health improved, but he needed to face the fact that it might not. He had to get his great-grandchildren, and quickly, before he lost the energy to show them how leaders of Black Blood behaved.

Before he lost the energy to teach them himself.

Or bend them himself, if he had to.

He hoped he wouldn't have to.

But it was looking more and more likely. The girl was strong and willful. The golem had gotten his personality through the boy, and that would also mean he was willful. They hadn't been brought up as proper Fey. There was much conditioning to undo.

Rugad sighed. He had made only one serious mistake in his entire career, and he was still paying the price. He had let Jewel go with her father, let her come to Blue Isle, and here she died. If Rugad had kept her by his side, none of this would be happening now.

He wouldn't have these wild great-grandchildren, and the future of the Fey Empire wouldn't be in doubt.

One mistake was going to take years to rectify.

One mistake.

He sighed again, tilted his head back, and then, suddenly, smiled as an idea reached him.

One mistake. If that was all it took to put something as grand as the Fey Empire in doubt, imagine what one mistake would do to a place as tiny as Blue Isle.

Nicholas had yet to make any serious errors with the Isle. He had shown great strength in all things, turning great odds against him into his favor.

But he had a serious weakness, and it became clear as Rugad had struggled inside Nicholas's daughter.

The man loved his children. He would sacrifice his country for them. And that, as any leader knew, was a great mistake.

Rugad's smile grew.

A mistake Rugad could use to his own advantage.

SIXTY-FOUR

GIFT sat at the base of the steps, arms wrapped around himself. He knew he had shocked them with his vehemence, but they didn't understand. Some people did not deserve to live. Some people caused such destruction in their wake that they deserved death.

This Matthias was one.

The Black King was another.

Gift could do nothing about his great-grandfather—there were strictures against that—but he could do something about Matthias.

And he would.

He started to stand when he saw a movement beside the fountain.

"Coulter," he said, wanting Coulter at his side. Coulter was the only other one with magick in this cave—at the moment. If Gift could see something, chances were that Coulter could too.

"What?" Coulter asked. He came partway down the stairs.

"Did you see something?"

"No," Coulter said.

The movement behind the fountain grew. Shadows rippled and changed, then Gift's mother slid out from behind it. Her braid was tangled, her eyes wild. She looked terrified.

"Gift," she said, "do you have a Link to your sister?"
"What?" he asked. Then he realized what he had done. He was responding to her without letting the others know she was there.
"Coulter," he said again. "Do you see anything near the fountain?"
"No," Coulter said.
The others were looking as well. Adrian was actually squinting, as if that would make him see better.
"No," Coulter said, this time more slowly, "but I feel something." He hurried down the steps and crossed the floor.
"Careful of the water," Adrian said.
Coulter seemed to ignore him.
Gift's mother frowned at him, as if he were a gnat, then made her way past him. "Gift," she said. "This is important. Do you have a Link to your sister?"
"I don't know," he said. "I don't think so. Why?"
"Because your father is bringing her here, and without your help, she is lost."
"My father is coming here?" Gift said.
"The King?" Adrian blurted, then put a hand to his mouth, looking surprised at his own reaction.
Coulter had turned. He clearly did sense her. He was following her closely. If she stopped moving, he would walk right into her.
"Listen," his mother said. She stopped close enough to Gift that he could touch her without moving his arm. "That's why I left you so suddenly. It had nothing to do with what you said. I had to go to your sister. To your father, actually. My grandfather—" she stopped speaking, shook her head, and then sighed.
"What did he do?" Gift asked. Her urgency was contagious.
"The King?" Adrian asked.
"No," Gift said. "The Black King."
"He tried to take her mind like he tried to take yours," his mother said. "Only she doesn't have"— she raised her head, turned, and faced Coulter—"an Enchanter for a friend. All she has is my pathetic golem."
She spoke the last words with distraction. Coulter was looking at her, but his eyes were gazing at a space just beyond her. He didn't see her, but he seemed to know where she was.
"A golem?" Gift asked. He didn't understand her urgency or

her concern. Wasn't she a Mystery? Couldn't she do a lot of these things on her own? Why would she need him?

"Does she mean Sebastian?" Coulter asked. He was now looking at Gift.

Gift shook his head. "Sebastian is dead."

"Sebastian," she said, "is a golem. They don't live, so they don't die. I thought you were raised Fey, Gift."

"I was," he said.

"Then you should know that."

"I didn't learn everything," he said.

Coulter put a hand on his arm. "There's a great deal of magick energy right in front of you. Is that what you're seeing as your mother?"

"Yes," Gift said. "It is her. I can touch her."

"I'm going to try," Coulter said.

"We don't have time for this," his mother said, glancing at Coulter. "I need to know if you can help your sister."

Coulter reached out to her. Gift's mother took a small step backward to remain outside his grip.

"Let him touch you," Gift said.

She raised an eyebrow, as if to say that he didn't know what he was asking, and then stopped moving.

Coulter's right hand touched her and sparks rose as if he had put steel against a grindstone. He cried out in pain and grabbed his wrist with his left hand.

"It is real," he said.

"And not very safe for him," Gift's mother said. "I'd advise him not to do it again."

"Are you threatening him?" Gift asked.

Adrian had come closer. Leen had her dagger out, for all the good it did her, and the Cap had moved farther up the stairs, as if having the others there gave him an excuse to save himself.

"No," his mother said. "But it is as I told you. I am allowed three people—"

"I know," Gift said. "I remember."

"All others must deal with me, not as Jewel, but as a lower-end Power. A Mystery. It would not be good for him to touch me again."

"Was it a threat?" Adrian asked softly.

Coulter's fingertips were red. He cradled his hand to his chest.

"She says it's because she can only appear in Fey form to three people, and Coulter's not one of them."

"All magick has rules," the Cap said.

"So now you believe her," Gift snapped.

"I believe the rules," the Cap said.

"Something is there," Coulter said. "This is not a hallucination, and Gift doesn't have the kind of magick to create a magick energy column like this. Right, Scavenger?"

"So far as I know," the Cap said. "I don't know everything about all magicks."

"But you know more than we do," Adrian said.

"True enough." The Cap sounded pleased with himself.

"I'm not going to let it harm any of you," Leen said. "Tell it that."

"What are you going to do?" the Cap asked. "Stab it with your pathetic knife? Come on, girl. You know that physical objects have no effect on pure magick."

"I don't know that," she said. "And if it were true, then Coulter's fingers would have had no effect."

"It was his magick colliding with mine that created the sparks," Gift's mother said. But Gift did not translate. She focused on his face again. "Please, Gift. Can you help your sister?"

"I'm not sure I want to," Gift said. And he wasn't. She had attacked him, that sister of his. She had turned into a bird and tried to peck his eyes out. She might even have killed him if Solanda hadn't tried to stop her. And then what would have happened?

"You and she are the only defenses against the Black King," his mother said.

"Why would you want defenses against the Black King?" Gift said. "Why would you care?"

"Rugad is too close to true power," Gift's mother said. "He is a great warrior, and has a brilliant military mind, but he is not the person who should touch true power."

"Who should, then?" Gift asked.

She shook her head. "A person who knows the pain such power can bring. A person who knows its anguish, and who does not want it. Rugad wants power too much."

"And that's bad?"Gift asked.

"It was good for the Fey until we came to Blue Isle," his mother said. "But it isn't good any longer."

"How does my sister fit into this?"

"You and she are the heirs to the Black Throne. She knows the Isle, Gift. You know the Fey. Together you would be a formidable team. And an acceptable one to both the Islanders and to the Fey."

"I thought the Fey didn't care about the Islanders. Why do you?"

Her gaze darted to the fountain and then back to him. It was as if her look encompassed the entire room. "A person's perspective changes when they cross over to this plane," she said.

"When they die, you mean," Gift said.

"I'm not completely dead yet, son," she said. "If I were, I wouldn't care about this at all."

He shook his head. He wasn't sure he understood her. "So what are you, then?"

"Enough questions about me," she said. "I already warned you about that. I need to know if you can help your sister. She'll be here soon. And your father will not have the Shaman's help."

"Why not?"

His mother bit her lower lip, then sighed. "She will make the wrong choice as far as your father is concerned."

Coulter crouched near her feet, as if he were studying her magick from the ground up.

"Will make?" Gift asked.

"Made," his mother said, but she sounded less sure of herself.

"I don't have a Link with my sister," Gift said. "You know how we were raised."

"But you saw her a lot. You knew her, through Sebastian."

"And through Sebastian's body, not my own. She's his sister by love, mine by blood. There's a big difference."

His mother let out a sigh that echoed in the room. Even the others seemed to hear it. The Cap looked up. Adrian put a hand to his ears, and Leen swung around in a slow circle, knife out, like an ancient warrior.

"Whistle?" Coulter asked.

"Sigh," Gift said.

When Coulter spoke, Gift's mother looked directly at him as if seeing him for the first time. "Your Enchanter," she said. "When he closed your Links, how did he do it?"

"We have our own Link," Gift said. "He came through that."

"But how did he close the Link between the two of you?"

The details she did know astonished him, more than the details she didn't know.

"I closed it," Gift said.

Coulter was watching him now. "What's going on?" Coulter asked softly.

"But you're still Bound," Gift's mother said.

"We'll always be Bound," Gift said, and felt a flare of anger. At her. If she hadn't died, he wouldn't be Bound to Coulter. Sebastian would have lived—

—or was he really dead? Gift was no longer certain about anything any more. And if he didn't have a body, but he lived, how did he do that? Was he like that bit of energy that filled the Fey Lamp, something to be burned up and discarded? Or was it something more than that?

"What does it matter?" Gift asked.

Coulter had moved closer to him, as if to protect him. Gift moved away. He didn't want Coulter's protection. He hadn't wanted Coulter's protection since the night Coulter had closed his Links.

"It matters," his mother said, "because he can help save your sister."

"Can he?" Gift said.

"Along with you and your father. If you let him."

"And if I don't?"

"Your sister will be lost forever." His mother wrung her hands together as if the thought terrified her.

"Why don't you do something?" Gift asked.

"I can't," she said.

"Because—?"

"I chose you," she said. Her hands were clasped together so tightly that her knuckles had turned a brilliant white. "I thought you needed me more."

He felt an odd elation at that. His mother had chosen him over his sister. No one had done that before. His sister had been the favored one, even with the Shaman. Everyone had always gone to her rescue. Everyone had always catered to her. He had been abandoned and lost to both parents and they hadn't cared. They hadn't even recognized Sebastian as the replacement.

"Please," his mother said. "She'll be here any moment. Help her."

Finally they needed him. Finally he was more important than the sister who had grown up in the palace where he had been born. His mother's words, strange as they were, eased an ache in his heart that he hadn't even known he had.

"All right," he said. "Tell me what to do."

SIXTY-FIVE

RUGAD was still staring at the maps of Blue Isle when Seger returned to the Audience Room. Her manner was subdued, her head bowed as she approached him. She had been his personal healer for a long time, and she knew better than to rebuke him for things he had done, but he could feel her disapproval.

She had stayed longer with Wisdom than she needed. Rugad would have one of his assistants discover what she had done. He hoped she had done nothing more than stop the bleeding and give him a bit of strength to leave the palace—an ability to survive the trauma to his body and the changes which he would now suffer.

Rugad would hate to have to break in a new healer as well as a new adjunct. But he would do it if he had to. Sometimes changes in location led to changes in personnel. He knew it, but he never liked it.

"You will let me see to you now?" she asked.

He nodded. She sat across from him, her fingers probing his new wounds. He had several cuts and scrapes from the explosion, some bruises from his fall onto the chair, and a rather serious pain along the right side of his rib cage.

She probed the wounds, removing small bits of rubble. The

golem's stone. She made a pile on the table as she did so. The shards were good-sized; all were about the size of a fingernail, and as slender. He wondered that he hadn't felt them.

She helped him remove his shirt, and she treated the bruises on his back. She paused for some time over his rib cage.

"You've broken two ribs," she said. "You should rest."

"I have no time," he said.

She nodded, once.

"I can't spell you forever," she said. "At some point, you will need to let the body's own healing powers work."

"As soon as the Isle is secure," he said.

She said nothing, but he could feel it again, that current of disapproval rising from her.

"You may as well say what you're thinking," he said. "If it has to do with Wisdom—"

"I have learned to accept incidents like Wisdom's over the years," she said, making her discomfort known without actually criticizing him. "You must do such things to maintain your command. I understand that, and do as you ask in treatment. Sometimes it goes against my healing instincts, but you explained that to me when you brought me on as your personal physician. Many things you do go against my healing instincts. The fact that you have continued to speak without letting your throat heal properly is a choice I would not have made. You will always pay for that."

More than she knew, he thought. His real voice was gone. And, unlike a soul, there was no way to capture it and bring it back.

"I need my voice," he said.

"I know," she said. "You made a leader's choice, not a healer's choice."

"Then what do I feel from you?"

She smiled a little. "You think I would criticize you after that display tonight?"

She had a good point, but an invalid one. He always accepted honesty in conversation with his advisors. It was when they tried to usurp his power that he drew the line. Wisdom had crossed the line several times since arriving on Blue Isle.

"Seger," he said, "you have not committed any acts of treason that I know of, unless you gave Wisdom his tongue back."

She paused from her ministrations at his ribs. Her eyes were dark and almost unreadable. Her wrinkled skin appeared pale with fatigue.

"I do not disobey your orders," she said.

"Then you have nothing to fear from me," he said.

She took a deep breath. "I took extra time in returning to you."

"I noticed," he said.

"Not because of Wisdom. It took little to staunch the blood flow. I gave him some extra strength which will get him from here, and help him survive a few days. I figured you would not object to that."

"The last thing I wanted was for him to die too soon," Rugad said. "It would not impart the lesson I had hoped he'd learn."

She nodded once. She did a small binding spell over his ribs. The pain changed as she did so, from a sharp tug to a dull ache. Then she wrapped a cloth around his torso.

"I overheard some gossip among the guards," she said. "I stopped to listen."

He didn't move as she brushed his bruises, sending more pain through him. He needed to hear what she had to say, but he didn't want to show too much interest.

"They were talking about your run-in with the golem."

She had bowed her head. Her cheeks were flushed a dusty rose color. He had never seen her blush before. So the news disturbed her. Or imparting it to him did.

He sensed no fear in her though, only caution.

"They believe the magick on this Isle is as strong as Fey magick. They believe that we'll all die here."

That did startle him. His heart rate increased and so did his breathing. A light sweat coated his body. He couldn't pretend it was from the injuries.

She brought up her head. Her eyes had shadows beneath them that he hadn't noticed a few moments before.

"They were saying that if the great Black King of the Fey could twice be injured by Islanders, then all Fey were in danger."

And they were. They didn't know it yet. They were in danger because, for the first time since he had become Black King, for the first time in his lifetime perhaps, even for the first time in several lifetimes, the Fey did not believe they were invincible. Soldiers who thought they were invincible tried all sorts of things frightened soldiers did not.

He opened his mouth to ask who the guards were, but she put her cool fingers across his lips.

"No need to ask about the guards," she said. "Save your injured voice this once. I was preparing to let you know their names. I recited them as I returned here, so that I would remember them. But then I passed the kitchen, and heard the same story repeated. The rumor is already out, Rugad. There is little you can do to stop it."

He swallowed, and felt, suddenly, the pain in his throat. He had been ignoring it, but he could ignore it no longer. His raspy voice, the cuts on his forehead, the bruises on his body, were all signs to his people that he could be hurt.

And if he could be hurt, so could they.

He mentally cursed his great-grandchildren.

He mentally cursed that golem, and then he threw in the Islander King for good measure.

Seger took her fingers from his lips. "I'm sorry to be the one to tell you," she said.

"Few others would have bothered," he said, "and I needed to know."

She put balm on his cuts. "Your bruises will heal in a few days," she said. "I'd tell you to be cautious of the ribs, but I know you will not. Just send for me if you suddenly discover you have difficulty breathing."

He remembered the instruction from the six times previous that he had broken ribs. But they all predated her. He did not need to tell her he had been through this before.

"My concern," she said, "is the stone shards in your cuts. They belong to another's magick, and may infect you. The infection would not be physical. It would harm your own magick."

"How will I recognize the signs?"

"You will not," she said, "until there is damage. Let me tend to you daily. I will check your aura for signs of change, and I have a friend, another healer, who will be able to see your magick. If you trust her."

"If she does not speak to my people of this."

Seger's smile was small, as if she had found no amusement in his words. "Healers keep confidences, sir," she said, a bit too formally.

He knew that. He also knew that with a famous and important patient, such as himself, healers could sometimes not resist the temptation to talk. He was merely letting her know that such conversation would be punished.

She would never do it. But her friend might. And with morale at the level it was at now, he could not afford that.

She gathered the shards in her right hand.

"I want those disposed of," he said. "I am making certain that the golem does not return."

She glanced at them. The pile was so large she could barely close her fist over it. "I would like to keep these," she said, "at least until we know if you are infected."

"What good will that serve?" he asked.

"I can analyze the magick. Do we know whose golem this is?"

"Rugar's people created it."

Her smile faded. "I know that,sir. But who sustains it?"

"My great-grandchildren," he said.

"Odd," she said. "I would have thought the magick came from elsewhere."

"You believe this golem is part of the Mysteries?"

"It has survived one shattering, sir," she said. "And from descriptions I have heard of its earlier appearance, it might have survived one more. There are few golems with such longevity, and rarely are they supported by a living creature."

"I want it destroyed," Rugad said.

She closed her fists over the shards. "It might be a tool of the Powers, Rugad," she said.

"I do not care," he said. "It tried to kill me."

"Perhaps," she said slowly, "it thought you were violating a magick law."

She was breathing hard, as if speaking that last sentence terrified her. He raised his eyes to her face, put all the sternness he had into his gaze, and watched her breathing increase even more.

"Do you believe the Fey will die here?"

"I am a Healer, sir," she said. "I would do everything I can to prevent it."

"You haven't answered my question."

She swallowed so hard he could hear it. She cradled her cupped hand with the other. He wondered if she meant the tenderness that he saw in the gesture. He wondered if he needed to take the shards from her.

"I believe there is a magick here like we have never encountered before. It is stronger than any other."

"Stronger than ours?" he asked.

"The same, I think," she said. "But that renders us vulnerable." She smiled, a small almost frightened look. "I do not like being vulnerable, sir."

He didn't either. So that was what he had been feeling. Not older, so much, as vulnerable. He had been hurt twice by these people. By the very people he had come to recover for his Empire.

"Nor do I," he said. "But we are flesh and blood. Unlike that golem there, we can die, all of us. Or lose our minds and kill ourselves as the Enchanters do."

He shuddered once, grateful he had been spared that magick.

"I do not feel safe here," she said.

Her word choice amused him. "You felt safe in the Nye campaigns?"

"Of course," she said. "I knew we would win."

"Yet you treated our wounded. You know how many we lost."

"You were uninjured," she said.

"But my son wasn't," he said.

"Your son wasn't Black King. It is not the same thing."

No, he supposed, it wasn't. And therein lay his dilemma. There were some things only he could do. Only he could have traveled the Links through that golem, and he had to be alone to do so. He couldn't have let anyone know how vulnerable he was at that moment. If the guards had been in the room, they might have separated his body from the golem's too soon, and he would have died in that explosion.

Or he would have found out what else could happen.

"We are weak here," she said.

A shiver ran through him. Even those who lived here with him, in the palace, had the wrong perspective. "How strange you say that," he said, "when we own the entire country."

"But we do not have what we came for," she said.

"We came for Blue Isle," he said.

"I thought we came for your great-grandchildren."

"I came for them," he said. "And dealings with the Black Family are never easy." He smiled at her, even though he didn't feel like smiling. "You should know that."

She nodded once, then shrugged. "I have spoken out of turn."

"No," he said. "You have told me what you believe. It is not out of turn at all."

"Then I shall tell you one more thing." She squared her shoulders as if bracing for his reaction. "Wisdom believed you were making errors here on the Isle, and he thought you were doing that because of your injury. That is why he was questioning you, why he was speaking for you."

"So you're telling me he had the best of intentions."

"Yes," she said.

"So I should evaluate intentions when I investigate treason?" Rugad asked.

She sighed. "I knew you would take this the wrong way."

"How should I take it then, Seger?" he asked.

"Wisdom is but one example of the dissent around you, Rugad. The worries about the Isle are but another. There is a problem among our people that I have never seen before. We no longer trust each other."

"We have never trusted each other," Rugad said. "Spell Warders fight with Shape Shifters; Shape Shifters dislike Red Caps; Red Caps hate those of us with magick. It is the way of our people."

"But we've managed to work around those differences before," Seger said. "I'm not sure we can now. We had a common vision of our people, of our strength. It seems to be gone."

Because he had fallen. Because he had not been there to lead them. He had started to change this with Wisdom. He would have to do more. He would have to lead his own people back into faith in themselves.

"It'll return," he said, and hoped his long pause didn't seem to her like a lack of belief on his part. Blue Isle was a complicated place, but it would not defeat the Fey.

Only the Fey would defeat the Fey.

Somehow he had to show his people that, to remind them that they had used methods similar to the ones they were suffering now to defeat other races.

A knock on the door made Seger start. She bowed slightly. "I should go," she said.

"Thank you for your honesty," Rugad said to her.

She nodded, took her bag and the bits of golem-stone she had pulled from him, and headed for the door. When she opened it, the Lamplighter stood outside, his hands clasped against his chest.

"Let him in," Rugad said.

The Lamplighter entered. His face was blotched, his eyes wild with fear. Rugad could smell him, even across the distance between them.

"You have a report," Rugad said, even though he could tell from the Lighter's demeanor what the report was.

The Lighter swallowed. "I used every skill I had," he said. "I scanned the room in darkness. I Charmed, wooed, and coaxed. Then I did a search with my own abilities, feeling the air for the golem as you requested. But he was not there."

Rugad had suspected this would happen. This golem had been too much trouble from the beginning. And it was linked to the Black Family. Golems like that were always unpredictable.

"You are certain you had the right room?" he asked.

The Lighter nodded. "To make certain, I did other rooms on the floor. I did the corridors and the balconies. I even had the guards show me what they did with the rubble." He ran a hand through his thinning hair.

"I'm sorry, sir," he said. "The golem's soul is gone."

"Gone," Rugad said.

"I could not find it," the Lighter said. "And I should have been able to. I used all my skills and I am the highest ranking Lamplighter we have. I have more abilities than my fellows. I once pulled a specific soul across a Nye battlefield for use in a Healer's tent. I cannot find this golem."

"Why do you think you can't find it?"

The Lighter took a deep breath. "Perhaps too much time has passed."

"But you don't believe that."

"No, sir."

"Well?" Rugad asked. He understood fear. He understood that the Lighter was worried he would be punished for his failure, even though Rugad had promised him he would not be. But Rugad was not going to waste his own time prying information from the man, not without specific return.

"Sir," the Lighter said, head bowed. His thin hair had formed a small wispy circle on the top of his skull. "This golem is strong enough to injure you. It has considerable power, which means that it has considerable magick."

"More than you?" Rugad asked.

"Something has given it its strength," the Lighter said, "and it's not just Fey magick. In all our history, I know not of a golem that has twice attacked the Black King."

Actually, Rugad wanted to say, it was only once. The other time it had been defending the man it considered a father.

"The golem," he said carefully, "shattered. Golems do that under pressure. Could it be that the golem had not enough of a soul to capture?"

The Lighter closed his eyes tight, as if blocking the answer in his own mind. Then he sighed and opened them. Clearly he didn't want to answer Rugad's question. But he would. His fear was too powerful for him to lie.

"No, sir," the Lighter said. "There were traces of his soul all over the room. If anything, sir, his presence is stronger than any I've seen. Except yours."

Rugad had not expected that answer. It sent a shiver through him. He had seen a golem like that in the past: his grandfather's golem, which had lived for decades. Its eyes had held a power that Rugad had seen only in the Black Family, its magick fairly crackled off it, and its power was undeniable.

And dangerous.

"If there were traces, why couldn't you track it?" he asked.

"Because the traces came from the shattering, not from its flight," the Lighter said.

Stronger than any he'd ever seen. Rugad clenched his right fist, then slowly released it.

"I want you to keep searching for the golem's soul," Rugad said. "Put most of your people on it. They should be done with the results of the last battle."

The Lighter nodded.

"It has to have gone somewhere," Rugad said, "and we will find it."

The Lighter opened his mouth as if to add something, but Rugad had had enough. His guards in the listening posts were good about keeping state secrets, but they hadn't needed to hear this last. This golem would spook them all.

"I understand that your inability to capture the golem is in part my responsibility since I did not have you come immediately to my suites," Rugad said. "I will tolerate this mistake. It can be rectified by finding the golem."

"Aye, sir," the Lighter said.

"You are dismissed," Rugad said.

He did not watch the Lighter go. The man was terrified, and justifiably so. Things were not working out as Rugad wanted.

He would have to change that. He could not focus on the setbacks as his people were doing. He had to focus on the successes.

It was time to make Blue Isle completely his.

No matter what the personal cost.

SIXTY-SIX

DAWN'S light was thin over the mountains. Boteen peered out of the window of his carriage. They were heading toward a village. It was still a distance off, but he had seen it from the hilltop earlier. The village was small, stone cottages nestled against the base of the mountains.

But the mountains, the mountains were spectacular. He had never seen mountains that tall, not in all of Galinas—or at least, the half of Galinas he had traveled through. They were tall and peaked, snow-covered and treeless at the top. The mountains themselves were red, giving them the name, he supposed, of the Cliffs of Blood.

He had felt uncomfortable since the sky began to lighten. His stomach hurt and there was a slight buzzing in his ears. He couldn't pinpoint the cause, but it didn't feel physical. It was growing worse the closer he came to the village.

His sense of the other Enchanter, though, had grown stronger. Much stronger. He got a sense, just before dawn, of a great magick being used, and thought he saw fire against the sky. But he checked with his traveling companions, and none of them saw anything. It meant nothing, of course. He saw a great many things others did not, but still, the fire had been so vivid, he felt as if everyone for miles around had been able to see it.

He had been wrong.

And then there was the other feeling, the one that had been growing as the Cliffs of Blood drew closer.

He felt a longing, a desire, to climb the mountain, to go to a place deep within it. The longing made him think of his boyhood and the family he had left decades before. A feeling that, if he climbed, he would be going home.

So many contradictory feelings, and none of them affecting his traveling companions. He knew what this was; it was a caution for him, an acknowledgment throughout his body that he was going to a place filled with magickal people. He was so used to the feeling among his own kind that he often ignored it.

But these people were not his own kind, and he could not ignore this.

Not now.

He rapped on the roof of the carriage. He had been told, before they started, that that was his signal to stop. He had also been warned to use it sparingly—which meant, in Fey terminology, not to use it at all.

Still, this trip was being taken in the most part because of him. He had the right to stop, no matter what the cause.

This uncertainty was unlike him as well. It wasn't coming from within, but from without.

The carriage rumbled to a halt. Voices, calling in Fey, warned each other of the suggested stop. No one approached him.

That was as he expected.

He got out of the carriage and didn't look at the others. They had stopped on the dirt road. It ran above a fork of the Cardidas River. The fork had carved a path through the mountains. The drop here was significant—it would kill someone who fell—but certainly not as spectacular as it was on the other side of the river.

The Wisps assured him that the fork would return to the main branch of the Cardidas. They had flown ahead, discovered that the carriages were reaching the northeastern edge of Blue Isle. The Cardidas started here, between the Cliffs of Blood and even more deadly-looking cliffs called the Slides of Death. It would take, one of the Wisps told him, a military mind more brilliant than Rugad's to enter Blue Isle from this side.

His companions got out of the second carriage. The Horse Riders were staring at him. The Bird Riders were landing all around him. The Wisps were growing to full adult size.

He spoke to none of them. Instead, he looked at the mountains. They were covered with silvery morning light, making the red stone appear shiny, as if it were made of red blood. He shivered once.

The mountains had brought dozens to their deaths.

This was not a good place, at least not for his kind.

He shaded his eyes with his hand. A rock quarry had been hollowed out of the mountainside, and behind it, a maze of trails. Above those trails, a diamond glimmered.

It couldn't be a diamond. He couldn't see it from this distance. It had to be something else.

Home.

The voice whispered in his head. It was soft and seductive, and powerful.

The other Enchanter was up there. Not at the diamond, but near it.

Boteen blinked. He had heard of something like this, but the buzzing in his ears made it hard for him to concentrate. A block, almost as if someone knew he was coming and was trying to prevent it. But it wasn't the other Enchanter. He seemed too concerned with himself, from what Boteen could tell.

Something was happening on that mountainside.

Something important.

"We need to go up there," he said to no one in particular.

"Where?" Ay'Le, Rugad's Charmer, asked, shielding her eyes. She wasn't as tall as Boteen, but she was nearly as thin. Charmers usually came into the magick late, but the Fey had known early that Ay'Le would come into hers. She had been too lean, to lithe to be a magickless Red Cap.

He pointed to the mountainside. "Do you see something that resembles a diamond up there?"

She squinted, then put a hand over her face, much as he had, to shield her eyes. "No," she said.

He let out a small sigh. He had expected her answer, but didn't welcome it. "Are you hearing a slight buzzing in your ears, feeling a bit of nausea?"

"No," she said, and this time she looked at him. "Perhaps you're coming down with something?" She signaled for Erbok, the Domestic. He had been talking with one of the Wisps. When he saw the signal, he came over.

"I'm fine," Boteen said. "The symptoms aren't physical."

"What symptoms?" Erbok asked.

"He's hearing a buzzing, feeling ill," Ay'Le said. "See what you can do for him."

She left his side, then and he wondered how Charmers ever got their name. He was an impervious to their magick as Visionaries were. And like Visionaries, Charmers angered him more than they pleased him. Still, he supposed, they were useful to have around. They did do the talking—and the convincing—where it was needed.

"How serious is this?" Erbok said.

"It's got a magickal cause," Boteen said. "I've felt it before." He moved slightly away from Erbok. "Do you see that glow on the mountainside?"

"The sun?" Erbok said.

"No," Boteen snapped. "It looks like a diamond."

"No," Erbok said.

Boteen groaned. Why did he have to be traveling with lesser magicians? Why couldn't he travel with a Visionary or a Shifter? Someone whose powers at least had a hope of matching his own.

"There are currents up there," one of the Wisps said.

He turned. She was an older Wisp, delicate and very pale for a Fey. The lightness of her skin came from mixed blood several generations ago. It paled Wisps, sometimes making them the color of their wings.

Because of her coloring and fragility, she had been named Gauze.

"Currents?" he asked.

She nodded. "When we fly, we note magick currents. We've lost some people in magick swirls. We're quite cautious about such things."

Another Wisp, whose name Boteen had heard before they set out but had forgotten, said, "We've been having a lot of trouble around this mountain range. The magickal currents are the strongest we've ever encountered."

"Wisps are so fanciful," said a Gull Rider, landing on the top of the carriage. "They are so light they make up various currents to explain why they can't stay a course. It's because you weigh nearly nothing."

Boteen shook his head. "I've been feeling this as well. Perhaps you're too large to feel what they have."

He stepped around the carriage. The Horse Riders had retained their shape. The Fey on their backs were peering around their horse necks, apparently trying to gauge the road ahead.

"Where else have you encountered currents like this?" he asked Gauze.

"Coming up the mountains to the south," she said. "There were strong magick currents there, but not as strong as these. They're all over the Isle."

"But have you discovered them anywhere other than Blue Isle?"

"Around a Shadowlands."

"We always have to teach young Wisps how to enter a Shadowlands safely," the other Wisp said.

Boteen remembered something of that. When he had been a young boy, there had been a bit of a scandal when a Wisp child was crushed in a Circle Door. The Visionary who made the Shadowlands, some minor member of the Black King's family, had called it an accident. The Wisps had chastised the parent Wisps, claiming negligence, and the remaining Fey had thought it all a great waste of time.

"Anywhere else?" he asked. He was standing on the edge of the road. Beneath his feet, it angled down the mountainside and toward the fork of the Cardidas. From here, the river looked deep and powerful. There was white water where it hit a series of rocks.

"Not that I've encountered," Gauze said.

"What about places you've heard of?"

"I've heard the Eccrasian Mountains have difficult magick currents," the male Wisp said.

"Air currents," The Gull Rider snapped. "It's because of the mountains' unusual height."

Unusual height. Boteen turned to her. "Are they as tall as these mountains?"

"Don't know," she said. "But I would think so. They were supposed to be the tallest in the Fey Empire, at least they were when we had gone as far as Nye."

That fact was significant somehow. And Boteen didn't think it was because of the air currents, as the Gull Rider suggested. The buzzing in his head was increasing, making it difficult to concentrate.

He squinted at the mountainside. The diamond burned bright in the growing sunlight. The mountains were reflecting red onto the river below. Flowing blood, constantly moving. No wonder the mountains had gotten their name. He was getting continual reaffirmation of that name in the sunrise.

"We need to go up there," he said again.

"There's no way we'll get the carriages up those trails," the Gull Rider said. "They're narrow and rocky and seldom used."

"I need to get up there," Boteen said.

There was a clatter from farther down the road.

"Hey," one of the Horse Riders said.

Boteen turned, as did the others standing with them.

"We've got company," the Gull Rider said.

Five Islanders on horseback came over the rise. One of the Horse Riders neighed, and its Fey self looked distressed. The Rider patted himself on the mane with one small hand

The Islanders stopped in front of Boteen's carriage. Boteen walked around it, hands clasped behind his back. The buzzing, which had been so loud a moment before, had stopped.

So these Islanders were the source of it. Strange. They didn't seem to be doing any magick at all.

The five Islanders were all male. The man in front was clearly their spokesman. He appeared to be middle-aged, his long hair faded to a blondish gray, his eyes a watery blue. Islanders did not age well. Their pale skin showed every bruise, every broken blood vessel, every scar.

The man in front was carrying an extra forty pounds on his short frame. He hid most of it in a sweater and bulky pants. His boots were old and scuffed, and he griped the horse too tightly with his legs. He wasn't that used to riding, then, or he hadn't done it for a long time

"Tall ones," he hissed, looking down at Boteen.

Even though he sat on the horse's back, the man's head wasn't that much higher than Boteen's. Boteen wondered how tall he would be if he were standing beside him. The man probably came up to Boteen's waist.

"Actually," Boteen said, "We're Fey."

"We don't care what you are," the man said. "We've come to warn you away from Constant."

"Constant being?"

"Our town."

Ay'Le pushed her way forward. She put a hand on Boteen's arm, signaling that he should be quiet. Rugad had probably sent her for an occasion just like this one.

"We've come to introduce ourselves," she said with a smile. "We're the new rulers of Blue Isle. Your King has abdicated. His family is gone."

"We don't care about the Isle," the man said. "Just our small corner of it. And we don't want tall ones here."

Her smile grew. "We don't know what your objection is to taller members of your race, but we—"

"It's all tall ones," the man said. "Your race, ours. It makes no difference. The important thing is height. You know that."

"Because height implies magick ability?" Boteen asked.

Ay'Le shot him an angry look.

"Because height guarantees it," the man said.

"Then I should think you'd be wary of me," Boteen said. Ay'Le's grip on his arm tightened. She was reminding him that Rugad had placed her in charge of this mission. Boteen felt that the mission had changed the moment he saw the diamond and felt the impact of a strange magick.

He shook her off. He nodded toward the mountains. "What's up there?"

The man's face shuttered. "Where?"

"That diamond of light off the side of the mountain, quite a ways above tree line."

The men behind the spokesman stirred. Their horses shifted from leg to leg as if the riders' nervousness translated to them. So there was something in the mountains. And these Islanders didn't want him to know about it.

The spokesman's face had flushed a deep red. "We have had an infestation of tall ones in the past few days. We want no more. We've driven the others out. But we can't have you overrunning us. Go back to your kind. Tell them they're not welcome here."

"Or what?" Boteen asked.

"Or we'll have to look upon you as Soldiers of the Enemy."

Obvious that statement had some great meaning to the Islanders. He understood the intent clearly enough. But he wondered what else it meant, and why it was spoken with such clarity. Usually threats were less subtle than that.

"Is that like killing us?" Boteen asked.

The man's flush deepened. "You have been warned," he said. Then he clucked to his horse. The riders behind him turned, and he did the same. They galloped off in the direction they came.

"Wonderful work," Ay'Le said. "You've alienated them totally. I was supposed to Charm them into a peaceful surrender."

Boteen shrugged. "Go try."

She uttered a Hiere curse, executing that language's glottal stops and clicks perfectly, then she turned her back on him and started toward the carriage.

"What did he mean," the Horse Rider nearest Boteen asked, "an influx of tall ones?"

Boteen froze. He hadn't thought it through. What an excellent question. "What's your name?" he asked the Horse Rider.

"Threem," the Rider said.

Boteen smiled. He'd heard of Threem. Threem had distinguished himself in three battles on Nye and was well known within fighting circles. Rugad had taken no chances on this trip. He had sent the best.

"The only tall ones," Threem said, "would have to be Fey."

"No," Boteen said. "An occasional Islander gets tall."

Like an Enchanter. Like the man he was looking for.

"But would they consider one of their own an influx?"

"I don't know," Boteen said. He stared at the road. A small cloud of dust rose ahead of them, where the other riders had disappeared. "I doubt it."

"The Infantry is still behind us," the Gull Rider said from above. "I have seen no other Fey."

"If you're isolated, even five Fey would seem like a lot. And now they know of us. Someone had to have been monitoring our passage for sometime. Those riders knew we were here," Boteen said. "And these Islanders have no flying magicks that we know of."

"A simple message system along those hills wouldn't be hard," Threem said. "A flash of light, using silvered glass, could be interpreted a dozen ways."

"And if they already felt threatened, they might set up such a system," Boteen said slowly. The dust cloud had vanished. "An influx." He stretched, looked up at the mountain, at the diamond of light no one else could see. "Rugad destroyed the Failures and, according to all we learned, they never traveled this far north and east in the first place. We know we are Rugad's first people up here, and I have not heard of any defectors from our own ranks."

Threem snorted. "No one would dare."

That much was true. The last time someone tried to leave

the Fey army, Rugad had ordered a death so terrible that those who saw it would tell of it in hushed whispers, tell of it for generations. Boteen had seen it. He had never thought of crossing Rugad, not since that.

"There are only two Fey from that first group left alive that we know of," Boteen said.

"Rugad's great-grandchildren," Threem said.

Ay'Le had come back to Boteen's side. She was unnaturally calm. "They might have had traveling companions."

"Who would have been spared if they weren't in Shadowlands," Threem said.

"The great-granddaughter was raised in Jahn, among the Islanders," Boteen said.

"But the great-grandson wasn't." Ay'Le's calm was a facade. Boteen felt the excitement in her. "If we find even one of them—"

"Don't plan your success before it happens," Boteen said. "It will divert you from doing the work."

She shot an angry glare at him. "You diverted me from my work the first time."

"Oh, it's my fault now, is it?" Boteen said.

"Stop," Threem said. "This won't get us anywhere."

"He said that they forced the other tall ones out," the Gull Rider said. "I wonder how long ago that was."

"It couldn't have been too long," Boteen said. "They're acting like people in a panic."

"I'll search for these Fey," the Gull Rider said.

"You'll wait until I tell you to do so," Boteen said.

The Gull Rider peered down at him from the carriage.

"You're not in charge of this mission," Ay'Le said. "You were along on a mission of your own. They weren't supposed to mix."

"They have mixed," Boteen said, "and since I have the ranking powers, I am the one in charge." He looked up at the diamond of light. "We need to go up there."

"There's no guarantee that these Fey you're looking for are there," Ay'Le said.

"And there's no guarantee they're not," Boteen said. "If they're still nearby, they're in the mountains."

"How do you know that?" the Gull Rider said.

"Easy." Gauze spoke from her place beside the carriage. She had been listening silently up to this point. "We've been all over this area. We haven't seen any Fey on the roads besides our people. We haven't seen them anywhere, have you?"

"No," the Gull Rider said a bit sullenly.

"If there are signalers on the mountainside, we haven't seen them, either," the other Wisp said.

"It's easy to hide in a tangle of boulders," Boteen said.

"But it's pretty open down here, on the road, and near the river," Gauze said. "If they ran the Black Heirs out of that village within the last few days, we would have seen them."

Ay'Le let out a small breath of air. "If they drove the Black Heirs out of their village, they must have some amazing powers."

"They might," Boteen said. "But the Black Heirs are Visionaries, and the girl is a Shifter. These are not offensive magicks. The Black Throne is vulnerable, more vulnerable than you'd like to think."

"Then why aren't you in charge, Enchanter?" Ay'Le said.

Boteen looked at her, fairly astonished. "Your history is poor, isn't it, girl?"

Then he stepped away from her.

"Her history and her knowledge of other magicks," Threem said. He laughed, and the sound came out as a small neigh from his Fey mouth. His horse's head hadn't moved.

"A small group of Fey," Boteen said. "I should be able to find them. We need to get me across that river, and up that mountainside. But before we do, I want to know what we're facing. Gauze, I know you can't see the light I was speaking of, but let me describe its location to you. I want to know what's there before we make the climb up the mountain."

"The carriages aren't going up any mountain," Threem said.

Boteen put his hand on Threem's back. "We don't need any carriages," he said.

"A horse could break a leg up there," Threem said.

"Then go up as Fey," Boteen said.

"You think you know what's up there," Threem said.

"No." Boteen sighed. "But something is. I can feel it."

And so was the other Enchanter. But he didn't tell them that. They didn't need to know everything.

"Should I send for the Infantry?" Ay'Le asked. Her question, though a good one, was asked with a bit too much sarcasm, as if she wanted everyone to know how displeased she was with her loss of leadership.

"I think so," Boteen said. "Let's take over the roads leading into that little village. We were supposed to take this place for Rugad. We'll let a show of force start it. Then you can go Charm them, Ay'Le, if you're so inclined."

"You make my work so easy," she said.

"I will do your work if you continue to be insubordinate," Boteen said.

She closed her mouth and raised her head slightly.

"Go on, Gauze," he said. "We'll take care of things here while you investigate."

She shrank to a small version of herself, barely as large as Boteen's thumb. Then she took off, letting her small spark shine so that he could follow her passage across the river.

The pull of the diamond grew. He had stumbled on something far larger than he expected.

A power he hadn't known existed.

Gauze disappeared into the growing sunlight.

He hoped she would be able to return.

SIXTY-SEVEN

THE sun was coming up, and the fires had gone out. Only wisps of smoke remained, trailing up toward the blue sky. Matthias leaned against a boulder, arms crossed over his chest. The morning air was cold, colder than it had been during the night—or perhaps that was caused by the fires going out.

Tri was asleep by another boulder. Denl and Jakib slept in the burning boy's old camp. Pausho and her companion had gone down the mountain after Matthias had tried to question her some more. She would not listen to him, and she would say nothing after her pronouncement about the Hand of God.

He hadn't slept. He was tired and hungry and shivering, but he couldn't sleep. His mind was too busy.

And the Fey were above him. He could see their trails leading to that shimmer.

That place that Pausho had said the Roca had been.

He had died there.

He had been born there.

He had been *re*born there.

Matthias, the greatest scholar of Rocaanism, had never heard of this. Nor had he heard that the Words still existed.

And he had studied here after he had left the Tabernacle. He had found old things, and dug through old records, never thinking of asking the Wise Ones. Never thinking of checking with the ones who had left him for dead.

For religious reasons, they said.

Ordered by the Roca.

He shook his head.

Thinking about this was no easier than thinking about the burning boy's accusation.

You are just like me.

Or the flame that had traveled from one finger to another.

He was just like the boy and just like the Roca.

Only the Roca's powers had come from God and Matthias's from the Evil One, at least according Pausho.

He never asked how she could tell.

Demon-spawn. Perhaps he truly was demon-spawn. She said he would find out.

If he went to that shimmer.

The place where the Roca had been reborn.

He gazed up at it. The shimmer continued, strong and silvery in the growing morning light. He could feel it calling him, feel the pressure it put upon his very soul.

He glanced over his shoulder, down the mountain toward Constant. Marly was there. She had made Denl and Jakib promise to bring him home safe. Despite his height, despite his ruined face, she cared about him.

Maybe, in time, it would grow to love.

He should probably just go down the mountain, hide in his small house, and find a way to survive the inevitable Fey invasion. He should live with Marly and her band of former thieves and try to have a normal life

With flames that danced from his fingers.

He sighed.

He would never be able to let this go. Never. The mountain had always called to him, and he had thought it was part of his heritage, part of the fact that he had survived its cruelties. He had never thought of climbing it before

Not until he saw the Fey trails, and knew he had to.

He still had to. He couldn't stop now.

And the boy had given him something. The boy had given him a way to harness his own powers.

Matthias held out his right hand, cupped it, and imagined a ball of flame in the center of his palm.

A small ball appeared, the fire gold blended with orange, the colors swirling against his pale skin.

He closed his hand, willing the ball away, and when he opened his fingers, there was nothing on his palm. No fire, no scorch marks.

No burns.

You are just like me.

You have a great magick, holy man.

A great magick.

What if Pausho was wrong? What if Matthias's magick was of the Roca? History traced the Roca's line through Nicholas and his half-breed children, but it did not trace what happened to the Roca's second son, the one who was the religious leader on Blue Isle. Did he father children? Was Matthias part of his line? Was that burning boy, that Coulter? Over the generations, the line would have thinned enough so that both of them could be part of the same line and not know it.

Maybe he shouldn't have listened to the others all that time. Maybe he should have realized that he had a gift no one else had.

Maybe the mountain had let him live for a reason.

And maybe he could see the shimmer above him for the same reason.

His shivering had stopped, but his back, pressed up against the boulder, had grown cold even through the clothes he was wearing.

His headache was going away, too.

The Fiftieth Rocaan, a deeply religious man who seemed to think he had heard God's still small voice, believed that the Fey were the Soldiers of the Enemy. He believed that the Rocaan's duty had been the Roca's duty, to clear Blue Isle of the Soldiers of the Enemy.

But the Fiftieth Rocaan, for all his belief, had not been a descendent of the Roca. The Fiftieth Rocaan had been merely a second son of a farming family, and while he led the religion, he did not have the powers of the religious leader.

What if Matthias did? What if his kind were the actual designated leaders of Rocaanism? What if they were the ones who had been thrown out in the schisms all those centuries ago?

Was that what the Wise Ones were guarding? But that made no sense. Because if Matthias was a direct descendent of the Roca, then the Wise Ones would have struggled to keep him alive, not kill him.

Wouldn't they?

He felt as if he had gone to sleep and awakened in a world he no longer recognized. When he was a young man, he had joined the Tabernacle because it had order. It also provided him an education, a way to live in his mind. Then, as he rose in its ranks, he discovered he had a specialty. His scholarship was unique, valued, important. He could do it while living within the orderliness that was the Tabernacle.

Day to day he knew how his life would be. Then he became an Elder, and reached the highest level he wanted to achieve in the Tabernacle.

He had never wanted to be Rocaan. He hated power, feared it within himself.

Because he was demon-spawn? Because he was raised believing he was unworthy?

Or because he truly was lacking belief, lacking the ingredients he admired in the Fiftieth Rocaan?

Who had seen something in him. Who had appointed Matthias to be his successor.

Matthias sighed. The world no longer was orderly. The Tabernacle was gone. He no longer understood his own place in the world, and each time he tried to figure it out, something came along to change his understanding.

He was not a dumb man. But he was flawed.

Pausho and her kind believed he had been flawed from birth.

He glanced at the shimmer again. He could go to it, and face the future, the uncertain future which the Fey had brought with them, see what other darkness lived within himself, or he could go back down the hill, down to Marly, and hope he survived.

He was never very good at hope.

He got up, brushed himself off, then went to Tri, and shook him awake. Tri opened his eyes slowly, awareness a few moments behind.

"I must have fallen asleep," he said. "Who'd have thought I could after this night."

"We're going up the mountain," Matthias said.

Tri nodded. "I knew we would. You can't keep away from a puzzle."

"You think this is a puzzle?"

"It's something Pausho knows that you don't," Tri said.

"Do you?"

Tri shook his head. "I was a bad Wise One. I didn't do any of the study I was supposed to, and I associated with people like you."

Matthias let himself smile. The movement tugged on his still-healing wounds. He patted Tri on the back and went to Denl and Jakib. They were leaning on each other beneath the stone roof. The place the burning boy had found to camp was a cozy one, despite its location.

"We're going up the mountain," Matthias said.

Denl opened his eyes quickly, as if he had only been dozing. "Wouldn't it be best if we got help afore we went? Weapons n such?"

Matthias clenched his fists, remembering the feel of the fire above his skin. "We'll be all right."

"I promised Marly that ye'd come back," Jakib said. He had a hand to his head, and he was looking groggy.

"I will," Matthias said.

"What do ye think is up there?" Denl asked.

"The Fey," Matthias said. And something else. Something that called to him. Something that drew him like nothing ever had before.

He stood and gazed at the shimmer.

He would learn much this day.

If the mountain let him.

If the mountain helped him survive.

Again.

SIXTY-EIGHT

HIS daughter was heavy.

Nicholas had shifted her position. He had been cradling her in his arms. Now he carried her over his shoulder. Her arms dangled against his back, her chin banged into his spine, and her feet bounced against his legs. He hadn't realized how long she was or how big. That tall, slender girl carried a lot of weight, and right now it was dead weight. It almost felt as if he were carrying a body instead of a living creature.

At least she still breathed on her own. And as long as he had his hands on her, the Shaman said, she wouldn't Shift. As long as he imagined her as Arianna and not as something else.

Although he found himself wishing she had remained in her lizard form. He could have cradled that in the palm of his hand and still negotiated this trail.

If he wanted to call it a trail.

The sun had come up on his section of the mountain now. The ground was red, the rocks were red, and he was covered in red dust. The air was cold, though, and on the rocks above him, he could see snow.

The Shaman had some water, which she was giving to him regularly, and he ate part of their stash of tak as he walked. The Shaman scurried before him, her robes catching on the spindly plants that grew in this strange environment. She carried their bundles and Arianna's boots. Farther up, before the snow started, there were no plants at all. Only rocks and dirt and signs of slides.

Slides. He didn't want to think about them. The ground had shifted beneath his feet more than once already. He had one arm wrapped around Arianna's hips, and he used the other for balance. He wasn't certain he'd be able to catch himself if he fell.

And he wasn't certain what would happen to Arianna.

When they left the place where Arianna had been attacked, the Shaman had scurried around Nicholas and had led them along an upper path. There was a lower path that he could see if he glanced down, winding its way around the sides of the mountain, wider and more traveled than this path. But the Shaman was avoiding it purposefully.

She seemed to know where she was going.

And she was moving as fast as he had ever seen her move.

The worry that had been in the pit of his stomach since he fled the palace had grown worse. He just might lose his daughter on this mountainside, lose her to her great-grandfather.

If her great-grandfather's invasion of her mind—and that's what it sounded like to him, no matter how the Shaman explained it—killed Arianna, would that trigger the curse they had always warned him of? The Black Blood against the Black Blood?

Wouldn't the Black King have known of that risk? Wouldn't he have cared?

Or was that something else the Shaman had made up to scare Nicholas?

As they had walked on this trail, his mind was going over each conversation he had had with her. She had often been obtuse, sometimes purposefully so. She had implied that Sebastian was not his child—but she had never told him of Gift.

She had done many things, always, he thought, to save him.

But what if she had had another motive, one he wasn't sure of?

It couldn't be a Fey motive, could it?

She couldn't still be working for the Empire?

But she too was a Visionary, and she could travel across these Links. Sebastian had claimed that he and Gift had spoken all the time through their link. Was the Shaman communicating with the Black King?

But if she was, then why would she have urged Nicholas to kill him?

Unless it was a ploy to cause Arianna's death.

He shook his head. It made no sense. None of it made any sense. Why would the Shaman risk everything to attend Arianna's birth when she would later urge Arianna's death? And why would she have told Nicholas all these things about the Fey when she had not supported the Islanders after all? And why would she have claimed to be his friend?

He stumbled on a narrow section of trail and caught himself with his free hand. Arianna bumped against his back so hard that the air almost left his body.

The air felt thinner here, anyway. It seemed harder to fill his lungs, but he didn't know if that was due to his own exertion or not. He wasn't used to this much exercise any more, all the walking and climbing he was doing. Wasn't used to it at his own weight, let alone carrying a daughter who was taller and who might even weigh more than he did.

He couldn't lose her. That was the thing he kept coming back to. He couldn't bear to lose her. He had lost everyone else.

Jewel.

His father.

So many friends.

Even Sebastian was gone, and Nicholas didn't know his real son.

And in its own way, he had lost his home. The Isle wasn't his any more. Even if he recovered it, it would be different.

The Fey had left their mark on it. He would never be able to change that.

The Shaman scrambled over a series of boulders. Nicholas stopped to catch his breath.

The trail had disappeared. They seemed to be following her instincts now.

"Wait!" he called.

His voice echoed down the mountain.

Wait.

wait

wait

She stopped.

"Where are we going?" he asked.

She pointed. She was breathing hard, too. He could see it,

even from this distance. She still had a wild look about her, a look that made her seem like a completely different person.

Her white hair frizzed around her face. Her dark eyes flashed in the sunlight. Her nut brown skin seemed even more wrinkled than it had before. She had always seemed so serene to him, and now the serenity was gone.

He wondered what had taken it.

"Isn't there a path?" he asked.

She ran a hand through her wild hair. "There are others on that path, Nicholas. We have to go this way."

He stared at the boulders, wondering how he would carry Arianna over them. His strength had limits. And he was reaching them.

"How much farther?" he asked.

"Not much," she said. "Please, Nicholas, we haven't much time."

Why not? Because of Arianna? Or because of something else?

"Will Arianna die if we don't make it soon?"

The Shaman glanced over her shoulder as if she expected to see someone. Their voices were echoing down the mountain. If there were others on the trail, he wondered if those people could hear them.

"I need to have time to help her, Nicholas. I need to get there first."

"I understand that," he said. "But I'm not sure I can climb this."

"You have to," she said. "And you don't understand. I have to arrive before the others."

"What others?" he asked.

She said nothing more, just turned her back on him and started climbing again.

You have to.

The implication was that he would have to climb this mountainside if he wanted Arianna to live. He tentatively took his hand off her hips and leaned forward. Her weight seemed to keep her in place.

"Come on, baby girl," he whispered. "We're going to make this."

And then he started to climb.

SIXTY-NINE

BOTEEN paced. Gauze had been gone much longer than he'd expected. Had the magick currents she'd been talking about done something to her? Had she encountered something she should not have?

He didn't know.

All he knew was that the siren song of the mountain was growing stronger. He felt it even if he didn't look at it. The buzz had left his ears and the nausea was gone from his stomach—those things had disappeared as the riders got farther away—but the feeling that he needed to climb up that mountainside had grown stronger and stronger with each passing moment.

The Gull Rider let the wind ruffle her feathers. She raised her wings slightly as if she were contemplating flight, and then lowered them again. The Horse Riders stood patiently, although Boteen knew it was not their nature to do so.

Ay'Le kept watching him through the corner of her eye. She seemed to think he didn't notice, or maybe she didn't care. She had sent the other Gull Rider for the Infantry, and then she had started pacing.

She hadn't liked the waiting, and she wouldn't like it if Boteen decided to go up that mountain.

Not that it mattered. She was a third-rate Charmer, no matter what Rugad said. She was more interested in her own power than in the work she had to do.

Although he had noticed that was common among Charmers.

The sun had risen far enough above the mountains to shed a warm light on this section of the road. It sparkled on the blood red water below them, making it look as if rubies floated on the surface of the water. There was a sort of drama here, an expectation in the very build of the mountains that something spectacular was going to happen.

Or perhaps it already had.

He liked the magickal feel of the place. Most of the countries he had traveled to on the Galinas continent had the charm of age, the fascination he always found in a new culture, and nothing more. Not this sense of challenge that he felt here, not the sense that he had come home.

He stopped moving at that last thought.

Home.

What had made him think that? He had been born on the road, the son of a Spy and a Domestic whose lust hadn't lasted beyond his childhood. Neither of them knew how to raise him. They had turned him over to Rugad's Spell Warders at a very young age, and he became the tester for many of their spells. It enabled him to learn all the magicks of the Fey—even the handful he could not perform, like Shifting—but it had also ensured that he would never have a permanent residence. He had been part of Rugad's troop since he was three years old, part of his parents' strange traveling household before that.

He had never had a home.

So where was this feeling coming from?

But he knew. It was coming from the mountains. And the magick in the air.

It was coming from the very wildness of this place.

He had to be prepared, prepared to let Rugad know exactly what was going on.

"Get the Scribe," he said to Ay'Le.

She frowned at him, then knocked on the door of the other carriage. The Scribe was like all of his kind, a rather dull fellow who seemed frightened by anything out of routine. He had disappeared into the carriage when the Islanders rode up.

Boteen hadn't seen him since.

The carriage door opened slowly. The Scribe came out.

He was older than Boteen by at least a generation. He might

even have been older than Rugad. His eyes were large and deep, his mouth small, and his ears the size of hands.

He bowed to Boteen, who shook his head.

"I'm not someone to bow to, Scribe," he said.

"I'm sorry, sir," the Scribe said and started to bow again, but seemed to think the better of it. He seemed uncomfortable at being noticed, uncomfortable at the strange place. He glanced more than once at the river, frothing pink foam below them.

"You knew this would be a difficult trip, did you not?" Boteen asked.

The Scribe shook his head. "I was only told that I was needed."

"And you normally sit in a corner and listen."

"Yes, sir," the Scribe said.

Boteen let some air out of his nostrils. Of course. This man was next to worthless. But Rugad had sent him for a reason.

"If you had let me talk to those Islanders," Ay'Le said, "he could have recorded that."

"You did talk to the Islanders," Boteen said.

The Scribe was watching them intently. What else was he supposed to report back to Rugad?

"You are mine now," Boteen said. "This whole trip is mine now, and you will do as I say. Is that clear?"

The Scribe nodded once.

Boteen almost asked him for his name, then remembered. Scribes were forbidden to give their names when they were working. It was better for them to be anonymous. Better for them, better for their magick, and better for those who used their services. That way a perceived error would not be taken out on the individual Scribe, but on the entire group.

As timid as this one was, that was probably good for them.

"You will be at my side, and you will be prepared to take a message back to Rugad. I suspect the message will be a very specific one."

"That's what I am for," the Scribe said. "Specific messages."

"Good," Boteen said. He glanced at the mountain. The Scribe did too, and shuddered. Boteen got the sense that the Scribe rarely went outside.

"Do you ride?" Boteen asked.

"No," the Scribe said.

"Wonderful," Threem mumbled from beside him.

"Well, then, you'll have to learn. There's no way a carriage will make it back to Jahn in the time I suspect we'll need."

"So you'll burden us with him," Threem said again.

Boteen smiled at him. "Maybe even you, Threem."

The horse's head moved, neighing as if in protest. Threem patted the horse's neck, his own neck, unconsciously. Such twitches these strange magicks had. Boteen shook his head.

His own twitches would come later.

"May I return to the carriage now?" the Scribe asked.

"No," Boteen said sharply. "I told you to remain beside me."

"But there is no one else here," the Scribe said.

"This is not going to be a normal assignment for you. You are simply going to be my messenger boy, not the recorder of a long diplomatic meeting."

"Surely, sir," the Scribe said, his voice humble, his head bowed, "one of the others—the Gull Rider, perhaps—can serve as a better messenger."

"Not in this case," Boteen said, and all but rose on his toes with excitement. "If we are facing what I think we're facing, Rugad needs to know the exact wording of the message from me. He would grill a Gull Rider. He will believe you."

"True enough," the Gull Rider murmured from above.

"I'm the head of this team of Horse Riders," Threem said. "You can't make this creature ride on my back. I will send one of the others."

"Only if he's quicker," Boteen said.

"I'll make certain of it," Threem said.

Boteen smiled a little, then paced to the edge of the mountainside. He didn't expect the Scribe to follow him this far, but the old man did, finally understanding his assignment. He peered down at the red water, and turned so pale that for a moment, Boteen thought he was going to pass out.

"Afraid of water?" Boteen asked.

"Heights," the Scribe whispered.

Wonderful, Boteen thought, and they would be going into the mountain. Ah, well. He couldn't worry about the Scribe. The Scribe would have to take care of himself.

Something glinted over the water. Boteen squinted. The glint was moving. It looked like a spark. It was growing closer and closer.

Gauze.

He had just about given up on her.

She arrived on the side of the road, landed, then grew to her full height. For a moment, she looked as if she were dusted with sparks, her body and her wings alight with internal fire. Then the image faded, leaving her delicate face untouched.

"Boteen," she said. "I think we need to speak alone."

He glanced at the Scribe, wondering if he should order the man along, and then decided to trust Gauze's judgment.

"I guess you get to go to the carriage after all," Boteen said.

The Scribe bowed and almost ran to the carriage. Boteen suppressed a smile. This trip would be the challenge of the man's career.

Then he turned to Gauze.

She was rocking back and forth on her small feet, her wings fluttering with the breeze off the river. When she saw him looking at her, she beckoned him away from the carriages, down the side of the road to a small outcropping.

The outcropping bulged over the river. On three sides, he could see the water frothing below him. The river boomed over the rocks below, sounding as furious as the ocean.

Above him, real birds swooped and dived, hunting in the rapidly moving water. The diamond glow on the mountainside beckoned him, and he glanced at it, just once.

"What did you find?" he asked.

"One of the most terrifying places I've ever seen," she said. "It's a cave, with marble steps and an interior hollowed out by human hands. It's guarded by the Islanders' holy swords, and inside are all the tools of their religion."

"You went in?"

She nodded.

He would have to remember to tell Rugad of this, of her great courage.

"There's more, isn't there?" he asked.

She nodded again, a small smile playing on her lips.

"What is it?" He knew she was milking the information, and he didn't care. He needed to know.

"Rugad's great-grandson is inside, along with some Islanders and some Fey. They're expecting the arrival of the great-granddaughter and the Islander King at any moment."

All of them in one place. Boteen's heart skipped. He had found them. His instinct had been right.

"Inside the Islanders' religious place?"

"I'm not sure what kind of place it is," Gauze said. "The

magick currents outside of it are so strong, I nearly landed on one of the stone swords."

He still had to see this place. He knew it. And he also knew that he couldn't wait for the Scribe to reach Rugad. This news was too great.

"You are sure these are the Black King's great-grandchildren."

"I am certain of the son," she said. "And I know they were talking of the others coming."

He squinted. Her voice sounded odd, as if there were something else, something she was unwilling to admit to.

"What happened to you in there?"

"Magick currents," she said. "I told you."

"And what else?"

She blinked, then looked away. Her wings fluttered again, but this time the fluttering wasn't caused by the breeze.

It was caused by her nerves.

"You need to tell me," he said. He put a bit of Charm in the words. He rarely did that. He rarely used spells unless he needed to.

"My grandmother," she said. Then started, backed up, and nearly tumbled. He reached for her, but she righted herself and smiled at him.

"Your grandmother?"

"She was—" she shook her head.

"Your grandmother was Eklta, one of the great Wisp messengers of the L'Nacin campaign. I've heard of her," Boteen said. "And was sorry to hear how she died."

Gauze nodded. "She knew secrets; she was killed for them. It happens. At least I got to spend some time with her on Nye."

Boteen knew that Gauze had to get to this in her own time. But he felt the impatience in his own stomach. The great-grandchildren. Here, in this place of wild magick.

"Murder is never something we live with easily," he said soothingly, fighting the urge to use a spell more serious than Charm. Something that would compel her to talk. "But I don't understand how it fits now."

"I—" Gauze swallowed hard, then shook her head. "I nearly slammed into one of those stone swords. They're bigger than you, Boteen, and they are stuck into the mountainside. I don't know if they have Islander magick, but the current around them was so strong. I was falling toward one, unable to stop myself, when my grandmother appeared beside me. She pulled me out, and by then, I was inside the cave. Then she kissed me on my cheek, told me I would be forever loved and forever remembered, and led me down the stone stairs."

Boteen's heart sank. "And that's when you saw the great-grandson."

Gauze nodded. She saw his disbelief. "The boy was talking to someone who wasn't there. And there was a clean Red Cap with him, as well as a woman from Rugar's infantry. They were whispering to an Islander, trying to explain the Mysteries to him."

"The Mysteries?" Boteen repeated. He looked at the diamond on the mountainside.

The Mysteries?

It couldn't be.

But it all made sense. Complete sense.

Gauze had stumbled on a Place of Power. Here, in Blue Isle. And it was controlled by the Islander religion. That was why they were able to defeat the Fey. They had the same powers. They just used them differently.

A Place of Power. Where the Mysteries lived, and the Powers ruled. Where, if a man went deep enough into the cave, all time disappeared.

"You're certain of this?" Boteen asked.

She nodded. "I'm sorry about my grandmother. I wasn't going to tell you. I was afraid you wouldn't believe me."

He didn't want to hear her apologies or her worries. "Who was the great-grandson talking with?"

"I don't know. It appeared as if he were talking to the air."

Another confirmation, if he chose to see it as that. "I understand. But who did he think he was talking to?"

"His mother," she said.

"Jewel?" Boteen asked.

Gauze shrugged. "There were no names used. None at all."

Mysteries. It was said Mysteries could appear to three people, and three people only. The Mystery's greatest love in life, the Mystery's greatest hate, and a person of the Mystery's choice.

"You and your grandmother were close?" Boteen asked.

Gauze nodded. "I loved her more than anything."

"And how did she feel about you?"

Gauze smiled. "I was the only family she had. She said she loved me to distraction."

Boteen nodded. Greatest love. It wasn't a real confirmation, but it was good enough.

"You need to go to the Black King and tell him what you saw. You need to get to him as soon as you can. *Do not* tell him of your grandmother. And do not tell him what's in the cave. Just that his great-grandson, great-granddaughter, and the King of Blue Isle are meeting in this remote location. Do you understand?"

"Doesn't he need to know the danger?"

"Tell him I'm going to investigate. Tell him I will send word when we know more. Tell him—" Boteen paused, thought. "Tell him to send as many troops as he can here. Tell him there are strange magicks here and we have not yet located the source of them."

"Should he come?" Gauze asked.

Boteen shook his head. He didn't want the Black King here yet. He didn't know what would happen if Rugad came.

"That's his decision," Boteen said. "But it would be better if he waited until we knew more. Can you do all this without revealing the cave?"

"Of course," she said.

"Then go," Boteen said. "Go now. And tell no one but the Black King of this."

She nodded to him, shrank, and rose in the air, her spark glinting off the sunlight like the diamond across the way.

A Place of Power. The Black Family, and another Enchanter.

All the power of Blue Isle, here in this place.

Boteen smiled.

The advantage had just returned to the Fey Empire.

Three Places of Power in the world, and soon they would have two.

Rugad would be so pleased.

SEVENTY

MATTHIAS felt as if he were growing stronger. He climbed the thin trail that kept disappearing on him. Behind him, Denl and Jakib complained softly. Tri said nothing, but did grunt occasionally as if in pain.

They had just gone through a boulder field and were coming up on some flat rocks that looked as if they had once been part of a staircase. Decades, maybe centuries, before, a slide had covered part of the stairs.

Matthias had to use his hands for balance as he climbed, but he didn't care. He felt a sense of urgency he had never felt before. He knew that the Fey were above him, but that wasn't where the urgency came from.

It was coming from the shimmer itself.

Above him, he thought he heard other voices, familiar voices. Once he even thought he heard Nicholas, although he knew that was an impossibility. Nicholas was somewhere else, if he was alive at all. Nicholas would never be in such a treacherous place so far from his precious home.

Or his half-breed children.

The sun's full rays were on Matthias, but they didn't warm him. The air grew colder as he climbed. The shimmer still rippled above him, but he felt it more than he saw it. It seemed to be giving him strength, pulling him forward. The feeling he had had about the mountains ever since he was a small boy had grown, and he wondered, as he grabbed the rocks and pulled himself forward, why he had never done this before.

Why he had never climbed to this place before.

He had always resisted it. He had always felt as if the mountain's call to him had been a call to his own death. He had nearly died here once; he figured the mountain wanted to finish the job.

He hadn't realized that perhaps it was calling him home.

The rocks had cleared off the stairs. The stairs were broken, but they were still easy to manage.

He hurried.

"Holy Sir!" Denl yelled from below. "Please dunna lose us here."

He didn't answer. They would be able to catch him.

They knew where he was going.

The steps led to a rock ledge, and behind it, the shimmer pulsed. He could feel each pulse. With it came another pull, as if each pulse were timed to draw him forward.

The exhaustion he had felt earlier was gone.

His hunger was gone as well.

And so was the headache that had formed after his meeting with the burning boy.

"Matthias, please," Tri called. "Wait."

Matthias took the last few steps, and then hauled himself onto a large rock ledge. When he stood on the ledge, he stopped, and took a deep breath.

The air was thinning. He had trouble breathing. He should have realized that would happen, but he hadn't thought it through. He had only been thinking of coming up here, of reaching the top, of getting to the shimmer.

He was nearly there, if he could only catch his breath.

If he went on like this, he wouldn't make it any farther. He knew that, no matter how hard the shimmer pulled him.

He turned his back on it, and stared over the ledge into the valley below.

Far below, the river twisted, its coppery red color a wound in the valley floor. Beyond it were the roads and trails that led to Constant. The town was nestled against the mountain, with gray stone houses looking as if they had been formed just for the people of the town.

The Roca had come from here, from this desolate place, and

beneath the town, if Pausho and Tri were to be believed, were the Words Written and Unwritten.

And above, in the shimmer, was the cave where the Roca had been reborn.

What would happen to Matthias there? Would he experience some sort of magickal event?

He didn't know. He did know that he would have to clear the Fey out of there first, and he couldn't do that alone.

Tri reached him before the others. Matthias took Tri's hand and pulled him onto the ledge.

Tri was breathing heavily. "It's quite a climb."

"Yes," Matthias said. He was still watching the stairs. Denl and Jakib were making their way up carefully. Denl kept looking over his shoulder as if he were afraid of falling backward and tumbling all the way down to the river.

"Hey," Tri said. "This is man-made."

He was looking down at the ledge. Matthias looked down too, and wondered why he hadn't noticed it before. The rocks were mortared together and time had worn them flat, although several had worked their way loose. It looked like a poor version of the flagstone leading into one side of the Tabernacle.

Now gone, probably.

His heart twisted a little.

He would miss the Tabernacle. For the rest of his life he would miss it. It hadn't mattered that he had left it. It mattered that it remained, that it existed, that it continued without him.

He had loved it so much that he had given up himself for it.

And now it was gone.

Denl and Jakib made the final climb to the ledge. They stopped beside him, breathing as hard as he had.

"We're almost there," he said. He could still feel the pulsing, the shimmer, pulling at him. "Let me go first."

"I dunna think twould be wise," Jakib said. "Marly—"

"You'll keep your promise to her," Matthias said. He was smiling. He liked to have Jakib worried about this. He liked the strength that Marly had, the command she had over all the men in that small crew.

"He might have a point," Tri said. "You're the one who has the Secrets."

"And I'm the only one who seems to know where this place is," Matthias said. "Don't worry."

"They know we're coming," Denl said.

"I know," Matthias said. "I've already thought of that."

It was one of the reasons he wanted to go first. He wanted to use the newfound power, the one that the burning boy had taught him, and he didn't really want his friends to see it.

He still hadn't come to terms with it.

He still wasn't sure it was magick.

"Is that where we're goin?" Denl asked. He was pointing behind Matthias.

Matthias turned slowly. He had been unwilling to look before this. A cave opened against the mountainside, its mouth as wide and huge as the entranceway into the Tabernacle. Around its mouth were swords.

Rocaanist swords.

His mouth went dry.

The Fey couldn't be here. They couldn't. They wouldn't go inside something guarded as that was, with swords that large.

He hadn't seen swords that size outside of the Tabernacle. One had hung from the sanctuary ceiling, point down, and visitors had often worried that it would fall and hurt them. These swords did not look as precarious. They were made of stone.

The first two were embedded in the rock platform like columns rising in front of a large building. They were tall and imposing, and he could feel their strength.

Fey trails led around them, and down, into the mouth of the cave. The burning boy was here as well.

Matthias could sense him.

Two other swords were embedded in the sides of the cave's mouth, as if someone had thrown them there in a fit of anger. The swords extended straight out. If they weren't so large, someone could grab them and fight with them.

If they weren't larger than a man himself.

And above the cave's mouth was the final sword. This one was carved into the rock, point extended downward, as if it would fall on anyone who went inside.

Matthias wondered if the Fey had been afraid as they entered. He wondered if they had looked up at that sword and seen their doom.

"They're inside the cave," he said.

"Na Fey would go in there," Denl said. "Tis Rocaanist."

"Nonetheless," Matthias said.

Tri cleared his throat and stood, brushing off his clothes as he did so.

"If we do this right, we have an advantage."

"They're trapped," Matthias said.

"Who knows ha far the cave goes, though," Jakib said.

"It doesn't matter," Matthias said. "They'll be trapped inside without food or water."

"There might be water inside," Tri said. "If it is truly a Rocaanist cave, it should have holy water."

"Which will poison an unprepared Fey," Matthias said.

"Aye," Denl said. "They might be afeared ta drink it."

"All the better," Matthias said. "I'll go first, as I said, then I'll beckon you forward."

"How can we hold a siege with only four people?" Tri asked.

Matthias grinned. "If we do this right, they'll think there are more than four out here."

He started toward the cave, walking slowly, quietly, past the first two swords. They were Rocaanist. The symbols on the hilt were ancient, dating from the Roca's time. Their meaning had been disputed for centuries, their true translation lost. It didn't matter. Matthias felt as if he were seeing an old friend.

As he approached the swords that stuck outright, he noticed that someone had scraped dirt off one of the hilts. A jewel gleamed redly from its place near the markings.

His stomach jumped. A passage from the Words flitted through his mind, but he couldn't catch it. Or was it from the Secrets? He couldn't remember, not right now. He was thinking of too much.

But he knew it was something about jeweled swords held by giant hands.

The Hand of God.

He shuddered.

What had Pausho said?

I discourage no one from touching the Hand of God.

He stood on his toes and ran a finger along the jewel. It tingled against his skin.

There was so much here. So very much for him to learn, to understand. And he had no time.

He had to take care of the Fey first.

Denl and Jakib stayed a good distance behind him. Tri was a bit closer, staring at the swords openmouthed.

Matthias looked away from them, and up at the sword above him. He had been wrong. It hadn't been carved above the mouth of the cave, but mounted there instead. Its mounting was thin, a single bracelet, as if the sword were in a stand on the ground instead of hovering above the ground.

If the Fey hadn't been afraid as they had gone in here, they should have been.

He felt a nervous jumping in his own stomach. They were expecting him. What had he done that day when he killed Burden so long ago? What had he done on the mountainside below? He had built a shield, an invisible shield in front of himself.

He wondered if he could do it, without an immediate threat.

He took a deep breath, imagined it, and then hoped it was there.

It was the best he could do.

A light as bright as sunshine poured out of the cave. With it came a calmness that he hadn't felt since he was an Aud, decades before. He would go to the edge of it, just inside, and see what he faced. If they attacked him, he would use his newfound powers to attack back. If they emerged, then Denl and Jakib and Tri could handle them.

There couldn't be that many of them.

He didn't see that many trails.

He took a step beneath the giant sword, stopping in the light at the cave's mouth. He peered inside, saw chalices and marble steps, and heard the splashing of water, mingling with voices.

Then a man's voice cried out, and a woman appeared from nowhere. She was as tall as he was, taller maybe, and Fey. She rammed her fist through his shield, making it visible and shattering it at the same time. Pieces flew all over the cave, skittering on the marble, cutting through the air.

Her hand wrapped itself around his throat so tight that he couldn't breathe, and she tugged him just inside.

He struggled against her. He had never felt anyone so strong. She grabbed him with her other hand, preventing him from using his right arm. The pain in his throat was intense. He couldn't breathe. He pulled against her, trying to think of a spell, trying to imagine magick, but each time he did, it disappeared. The thought went away as if it had never been.

The woman put her face close to his, and with a start, he realized he recognized her.

But he couldn't.

He was dying.

It was the only explanation.

She smiled and loosened her grip just a little.

"Frightened, holy man?" she asked.

He brought a hand up to her wrist, trying to pull her fingers away. His air was going. He had felt this before, this desperate ache in his chest. He was gasping this time, though. He was trying to bring air into his lungs, but it wouldn't go through his throat.

Her grip was too tight.

It was too tight.

"Do you want to beg for mercy, holy man? I'll let you go if you do." Her smile grew. Her hand was warm, her skin was clear. The top of her head was unharmed. She didn't look like she had when she had been carried out of the Coronation Hall, that foul mist rising from her hair.

Black spots floated in front of his eyes. Beg for mercy? Have a second chance? Undo the very thing Nicholas had nearly killed him for all those years ago?

Matthias nodded, once.

She loosened her grip enough for him to draw air. It felt like life going into his lungs. He gasped once, twice, three times. The spots had gone away, but the ache in his chest remained. And he was getting light-headed.

"Jewel," he said, knowing how ridiculous it was. She was dead. He had killed her. Intentionally, no matter what he had said to Nicholas. Matthias had killed her because he thought her evil, because she had polluted his people, the Roca's direct line. Because her children would inherit unless he could change it.

He had called it God's will.

Had it been?

How could it have been if he were demon-spawn?

And if he wasn't?

She had her head tilted slightly, her brown eyes watching his every move. He could feel her breath on his face. How could she be alive? And younger than he remembered?

"Can't say it, can you, holy man?" she asked, but her fingers didn't tighten.

"Jewel," he said again. "I'm sorry. Please let me go. I didn't realize—"

Her fingers dug into the skin of his neck, shoving his Adam's apple backward and making him choke. He tried to cough, strangled, and felt a searing pain as muscles strained against her touch.

"You couldn't do it, could you, holy man?" She pushed her face close to his. Her nose nearly touched his. "You couldn't apologize. I thought maybe after all these years, after learning what you had done, and figuring out what you are, that you might actually be sorry. Deep-down sorry, but you're not."

He clawed at her wrist, shoved with the arm she gripped, and pulled backward with his feet. His head ached, and the pain in his chest turned into a burning. His entire chest felt as if it were on fire, and he didn't know how to stop it.

The black spots had returned. They were growing larger and larger.

"I am sorry," he mouthed, but the words didn't come out. Not a sound came out.

She understood anyway. "You said, 'I'm sorry. Please let me go.' *Me*, Matthias. Me. Me. Me. Everything is always about you. You destroyed a marriage, nearly killed a newborn, and those actions led to the destruction of a culture, the loss of hundreds, maybe thousands of lives. 'I'm sorry,' you say. 'I'm sorry. Please let *me* go.' "

This time she did press her nose against his.

"Never will I let you go," she whispered. "The Powers have promised you to me, and I will take you, Matthias. I will never let you go."

The pressure of her fingers increased. The pain brought tears to his eyes. He struggled against her, but his struggles were growing weaker now. He could feel himself slipping away.

You have a great magick, holy man.

But this time the comment running through his head was a memory, not a command. He couldn't find the magick, couldn't find a way to save himself.

He took the last of his strength, shoved—

—and she didn't move.

It made no impact on her at all.

"Please," he tried to say, but nothing came out.

Please, he thought.

Please. Stop.

But he couldn't stop her. The blackness had covered his eyes. The pain was receding and he was tumbling inside himself, backward, backward.

To the awaiting darkness.

Now she could kill him.

Now she could have her revenge.

And she deserved it.

He knew that, deep down.

She deserved it all.

SEVENTY-ONE

HIS mother had been talking to him. He had just asked her to tell him how to save his sister, when she had tilted her head as if she were listening. She got a terrifying expression on her face, sharp and furious and hateful all at the same time, then she had run up the stairs so fast that he couldn't keep up with her.

Gift just started after her, stupidly, as if she had fled from him. Perhaps his sister was coming. Perhaps his mother was going to help her into the cave.

Coulter was staring up the steps, too, but his expression was not one of confusion.

It was fear.

"What's going on?" the Cap asked.

"He's here," Coulter said.

Gift shot a glance at him. He? Not Nicholas's father. Coulter wouldn't use that tone about him, would he?

"The Rocaan?" Adrian asked.

"Yes," Coulter said.

Gift felt a shudder run through him. The man who had come back from the dead—or what he and Leen had thought was dead. Outside.

And his sister about to arrive.

His half-Fey sister.

And his mother, disappearing up the stairs.

Outside there was a male cry, sudden and abrupt. It almost sounded as if it had been cut off in the middle.

Gift started up the stairs. The Cap grabbed for him, but didn't stop him. Coulter kept pace with him. Leen joined them, her expression hard.

Adrian and the Cap didn't follow. The Cap handed Adrian a sword from his stash and then Gift didn't look at them any more.

The outside of the cave was light. It had become day while he was inside that place and he hadn't even realized it.

His mother was standing in the mouth of the cave, her hand around the throat of the man who had killed her. She was holding him away from her with her other hand. His face was red, his eyes bulging, his lips moving, but making no sound.

"My God," Leen whispered. "What is it? What's happening to him?"

And then Gift realized that she couldn't see his mother. Leen saw the murderer of Gift's mother gasping for breath, one hand in the air instead of clutching Gift's mother's wrist.

How odd it must look.

And terrifying.

"She's killing him," Gift said.

"Who?" the voice came from behind him. He turned slightly. Adrian.

"My mother," Gift said.

Adrian was holding a sword and peering around Gift's shoulder. He didn't seem upset. He seemed stunned, worried, almost frightened.

Gift took a step closer. Coulter put his hand on Gift's arm. "If she is killing him, let her," Coulter said. "It is between them."

Gift wasn't going to stop her. He had been going to help her. But in stepping closer, he realized something: the Rocaan's companions were behind him, watching with the same terror that Leen was. They must have assumed he was under the influence of a great magick—

And maybe he was.

The Rocaan's mouth was moving, forming words. *Please,* he was saying in Islander. *Please.*

Gift's mother seemed to be ignoring him. And she seemed to be enjoying herself. Then the Rocaan's body collapsed. Gift's mother didn't move. She kept her hand on his throat, kept holding him upright. She was like a cat who was playing with a bird long after it died. She would hold him until all the life had drained out of him.

Gift felt oddly detached, watching her. This wasn't what he had imagined from his mother. Or what he had expected. He had thought that she would be a good woman, a woman who knew no cruelty.

How could he have thought that?

She was Fey.

Suddenly Coulter looked beyond the two of them, as if he saw something else.

Adrian noticed too. He came up beside Coulter, and said softly, "What is it? What do you see?"

"Nothing," Coulter said.

"Something has changed," Adrian said. "I can tell from your face."

Coulter looked at him, gaze flat. Gift felt it too. For all he tried to remain separate from Coulter, he couldn't entirely. They were Bound. Parts of their emotions leaked back and forth, rather like a heightened awareness, a knowing of things they wouldn't normally know.

Something was wrong.

Was it Gift's mother? Was she wrong in getting her revenge?

"What is it?" Gift asked.

Coulter looked at him, and Gift realized he had misinterpreted Coulter's earlier expression. Coulter's gaze hadn't been flat, hadn't been hiding things.

It had been frightened.

"Coulter?" Gift whispered.

"There's another one," Coulter said. "The third one."

"The third what?" the Cap asked.

"The third Enchanter," Adrian said. "Right, Coulter?"

Coulter nodded.

"What about him?" Gift asked, even though he had a hunch he already knew.

"He's here," Coulter said. "And he knows we are, too."

SEVENTY-TWO

SHE had to hurry.

The Shaman glanced over her shoulder. Nicholas struggled behind her, his face dripping sweat, Arianna slung over him as if she were dead already.

They might lose everything. In the next few moments, they might lose Arianna and all their power in the battle against the Black King.

If she didn't hurry.

The Place of Power was over the next rise, behind a boulder, and down. They would be coming at it from the side, not from below.

For the first time in her life, for the only time, she wished that she had more than one type of magick.

She wished she could fly.

"Hey!" Nicholas said, and she could hear how out of breath he was. "Slow down!"

But she couldn't slow down. She had to get there.

She had to be there.

Now.

She scurried across the thin trail, her feet catching on the rocks that had fallen and embedded themselves in the dirt. She dropped the bundles and Arianna's boots, and held her arms out for balance. She was breathing hard.

She hoped Nicholas would forgive her.

She hoped he would understand.

The future was the most important thing. She had to prevent Black Blood fighting Black Blood.

There was only one way to do it, at least according to her Visions.

"Wait!" Nicholas called, his voice growing fainter.

She didn't say anything. She had reached the top of the rise. Below her, she could see the glow that indicated the Place of Power. Three Islanders stood outside, looking terrified, looking shocked.

She was too late.

She was already too late.

She slid past the boulder, grabbing it as she went. No one seemed to hear her coming despite the shower of rocks that preceded her. They fell onto the flagstones below—or what used to be flagstones. Moss had grown between them, and the rocks had chipped and broken.

This was an old place, as old as the place in the Eccrasian Mountains.

It felt the same: all full of magick and power; full of evil and good; timeless, soulless, and somehow the center of everything.

Rocks rained on her.

She glanced up.

Nicholas had reached the top of the rise. He too saw the Islanders below. He had one arm wrapped around Arianna's legs. The other was free so he could climb down.

"Wait!" he said when he saw the Shaman looking at him.

She shook her head and skidded the rest of the way. The movement scraped her thighs and buttocks, but she didn't care.

In a few moments, minor pain wouldn't matter.

Nothing would matter.

She ran across the flagstones. The Islanders turned when they saw her come. One had a knife.

She didn't have any weapons.

She had no way to fight him.

Except with herself.

She ran between the three of them, shoving them aside. The one with the knife fell against a rock. The other two stumbled, surprised, probably, that someone would attack them when they were armed.

Then she saw it:

The Islander, their Rocaan, the one who had married Jewel and Nicholas alongside the Shaman, the one who had killed Jewel so horribly on that day long ago.

He was still standing, but his face was blue. His eyes were closed, and his tongue was sticking out of his mouth.

No one was touching him, yet she could see the marks of fingers in his neck.

He was in the thrall of a Mystery.

A Mystery that was focusing all its Power on the kill.

He, apparently, had thought the Mystery was strangling him, but it didn't matter. The magick was what mattered.

The magick of the Mystery, serving one of its goals.

The justifiable homicide of a hated person. So few were granted the right.

The Power at the moment was so finely focused, so hard to stop.

She knew it.

And she feared it.

She had feared this moment for a long, long time.

His aura was fading.

He was dying.

And he deserved to die for the things he had done. The lives he had cost, the destruction he had brought.

The hatred he felt.

He deserved to die.

But she didn't hesitate. She ran the few feet across the flagstones, grabbed his shoulders and flung him away. With the same movement, she shoved her neck where his had been.

Then she saw her assailant:

Jewel, looking at her.

Jewel, trying to pull back.

"No," Jewel said. "Not you. This is wrong."

She tried to pull away, but it was too late.

The Shaman saw her own life force coloring Jewel's fingers, weaving its way through Jewel's body, becoming part of the Mystery, then seeping into the door of the Place of Power, to go wherever unfettered souls went.

Such a slow filtering.

"No!" Jewel called, but she didn't say it to the Shaman. She called it to the skies, to the Powers. "It's not fair! Take someone else! Take a different price!"

The Shaman saw them, floating above.

She heard the Powers murmur something about choice, about information and Gift, about the way things should be.

"I'm sorry," Jewel said, and then she disappeared.

SEVENTY-THREE

DENL heard his knife clatter to the ground. The old woman had blundered past them as if she hadn't even seen him. She had knocked him aside with her body, and had hit Jakib and Tri at the same time.

Then she had hesitated when she had seen the Holy Sir in the throes of his magick fit. She had hesitated, but only for a moment.

And suddenly she was running toward him, grabbing him, flinging him aside, and taking his place. Her face was contorted, but she didn't look as terrified as he had.

Only she was going to die.

Denl knew it.

They all knew it.

She had taken the Holy Sir's place.

An old Fey woman.

What had she been thinking?

It didn't matter what she had been thinking. She had thrown her life away for the Holy Sir's.

Denl had never known the Fey to be so altruistic. She had to have a reason. A real reason.

Perhaps they needed the Holy Sir for something even worse.

Denl glanced at Jakib and Tri. They were staring at the

woman. Jakib still lay where he had fallen. Tri was getting up, but he looked stunned.

It was up to Denl.

He paused to pick up his knife, just in case he would need it, then he ran across the rock ledge. His breath was coming in sharp gasps. Something in his chest had been injured in his fall.

He didn't care.

He had to hurry.

He reached the Holy Sir. The imprint of fingers marred the man's neck. His face was red, but he was breathing, great gasping breaths. His eyes were open, but glazed, as if he didn't know where he was.

He probably didn't know the danger he was in.

Denl grabbed the Holy Sir by his armpits and pulled him away from the old woman. She wasn't fighting, even though the red marks on her neck were growing. She was staring at something far away, as if it were her destiny.

As if it were her fate to take the place of the Holy Sir.

She didn't even notice Denl behind her, didn't notice that he was hauling the Holy Sir away.

As he got closer to the swords, Tri came forward and grabbed the Holy Sir's feet.

"We ha ta get him out a here," Denl said.

Tri nodded. Carrying the Holy Sir had suddenly become easier. His body swung back and forth as they started toward the path down.

Jakib hauled himself up. He glanced again at the old woman as if he couldn't believe what he saw. Then he started after them.

The Holy Sir's eyes were still glazed. His breath was rasping but even. The marks on his neck were turning purple. He had been badly bruised.

Denl reached the edge of the flat stone area and looked behind him for the path. There it was, descending sharply. Going down carrying the Holy Sir like this would be very difficult.

Maybe even impossible.

"Stop," Denl said.

No one was chasing them. The old woman was still in her place up front. The Fey that the Holy Sir believed to be inside the cave hadn't come after them.

Denl raised his head to scan the area.

No one.

Except a stricken-looking man on the edge of the flat path.

He was short and blonde and looked somehow familiar. He had a woman slung over his shoulder. A tall, slim woman with dark hair and dark skin.

A Fey.

The familiar man was staring at the old woman and beyond, his face so white he seemed to be seeing a ghost.

Then he turned his head slowly, and his gaze came to rest on the Holy Sir.

"No!" the man shouted, and the word echoed through the mountains.

It was filled with such anguish that Denl felt the pain.

No!

The man scurried across the flat rock, the woman's arms bumping against his back.

"We ha ta hurry," Denl said.

He would use the idea from the other man. A shoulder carry might work.

"Here," he said. "Let me carry him."

He switched his grip on the Holy Sir, turning him, then using his back and body to pick him up. The man was heavy and longer than Denl realized.

"I'll carry him part a the way. Then the two a ye need ta help," Denl said. "Tri, ye go first down this trail, and tell me what to expect."

The Holy Sir twisted slightly. Denl tightened his one-handed grip on the Holy Sir's back. "Ye," he said softly, "don't move. I ha ye. We'll get ye out a here."

The Holy Sir said nothing, but he relaxed against Denl's shoulder.

"Jakib," Denl said. "Make sure na one follows us. Watch our backs."

Jakib nodded, looking a bit stunned that he was taking orders from Denl. But neither of the others seemed to understand the significance of this.

The Holy Sir had nearly died.

He was the only link left to Rocaanism.

He knew things no one else did. He had explained that to Marly and Denl had overheard.

And then there was that vision last night: the burning boy who tried to get the Holy Sir to use his powers.

Maybe if the Holy Sir had used powers, he wouldn't have needed rescuing.

When Denl got him below, to the city, he would talk to the Holy Sir about this.

The Holy Sir might save them all from the Fey.

Although he had nearly died in this place filled with religious symbols.

Something had nearly killed him.

Something Fey?

Then why had the old woman tried to save him?

Why had she taken his place?

"Hurry," Tri said, the urgency now in his voice.

Denl took a deep breath and started down the path. His side hurt. He didn't have time for questions now.

He had the Holy Sir's life in his hands.

And he would do everything he could to save it.

SEVENTY-FOUR

NICHOLAS saw it, but he didn't believe it. A Fey woman, standing in the doorway to a cave, her hands wrapped around Matthias's neck.

A Fey woman who looked just like Arianna—just like Jewel—killing Matthias.

And then the Shaman ran across the flagstone, ran so fast that she knocked aside three Islanders Nicholas didn't recognize, and shoved Matthias out of the way.

The Fey woman was horrified, took her hands away, and still the Shaman was in pain.

She still seemed to be dying.

Nicholas scrambled across the boulder, stopping when he saw the three men taking Matthias away.

"No!" he shouted, but he couldn't go after them, not with Arianna over his shoulder.

And he couldn't leave the Shaman to this.

He ran across the flagstones as quickly as he could. Arianna bounced against his shoulder, his grip on her so tight he wondered if she would get bruises. He wanted to set her down, but he couldn't. He didn't dare.

What if she Shifted again?

But he was alone here, alone with the Shaman and the

woman who looked like Jewel and Matthias and his three friends who were carrying him away.

He would have to let Matthias go.

Again.

Matthias, at this moment, meant nothing.

Not compared to the Shaman.

Not compared to Arianna.

Not compared to Blue Isle itself.

Nicholas wouldn't have the Isle without his daughter.

He wouldn't have his daughter without the Shaman.

He kept running toward her. The Shaman was turning red in the face, and there was a growing discoloration on her neck, even though the Fey woman, the one who looked like Jewel, had backed away.

He could hear the Fey woman now.

"No, not you," she said. "This is wrong."

She sounded like Jewel.

She backed away from the Shaman and held her fists to the sky.

"No!" she shouted. "It's not fair! Take someone else! Take a different price!"

The sky was cloudy suddenly as if a haze had fallen over the sun. Nicholas had nearly reached the Shaman. He was close enough to the Fey woman, to Jewel, to see the lines in her face.

There were none.

He reached for her with his free hand.

She bent her head back toward the Shaman. "I'm sorry," she said, and disappeared.

A line, a glow like the sun itself, had attached itself from the Shaman to the Fey woman. The Fey woman's end disappeared when she did, but the line remained. It looked as if it were pouring the Shaman's essence into nothing.

The Shaman fell to her knees.

Nicholas hurried to her side. He kept Ari on his shoulder with one hand. With the other, he eased the Shaman down. He reached for the line, but he could no longer see it.

"What can I do?" he asked.

The Shaman shook her head weakly. "I told you," she said, her voice coming in breathy gasps, "you would not like it."

"You did this on purpose?" he asked.

She smiled.

"We need to get you some help."

"There is no help, Nicholas. I'm dying."

"You can't," he said. "I need you."

And then he realized how awful that sounded. How selfish. *She* was dying.

"There must be help. There must be."

"No, Nicholas," she said.

"But Arianna—"

"Perhaps your son," the Shaman said. Her voice was trailing out. Her lips weren't working as well as they had just a moment earlier.

He couldn't lose her. She was his help, his lifeline, his doorway to the Fey. "I'm sorry," he said. "Sorry I got angry with you about Arianna."

"I thought you'd be angry about this," the Shaman said. She took his hand with hers. Her fingers were surprisingly strong.

"You *knew* about this?" Nicholas asked. "About Matthias?"

"Yes," she whispered.

"He murdered my wife. He was one of the causes of this war. You know what he is, and you still did this?"

"I know what he is," she said. "You don't."

"No," Nicholas said. "He can't be worth your life."

"He is worth mine and a dozen more," she said. "I mean nothing to the future of the Fey. He can stop the Black Blood against Black Blood."

"Matthias?" Nicholas asked, feeling stunned. "He's a pathetic man filled with hatred."

She shook her head again. Her lips were turning blue. Her face had gone pale. It was as if she were losing blood but he couldn't see where she was bleeding.

She pulled him closer with the remaining strength in her hand. "He is important, Nicholas. Know this. You must know this. He is your God."

"What?" Nicholas asked, unable to believe what he just heard.

"Your God, Nicholas," she whispered. "Matthias is your God."

Then she let go of his hand, and brought her hand to his face. She smoothed his hair away, and touched his cheek lightly.

"I have loved you," she said softly. "Perhaps too much . . ."

And then her hand fell away. She smiled at him and it took him a moment to realize she was gone.

With his free hand, he cradled her to him. His wisdom, his strength, the person who was always there for him, from the day he married Jewel. The Shaman was thin, so thin, and already growing cold.

"No," he whispered. "Not you too. I can't face this. I can't face this all alone."

He buried his face in her hair, the white strawlike hair, and rocked back and forth, holding his nearly lifeless daughter and the body of his last—and best—friend.

THE RESISTANCE

SEVENTY-FIVE

MATTHIAS came to himself when Denl set him down. They had reached the camping spot, the spot where the boy Coulter had started all the fires. Denl had placed Matthias on the cool ground, and Matthias's hand brushed against one of the boulders.

It was cold and warm at the same time. It seemed to remember the fires from the night before.

He didn't know how he knew what a boulder was thinking, and that startled him into awareness.

He wasn't dead.

He had survived that attack.

Jewel.

He brought a hand up to his throat. Jewel had attacked him.

Jewel.

She was dead. He knew she was dead. He had seen her die. He had watched the holy water seep into her brain.

He had killed her.

And just a few moments earlier, she had tried to strangle him. Then something had happened, Denl had pulled him away, and he awoke here.

With an aching throat, burning lungs, and the worst headache he had ever had in his life.

Alive, though.

He was alive.

"Holy Sir," Denl said, peering down at him. "Tis everathin all right?"

Matthias made himself smile. The wounds on his face didn't hurt nearly as bad as they had before. Not now. Not with the new problem in his neck.

"I'm all right," he said. His voice came out raspy and hoarse, but still his. He extended a hand to Denl. "Help me up."

Denl took it and pulled. Matthias got to his feet and swayed a bit, then caught himself on the boulder.

"Tis sorry I am, Holy Sir," Denl said, "but I dinna think we have time ta rest. I been carryin' ya. Tri was about to . . ."

Matthias had no idea how small Denl had managed to carry him down that mountainside. "No," Matthias said. "It's not necessary."

"Ye may have anather fit, beg pardon, sir," Denl said.

Matthias raised his head. "Is that what you think I had?" he asked. "A fit?"

"Aye, sir. We dinna know what else it could be."

"Although you do have fingerprints on your neck," Tri said.

Matthias touched the skin gently. It was swollen and painful beneath his fingers. The three men hadn't seen Jewel. They hadn't seen his attacker. Had she been a ghost?

Or the Hand of God, as Pausho said?

Or something else? Something the Fey inside that cave had sent him?

Something the burning boy had done?

"It wasn't a fit," Matthias said. "It was Fey magick. We got too close to them."

He glanced back up the mountain, but the effort of moving his neck almost proved too much. Pain stabbed through his spinal column into his head.

"If so, then why would a Fey save you?" Tri asked. He looked at the others. "That's what that old woman was, isn't it? A Fey?"

Denl nodded and didn't meet Tri's gaze.

"A Fey saved me?" Matthias asked.

"Twas an old woman Fey," Denl said. "She had a cloud of white hair around her head and she shoved ye away, taking yer place."

"What happened to her?" Matthias asked.

"I dinna know," Denl said. "We dinna stay to find out."

Matthias rubbed his neck absently. An old woman with white hair. The Shaman? Why would she save him?

Or perhaps it was all part of the magick.

Perhaps it was a warning.

Perhaps it was something else.

He didn't have time to think about it.

"We know where the Fey are," he said. "I saw them inside that cave before I got attacked. Pausho will want to know. She can get her tall ones now."

"You're going to hook up with the Wise Ones?" Tri asked.

Matthias looked at him. "That cave is an interesting place, Tri. Do you know what it is?"

Tri shook his head.

"Nothing in all your days as a Wise One told you about it?"

Tri looked down. He had already apologized a dozen times for not doing the work of a Wise One. Any of it.

"Pausho seems to know, and she seems to know how to get inside without getting hurt. I will trade her some tall ones in exchange for information."

"How do you know she'll work with you?" Tri asked.

"She didn't think I'd survive that place. I have. The mountain has spit me back a second time. She can't deny my survival. And she needs me. This place will be different now. The Fey have found it. She'll need my help making Constant safe."

"Do you think she knows that?" Tri asked.

"If she doesn't now, she will soon," Matthias said. He leaned on the boulder. Talking hurt. His entire body hurt, and he was exhausted. He'd have to get down this mountain, even with the headache. Marly would help him when he got to town. Marly would heal him.

Suddenly he missed her. He had never missed anyone like that before.

He needed to see her.

"Do ye think them Fey will come after us?" Jakib asked.

Matthias ran a hand through his hair. It was matted and tangled from this long, event-filled night. He squinted, felt what he had never allowed himself to feel before.

He could feel the boy Coulter up the mountainside. It didn't seem as if he moved.

But Matthias could feel another one, another person just like him and just like Coulter—or an echo of one—not too far away from him. He looked across the valley. The other one, the third one, was on the other side of the river. The river bubbled below; he could hear it rather than see it. And he could see nothing unusual. He could only feel something there. Something he had never allowed himself to feel before.

"Holy Sir?" Denl asked. "Do ye think them Fey'll come?"

"No," Matthias said, and felt the certainty of it. If they were going to come after him, they would have done so by now. And they would have caught him. No matter how fast Denl had gone down that mountainside, it would have been slower than an unencumbered group. "They're not coming yet. But they will. Tri is right; we have no time to rest. We have to get to Constant."

"Do ye think they'll take the town?" Denl asked.

Matthias put a hand over his eyes, careful not to brush his wound. Even shaded he could see nothing.

"I think," he said, "that group has found something special in the cave, and they're not leaving. But more Fey will be coming here now. And we need to be ready."

"Maybe I should bring some folks back up here and get rid of the group in the cave," Tri said.

"And risk having what happened to me happen to you?" Matthias said. "We don't know if that's a magick lock, some way of keeping certain people out."

The idea fit with what Pausho had told him. She hadn't been certain how he would be received.

"No," Matthias said. "You're better off coming with me. I'll need your help with the Wise Ones anyway."

"They won't want to hear from me," Tri said.

"They might," Matthias said. "When they realize you're with me."

He started toward the path. He was certain the Fey in the cave wouldn't follow. But he didn't know about the other powerful one he felt. That person was too close. And Matthias wasn't ready for him.

Matthias wasn't ready for anyone. He needed to sleep. He needed to heal.

But most of all, he needed to think. The boy had shown him powers Matthias hadn't dreamed of and wasn't sure he wanted, then the boy had disappeared in that magick cave. A vision of a woman long dead had tried to kill Matthias and another woman, a Fey woman, had saved him.

Perhaps he had been rescued by the mountain again. He

only had the word of Denl and Tri that the woman was Fey. Tri had never seen a Fey before. For all Matthias knew, the woman could have been merely tall. Everything happened so fast, not even Jakib and Denl were certain.

Matthias had gone up the mountain twice in his life. The first time unwillingly, the first time to die, and the mountain had spit him back, had let him live.

The second time he had gone up willingly, to kill, and he had not done that either. He had nearly died, and again, the mountain had spit him back.

Each time he had gone up, he had come back changed. This time he was physically weaker, mentally shaken, and yet feeling stronger than he had ever felt in his life. This was the place he belonged, the place that gave him meaning.

He would have to discover what that meaning was.

And to do so, he would have to help the people of Constant survive the Fey.

Whether they wanted his help or not.

SEVENTY-SIX

HE kept expecting her to come back. Nicholas rocked the Shaman, holding her close. She had great powers. She had great wisdom. She had to come back.

She had to.

But she wasn't moving against him, and he couldn't feel the rise and fall of her body as it took in air.

She was dead.

She was dead, and he didn't understand why.

Matthias a god?

She must have meant something else. Perhaps she meant that he had the Secrets, although how she could have known about those, Nicholas didn't know.

Or perhaps she meant that he was the only Rocaan now.

But why would that matter? Why would any of it matter more than her life?

And Arianna's. Without the Shaman, he couldn't save his daughter. He didn't know what to do. They had come too slowly, apparently.

He had come too slowly.

The Shaman had said that she needed to get here *first*. Apparently that meant before Matthias.

And she hadn't.

She was dead.

And now Arianna would die.

He felt a hand on his arm. He looked up and saw his wife. His beautiful wife, looking younger than she had the day she died. Her brow was clear, her hair was braided and her eyes, her lovely upslanted eyes, were filled with tears.

"Jewel," he whispered. "How can it be you?"

Maybe he had died, too. Maybe he just hadn't realized it.

She brushed some hair away from his face. "The Shaman told you," she said. "This is a Place of Power. You can see me here."

Somehow that made sense to him. His view of the world had so altered from the time he was a boy—a view where everything remained the same to one that accepted magick beyond his imagining—that he could believe, somehow, that he could see his wife, his long-dead wife, here in this place.

"I've been with you since Ari was born," she said. "Beside you, helping you where I can."

He had felt her. Sometimes. Dear God, he had felt her. All those imaginings, his inability to let her go, had been because she was still with him?

She crouched beside him. "I'm sorry, Nicholas," she said. "This went so horribly wrong."

She was indicating the Shaman, but she hadn't touched her. Only him.

"You were trying to kill Matthias," Nicholas said.

"He was promised to me," she said. "But she interfered."

"She said—"

"I heard." Jewel sighed. "I haven't Seen that, Nicholas. I never told the Powers who my greatest hate was. But they had to know, didn't they? They had to know."

"It doesn't matter right now, Jewel," he said. "The Shaman is dead. Arianna is dying. I can't save her. Can you?"

"Yes," she said. She moved her hand from his back. He felt the loss of warmth as if it were another death. "I'll be right back."

She got up. He cradled the Shaman, then eased her back. Her face looked very young in death. The wrinkles had smoothed, and he saw that she too had that Fey beauty. He had never recognized it before.

As he moved, Arianna slid slightly against his shoulder. He

didn't know where Jewel had gone. He wondered if he should follow her.

He was amazed that he could trust his wife after what he had just seen, after she killed the Shaman.

But he had seen enough to know that Jewel had been trying to kill Matthias, and the Shaman had chosen to get in the way.

She had told him that she would choose her death.

He glanced around for Jewel, but didn't see her.

She had to hurry. They didn't have much time.

He could sense it.

They had to do something now, or he would lose Arianna.

This had happened twice in Arianna's life—her own life being at risk because someone else died.

And he could do nothing about it.

He wrapped his arm tighter around his daughter.

"I'll do what I can, baby," he whispered.

"Nicholas." Jewel's voice sent shivers through him. It was exactly as he had remembered, exactly as it had been all those years ago. Time had not diminished his memory at all.

He looked toward her voice. She was standing beside a tall Fey, a Fey Nicholas had never seen before, even though he had elements of Jewel and Nicholas both in his face. The boy had bright blue eyes, like Arianna did, and smooth skin.

He would have looked like Sebastian but for that smooth skin and those blue, blue eyes.

And that sharp, intelligent, mobile face.

"Nicholas," Jewel said, her voice husky. "This is our son. This is our Gift. Do you remember?"

Of course he did. Here was that baby, the one Nicholas had had such high hopes for. He remembered that face, that mobile, expressive face that had disappeared one night, replaced, he later learned, by a bit of magick that should have died within weeks. Instead, the magick had become a child he loved not for his expressiveness nor his quickness, but for his compassion.

"Gift," Nicholas said. He wasn't equipped for this moment. The death of a friend, the resurrection of his wife, and the introduction of his son all at the same time.

Nicholas stood as carefully as he could, holding Arianna tight for balance.

"Forgive me," he said. "But are you real?"

"As real as I am." The voice came from inside the cave. Nicholas glanced in that direction. A man emerged, an Islander, who was short and blond and as young as Gift. "I'm Coulter."

Nicholas nodded. He wasn't even sure how to identify himself. As King?

"I could ask the same thing of you," his son said, and in the voice, he realized that Gift was a different person, not a duplicate of Sebastian at all. Gift's voice was deep and strong, with elements of Nicholas's own voice. It also had a Fey accent, and he placed the wrong emphasis on the words, like so many Fey did.

Islander wasn't even his native tongue, this heir to Blue Isle's throne.

"My daughter," Nicholas said. "Your sister. She's dying. Your mother"—he glanced at Jewel—"says you can help her. The Shaman was going to, but she's dead."

His voice broke again. This was too much for him. Too much after all the losses. He didn't feel it consciously yet, but it stopped his throat.

His son, Gift, looked at his mother, then looked back at Nicholas. "You see her, too?"

"Of course," Nicholas said. "Doesn't everyone?"

"No," Gift said, and the response was curt.

"Let's get her inside," Coulter said, and he led the way. Gift followed without a glance back at his father. Jewel nodded.

Nicholas had no choice. He left the Shaman half-in and half-out of the doorway and went inside the cave. As he did, he asked, "Is there any way we can bring the Shaman inside? If this is a Place of Power, as she said, then maybe something here can help her."

"I'll do it." Another voice spoke, a voice that also had Fey accents on his Islander. A short Fey scurried past Nicholas. He frowned. He had heard of short Fey, but had never seen one up close.

A Red Cap?

With his son?

"Nicholas," Jewel said.

He stepped farther inside. The cave was huge and so light that it was almost blinding. Marble stairs led down to an Islander man and a Fey woman on the floor. A fountain bubbled beyond, and all around were symbols of Rocaanism.

The hair on the back of Nicholas's neck rose.

"I don't think Ari can be here," he said.

"Nonsense," Jewel said.

"I'm here," Gift said. "And I'm all right."

He was. As long as Arianna didn't touch anything religious, she would probably be, too. Nicholas didn't have the time for the niceties at the moment.

He carried his daughter down the stairs and laid her on the marble floor.

Arianna was as gray as the floor itself. The strange light fell on her face, illuminating its lifelessness.

Coulter bent over her, then brushed a strand of hair away. Nicholas felt the urge to push the boy back. Coulter looked up, his expression odd. He was staring at Gift.

"She looks like you," he said.

Gift shrugged. "She tried to kill me once," he said. And in the flatness of his voice, Nicholas heard one of his own tones. A diffidence covering fear.

"What now?" Nicholas asked.

"Gift is going to help his sister," Jewel said.

Nicholas's stomach twisted. "How?"

"He'll travel your Link and go in after her."

Nicholas looked at the son he had never seen, the boy he had longed for ever since he had learned what happened, and felt his mouth go dry. "No," he said, even before he could think. "We don't know what's happened to her. The Shaman thought the Black King did this. If he's still within Arianna, then he could trap Gift, too. It's not safe, Jewel. Can't you do something?"

"No," she said.

"I said I would go," Gift said. "It's something I can do."

"I know," Nicholas said. He wanted to explain things to his son, but there wasn't time. "But we can't lose you too, Gift. What if you get trapped?"

Coulter listened closely. He rocked back on his heels, squinted at Nicholas, and then said, "Why don't you do this?"

"Because only Fey can," Nicholas said.

"I'm not Fey," Coulter said.

Nicholas frowned at him. Of course the boy wasn't Fey. "Are you saying you could do this?"

He certainly didn't look Fey. He looked as pure Islander as Nicholas did.

Coulter shrugged. "I think so."

"You think so?" Nicholas repeated. "You're an Islander."

"He's an Enchanter," Gift said. "He can do it."

"But he'd have to use Nicholas's Link," Jewel said.

"So would I," Gift said.

"But—"

"It would be easier," Coulter said, speaking to the air. Then Nicholas realized he was trying to talk to Jewel. "I can see the Link clearly. I can try to travel across it."

"Enchanters can do that," Jewel said, "but they don't have as much time and flexibility as a Visionary. Enchanters have most Fey magick, but it is always shortened, its power truncated, because of its abundance."

"She says," Nicholas said. "That you won't have as much time as Gift."

"I know," Coulter said. "But I have more magick available to me. I might be able to find Arianna faster."

And fight the Black King if necessary.

"You don't have Black Blood, do you?" Nicholas asked.

"He's an Islander," Gift said.

Jewel was looking at Nicholas.

Nicholas kept his hand tightly on Arianna. "If Gift finds Arianna, and the Black King is there, then we have the exact situation the Shaman was afraid of: Black Blood against Black Blood. Sending Coulter would prevent that."

Jewel let out a sigh. The vials around them tinkled softly as if they felt a breeze. "I hadn't thought of that."

"I'm not afraid of the Black King," Gift said.

"You should be," Nicholas said. "Let Coulter go first."

"Only if I can go if it takes him too long," Gift said.

"It's too dangerous," Coulter said. "Your father's right."

"I'll go with or without your help," Gift said.

"I thought you didn't like your sister," Coulter said.

"I *said* I'd help her."

"Fighting won't help at all," Jewel said.

Gift stopped. Then he looked at Coulter. "All right," he said. "But don't do anything without her permission."

"If I find her," Coulter said.

"Not good enough," Gift said.

Nicholas felt a shiver run through him. What was Gift warning against? He didn't have time to find out.

"Let's do it now," Nicholas said. "Coulter, find my daughter."

Coulter nodded once. He glanced at Gift who pursed his lips, and crossed his arms.

"I don't know how this will feel," Coulter said to Nicholas. "I have to use your Link. I'm not sure what it will do to you, do you understand?"

Nicholas took a deep breath. It was a risk he was prepared to take. His future was in this cave. His future and Blue Isle's.

And as the Shaman said, sometimes that took a sacrifice.

"Yes," he said. "I'm trusting you to bring my daughter back."

"I'll make sure you're all right," Jewel said.

Nicholas smiled at her. She would.

Gift swallowed so loud, the sound echoed. "I'll be the backup," he said. "We can't lose you and my sister."

Coulter was staring at him sadly as if waiting for Gift to list him too.

"Or Coulter," Gift said, but the words sounded reluctant.

Couler nodded once, as if that were enough. "Ready?" he asked Nicholas.

"Ready," Nicholas said.

Then Coulter reached forward and touched a small area in front of Nicholas's heart. It felt as if someone had plunged a knife into him.

Coulter's eyes glazed, and Nicholas traced the boy's presence in Nicholas's Link through the pain that moved from his heart into his very soul.

SEVENTY-SEVEN

HE felt every one of his ninety-two years this morning. Rugad bent over, pulled on his boots, and sighed. His body ached from its fall after the golem's attack, and his throat hurt from all the talking he had done the day before. Each muscle, each movement reminded him of the stresses he had put himself under.

He would put himself under even more.

This Isle had bested his son.

This Isle had killed his granddaughter.

It had taken his voice.

It would be his, no matter what. He would have the Isle, and he would have his great-grandchildren, and he would move on to Leut, no matter how much pain he felt, no matter how old he felt, no matter how injured he was.

He would conquer Blue Isle, and use it as a stepping-stone for the rest of the world.

This morning was the start of it all.

He had made the decision before coming back to his rooms. The guards had cleaned them, removing the broken chair and the bits of stone as he had requested. The golem had been disposed of, pieces of him flung into the river, the rest scattered about Jahn.

He could never be assembled again.

Another obstacle down.
Several more remained, but Rugad had confidence that he would take those as well.
He stood and stretched. He had felt like this after difficult battles, all bruised and battered, and yet satisfied that he had won. Only the satisfaction was missing on this day.
He had won the Isle, but he didn't hold it.
The loss of the King, the loss of his great-grandchildren—and their ability to injure him—had caused panic among his own people.
He would put that panic to rest.
He threw on his cloak and headed for the door. He passed the empty Fey lamp and shook his head. The golem's soul should have been here. It disturbed him that it wasn't.
Rugad opened the door. A breakfast waited outside as he had commanded. He stopped, sipped the water, and then took the slices of bread, leaving the rest for his guards.
"I will not finish this," he said to the guard who faced his door. The guard knew, as all his guards did, that they were allowed his leftovers. It was one of the perks of serving the Black King.
The two hours' rest he had gotten had made him even more tired. If he were being honest with himself, he would admit that the defeats had gotten to him as well. Amazing how such small things, a few setbacks of the right type, were enough to demoralize even the strongest men.
And he had focused too much on Wisdom and not enough on the real problem. Wisdom had been dealt with. Rugad had learned that the Islanders' King was in the northern mountains somewhere, and the golem was gone.
This was progress.
He would have to treat it as such.
But first, he had to raise the morale of his own people.
He had taken some time with his appearance that morning, making certain he wore the polished boots and his darkest cape. His hair flowed freely about his face, making him look younger and having the effect of hiding some of the worst bruises from the day before. He wore a scarf, something he had done as a younger man, to hide the scar around his throat.
No need reminding the troops that he had been injured.
He no longer had his full voice, but on this day, he didn't need it.

He took the stairs two at a time, finishing the bread as he went. He nodded to each Fey he passed, and they nodded back, most of them looking surprised at his recognition.

If he had to look each and every one of his people in the face in order to raise their morale, he would do so. The word would not get out through Jahn and the surrounding countryside that the Black King was injured, too injured to rule them.

That would cause even more dissension.

When he reached the base of the stairs, he saw his new assistant, Selia, standing by the main doors. She had her hands behind her back, her posture perfect, her demeanor fine—or it would have been, if she weren't rubbing her thumb and forefinger together nervously.

"Selia," he barked. The word came out as a rather loud nasal rasp. It sent a shuddering pain all the way down his throat, but he didn't mind. It was a small price to pay for a voice that carried.

She jumped, then nodded when she saw him.

"Is my carriage ready?"

"Yes, sir," she said. "I have extra guards who are willing to go alongside—"

"No," he said. He wanted minimal guards, and none in the carriage with him. The rumors had started because of his injuries. He wanted to show his people that he had no fear of this Isle, and that he was strong enough to take care of himself. "Only the Spies as we talked about and the Wisps floating above."

"Yes, sir." She bowed her head.

He came closer to her, put a finger under her chin, and lifted her face toward his. "You don't like that, do you, Selia? The fact that I go out unprotected?"

She chewed on her lower lip. He wondered if she were even aware that she was doing it.

"No, sir," she said softly.

"You do not believe in your own people? It's them that I go to see."

"But what of the Islanders, sir? If they see you alone and unprotected—"

"They'll kill me?" he asked. He knew morale was bad, but he didn't realize how bad. The Black King should be invincible, not a sniveling weakling that his own people had to worry about each time he showed his face.

He had never suffered a morale problem of this nature before.

He would solve it.

He would solve part of it now.

"Yes, sir," she said. "I'm afraid they might have a chance."

He tilted his head back so that he was looking down on her. He let his nail dig into the skin covering her jaw.

"You believe that I will go out among my own people, survey the damage we have wreaked on a city that once stood tall and proud and untrampled, and that some rogue Islander will get through the hundreds of Fey, get close enough to me, and injure me?"

She blinked once, but that was enough. He saw the doubt creep into her face.

"I hadn't thought of it like that, sir."

"What has happened to me," he said, taking the time to explain to her because as his spokesman, she would have to explain to others, "is normal when the Black Family has dissension in its ranks. You don't know that because the Black Family has been unified in your lifetime, and in mine. But the separation caused by my son's blunders have created this mess, which I am repairing. No random Islander can touch me. My great-grandchildren don't dare. Their father's power has been taken from him."

Rugad smiled. Selia's eyes widened.

"Nothing," he said with emphasis, "can harm me."

"But in your rooms," she said then covered her mouth, looking terrified. He could see the thought on her face. She was already protecting her tongue.

Good.

Wisdom's example would stay with her always.

Rugad's smile grew. "The golem. You feel that he damaged me?"

"You have injuries, sir." She spoke through her hands because she was smart enough to realize that she had started the conversation, so she had to finish it.

"Yet you think nothing of some of our soldiers who have seen Domestics to heal arrow wounds or sword slashes from the attack on the Isle."

"Sir?" she said, letting her hands drop.

"I knew that the creature was a golem when I chose to be alone with him. He was a creation that looked like my great-grandson and, I feared, harbored family secrets that no one but myself dared hear. When I learned from him what I needed to know, I destroyed him. He was a dangerous bit of magick that we didn't need roaming the Isle."

A slight frown built between her brows. "So you have war wounds?"

"I am the leader of this invasion," Rugad said coldly. "It is only natural for me to bear a bit of the burden of it as well."

"Right, sir," she said. She shook her head a little as if she had to physically reorganize her thoughts. "I will not add any guards to your trip. It was foolish of me to even inquire."

He put a hand on her arm. "It was not foolish," he said. "Inquiries I like because I can approve or disapprove of them at will. Wisdom made the mistake of taking the action before consulting me. See to it that you don't do that."

"I will never make that error, sir."

"Good," he said. "I put you here for your talent at Charming and for your common sense. See to it that I benefit from both."

"Yes, sir," she said.

He nodded to her, then went through the doors.

The carriage was open, as he had requested. It was black with a slight dip in the center and a step on the side. Two seats faced each other in its main section, and another seat was along front for a driver, something Rugad didn't need. Two Horse Riders made up the team, and he was familiar with both of them. They would take his instruction directly.

He loved the look of them. Two Fey appeared to be riding on back of the horses, although from the side, it was clear that they had no legs, that their torsos sprung from the horses' backs. The Riders were male and female. In deference to him, they wore a uniform over their torsos, something he knew was quite uncomfortable for Riders in their animal form. He nodded his pleasure and used the small railing to get into the carriage.

All of the insignia of the Isle's ruling family had been removed. There were still the faint marks of swords on the sides of the carriage. The cushions had been obviously—and hastily—replaced with black velvet cushions, Domestic-spelled for comfort.

He sat down and clucked softly, letting the Riders take the lead. This was Selia's first test. If she had deviated from his instructions, he would know it immediately.

But apparently she hadn't. The Riders took the carriage on a wide arc around the palace. All along, Fey had turned out, despite the earliness of the hour. They saluted him, or bowed, or nodded slightly. Fey did not applaud or cry out at ceremonial events, like so many other cultures did. Fey cried out during battle. This was merely a review, an acknowledgment, a way of establishing Fey dominance.

He nodded in return. At times, when the carriage was going slowly enough, he stood, as if to inspect something.

There was nothing to inspect while they were on the palace grounds. He had seen them all from his windows, and knew that they were relatively unharmed. The only damage had come from the attack the Islanders' King, Nicholas, had started, and that was minor: a few marks in some of the side buildings, bloodstains all over the flagstones, which had taken some Domestic a week to clean properly, and a badly trampled area on one side of the garden.

But the palace was an island of normality in the ruined city. He had seen that from his window as well.

And the ruins, as he would remind his people, had come through their good work.

Without Jahn, there was no Blue Isle. The heart of Blue Isle was its city, and it would soon have a new and different sort of central government, one that answered only to the Fey.

If any Islanders turned out this day, they would learn that as well.

He doubted that any of them would show their faces.

He stood as the carriage went through the gates of the palace. More Fey lined the central road, so many in fact, that they stood five deep in order to see him. He had done this sort of thing before; he had reviewed the troops after a great victory, but then, as now, it had been optional to come see the Black King.

In the past, only a small portion of his troop had come out to see him. He hadn't minded. It meant the rest were working or resting after a job well done.

This time, it seemed, everyone had turned out.

To see if he lived?

To see if he were in good health?

Apparently.

He did not smile. It would have been inappropriate to smile. But he did nod when he saw familiar faces. The carriage took him slowly toward the river, and the great bridge. He would see, and perhaps applaud, the destruction of the Tabernacle, home to the Black Robes. Then he would go neighborhood by neighborhood, inspecting the damage, perhaps ordering another building burned.

He would have to stand through all of this, to prove to them that he was fine, even though he had been better.

They didn't need to know that.

Morale was bad enough, and none of his injuries were life-threatening.

Any longer.

Blue Isle had nearly had him, twice, and that was all it would get of him. From this point on, the Isle belonged to him, and he was letting his people know it.

And he was confirming the victory that he knew he already had.

Remembering it.

Feeling it.

The injuries had taken their toll on him as well, as had the surprise at being bested.

He should have been pleased. If he wanted confirmation that he had made the right decision in coming to Blue Isle, the two times his great-granddaughter and her golem had taken him were proof enough.

And despite the difficulty he had had with the golem, he had done what he could when he saw his great-granddaughter. He had taken the first step toward making her a true member of the Black family, something he had not had time to do when he contacted his great-grandson.

His great-granddaughter would make a superb leader of the Fey. She had the fire, the intelligence, and the magick.

She would be among the best.

Now all he had to do was get rid of her father and bring her to him.

That was all it would take to secure the Isle.

Two small acts.

And he knew he could accomplish them.

SEVENTY-EIGHT

SHOOTING pains ran through her leg.

Arianna cursed again as she allowed herself to get pulled back to her foot marker. She rubbed the leg, waiting for the pain to ease.

She had made it farther this time, but she had still stopped herself. One false thought, one change, and she would be back here, where she started.

She had no idea how much time had passed. This darkness was unchanging, and she had no way to mark the time.

A person could go mad here, over time. No sound. No light. No smells. Nothing.

Totally and irrevocably mad.

She could feel the edge of panic creep up, and she fought it back down.

Arianna?

A voice she had never heard before echoed far away.

She shook her imaginary head. And she had caused it. She had caused that sound by worrying that she wouldn't ever hear anything again.

Arianna?

If she were going to make up a sound, though, wouldn't it be something else, like the sound of blood rushing through her veins or the sound of her lungs breathing in and out?

And if she were to make up a voice, why not use one she was already familiar with, instead of this one? This voice was deep and husky, with a lot of youth in it, the promise of a voice that would someday settle into something other than what it was now.

Arianna?

And it sounded as if it were calling for her.

Was it her great-grandfather? Had he come back?

But she had heard his voice, and it sounded nothing like this. Besides, it spoke with a Fey accent mixed with Nye emphasis on the Islander language. The Black King was fluent in her native tongue, but he had learned it from nonnative speakers. It had shown, even when he had been trying to hide it.

The pain in her leg was gone. The voice had given her something else to think about.

Arianna?

What harm would it be to shout back, even if it were her great-grandfather? He could show her the way out, and then she could fight him. Even without Sebastian's help, she had managed to trap him. The Black King wasn't as all-powerful as he thought.

Sebastian. Her heart ached at the thought. What had he been doing? He had been hiding, alone, and then he had managed to save her. He had seemed so wonderful in this place, without his stone body to slow him down.

Arianna!

The voice sounded a bit strained now, as if it were creeping into panic. What would cause someone to panic? Was she actually hearing something outside herself? Was the person panicking because of something Arianna was doing? Was she Shifting without being conscious of it? Babies did. Maybe Shifters who didn't have control of their own bodies did too. Maybe that's why Solanda had warned her that any Shifter who got terribly ill died.

Or maybe the voice was inside her. She hadn't closed those doors as Sebastian had told her to do.

The thought made her imaginary body tremble.

Hey! Arianna shouted. *I'm here! I can't get out! Mark your way!*

There was no answer. She sighed. She *had* made up the voice. She would have to gather control of her mind and try to find the way out again. It sounded so easy, controlling one's mind, but it wasn't. It was the most difficult thing she had ever done.

Arianna? Call me again. It's really dark back here.

Her heart leapt. This time, she hadn't been thinking of the voice at all. Maybe it did belong to someone else.

But who?

Look, she said, trying to keep her excitement down. *Maybe it would be better if I found you.*

There was a pause before the answer. He had to be very far away.

Nope, he said. *I have some talents you don't. It's better if I come to you.*

All right, she said. *You want me to sing or something? Or maybe not. I don't sing well in this form.*

Of course she could switch to a robin. She didn't really have to Shift. She didn't have control of her body. She didn't know which part of her body she was in, exactly, just somewhere in the brain, she assumed, and she wasn't even sure about that.

You can do whatever you want, he said. *I finally got used to the darkness, but some conversation might help.*

Who are you? she asked.

It took less time for his replies to reach her now. She could sense someone approaching.

Perhaps she was wishing again.

My name is Coulter.

Coulter, she said. *Do I know you?*

I think you do now, he said. *Two people can't get a lot closer than this.*

I mean outside. Have I met you before?

No, he said.

Then how did you get here?

I'm traveling on your father's Link. We don't have a lot of time on it either. My powers are large, but time-limited.

Where's the Shaman? Why isn't she helping?

There was a pause, but Arianna didn't think this one was caused by distance.

She helped as much as she could. She got you to me.

A light appeared in the distance. It was faint, and it seemed to be moving.

Are you wearing light? she asked.

I thought it would be easier, he said.

The light illuminated gray, winding coils that were as large as tree limbs. They seemed tightly packed together and if she looked at them closely, she could see blood and other liquid moving through them.

Was this her physical brain? If so, where was she exactly?

Then he turned the corner.

She had been expecting a Fey.

Instead she saw something she had never seen before. A tall blond Islander boy with upswept eyes and high cheekbones. He had pointed ears and was startlingly handsome.

Breathtaking, in fact, if she had had any breath to take.

What are you? she asked. *Are you a half-breed like me?*

I don't know, he said. Then he spread out his hands. The light moved with him. He glowed all over. *I don't really look like this. Except in my own mind. That's how this works, you know. Your own image disappears. Your self-image appears. You'll see me soon enough. I'm not much to look at, really.*

She smiled. *You are now.*

She could get a sense of her father about him, but it was as if he were wearing her father's coat. She understood now why he said his time was limited. She could feel a pull from that coat.

How far do we have to go to get out of here?

It's like a maze, he said. *The distance is short, but the trail is long.*

How did you find me?

We all leave small trails. Yours was nearly invisible. You must have come through here fast.

I barely remember it, she said.

He nodded and held out his hand. The moment of truth, the moment when she discovered if he was real or not.

If he was real as anything could be here.

She let her fingers touch his. He was real. The power of him, the essence of him ran through her. It left her imaginary skin tingling. She had never felt such magick all in one place. And a bit of darkness, toward the back of his skull, as if it were a dot that he were unaware of.

Yet there was such warmth in him, such light.

She let him pull her forward.

Let's bring you back to yourself, he said. He tucked her hand under his arm. She looked down at herself. She was glowing, too. His light had extended to her, illuminating the way.

Why did you come for me? she asked.

I was helping your family, he said. *I was a bit worried about it at first, but now I'm glad I did.* He cradled her closer. He was so warm. She hadn't realized how cold she had been, how cold and alone.

And frightened.

The fear was easing now.

They were climbing uphill. Every few steps they made a turn. She understood now why she had gotten lost. It was amazing she had gone as far back as she had.

Finally they reached a plateau, and she recognized the place where she had fought her great-grandfather. Her real eyes were just below that, and the light they received poured in, nearly blinding her.

She felt so much relief that she staggered against Coulter.

It's all right, he said. *You'll be all right now.*

He stroked her hair away from her face, then he held it between his hands. She let him. He felt so good, so familiar. So strong.

He was taller than she was. He had to look down on her. She had never been near a man who was taller. Sebastian had been the same height, and so had her brother.

The thought of him made her shudder.

Her brother and the Black King. They were as tall as she was. Not taller.

Coulter's gaze dropped to her lips, then met her eyes again. He wanted to kiss her. She leaned into him, letting him. He bent down, touched his imaginary lips to hers, and that feeling—that stunning sense of him—ran through her again.

When he pulled back, she whispered, *Thank you.*

But not for the kiss. For rescuing her.

He seemed to understand that.

He tucked a strand of hair behind her ear. *I have one more thing to do,* he said. *And you need to watch me, so you can do it when I'm gone.*

You're leaving? she asked, feeling a sudden loss at his absence.

I have to. I can't stay here long. He ran his fingers along the side of her face. *Your great-grandfather traveled a Link to get here. I can close your Links, all but the one I took. You have to close that yourself.*

She remembered Sebastian when his Link to his brother closed. He claimed he was all alone.

She had never traveled a Link, at least not to anywhere in

particular. It had been in exploring a Link that she had gotten into trouble. She didn't mind closing the Links. She probably wouldn't miss them.

But Coulter misunderstood her silence. *You'll feel alone, but you won't be. If you want, I'll close the Links so that you can reopen them yourself.*

She heard something else in his voice, something that made it seem as if that weren't a good idea.

Do it the way you think best, she said.

He smiled, and it felt as if the sun had come through very dark clouds. Why was she so drawn to him? Because he had rescued her? Because he was here, in her mind? Her great-grandfather had come uninvited and she hadn't felt drawn to him. And then Sebastian had appeared and she had felt the same old love for him she always had. Did this place merely reflect already existing feelings?

Or possible ones?

She didn't know.

I only have a few more moments, he said, letting her go. He walked back toward the darkness and touched it lightly. The doors she had seen earlier reappeared. He touched the first one.

This is your Link to Sebastian, he said. He put a lock on the door, turned the key, then he held the key up to her. *Do you want it?*

She did, suddenly. She didn't want someone else that she barely knew, someone she would not recognize outside herself, holding an important piece of herself.

Yes, she said.

Only open this when your great-grandfather is dead, he said as he gave her the key. *Please. You don't know how dangerous he is.*

Oh, she thought she did. But she said nothing.

Coulter went to other doors, some large, and some small, some belonging to people she hadn't thought of in a long time. The last belonged to Solanda.

He sighed, and when he looked at her his eyes were filled with sadness. *It doesn't matter if I close this or not,* he said. *Did you know?*

A chill ran through her. *Know what?*

That there no longer is someone on the other end of this Link?

No. She hadn't known it. But she had suspected it.

No one can travel this, he said to her silence. *Let's just leave it open.*

She nodded, once, then sighed. So much had happened, so much had changed, that she didn't have the energy to feel Solanda's death.

He went to the final door. *This Link is between you and your father. I traveled on it. I have to go through the door to leave. Then you must lock it behind me. Please do. If the Black King captures your father, he can use this Link to get to you. Anyone with the powers of a Visionary or an Enchanter can. Right now, you're vulnerable. Please. Lock it after me.*

He didn't need to emphasize this so hard. She remembered the invasive feeling her great-grandfather had caused. She would never forget it.

I will, she said. *I will lock it.*

Coulter smiled at her. He opened the door and stepped through it.

Wait! she said. *Will I see you again?*

When you open your eyes, he said. *I'll be right there.*

He smiled at her, blew her a kiss, then disappeared into the light, pulling the door closed behind him. She leaned against the door for a moment, wondering at the strangeness of it all, and then she put a lock on it, turned the key, and placed the key on the ring with all the others.

Amazing how things just appeared here, when she thought of them.

Then she sighed, the relief returning, and headed toward the center of herself.

As she did, she heard crying.

She didn't feel like crying.

How odd.

She turned toward the sound, and saw a tiny baby, barely outside the darkness. She didn't know how she and Coulter had missed it. She crouched beside the child, and looked down.

It was Fey. It was pure Fey, and it was a little boy. She imagined a blanket, and then she had one. She wrapped him in it.

He couldn't have been more than a few hours old.

She had a sense that she knew this child, and knew him well.

Sebastian? she whispered.

But of course, he couldn't answer. He didn't have the gift of language yet.

She carried him with her as she returned to the center of herself. Then she reconnected with her body. She felt her own hands—her real hands—move. She felt her legs, her torso, even the place where her Shifting was located.

Her body felt odd, as if she hadn't reassembled it properly, and she made a few adjustments. She wondered if she had Shifted while she was lost.

Then she stepped behind her eyes and opened them. For a moment, she felt a dislocation—her small self looking out large windows—and then she reconnected completely, forgetting how tiny she could be inside herself.

She was back.

She looked up and saw her father's face.

There were tears in his eyes.

"Arianna," he said with so much love, so much fear, so much relief, she could feel it as if it were her own.

He put his arms around her and cradled her close, and she felt safe, truly safe, all of her, for the first time in a long time.

"Daddy," she said, and felt as if she had come home.

SEVENTY-NINE

RUGAD made the Horse Riders stop the carriage on the bridge over the Cardidas River. The sun glinted off the brown water, making it beautiful, making the area brilliant. There were no Fey lined up on the bridge, and he could sit.

He did just that; he sat in his carriage and surveyed the entire city.

To the south, he saw nothing but ashes and burned-out buildings. He could still smell the faint whiff of smoke in the air. His own people worked in the rubble, rebuilding some sites, cleaning up the remaining bodies, clearing the land for eventual farming. Others worked near the water's edge, rebuilding warehouses. The southern side of Jahn would become fields and storage. When Rugad restored trade with Nye, the entire area would come alive again.

The ruins of the Tabernacle still stood. If he squinted, he could almost see the building as it once was—the towers rising out of the ground, the swords painted on the sides. But if he truly looked at it, he could see it for what it was: a hollow wreck. The towers remained, but the center parts of the building had been burned out. On one floor a charred blanket drifted from an open window—obviously someone had used it in an attempted escape.

The entire place spoke of destruction and death.

He would leave it standing, even though the land would be useful as farmland. He wanted to remind the Islanders of what they had, what they lost, and who had taken it from them.

He wanted them to remain in line.

Not that there were any Islanders to see it. Those that had survived had fled into the countryside. He would bring them back as he needed them, and convince them that he was not a bad leader. He had already convinced places like the Kenniland Marshes in the south that he was a better leader than Nicholas, better than all the Kings that had ruled Blue Isle before him.

Nicholas had never visited the south. He had done nothing to alleviate the poverty of the region. Rugad already had. He had his Domestics train the marshlanders in the growing of rice and other crops that benefited from damp land. He would make that section of Blue Isle one of the wealthiest, one of the most important, simply through the crops it grew.

They were seeing the changes already.

He turned and looked behind him.

The palace dominated the view behind him, untouched and proud in the early morning sky. Around it, several other buildings remained standing; indeed, whole sections of the town were still intact. The Fey had shooed most of the Islanders out of there, as per his orders, and were using the empty buildings as their own. As he rebuilt, he would make this part of Jahn into the whole city itself, and he would make it uniquely Fey, something he hadn't done in all the years he had conquered countries.

He had never rebuilt a city before. He had always torn them down.

But he had the opportunity now. Blue Isle's culture had to be subjugated to the Fey culture. Jewel had determined that when she had married an Islander. The cultures couldn't merge—the Fey never did that—so one culture had to become dominant. When Rugad's great-grandchildren ruled, they would do so as Fey.

He would see to that.

He looked ahead again, and clucked to the Horse Riders. They continued at a good clip. The bridge was long and well built, a triumph of engineering that didn't seem much in evidence in other parts of the Isle. He wondered who had ordered it and how it had come into being.

And why the tunnels had been built beneath the road, connecting both sides of the city.

The Horse Riders slowed as they came to the end of the bridge. Fey lined up three deep to see him. The numbers in which they appeared continued to impress him. He had made the right choice: the entire army had been worried about him. The rumors must have been out of control. He would spend the next few days putting them to rest, and then building success stories to counter them.

The carriage's wheels clattered onto the road. All around him, Fey nodded and half smiled at him in acknowledgment. He gazed on as many of them in turn as he could, and still evaluated the devastation that was this side of the river.

Then a spark flew before his eye. There were no active fires any longer, so he had to have seen a Wisp. The spark flew back, landed in the seat opposite him, and transformed into a slender woman with delicate wings.

He recognized her. It was Gauze. He had sent her with Boteen.

"Turn the carriage into the Tabernacle's gate and stop it," Rugad said. He would talk with her there, while it seemed to his people that he was viewing the ultimate destruction of the Black Robes.

The carriage turned and the Fey blocking the gate parted as if they had known the carriage was going to come their way.

The Tabernacle looked even worse up close. The towers had crumpled inward. Only the outer shells, facing the river, remained. The remaining walls had tumbled. The smell of blood and death still lingered in this place, and he wondered if all of the bodies had been located, or if the Red Caps had left this place for last.

The carriage stopped.

He said to the Horse Riders, "Please detach yourselves and go to the gate. I need to talk with Gauze alone."

The Fey part of the Riders unhitched their horse parts, and trotted to the gate. The carriage shook with their passage.

"Well?" Rugad asked.

"Boteen assures you that our party is fine," she said, and Rugad suppressed a smile. Of course he would do that. He knew how Rugad thought.

She looked exhausted, but she did not look as if she had come from a battlefield.

"He wants you to know that there are strange magicks to the north. The air is full of them, and in fact, I rode a current of one halfway here or I would not have arrived yet."

She wiped a damp strand of hair from her face.

Rugad tensed. He knew that Boteen hadn't sent her all this way for strange magicks.

"He also wanted me to tell you what I saw. Boteen had me investigate a cave in the mountainside. In it, I saw your great-grandson, and overheard him talking with his companions: one Fey, a clean Red Cap, and two Islanders. He was expecting the arrival of his sister and his father at any moment."

"You did not wait for them to arrive?"

"No, sir. I was to report what I saw immediately to Boteen. He told me to come to you."

So Boteen was alone with his great-grandchildren.

"I am also to tell you that we had not yet reached the cave. It is considerably high up a mountainside. It will take our party some time, maybe a day or more to reach it."

Rugad's mouth went dry. If he assembled enough Bird Riders and his chair, he could be there in a day.

"Boteen says also to tell you that the Islanders in the area have some of that strange magick and they are hostile. We have Infantry moving in, but he believes you should send troops."

"I already have," Rugad said, remembering his own order from the contact with his great-granddaughter. Troops were on the way. Now he just had to direct them to the right place. "Does he believe my great-grandchildren are going to move?"

Something passed across her face then, something so brief that he almost didn't see it. But it had been there. "They won't move," she said.

"How do you know?" he asked.

The look again. A cross between fear and panic, and something else, something softer. Memory? Fond memory?

"What aren't you telling me?" he asked before she could answer his first question.

"I have told you all of Boteen's message," she said.

"But there's more, isn't there?" he asked.

She nodded.

"Something to do with the special magick you mentioned."

She nodded again.

"Does Boteen want to tell me, or is he keeping this for himself?" Rugad asked.

"Neither," she said, then bit her lower lip. She had realized that she had admitted something.

"Go on," Rugad said.

She sighed. "I think he wants to confirm before coming to you."

"But it has to do with the special magicks," Rugad said. "There is a reason my great-grandchildren and their father are meeting in this place, isn't there?"

"Boteen thinks so," she said.

"But he doesn't know."

"No," she whispered.

"When did he send you?"

"At dawn, sir."

She had come rapidly. As rapidly as she said. And Boteen could have sent the Scribe or a Gull Rider. He sent a Wisp. The fastest Fey he had with him.

Rugad let the mystery go for a moment. He would verify what the strange magick was.

His great-grandchildren and their father in a cave on the mountainside.

Excellent.

He nodded to Gauze. "You have done well, my child," he said. "Go back to the palace and rest. When I return, you will show me where my great-grandchildren are."

"Yes, sir." She shrank and flew away, as if she were happy to be gone, as if she had gotten away with something.

It didn't matter. He would discover what it was.

After he killed Blue Isle's King.

Publicly.

For daring to lay a sword on the Black King of the Fey.

And then he would work on his great-grandchildren, and he would secure Blue Isle.

He smiled.

Finally, victory was within reach.

EIGHTY

NICHOLAS held his daughter in his arms. She was alive. She was all right. She had smiled at him and looked like his Arianna.

He had been so terrified of losing her. More terrified than he cared to admit.

It felt so different from holding the Shaman's lifeless body, or Arianna's body just a moment earlier. She stirred slightly, moved a little, as she always had.

Arianna had never learned how to be still.

After a moment, she pushed away from him, and looked around the area. Her gaze stopped on Gift's face. They stared at each other for a moment, then she looked away. She met each face with that strong stare, not finding what she was apparently searching for.

"Where's Coulter?" she asked.

Nicholas felt stunned. The boy had taken his hand away from Nicholas's heart moments before Arianna stirred. The pain had disappeared, and Nicholas had watched his daughter's face, going from immobile to mobile to becoming itself again.

"Right here," the boy said, and he sounded almost ashamed.

Arianna looked past him, then back at him.

The boy shrugged. "I'm not the same out here. I told you."

"You're not Fey," she said. "You're not even half-Fey."

"No," he said.

"Then how did you do that?"

He looked down, his face so red that Nicholas felt pained for him. A teenage boy in the presence of a pretty girl. Plus something else. They had spoken before she had awakened. She had expected him, but not like this.

"Coulter has all the powers of the Fey without all the curses of them," Adrian said. "Sometimes I think he absorbed them from the world around him."

"I was raised among the Fey," Coulter whispered. "I was kidnapped as a baby."

But there was more to it. Even Nicholas knew that. This place proved it.

"You look so different," Arianna said. She reached out a hand and touched Coulter's blushing face.

"I'm sorry," he said.

"I'm not."

Nicholas was, suddenly. He didn't like having his daughter look at a boy—a near-man—like that.

Jewel touched his arm. "She'll be all right," Jewel said, then put a finger to Nicholas's lips. "She can't see me. So don't say anything. It'll just confuse her."

He nodded.

"Let them be for a moment. I need to talk to you."

He stroked Arianna's hair. It was tangled and coarse from the days of traveling and the disorganized Shift. "I need a moment to myself," Nicholas said. "Will you be all right?"

"Don't leave me, Dad," she said.

"I'll be right over here." He pointed to the steps.

She took a deep breath, nodded once, then looked at Gift. "You're my brother," she said, and it sounded like an accusation.

"So?" Gift said.

"If you'd just said that, I wouldn't have attacked you that day."

"You wouldn't have believed me. You thought Sebastian was your brother."

"He *is*," she said.

Nicholas opened his mouth, and Jewel took his arm, pulling him away. "Let them settle this," she said. "You can't."

He looked at the Red Cap. "Keep them from going after each other, would you?"

"I don't get involved in Black Family affairs."

Adrian snorted and shook his head. "I'll watch them," he said.

"I won't do anything to this Gift, Dad," Arianna said. "I remember the last time."

"I know," Nicholas said. But he wasn't sure about his son. The Shaman had said that Gift reminded her of Nicholas's father. So far, Nicholas could see no similarities.

Jewel dragged him to the steps, then she hugged him so fiercely it took his breath away. He ran his hand down her back, and up again. His fingers bumped the ridges of her spine. Her skin was smooth, the muscles taut beneath it. She felt familiar, as if she had never left his arms.

He leaned into her, kissed her, and she tasted just as he remembered. He closed his eyes.

He could lose himself in her.

God, he had missed her. He had missed her more than he had ever thought possible.

She held him tightly for a moment, then she pulled back. That was one thing he had forgotten. Jewel was as mobile as her daughter. Jewel had never remained still, either.

She put a finger on his lips, stopping any questions he may have had. Behind him, he heard his daughter's voice rising.

". . . and you left him alone!"

"First you didn't want me to have anything to do with Sebastian, and then you're angry that I left?" Gift asked, voice rising too.

"Actually," Coulter said, loudly, to cover their voices, "that was my fault. . . ."

And then their voices softened again.

"The Black King knows where you are," Jewel said. "Or at least, he knows where Gift is."

Her finger left his mouth. He still wasn't sure what she was. All he knew as that some kind of Fey magick had brought her back to him.

"How did he find out?" Nicholas asked. "Has a member of this group betrayed us?"

She shook her head. "A Wisp flew in here just before you arrived. Since there are no more Fey from my father's invasion, she had to have come from Rugad. He will come here as soon as he learns of it, and he will try to take this place."

"Because it is a Place of Power."

"The Shaman told you that," Jewel said.

"Yes." He looked up the steps to the place where the Red

Cap had left her body. Nothing had happened to it. He had hoped that the magick of this place would help them.

At least he had gotten help for Arianna.

"Nicholas," Jewel said, "you have nothing right now, except an Islander and a Fey without magick, another Fey who has yet to come into her own, an Islander who has the skills of an Enchanter, and our children."

Nicholas sighed. He knew that.

"Your people are scattered, and they never were warriors. Matthias"—Jewel spit out the word—"is alive, and will come back here. You know that, too."

He suspected it. He didn't know it. He had hoped that Matthias's innate cowardliness would prevail. Perhaps it would still.

Yet the Shaman had saved Matthias.

"You need me," Jewel said. "You'll need to trust me."

Nicholas nodded. He did trust her. To a point. But he had learned in all the years around the Fey that sometimes things were not what they seemed. He wasn't sure if Jewel was the shade of his wife or something else, something that only appeared to be his wife.

"I don't know what you are," Nicholas said.

"I am your wife. Ask the Red Cap about the Mysteries. He seems to understand them. Gift sees me. You do. And Coulter has felt my presence. I am real," she said.

"I know," Nicholas said. He looked down, spread his hands, then sighed. "I'm just afraid that you're—say—a ghostly doppelgänger who only appears to be my wife."

She smiled and took his hands. "No," she said. "And I'll prove that to you later. There are things only you and I know. We'll discuss them." She glanced over her shoulder at their children. They were arguing softly, Coulter waving his hands at them as if to stop them. "Right now, we have another matter to take care of."

"Many other matters," Nicholas said.

"No," she said. "Between us."

He waited.

She touched the side of his face. "My grandfather is a warrior. The best of all the warriors. I was good. I was not yet great. I never had the chance. But I was raised by him. I know how he thinks. I know how the greatest warriors in the world work."

"But you can't fight any more," Nicholas said. "You're trapped here."

"There is more to fighting than holding a sword, Nicholas," she said. "You know that."

He did.

She said, "I don't want my grandfather to have the Isle. It is ours, Nicholas, and it belongs to our children. I'll help you keep it."

He had missed her. He had missed her so much. "I'll need your help," he said, leaning into her touch.

"We're better together," she said.

He smiled. "We always were."

". . . all the advantages!" Gift's voice rose.

"I did not!" Ari shouted. "*You* were raised Fey! You know all their tricks!"

"I was raised in Shadowlands. As if that's an advantage."

"It might be now—"

"Our children are fighting," Jewel whispered.

"What's so surprising about that?" Nicholas asked. "We were fighting from the moment we met."

Jewel laughed, and to his surprise, he did too.

His family, together for the first time. Maybe the only time. The Fey had taken so much from him, and they had given him so much.

They had given him this second chance with Jewel.

They had given him such spectacular children.

They had given him his family again.

He let Jewel lead him back to the group. Arianna and Gift were leaning toward each other, their profiles male and female versions of the same face. They were shouting at each other, their words mingling and getting lost. Coulter was trying to come between them, and the Red Cap had his hands over his ears. Adrian, who had promised to watch them, was doing just that.

"I don't think we're going to win any victories if you two are at each other's throats," Nicholas said calmly. His children looked at him as if his presence were a surprise.

Jewel moved to the side. Gift watched her.

Nicholas didn't. "We have a lot to work out," he said. "And not a lot of time. Let's save the fighting until we've won the war, all right?"

"Daddy—" Arianna said.

He held up his hand and smiled at her. "You need food and rest, my girl. And while you do that, we need to think about fortifying this place. I suspect the Black King will want it for his own. And I won't let him get it."

He spread out his arms. "The Fey call this a Place of Power. It is something they've been searching for since they started invading other countries. I suspect there may be things here that can help us. We need to find them."

"So we're staying here?" Arianna asked.

Nicholas nodded. "It's the new seat of government for Blue Isle. Not as cozy as the last, but it's the best we can do."

"It might be real good," Coulter said.

He looked at the boy. That was one person he would have to figure out. A possible ally. A source of great power.

"Yes," Nicholas said. "It might be."

He glanced up at the top of the stairs. His dear friend was up there. She had brought him here. She had known something, and she hadn't been able to tell him all of it. But this was where she wanted him to be.

How sad that he could trust her now, when he hadn't been able to trust her during the last day of her life.

"I think we'll be fine here," Nicholas said.

"But do you think we can defeat the Black King from here?" Adrian asked.

"If we can't," Nicholas said, "no one can. We have the heirs to the Black Throne, a Place of Power, an Enchanter, and several great minds all in this room. We have a chance. We will make the best of it."

And, he thought to himself, when the time came, he would kill the Black King. He would do it right this time, and he would give his children the opportunity they deserved.

He glanced at his wife, who smiled encouragingly at him. Then he went and sat between his children. They were magnificent, tall and Fey and magickal. Yet they had some of him in them, too. And they were their own people. He could feel their strength.

He would need it.

They would all need it.

But at least they had hope now.

They were together. And that gave them power. Like this place gave them power.

He had the tools for victory in this place with him.

And he would sacrifice everything—except his children—to keep the Black King from taking Blue Isle.

Nicholas would sacrifice everything to keep the Place of Power from the Black King's hands.

Everything, to keep his children away from the Black King.

He would sacrifice everything, if he had to.

Even the Isle itself.

ABOUT THE AUTHOR

Kristine Kathryn Rusch is an award-winning fiction writer. She has published fifteen novels under her own name: *The White Mists of Power*, *Afterimage* (written with Kevin J. Anderson), *Facade*, *Heart Readers*, *Traitors*, *Sins of the Blood*, *The Fey: The Sacrifice*, *The Devil's Churn*, *The Fey: The Changeling*, *Star Wars: The New Rebellion*, and with her husband, Dean Wesley Smith, *The Escape*, *The Long Night*, *Klingon!*, *The Rings of Tautee*, and *Soldiers of Fear*. Her short fiction has been nominated for the Nebula, Hugo, World Fantasy, and Stoker awards. Her novella, *The Gallery of His Dreams*, won the Locus Award for best short fiction. Her body of fiction won her the John W. Campbell Award, given in 1991 in Europe. *The Fey: The Sacrifice* was chosen by *Science Fiction Chronicle* as one of the Best Fantasy Novels of 1995.

Rusch is the former editor of the *Magazine of Fantasy and Science Fiction*, a prestigious fiction magazine founded in 1949. In 1994, she won the Hugo Award for her editing work. She started Pulphouse Publishing with Dean Wesley Smith, and they won a World Fantasy Award for their work on that press. Rusch and Smith edited *The SFWA Handbook: A Professional Writer's Guide to Writing Professionally*, which won the Locus Award for Best Non-Fiction. They have also written several novels under the pen name Sandy Schofield.

She lives and works in Oregon.

And be sure not to miss
the final book in the series

THE FEY: VICTORY

ONE

LUKE huddled in the small trees that separated his neighbor Medes' farm from the farm the Fey had been using as a stronghold. He could barely see across the yard. The moon had set when he and his three companions had started on this mission. Luke wasn't nervous, but he could hear Jona's heavy breathing, and the rustle of Medes' clothing as he moved, and could feel Totle's occasional jumps of fright.

None of them had ever done anything like this. The three men with Luke were farmers. They had tilled land, grown crops, and worked in daylight since they were tiny boys. When the Fey first invaded Blue Isle twenty years before, Totle hadn't even been born. Luke had fought, but Jona and Medes hadn't.

Luke had been captured.

The Fey's treatment of him and his father had changed his entire life.

Now his father was missing, and the Fey's second invasion of Blue Isle had deposed the King, destroyed the main city of Jahn, and forced the farmers—all the Islanders—to work for Fey glory.

Luke had decided that he would do that, in the daylight. At night, he would concentrate on destroying the Fey.

The others had come along because they too wanted the Fey off the Isle. They knew, as he did, that this mission was probably futile—that they could as easily die as succeed—but they also knew that the Fey had a weakness.

Their weakness was in their own arrogance, their own confidence in themselves, their own belief in their undefeatability. Luke had seen what happened to the Fey who had lost that belief. They made mistakes. They died.

He hoped to shake that confidence to its very roots tonight.

He glanced at his companions. Jona, the neighbor who had helped him set up this small resistance force, was a slender man, almost as old as Luke's father, with the thin wiry look of a person who'd worked in the sun his whole life. His skin was naturally dark from all those years outside, but Luke had insisted in covering him with dirt anyway. Jona wore the darkest clothes he owned, and those too had been covered in the rich, black earth that gave the Islanders such healthy crops. Except for his bright eyes, he was nearly invisible in the dark.

Totle was the youngest of them. He was from a farm several away from Luke's. Luke had never met him before. He had come with Jona when Luke had sent out the word. Totle was in his early twenties, and had taken over his farm when his father had died the year before. He still had that leanness only the very young and the very active had. His skin had been burnt by the extra hours he put in the fields before the Fey forces had arrived in this part of the country, and he bore a bruise on his left cheek which he received when he tried to guard his farm from the invaders.

They hadn't killed him. The Fey respected farmers too much. They had taken Blue Isle for its strategic location—halfway between the continents of Galinas, which the Fey had conquered, and Leut, which the Fey wanted next—and partly for its incredible richness. With Fey scattered over half the world, their demand for supplies and raw materials was great. They had already given the farmers in this section of Blue Isle instructions on how to improve yields and on what the Fey expectations would be for the future.

The last member of Luke's party, Medes, was crouched beside Jona. Medes was a thick man, with corded muscles that ran the length of each arm. He had small, spindly legs, and he bore much of his weight in his torso, which was rounded with muscle. He too wore black dirt. His silver hair proved to be the largest problem. They had had to cake the dirt in it to hide the color, and even then Jona would occasionally glance at him, curse, and rub more dirt in his hair.

They were sitting on Medes' land. The small trees served as a windbreak between Medes' farm and the farm the Fey were now using. That farm had belonged to a man named Antoni and his family. The Fey had told Luke that Antoni and his family had gone to work for one of the southern farms, but he had learned differently last night.

He had been reconnoitering this place, searching for a first strike for his small band, when he had gone into the barn. Inside, he had discovered Fey pouches. The pouches, which contained skin and blood and sometimes bones from the victims of a battle, were used by Spell Warders to devise more magic spells for the Fey. The pouches also had other uses, things Luke did not understand, but had heard of.

He had found his target.

He had also found Antoni. Luke had hit his head on a small lamp, and its illumination had flooded the barn. Inside the lamp were tiny figures composed of light: Antoni and his family. The only way their souls could have been trapped in that lamp was if their bodies were gone.

They were dead; they just hadn't realized it yet.

The Fey often captured souls and used them for light. The

Fey were not wasteful conquerors. They used each part of a victim for their magic, and they used all the resources of the countries they conquered, renewing those resources whenever possible, and using them to continue to build the strength of the Fey Empire. This conquering strategy was, Luke believed, one of the many things that gave the Fey their power.

He respected the Fey. He did not fear them. They had already done the worst to him twenty years before when they had set him free, Charmed him, and made him into an unwilling assassin. The assassination had failed, thanks to the quick thinking of the victim, and Luke's Charm had been exposed.

Ever since, he had hoped he would get revenge on the Fey.

Through the copse of trees, he had an imperfect view of the farmhouse. Fey were inside it, and outside. The guard on this building was not traditional for the Fey. Usually, they put some kind of magic spell on the place, or they created a Shadowlands, marked by a tiny rotating circle of lights. He hoped that the fact the Fey used real soldiers as guards, instead of trusting their magick, meant that there were few magickal Fey around. The Fey guarding this place had looked, in the daylight, young. Most Fey did not come into their magick until their early twenties, forcing many of them to serve in the magickless infantry during those years.

Luke guessed that Infantry held this patch of land, not any of the higher orders.

He guessed, but he did not count on it.

He was fully prepared to die in this raid.

He would do his best to make sure that Jona, Medes, and Totle did not.

Their target was not the farmhouse, but the barn, and those magic pouches. There were only two guards on the barn, both near the main entrance. It showed, Luke thought, that the Fey, for all their military knowledge, and their demands regarding yield and production, knew very little about actual farming. He had gotten into the barn the night before by crawling through an open slat in the back.

The group would do the same tonight.

And tonight, the light was with them. The moon, which had been full the night before, had set. They had very little time before dawn to conduct their raid.

Luke nodded to his companions. Totle patted his side. He had rags hanging from two pouches. Medes held up the small bottle of grain alcohol that he had brought. He had said it would help them. Jona took the wicks and held them in one hand. Luke had the flints. He didn't trust anyone else with them. He also had a few rags, and a few wicks. He figured he could make do without the alcohol if he had to.

He pointed to the barn. Totle's shoulders rose and fell as he took a deep breath, then he crouched and scuttled away from the trees. Medes followed a moment later, and then Jona. Luke brought up the rear, as he had planned.

Luke had thought to go first when he set this plan into motion, but Jona had talked him out of it.

"You're the only one of us with knowledge of the Fey," Jona had said. "If they see anyone, it'll be the first. And then they'll kill him. The rest of us can get away."

Luke knew that wasn't the case; when he had been captured, he had been in the center of the attacking force, but he agreed with Jona anyway. Luke was less afraid of the Fey than he was of his small band backing down at exactly the wrong point. By going last, he could prevent one of them from turning around, running, and calling attention to the whole group.

He hoped.

Totle had reached the first hay bale. Luke's biggest worry was that Totle, who was the least familiar with this field and farm, would go in the wrong direction.

So far, he was following instructions to the letter.

Medes then left the hiding place at the copse of trees. He

scuttled across the field as well, but his larger form was more visible, at least to Luke. Luke glanced at the farmhouse. The Fey weren't talking like they had been the night before. He couldn't see the guards very clearly at all.

But he knew they were there.

All he hoped for was that their lack of magic would help him. He hoped they would shout, or converse among themselves, before coming after Luke's small group.

But he had seen the Fey in action too many times. They always appeared silently at first, and then they began their shouting.

He suspected that, if they saw this small band, things wouldn't be any different.

Medes made it to the first bale. Totle started for the second just as Jona left the copse of trees. Luke had set it up so that only two members of the group would move at one time. He figured that way only half of his force would get caught if the Fey weren't diligent.

If they were diligent, the group would die.

Or worse.

It was the worse that Luke feared.

Jona moved the best of all of them—so low to the ground that he was almost invisible. He looked like a shadow in the darkness.

Fortunately all of the men were farmers. They knew how to move on a cut hayfield without making any noise. They knew how to avoid the stalks that would crunch beneath their feet. They knew how to approach a bale without making it shake.

Luke was glad that these three had joined him. He had others in his small resistance movement, thanks to Jona's efforts, who would not have made as good stalkers. Indeed, Luke had been surprised: in the day since he had first spoken to Jona, Jona had gotten the word to a good dozen farmers who had, in fact, spread the word to at least a dozen more. The group had not met yet, and Luke doubted it would ever meet in full force, but they all knew of each other, and they had already developed signals and meeting places, and systems to fool the Fey—if the Fey could be fooled.

Jona had reached the hay bale. That was Luke's cue. He swallowed hard—his mouth was suddenly dry—and started across the field.

He moved much more like Medes, and he knew it. Upright and quick, placing his feet on the exact right places, he hurried toward the bale. As he did so, he scanned the field. The house was dark, unlike the night before, and the guards weren't so obvious. The two trees that served as a windbreak behind the house were completely still.

There wasn't even a breeze this night, which was, he thought, both good and bad. Good because the Fey couldn't smell something different on the breeze, and bad because every noise was amplified. One misstep, and they would have the guards' attention.

He reached the hay bale as Medes reached the next one. Ahead, he could see Totle pat Medes on the back.

Jona grabbed Luke's arm, pulled him close, and put a finger to his lips. Then he pointed at the barn. Luke squinted. Finally he saw what Jona did.

Three guards.

The night before they had only had two.

Well, that took care of one of his fears. With the farmhouse so dark, he had been afraid that the Fey had moved on without him knowing, that they were gone, and their pouches with them, and this entire raid had been for nothing.

But in taking care of that fear, it had given him another. Had they known about his visit the previous night?

The Fey lamp had gone on. He had made no attempt to hide the light. But he had leaned a rake against it, making it look as if the rake had fallen and jarred the light awake.

Maybe the Fey hadn't fallen for that.

Maybe they knew someone else had been in their barn.

But how?

He took a deep breath to bring down the panic. They were Fey. They had powers he did not. He shouldn't question how. He should merely accept it.

He would just have to be cautious.

He hoped that Totle would be.

He had tried to warn the boy. But he didn't know Totle well, and that worried him. He had checked for all the Fey signs, the ones his father's Fey friend Scavenger had warned him about, but Luke didn't trust the Fey in any way.

There might have been one that Scavenger left out.

Luke nodded at Jona just as Totle started for the third bale. Luke pushed Jona slightly, and he headed forward, moving as they planned.

The field wasn't very large, but this system made it feel as if it were the size of eight fields. The waiting made Luke nervous, and he checked the sky to see if there were any sign of the sun.

No. The darkness was still as complete as it had been before. There were clouds above him, and that added to the blackness. Some kind of luck was with him, just as there had been the night before. Something wanted him to get to that barn.

He only hoped that something wasn't Fey.

Totle and Jona reached their respective bales. Then Luke and Medes left their posts and moved forward. Luke felt exposed as he crossed the emptiness between bales. But he could see more of the barn. No Fey on the side closest to him.

And two Fey at the door of the farmhouse.

Two Fey only.

Maybe they hadn't known of his visit after all. Maybe the extra guard was someone there to add with the watch, or to facilitate the change to the morning team. Or maybe he had just come down to chat.

None of the guards noticed him as he crossed the fields. They didn't notice Medes either.

So far, so good.

Totle was nearly ready to start the long trek in the open to get to the back of the barn. Luke couldn't help him with that either, couldn't warn him any more than he already had about the possibility of more guards in the back.

And about how to find that loose board. Luke didn't know how hard it would be in this darkness. He wanted to set the fire inside the barn, not outside. It would be too easy for the Fey to spot if he set it outside, and they would be able to put it out.

He wanted the fire to rage before they even noticed it existed.

He made it to his second bale. Jona clapped him on the back. Luke smiled and nodded. Then Jona left for the third bale, just as Totle crossed the field toward the barn.

Luke held his breath. He watched the boy's frame, noting the low crouch, the rapid movement. Totle was doing everything he was told, moving with complete purpose, not stopping to check his surroundings, getting to the next site and then securing it.

This was the difficult one.

This was the unknown part.

Luke wondered if this was how his father had felt when Luke had volunteered to go on that first mission against the Fey.

When Luke *insisted* on going.

Luke felt incredibly anxious now, and he didn't even know the boy. Imagine how he would feel if the boy were his son.

Totle disappeared behind the barn.

Luke held his breath another moment—and heard nothing.

No scream.

No cry for help.

No announcement from the Fey that they had captured one of the Islanders.

Nothing.

Luke let out the breath he had been holding. He noted that Jona had made it to the third bale.

There was still no sound from behind the barn. Maybe a Fey had been there and grabbed Totle, wrapping a hand around Totle's mouth to keep him quiet.

Maybe the Fey were just waiting there.

Waiting to see who else would come.

And maybe they hadn't noticed the four invaders at all.

Medes glanced at Luke, as if he too were uncertain about what to do next. Luke saw Medes' movement, but he didn't know if Medes could see him clearly. Despite that uncertainty, Luke nodded, as if to tell Medes to go ahead.

Medes did.

Luke couldn't watch him because Luke had to cross to the third bale. As he moved, he saw that the three guards hadn't moved from their posts. Neither had the guards near the house. The sky was unchanged. Very little time had gone by, although to Luke, it felt like hours.

Days.

He hadn't been this tense in a long, long time.

Then he took a deep breath and forced himself to think of something else. Of the way his feet fell on the dying hay stalks. Of the way the bales' shadows added darkness to already existing darkness on the field. Of the bale looming in front of him, Jona hiding in its shadow.

Luke had the right to inform these people of the dangers. He had done that. And because he had done that, he had given them enough information to make their own decisions.

If they died, it was because they had chosen to be here this night.

Because they had chosen to fight the Fey.

When that thought reached him, he felt better. Much better. The anxiety that had haunted him when he first reached the copse fell away.

And he knew that was probably good. A leader couldn't be plagued by doubts. They would interfere with his ability to lead.

Luke reached the third hay bale.

Medes disappeared around the back of the barn.

Jona tensed beside Luke. At this close proximity, Luke could smell the scent of Jona's fear mingled with his sweat. Jona was as terrified of this as Luke had been just a moment before.

But Jona was still going forward.

There was silence from the barn. Even though Luke squinted, he couldn't see against the darkness. He wanted to see shadows, to know if his two men struggled.

To know if they needed help.

He touched Jona on the side and Jona jumped. Luke took Jona's arm, and moved it toward his side, toward the knife he had tied to his waist. Jona understood.

He removed the knife.

He would be prepared in case the others were in trouble.

Then he nodded once to Luke, and headed across the field. Luke watched as Jona made his way, like a wraith, against the darkness of the field.

Something snapped.

Jona had snapped a hay stalk.

Jona fell flat, and that time, his movement was silent.

Luke bit his lower lip. He crawled cautiously to the edge of the bale and glanced at the guards.

They were looking around, but they didn't seem to see anything. Then one of them laughed. The others laughed with him.

A leader then?

Or merely someone who told a good joke?

Luke turned his head toward Jona. Jona remained down, counting to fifty as they had planned. Luke looked again at the guards.

They hadn't moved.

Luke couldn't see the guards near the house.

Jona disappeared behind the barn.

Luke bit his lip so hard he tasted blood. He grabbed his knife and waited at the edge of the hay bale.

He was supposed to count to fifty too. But he couldn't concentrate. He started once.

Then twice.

Then glanced at the guards. They had moved closer to each other, but weren't talking.

Maybe they were listening.

Luke would have to be very, very careful.

It all depended on him.

He started into the field.

And immediately saw why Jona had made a noise. He was amazed no one else had.

The stalks from the field trimming were short here. There were long stalks that hadn't been wrapped into bales all along the ground. It was hard to see them in the dark, and even harder to find a place to put his feet.

He went slower than he normally would have. He didn't want to make a second noise. He didn't want to draw the guards' attention if, indeed, it hadn't been drawn already.

He was breathing shallowly, his heart pounding. His ears were straining for a sound, any sound other than the hush-hush of his feet on the broken hay stalks. Every noise he made, from the rustle of his clothing to the soft exhalation of breath, sent little shivers through him. He was convinced the Fey were listening as hard as he was.

Then he made it to the side of the barn. The wood was warm and rough against his palm. He peered around the corner and saw nothing.

It was dark in the back, darker than anywhere else. His eyes, adjusted to the night, hadn't adjusted to this. He squinted, trying to see, but he couldn't. He couldn't hear anything either: no breathing, no moans, no cries.

If his friends had been captured by the Fey, they weren't outside.

If they hadn't, they were inside the barn, waiting for him.

Him, and the flints, and the instructions.

He clenched his left fist against the barn's wood. Almost there. Almost there, and the night would be over.

The mission would be over, and he could return home.

He sensed no one else. His heart was pounding so hard, he felt that the Fey could hear the hammering. He had trouble keeping his breathing regular.

It was now, or not at all.

He kept his left hand against the side of the barn. He rounded the corner, knife out, and went to the back where the rotted board was, the board he had found the night before.

It was in the center as he remembered. He crouched down and felt the dug-out area. The board had been pulled loose, by one of his friends, he hoped, and not by the Fey.

He slid through the dug-out area, noting that the smell of dog was gone. The fur he had felt the night before was also gone, probably rubbed away by his friends.

The smell of rot remained.

If anything it was stronger. He resisted the urge to sneeze. The scent got into his nostrils, invaded his body, coated him. What a difference a day made. Those pouches had a stink all their own.

And then he was inside.

The darkness was so thick he couldn't see anything.

Mixed with the stink of rot was the pungent scent of the grain alcohol.

Hands touched him, pulling him up.

Familiar hands.

"Luke?" Jona whispered.

"Yes," he whispered back. "Everyone here?"

"Yes," Medes whispered.

"The pouches are to our right," Luke whispered. He knew that from memory.

"We have to be quick about this," Jona whispered. "They heard me on the field."

"But they haven't checked it yet," Luke whispered.

"Still," Jona whispered.

"Enough talking," Medes whispered. "Let's do this."

"All right," Totle whispered. "The rags are already soaked."

"Alcohol's poured all over those smelly pouches," Medes whispered.

"Wicks are in place," Jona whispered. "I'm holding one."

They were just waiting for him. Luke pulled the flints out of his own small pouch. He took the hand on his shoulder, put a flint in it. "Hands," he whispered. Two more touched him, and he put flints in those as well.

As if it were planned, all the flints sparked, and for a brief instant, Luke saw the pouches, the soaked rags, the wicks running to this section of the barn.

Then the sparks went out.

He crouched next to the wick Jona was holding, and lit it. It burned easily—it had been treated, as so many candle wicks had—and the flame moved quickly across it. The tiny flame shone like a beacon, banishing the darkness.

Luke's heart was trying to pound through his chest.

Totle picked up another wick and lit it, as Medes lit a third. Jona grabbed the last and lit that.

Luke's flame hit the first soaked rag and it burst into a brilliant blue flame.

"Now," he said, not whispering any more. They had to get out. He grabbed Totle, and shoved him toward the rotted board. Totle crawled through the dug-out area, followed closely by Jona, then Medes.

Luke glanced behind him. The rags were all burning, a bright high blue flame with orange on the top. He could feel the heat against his face and skin.

Then he flung himself into the dug out area, and crawled out of the barn.

His companions were running across the field, not caring about the sound their feet made. Fey were shouting behind him.

Luke pulled himself to his feet, saw tendrils of white smoke emerging from cracks in the barn wall. Fire crackled inside.

"This is for Blue Isle!" he shouted.

Then he too started to run.